D1147057

ST CLARE'S
The Final Years

ST CLARE'S

Enid Blyton

St Clare's
The Twins at St Clare's
The O'Sullivan Twins
Summer Term at St Clare's
Second Form at St Clare's
The Third Form at St Clare's (by Pamela Cox)
Kitty at St Clare's (by Pamela Cox)
Claudine at St Clare's
Fifth Formers of St Clare's
The Sixth Form at St Clare's (by Pamela Cox)

Malory Towers
First Term at Malory Towers
Second Form at Malory Towers
Third Year at Malory Towers
Upper Fourth at Malory Towers
In the Fifth at Malory Towers
Last Term at Malory Towers

The Mysteries
The Mystery of the Burnt Cottage
The Mystery of the Disappearing Cat
The Mystery of the Secret Room
The Mystery of the Spiteful Letters
The Mystery of the Missing Necklace
The Mystery of the Hidden House
The Mystery of the Pantomime Cat
The Mystery of the Invisible Thief
The Mystery of the Vanished Prince
The Mystery of the Strange Bundle
The Mystery of Holly Lane
The Mystery of Tally-Ho Cottage
The Mystery of the Missing Man
The Mystery of the Strange Messages
The Mystery of Banshee Towers

Enid Blyton

St Clare's
The Final Years

3 books in 1

EGMONT

EGMONT

We bring stories to life

Claudine at St Clare's first published in Great Britain 1944
Fifth Formers of St Clare's first published in Great Britain 1945
The Sixth Form at St Clare's first published in Great Britain 2000
First published as *St Clare's: The Final Years* 2014
by Egmont UK Limited
The Yellow Building, 1 Nicholas Road, London W11 4AN

ISBN 978 1 4052 6847 9

1 3 5 7 9 10 8 6 4 2

www.egmont.co.uk

A CIP catalogue record for this title is available from the British Library

Printed and bound in Great Britain by the CPI Group

55941/1

Contents

CLAUDINE
at
ST CLARE'S

Contents

1
Back at school again

Pat and Isabel O'Sullivan walked into the fourth form-room at St Clare's, and looked round.

'Fourth form,' said Pat. 'Golly, we're getting on, aren't we, Isabel?'

'Yes – fourth form seems a long way from the first form,' said Isabel. 'I say – do you remember when we were in the first form – ages go? We were called the Stuck-Up Twins then, because we hated St Clare's, and didn't want to belong to it.'

The twins thought back to the days when they had been first formers. They remembered how they had settled down at St Clare's, their first dislike of it turning to pride and admiration, and now here they were, fourth formers at the beginning of the summer term!

'Don't the first formers seem babies now?' said Pat. 'We thought we were quite big when we first came, but when I see the first formers now they seem very young to me! I shall enjoy being in the fourth form, won't you, Isabel?'

'I shall,' said Isabel. 'I hope we shall stay on at St Clare's until we are in the top form – and I hope our friends do too.'

'Well, some of them have left already,' said Pat. 'Pam

isn't coming back, nor is Sheila. Lucy Oriell has gone too – to an art school. She was going to stay on here, but she's too brilliant at her art, and she's won a scholarship to the best art school in the country.'

'Good for Lucy!' said Isabel. 'We shall miss her though. I wonder if there are any new girls this term?'

'Sure to be,' said Pat. She looked round the big form-room. 'I say, this is a fine room, isn't it – the nicest classroom we've had so far. There's a wonderful view out of the window.'

So there was. The twins could see miles of beautiful country. It was country they knew well now, and loved very much. Down below, in the school grounds, were the tennis-courts, the games fields, and the big swimming-pool. The girls could see the school gardens too, and the big kitchen garden full of fresh vegetables.

'Bags I sit by the window,' said Pat. 'Hallo, there's Bobby, and Janet!'

Roberta and Janet walked into the classroom, grinning. Bobby's freckled face had a very boyish look, and she was very like a boy in her ways, full of fun and tricks.

'Hallo!' she said. 'Come to look at our new home? Nice room, isn't it?'

'What's our new form-mistress like?' said Pat. 'Miss Ellis – she's supposed to be quite nice, isn't she?'

'Oh, yes – very calm and unruffled and dignified,' said Bobby. 'She'll be all right.'

'Got any new tricks to play, Janet?' asked Isabel. Janet always had a stock of tricks each term, most of them from her schoolboy brother, who seemed to be a real scamp. Janet grinned.

'Wait and see,' she said. 'Anyway, I suppose I'd better go carefully now I'm a fourth former. Can't rag about so much when you get high up the school. And I'm going to work for my finals exam too, so I guess I won't have much time for tricks.'

'I guess you will, all the same,' said Pat. 'Any new girls, do you know?'

'Two or three,' said Bobby. 'Hallo, Hilary! Had good hols?'

Hilary Wentworth came into the room, dark and smiling. She had been at St Clare's even longer than the twins.

'Hallo!' she said. 'Yes, I had fine hols. I rode every day, and I played tennis on our hard court every day too. I say, who's the angel?'

'What do you mean?' asked the twins and Bobby.

'Oh, haven't you seen her?' said Hilary. 'She's just arrived, complete with posh new trunk, three tennis-rackets, and a handbag with gold initials on. What do you bet your Cousin Alison will think she's one of the world's seven wonders? She's got pale golden hair, bobbed like angels in pictures, and a pointed face like a pixie, and a voice like a princess.'

'Golly! Where is she?' said the others, with interest. 'Will she be in our form?'

'She's down in the hall,' said Hilary. 'She arrived in the biggest car I've ever seen, with a crest on the panels, and two chauffeurs.'

'Let's go and see her,' said Pat. So the five of them went

into the corridor, and hung over the stair banisters to see the newcomer.

She was still there – and it was quite true, she did look a bit like an angel, if an angel could be imagined dressed in school uniform, carrying three beautiful tennis-rackets!

'She's lovely, isn't she?' said Bobby, who, not being at all lovely herself, always admired beauty in others. 'Yes – I bet Alison will follow her round like a dog. Alison isn't happy unless she's thinking someone is just too wonderful for words!'

Alison came up at that moment. She was the twins' cousin, a pretty, feather-headed little thing, with not many brains. 'Hallo!' she said. 'Did I hear you talking about me?'

'Yes,' said Hilary. 'We were just saying that you'd be sure to like that schoolgirl angel down there. Did you ever see anything like her?'

Alison leant over the banisters – and, just as the others had guessed, she immediately lost her heart to the new girl.

'She looks like a princess from a fairytale,' said Alison. 'I'll go down and ask her if she wants to be shown round a bit.'

Alison sped downstairs. The others grinned at one another. 'Alison has lost her heart already,' said Pat. 'Poor old Alison – the wonderful friends she's made and lost! Do you remember Sadie, the American girl, and how Alison was for ever saying, "Well, *Sadie* says so and so," and we made a song about it and sang it? Wasn't Alison cross?'

'Yes, and when she was in the second form she thought the drama mistress was simply wonderful, and when she was in the third form she lost her heart to the head girl and made herself a perfect nuisance to her,' said Janet. 'Really, the times Alison has lost her heart to people, and they never think anything of her for it.'

'Funny old feather-head,' said Pat. 'Look at her, taking the angel's arm and going off with her, all over her already!'

'There's another new girl down there too,' said Bobby. 'She looks rather forlorn. Well, I do think Alison might take her round as well. Hi, Alison!'

But Alison had disappeared with the golden-haired angel. The twins went down the stairs and spoke to the other new girl.

'Hallo! You're new, aren't you? You'd better come and see Matron. We'll take you.'

'What's your name?' said Pat, looking at the new girl, who was trying not to show that she felt new and lost.

'Pauline Bingham-Jones,' said the new girl in rather an affected voice. 'Yes, I'd be glad if you'd tell me what to do.'

'Well, Matron is usually here to see to all the new girls,' said Hilary, a little puzzled. 'I wonder where she is?'

'I haven't seen her at all,' said Pat. 'She wasn't here when we came, either.'

'Funny,' said Isabel. 'Let's go to her room and find her. We've got to see her, anyway.'

They went to Matron's room, taking Pauline with them. They banged on the door. They liked Matron, though they were very much in awe of her. She had been at St Clare's for years and years, and some of the girls' mothers, who had also been at St Clare's, had known her too.

A voice called out. 'Come in!'

'That's not Matron's voice,' said Pat, puzzled. She opened the door and went in, the others following. A woman in Matron's uniform sat sewing by the window. It wasn't the Matron they knew so well. The girls stared at her in surprise.

'Oh,' said Pat. 'We were looking for Matron.'

'I am Matron this term,' said the new Matron. 'Your old Matron fell ill during the holidays, so I have come to take her place. I am sure we shall all get on very well together.'

The girls stared at her. They didn't feel so sure about that. Their old Matron was fat and round and jolly, with a strong and comforting kind of face. This Matron was thin and sour-looking. She had very thin lips that met together in a straight line. She smiled at the girls, but her smile stayed at her mouth and did not reach her eyes.

'We came to find you,' said Bobby. 'Usually Matron meets the new girls. This is one of them. She has to give you her list of clothes and towels and things.'

'I know that, thank you,' said Matron, biting off the thread she was using. 'Send all the new girls to me, will you? How many have arrived?'

The girls didn't know. They thought it was Matron's business to find out, not theirs. They thought of their old Matron, bustling about looking after the newcomers, making them welcome, taking them to their form-mistresses, or finding girls to take care of them.

'Well – this is Pauline Bingham-Jones,' said Pat, at last. 'There's another new girl somewhere. We saw her. Our Cousin Alison seems to be looking after her.'

The girls disappeared from the room, leaving Pauline to the new Matron. They looked at one another and screwed up their noses. 'Don't like her,' said Isabel. 'Looks like a bottle of vinegar!'

The others laughed. 'I hope our old Matron will come back,' said Bobby. 'St Clare's will seem funny without her. I wonder where Alison has gone with the angel.'

Alison appeared at that moment, looking flushed and radiant. It was quite plain that she had made a friend already. With her was the 'angel'.

'Oh,' said Alison, 'Pat, Isabel, Bobby, Hilary – this is the Honourable Angela Favorleigh.'

The Honourable Angela bent her head a little as if she was bowing to her subjects. Bobby grinned.

'I had a doll called Angela once,' she said. 'She was a bit like you! Well – I hope you'll like St Clare's. Alison, take her to Matron.'

'Where *is* Matron?' said Alison. 'I've been looking for her.'

'There's a new Matron this term,' said Bobby. 'You won't like her.'

The Honourable Angela Favorleigh didn't like Bobby. She gazed at her as if she was something that smelt rather nasty. She turned to Alison and spoke in a pretty, high little voice.

'Well – let's go to Matron. I want to take my things off.'

They went off together. Hilary laughed. 'Well, we shall all know where Alison will be most of this term,' she said. 'In the Honourable's pocket!'

2 In the fourth form

'Look,' said Bobby, 'there's another new girl. She's got her things off, too. She looks as if she'd be a fourth former, I should think.'

The new girl came up, walking quickly as if she had somewhere to go. 'Hallo,' said Bobby. 'You're new, aren't you? What form will you be in, do you know?'

'Fourth,' said the girl. 'My name's Eileen Paterson.'

'We're fourth form too,' said Pat, and she introduced herself and the others. 'Do you want to be shown round a bit? Usually Matron is here to welcome people, but there is a new one this term who doesn't know the ropes yet.'

The girl looked suddenly annoyed. 'I know my way about, thank you,' she said stiffly. 'I've been here a week already.'

Without saying any more she swung off. The others stared after her. 'What's bitten *her*?' said Bobby. 'No need to be rude like that. And what did she mean – that she's been here a week? Nobody comes back before the first day of term.'

Mirabel came up, with her friend Gladys. 'Hallo, Hallo!' said the others. 'Nice to see you again. I say, have you spoken to that girl who's just gone – new girl called Eileen

Paterson. Seems to think the whole school belongs to her!'

'No, I haven't spoken to her yet,' said Mirabel. 'But I know her mother is the Matron now – our old one is ill you know. Eileen is the new Matron's daughter, and she's going to be educated here. She came with her mother a week ago, when her mother came to take over the job and see to the linen and things.'

Bobby whistled. 'Oh! No wonder she was annoyed when we said the new Matron ought to be welcoming the new girls, and didn't know the ropes yet!' she said. 'And no wonder she knows her way about if she's already been here a week. I didn't like her much.'

'Give her a chance,' said Hilary. 'You know how you feel sort of on the defensive when you come to anywhere new, and meet girls who've been here ages. You feel a kind of outsider at first.'

There were new girls in the other, lower forms, but these did not interest the fourth formers much. They were glad to see one another again – the twins, Bobby, Hilary, Kathleen, Doris, Carlotta, and the rest. They had all come up together into the fourth form. There were a few old girls left in the fourth form, most of whom the twins liked. Susan Howes was head of the form, a pleasant, kindly girl with a good sense of responsibility and fairness.

The fourth form settled down under Miss Ellis. She was firm and calm, seldom raised her voice, expected good work and saw that she got it. She was interested in the girls and fond of them, and they, in return, liked her very much.

The Honourable Angela Favorleigh looked more like

an angel than ever in class, with her bobbed golden hair falling to her shoulders, the ends curling underneath most beautifully. All her school clothes, though cut to the same pattern as those of the others, were really beautiful.

'Do you know, she has every single pair of shoes especially made for her?' said Alison in a hushed voice to the twins. 'And she has a handbag to match every single frock she wears, all with gold initials on.'

'Shut up,' said Pat. 'Who cares about things like that? Your darling Angela is a snob.'

'Well, why shouldn't she be?' said Alison, ready to defend her new friend at once. 'Her family is one of the oldest in the country, she's got a third cousin who is a prince, and goodness knows how many titled relations!'

'You're a snob too, Alison,' said Isabel, in disgust. 'Why must you always suck up to people like that? Don't you know that it's what you *are* that matters, not what you have?'

'I'm not a snob,' said Alison. 'I'm pleased that Angela has chosen me for her friend, of course. I think she's lovely.'

'Pity she hasn't got more brains,' said Bobby. 'Honestly, I don't believe she really knows her twelve times table!'

Angela Favorleigh certainly was a snob. She was intensely proud of her family, of its wealth, its cars, and her own well-bred looks. She was very particular about making friends. She liked Alison because the girl was pretty and dainty, had beautiful manners and quite plainly adored the lovely Angela from the bottom of her foolish little heart.

Angela liked very few of her form. Bobby she detested because she had said she was like a doll. Carlotta she would have nothing to do with at all.

Carlotta didn't mind in the least. The dark-eyed, dark-haired girl had once been a little circus girl, and she was not at all ashamed of it. Her mother had been a circus-rider, but her father was a gentleman, and now Carlotta lived with her father and grandmother in the holidays, for her mother was dead. She had learnt to be lady-like, to have good manners, and was very popular indeed – but she had never forgotten the exciting days of the circus, and she often amused the others by turning cartwheels, or going completely mad in a Spanish way that the girls enjoyed very much.

Alison had told Angela the histories of all the girls, Carlotta included, and Angela had turned up her delicate little nose when she heard that Carlotta had actually ridden horses in a circus.

'How *can* they have her here, in a school like this?' she said. 'I am sure my people wouldn't have sent me here if they had known that.'

'Why did you come to St Clare's?' asked Alison, curiously. 'It's supposed to be a sensible, no-nonsense school, you know – not a swanky one.'

'I didn't want to come,' said Angela. 'My mother wanted to send me to a much nicer school, but my father has funny ideas. He said I wanted my corners rubbed off.'

'Oh, Angela! You haven't any corners!' said Alison. 'Honestly, I don't think you've any faults at all.'

This was the kind of thing that Angela loved hearing, and was one reason why she liked Alison for a friend. She looked at Alison out of innocent blue eyes, and smiled an angelic smile.

'You do say nice things, Alison,' she said. 'You are far and away the nicest girl in the form. I can't bear that common Eileen, nor that awful Carlotta, nor that dreadful Pauline Bingham-Jones.'

Pauline certainly wasn't much of a success. In her way she seemed as much of a snob as Angela, but she could not carry it off so well, because her clothes were not beautifully made, and she had no marvellous possessions such as Angela had. But she too turned up her nose at Carlotta, and disliked the ready-witted Bobby. As for Eileen, she would hardly speak to her at all.

'I don't see why Eileen should be allowed to join the school just because her mother is here as Matron,' said Pauline, in her rather affected voice. 'Good gracious me – we shall have the cook's daughter here next, and the gardener's too! It's bad enough to have Carlotta. She always looks so wild and don't-carish.'

Carlotta always did look a little wild at the beginning of term, partly because she was no longer under the rather strict eye of her grandmother. But nobody minded Carlotta's untidiness and wildness. It was all part of the vivacious, amusing girl. Carlotta knew that Angela and Pauline didn't like her, and she took a real pleasure in talking slang, making rude faces, and unexpectedly walking on her hands in front of them.

Miss Ellis, however, did not encourage things of this sort in the fourth form. Her form was a kind of half-way house, where girls had to learn to shed their irresponsible ways, and to become more serious, reliable members of the school. As soon as they moved up into the fifth and sixth, they had studies of their own, instead of common-rooms, and were expected to take a good deal of responsibility.

So Carlotta was often called to order by Miss Ellis, in her low, firm voice, and then Angela and Pauline looked down their noses at the one-time circus girl, and whispered mocking things to the girl next to them.

Pauline and Angela vied with each other in their boasting. The girls sometimes giggled to hear them.

'My third cousin – the one who is a prince,' Angela would say, 'he has an aeroplane of his own, and has promised to take me up in it.'

'Haven't you *been* up in an aeroplane yet?' Pauline would say, with affected surprise. 'Good gracious! I've been up three times already. That was when I was staying with the Lacy-Wrights. Fancy, they had sixteen bathrooms in their house – well, it was really a mansion, of course . . .'

'I bet you haven't more than one bathroom in your own home,' said Angela, spitefully. 'We've got seven.'

'We've got nine, if you count the two in the staff quarters,' said Pauline, at once. The other girls stared at her in surprise. They could well believe that Angela had scores of bathrooms, for wealth was written all over the little snob – but somehow Pauline didn't fit in with a number of bathrooms, a fleet of expensive cars and things like that.

'Well,' said Bobby, 'let me count *my* bathrooms. Three for myself – four for Mother – five for Daddy – two for visitors – er, how many's that?'

'Idiot!' said Pat, giggling. Angela and Pauline scowled.

'I can't remember whether we've got a bathroom at home or not,' said Hilary, entering into the fun. 'Let me think hard!'

But no amount of teasing would make either Angela or Pauline stop their vying with each other. If it wasn't bathrooms, it was cars; if it wasn't cars, it was their beautiful, expensively dressed mothers; if it wasn't mothers, it was clothes. The others really got very tired of it.

Eileen Paterson did not seem to mind very much being cold-shouldered by Angela and Pauline. She only spoke with eagerness of one thing – her elder brother. He was at work somewhere in the next big town, and it was quite plain that Eileen adored him.

'His name is Edgar,' she said. 'We call him Eddie.'

'You would,' said Angela, cattily. 'And if he was called Alfred, you'd call him Alf. And if he was called Herbert, you'd call him Herb – or Erb perhaps.'

Eileen flushed. 'You're a beast, Angela,' she said. 'You wait till you see Eddie – Edgar, I mean. He's marvellous! His hair's curly, and he's got the loveliest smile. He's the best brother in the world. He's working terribly hard at his job. You see, Mother lost a lot of money, so that's why she had to take a job as Matron, and why Eddie – Edgar – had to go to work.'

'Your family history doesn't interest me, Eileen,' said Angela, coldly, and went off with Alison. Eileen shrugged her shoulders.

'Little snob!' she said, loudly. 'She wants a good scolding.'

Carlotta agreed with her. 'Yes – sometimes I feel like throttling Angela,' she said. 'But now I'm a fourth former – what a pity! I shall quite forget how to scold anyone who needs it!'

'Oh no you won't,' said Bobby, laughing at the solemn Carlotta. 'When you fly into a temper, you'll forget all about being a fourth former – you'll just be the same wild Carlotta you've always been!'

The arrival of Claudine

Before a week had gone by, a fourth new girl arrived. Mam'zelle herself announced her coming.

'I have a surprise for you,' she beamed one morning, coming in to give a French lesson. 'We shall soon have another companion in the fourth form. She arrives today.'

'Why is she so late in coming?' asked Pat, in surprise.

'She has just recovered from the measle,' said Mam'zelle, who always spoke of this illness in the singular and not in the plural. 'The measle is a most tiresome disease. Claudine had a very bad measle, and she could not come back any sooner.'

'Claudine?' said Isabel. 'What a pretty name! I like it.'

'Ah, and you will like the little Claudine too!' said Mam'zelle. 'For she is French. She is my niece!'

This was news to the girls. They hadn't even known that Mam'zelle had a niece. One coming to St Clare's too!

'I hope she will be happy at St Clare's,' said Hilary, feeling that someone ought to say the right thing.

'Ah, she will be very happy,' said Mam'zelle. 'She would be happy anywhere, the little Claudine. There never was such a child for happiness. Always she smiles and laughs, and always she plays the trick and the joke.'

This sounded good. The girls began to look forward to Claudine's coming. They looked at Mam'zelle expectantly, hoping to hear more.

Then Mam'zelle's face grew solemn. She pinched her glasses more firmly on her nose and gazed at the listening girls with her short-sighted, much-magnified eyes.

'I have especially asked for Claudine to come here,' she said. 'Before, she has been to a Convent School, but it was too strict for her, and always they found fault with the poor little Claudine. They said she cared nothing for anyone, nor for any rules or customs. And I thought to myself, "Ah, the good, hard-working Bobby was once like that – and see what St Clare's has done for her! Now she works for her finals and she is as good as gold! Maybe the same thing will happen to my little Claudine." '

Bobby looked uncomfortable as Mam'zelle made this speech. She wasn't at all sure that she wanted to be referred to as 'good as gold'. But Mam'zelle was so much in earnest that Bobby made no protest. It wouldn't have been any good, anyway! Mam'zelle swept on with her speech.

'And so the little Claudine comes today, well-recovered from the measle, and you will all give her a grand welcome, will you not? For your old Mam'zelle's sake?'

'Of course we'll make her welcome,' said Susan Howes, and most of the others murmured the same, except Angela, Alison and Pauline, who all put on a bored look, as if a niece belonging to Mam'zelle wasn't worth giving a thought to.

'Ah, you are good kind girls,' said Mam'zelle. 'I will

introduce Claudine to you as soon as she comes. She will love you all. She is a good girl though she seems to care nothing for what is good and proper. But you will change all that, *n'est-ce pas*?'

The girls thought that Claudine sounded distinctly amusing. It would be fun to have a French girl in the class! They glanced at one another, thinking that of all the new girls, this latest one sounded the most promising.

About five minutes before the lesson finished the door was opened, and a strange girl appeared. She was small, dark and smart. She had a very cheeky look and she gave a quick sidelong glance at the girls before advancing to Mam'zelle.

Mam'zelle gave a shriek, and then flung herself on the new girl. She kissed her several times on both cheeks, she stroked her dark hair, and poured out such a torrent of French that no one could follow it.

The girl replied in smooth, polite French, and kissed Mam'zelle on each cheek. She did not seem to mind her aunt's outburst in the least.

'Ah, *ma petite* Claudine, here you are at last!' cried Mam'zelle. She swung the girl round to face the class. 'Now see, here is the little Claudine,' said Mam'zelle, her glasses falling off her nose in her violent delight. 'Greet your new friends, Claudine.'

'Hallo, buddies!' said Claudine, amiably. The girls stared in surprise and then giggled. It was funny to hear such an American expression from the little French girl.

'What did you say?' said Mam'zelle, who was not well

up on American slang. 'Did you say, "Hallo, bodies"? That is not correct, Claudine. You should say, "Hallo, everybody." '

The class roared. Claudine grinned. Mam'zelle beamed. She was plainly very proud of Claudine and very fond of her.

The bell rang for the end of class. Mam'zelle picked out Hilary. 'Hilary, you will take the little Claudine with you, please, and show her everything. She will feel strange and shy, poor little one.'

Mam'zelle was quite mistaken about that, however. Claudine didn't feel shy, and certainly didn't seem to feel strange. In fact she acted as if she had known the girls all her life! She spoke easily and naturally to them. Her English was good, though, like Mam'zelle, she sometimes put things in an unusual way.

She had been to school in France, and then had spent a term or two at a convent school in England. It seemed that Claudine did not want to remain at her last school and they did not want to keep her.

'You see – it was most unfortunate – the science mistress went up a ladder into a tree to collect some curious fungus that grew there,' explained Claudine, in her little French voice. 'And I came along and borrowed the ladder. So we did not have a science lesson that day.'

'Golly! Do you mean to say that you left the teacher stranded up the tree?' said Bobby. 'Well, you have got a nerve! No wonder Mam'zelle thinks St Clare's will be good for you. You can't do that sort of thing here.'

'No?' said Claudine. 'What a pity. Still, maybe you have good fun. I am sorry I did not come back to school on the first day. But I had caught a measle.'

The girls giggled. Everyone liked Claudine, except Angela. Even Pauline listened to the new girl, and Alison was much amused by her. But Angela as usual looked down her nose.

'What did I tell you?' she said to Alison. 'First we have to have Matron's daughter, and now we have to have Mam'zelle's niece! I can't see what you find to be amused at in Claudine, Alison. I'm surprised at you.'

'Well, I like her voice and her manners,' said Alison. 'I like the way she uses her hands when she talks – just like Mam'zelle does. She's really quite amusing, Angela.'

Angela did not like Alison to disagree with her about anything. She looked coldly at her friend and then turned away sulkily. That was always the way she punished anyone – by withdrawing from them and sulking. Alison couldn't bear it.

Alison tried to make it up. She went after Angela, and took her hand. She praised her and flattered her, and at last Angela condescended to smile again on her willing slave.

Then Alison was happy. 'You needn't think I shall bother about Claudine at all,' she said to Angela. 'She's a common little thing, really.'

'Not so common as Carlotta,' said Angela, spitefully. Alison looked uncomfortable. She sincerely liked Carlotta, who was absolutely honest, truthful and straight, besides being amusing company. Even her hot temper was likeable. Alison thought that Carlotta was more completely herself, more natural than any of the other girls. And to be natural was to be very likeable.

Claudine settled in at once. She took a desk at the back of the room, and bagged a locker in the common-room. She arranged her belongings in the locker, and put a photograph of her mother on top. She had brought a fine big cake with her and shared it generously all round, though Angela refused a slice. Alison did too, after hesitating. She was afraid that Angela might go into a sulk again if she saw her sharing the cake.

At first the girls were very much amused with Claudine, but they soon discovered that she had very un-English ways. For instance, she thought nothing of copying from someone else's book! She had a quick brain, but she was often lazy – and then she would simply copy the answers set down by the girl next to her. This was Mirabel, whose brains were not of the highest order. So, more often than not, Claudine copied down mistakes. But she did not seem to mind at all.

'Look here – we oughtn't to let Claudine cheat like this,' said Pat. 'She keeps *on* copying from Mirabel. Mirabel says Claudine didn't bother to do a single sum – she copied the answers of all hers!'

'The funny thing is, she does it so openly,' said Isabel. 'I mean – I really don't believe she thinks it's wrong!'

Claudine was very astonished when Susan Howes, the head girl of the form, spoke to her about the copying.

'It's cheating, Claudine! Surely you can see that!' said Susan, her honest face glowing scarlet, for she did not like accusing anyone of cheating.

'No, I do not see it at all,' said Claudine. 'You all see me do it. Cheating is a secret thing.'

'No, it isn't,' said Susan. 'Cheating is cheating whether you do it in front of anyone, or on the sly. Besides, it's so silly of you to copy from Mirabel. She gets so many answers wrong. Miss Ellis will find out and then you'll get into a row.'

'You think then it would be better to copy from Hilary?' asked Claudine, seriously. Susan sighed.

'Claudine, you mustn't copy from *any*one. I know French people have different ideas from ours – Mam'zelle has, for instance – but you'll have to try and get into our ways if you're going to be happy here.'

'I am happy anywhere,' said Claudine at once. 'Well, Susan, I will perhaps not copy again – only if I have not done any of my prep at all.'

Another thing that the girls found irritating about Claudine was the way she borrowed things. She borrowed pencils, rubbers, rulers, books – anything she happened to want at the moment. And nine times out of ten she didn't give them back.

'I forget,' she explained. 'I borrow a pencil and I use it, and I am most grateful for it – and then I forget about it, and poor Hilary, she says, "Where is my pencil, I have lost my pencil" – and there it is on my desk all the time, not at all lost.'

'Well, you might *try* and remember to give back things you borrow,' said Hilary. 'After all, it was a silver pencil of mine you borrowed, one I like very much. And you might ask permission before you borrow things.'

'Oh, you English!' sighed Claudine. 'Well, I will be good, and always I will say, "Dear Hilary, please, please lend me your so-beautiful silver pencil." '

Hilary laughed. No one could help being amused by Claudine. She rolled her expressive black eyes round and used her hands in the same way that Mam'zelle did. After all, she hadn't been in England very long – she would learn English ways before the term was over!

4

Beware of Matron!

The first few weeks passed, and soon the fourth formers, those who had come up from the third form, felt as if they had always been in the fourth form! They looked down on the third formers, and as for the second- and first-form girls, well, they were very small fry indeed. No fourth former would have dreamt of taking any notice of them.

The summer term was always a nice one. There was tennis, and there was swimming. Angela proved to be an unexpectedly good swimmer, deft and swift. Alison, who disliked the water, did her best to shine in it in order to try to keep up with her beloved Angela.

Claudine frankly hated the water. She entirely refused to go in, much to the games mistress's annoyance.

'Claudine! What is the use of coming to an English school if you do not learn the good things in it?' she said.

'Swimming is not a good thing,' said Claudine. 'It is a horrible thing, wet and cold and shivery. And I do not like your habit of playing so many games. Tennis is also silly.'

As no one could undress Claudine by force, she did not go into the water. The others teased her by splashing her as much as they could. The games mistress saw that sooner or later Claudine would be pushed in, fully-dressed, and she sent her back to the school.

Claudine's tennis was even worse than Carlotta's. Carlotta had never managed to play properly. She was still very wild and uncontrolled in games, and the tennis ball was quite as likely to drop into the middle of the distant swimming-pool as over the tennis net! But Claudine did not even attempt to hit the ball!

'This is a so-silly game,' she would say, and put down her racket and go off by herself.

'But Claudine, it's your tennis-practice time. You *must* come,' Hilary would say.

'I must not,' was Claudine's reply, and that was that.

Angela played a neat and deft game. She always brought her three beautiful rackets out with her, in spite of everyone's teasing. Pauline was jealous of them. She tried to pay Angela out by being spiteful.

'I've two or three more rackets at home,' she said in a loud voice. 'But it isn't good manners to bring more than one to school. My mother says that would be showing off. No well-bred person shows off.'

Nobody liked Angela's conceit, but nobody liked Pauline's spite, either. In fact, few people liked Pauline for, rich and grand as she made out her people and her home to be, she was a plain and unattractive girl – unlike Angela, who was really lovely. Nobody could help looking at the angel-faced Angela without admiration and pleasure. Alison thought she was the prettiest girl she had ever seen.

Eileen was moderately good at both tennis and

swimming. She was moderately good at her lessons too. She took a liking to Alison, for some reason or other, and was very upset when Alison showed her far too plainly that she had no time for her.

'*Why* can't you sometimes walk with me when we go out in the afternoons?' Eileen said to Alison. 'You can't *always* walk with Angela. And *why* do you always refuse when I offer you sweets? They won't poison you!'

'I know,' said Alison, coldly. 'I just don't want them, that's all. And I don't particularly want to walk with you, either.'

'I suppose Angela told you not to!' said Eileen, angrily. 'You haven't got any mind of your own, have you? Whatever Angela thinks, *you* think! Whatever Angela does, *you* do! You're even trying to grow your hair the way she grows hers – down to your shoulders and curled under. Well, you look a perfect fright like that!'

Alison was very offended. She looked coldly at Eileen.

'Well, if you want to know, Angela doesn't approve of you, and as she is my friend, I respect her wishes. Anyway, I don't approve of you, either. You're a tell-tale!'

Eileen walked away, her face scarlet with rage. Alison's last hit had gone home. Eileen ran to her mother with tales, and there was nothing the fourth form did that the new Matron did not know about.

Worse than that, if Eileen told her mother that someone had been horrid to her, the Matron soon saw to it that that someone was called to her room, and shown a huge rent in one of her bed sheets to mend, or holes in her games stockings, or buttons off clothes.

'I believe she makes the holes on purpose and pulls the buttons off herself!' raged Angela, who had been given three stockings to darn in her spare-time. 'I've never darned a stocking in my life. What's a matron for if she doesn't keep our things mended?'

'Well, it is the rule at St Clare's that we do some of our own mending,' said Pat. 'But I must say, Angela, I can't think that you made all those enormous holes in your stockings! I've never seen you with a hole yet.'

'Oh, I *know* I didn't make them,' said Angela, trying in vain to thread a needle with wool. '*How* do you make the wool go through the needle's eye? I've been trying to thread this for ages.'

The girls laughed. Angela had no idea how to double over the end of the wool and thread the darning needle in the right way. Alison took the needle and stocking away from her.

'I'll do your darning, Angela,' she said. 'Don't worry. I bet it's that tell-tale Eileen that ran to her mother about something you said or did – and so Matron gave you this work to do out of spite.'

Alison darned the three stockings – not very well, it is true, because darning was not one of Alison's gifts. But Angela was grateful, and was so sweet to Alison that the girl was in the seventh Heaven of delight.

Pauline was the next to get into trouble with Matron. She, like Angela, turned up her nose at Eileen, and would have no more to do with her than she could help. When she told Bobby one morning that she had a sore throat, Eileen overheard. She went off out of the room, and in a short while Pauline was sent for.

'I hear you have a sore throat, Pauline,' said Matron, with a thin-lipped smile. 'You should report to me at once. Eileen felt worried about you, and told me. It was very kind of her. I have a gargle for you here, and some medicine.'

'Oh, my throat is much better now,' said Pauline in alarm. And it was – but Matron was not going to let her off. She made poor Pauline gargle for ten minutes with a horrible concoction, and then gave her some equally nasty medicine to drink.

Pauline went back to the others, angry and afraid. She glanced round the room to make sure that Eileen was not there.

'Eileen's been telling tales again,' she said. 'She told her mother I'd got a sore throat – and I've just been having an awful time. I feel quite sick. I know Eileen told Matron she didn't like me, and that's why Matron gave me such a beastly time.'

'We'll have to be careful what we say and do to Eileen,' said Alison, scared, for she hated medicine of any sort. 'Perhaps we'd better be friendlier.'

'I shall not be friendlier,' said Claudine. 'That is a girl I do not like.'

And, far from being friendlier, Claudine really seemed to go out of her way to be rude to Eileen! The result was that Matron came down heavily on Claudine, and gave her a whole basketful of mending to do!

'You have torn the hem of both your sheets,' she told Claudine. 'And you have holes in all your stockings, and you need a patch in one of your blouses. You are a very naughty, careless girl. You will do most of this mending yourself, as a punishment.'

Claudine said nothing. She took the basket of mending and put it on top of her locker. At first the girls thought she would simply forget all about it, and refuse to do it, as she refused to do other things. But, to their surprise, Claudine took down the mending and settled herself in a corner of the common-room to do it.

Bobby watched her needle flying in and out. 'I say – you do sew beautifully!' she said. 'You really do! And your darning is as good as embroidery. It's beautiful.'

'I like sewing and darning,' said Claudine. 'We are always taught that well in France. You English girls are clumsy with your needles. You can bang all kinds of silly balls about, but you cannot make a beautiful darn!'

'Claudine, put that mending away now, and come out and swim,' said Susan. 'It's such a nice sunny day.'

But nice sunny days did not appeal to Claudine at all. 'I can see the sun out of the window,' she said, sewing away hard. 'Leave me. I like sewing.'

Bobby stared hard at the bent head of the little French girl. Then she gave a chuckle.

'Claudine, you like sewing a whole lot better than you like swimming and games, don't you?' she said.

'Yes,' said Claudine. 'Sewing is very OK, I think.'

The others laughed. Claudine always sounded funny

when she brought American slang into her speech.

'I believe this is all a little trick of Claudine's,' said Bobby. 'She wants to have a real excuse for getting out of games! We all know we have to give up games time if we have mending to do – and Claudine has made Matron give her a punishment that will get her out of games, and give her something to do instead that she really likes!'

Miss Ellis came into the room. 'Hurry up and go out, girls,' she said. 'Don't waste a minute of this nice fine day. Claudine, put away your sewing.'

'I'm sorry, Miss Ellis, but Matron said I was to do my darning and mending before I could go to play with the others,' said Claudine, looking up with big innocent dark eyes. 'It is very sad – but I suppose I must do this, Miss Ellis?'

'Hmm,' said Miss Ellis, not at all taken in by the wide-open eyes. 'I'll have a word with Matron.'

But Matron was quite insistent that Claudine had been careless, and must mend her things, so Miss Ellis left the girl to her sewing. And Claudine had a very nice time, sewing away happily in a corner of the sunny room, hearing the shouts of the girls in the swimming-pool. She had no wish whatever to join them!

Horrible wet cold water! she thought to herself, and then looked up as she heard footsteps coming into the room. It was her aunt, Mam'zelle.

'Ah, *ma petite*!' said Mam'zelle, beaming. 'So you are here. Let me see your sewing. It is beautiful! Why cannot these English girls sew? Where are the others?'

'In the water,' said Claudine, in French. 'Always they are in the water, or hitting a ball, these English girls. Me, I prefer to sew, *ma tante*!'

'Quite right, little Claudine!' said Mam'zelle, who, for all her years in England had never been able to understand why English girls liked cold water, hitting balls, and running madly about. 'You are happy, my little one?'

'Yes, thank you, *ma tante*,' answered Claudine demurely. 'But I am a little dull. Does nothing ever happen in these English schools?'

'Nothing,' said Mam'zelle. But she was wrong. Things did happen – and they were just about to!

Angela gets a surprise

About the third week of the term, when everyone had settled down, and got into their work, Angela had a surprise.

She had been playing tennis, and one of the balls had been lost. 'Don't let's bother to look for it now,' said Bobby, who hated to stop in the middle of a game. 'It's sure to turn up. Tennis-balls always do. If it doesn't we'll look for it afterwards.'

The ball hadn't turned up, and Angela had offered to look for it. The others had music-lessons to go to, or elocution practice. Angela was the only one free.

'All right,' said Hilary. 'Thanks, Angela. You look for the ball, and pop it back into the box with the others if you find it.'

The other three girls ran back to the school, and Angela began to look for the lost ball. It was nowhere to be seen. The court they had been playing on backed on to a high wall, and Angela wondered if the ball could possibly have gone over it.

'I remember Bobby sending a pretty high ball once,' she thought to herself. 'Well, it doesn't seem to be *this* side of the wall – so I'll just slip out of the garden gate here and look in the lane.'

The girl opened the gate and went out into the narrow green lane. She looked about for the ball, and at last saw it. As she went to get it, she gave a start of surprise. A tall, rather thin young lad was behind the bush near the ball.

Angela picked up the ball and was about to go back into the school grounds, when the boy spoke to her.

'I say – do you belong to St Clare's?'

Angela looked at him and didn't like him. He had hair that was curly, and much too long. His eyes were small and puffy underneath, and he was very pale.

'What business is it of yours whether I belong to St Clare's or not?' said Angela, in her haughtiest voice.

'Now look here – don't go all stuffy and stupid,' said the boy, coming out from behind the bush. 'I just want a word with you.'

'Well, I don't want a word with *you*,' said Angela, and she opened the garden gate. The boy tried to stop her going through.

'Wait a bit,' he said, and his voice sounded so urgent that Angela turned round in surprise. 'I want you to take a message to one of the girls for me,' he said.

'Of course I shan't do that,' said Angela. 'Let me pass, please. You deserve to be reported for this.'

'Listen. You tell Eileen that Eddie wants to see her,' said the boy. 'Wait – I've got a note for her. Will you give it to her?'

'Oh – so you're Eileen's brother, are you?' said Angela. 'All right – I'll give her the note. But I can't think why you don't come right in and see your mother and Eileen too, if you want to. Your mother is Matron here, isn't she?'

'Yes,' said Eddie. 'But for goodness' sake don't go and tell my mother you've seen me. She doesn't know I'm here. I'd get into an awful row with her if she knew I was.'

'Your mother gets lots of people into rows besides you!' said Angela, taking the note.

The girl went through the gate and shut it. Then she stuffed the note into the pocket of her blazer, meaning to give it to Eileen when she saw her.

Eileen was not about when Angela went back to the cloakroom to change her shoes. The girl saw Alison there and began to tell her what had happened.

'I say, Alison!' she said. 'A funny thing happened just now. I went out into the lane to look for a tennis-ball, and there was a boy there, hiding.'

'Gracious!' said Alison, startled. 'What did you do?'

'He was an awful creature,' said Angela, beginning to exaggerate, as she usually did when she had a tale to tell. 'Honestly, he looked like the boy who brings the fish here every day – you know, that awful boy with the too-long hair and the piercing whistle! I half expected him to say, "I've brought the 'addock and 'ake and 'alibut, miss!" like the fish-boy said to Matron the other day, thinking she was the cook.'

Alison laughed. So did one or two other girls in the cloakroom. Angela loved an admiring audience. She went on with her tale, not seeing that Eileen had come in to put away gym shoes.

'Well, he asked me if I belonged to St Clare's, and I put

him properly in his place, you may be sure! And then he told me who he was. You'll never guess!'

The girls crowded round her in interest. 'Who?' said Alison. 'How should we know who it was?'

'Well, it was dear, darling wonderful Eddie, Eileen's big brother!' said Angela. 'As common as could be! I nearly asked him why he didn't get his hair cut!'

Someone elbowed her way roughly through the group round Angela. It was Eileen, her cheeks scarlet. She glared at Angela.

'You frightful fibber!' she said. 'My brother's nowhere near St Clare's! How dare you make up a story like that? I shall go and tell my mother at once – you hateful, horrid little snob!'

She burst into tears and went out of the door. The girls stared after her.

'I say,' said Alison, 'she really *will* go to Matron – and there's sure to be a row. You didn't make it up, did you, Angela?'

Angela raised her voice and shouted after Eileen. 'Well, go and tell if you like – but your darling Eddie begged and begged me *not* to let your mother know he was here. So you are just as likely to get *him* into a row, as me!'

Eileen turned round, looking scared. It was plain that she now believed what Angela said. It *had* been Eddie!

'What did he say to you?' she asked Angela, in a strangled voice. 'Did he want to see me?'

'Shan't tell you,' said Angela, in an irritating voice. 'I *was* going to do you a good turn and give you his message

– but if you behave like this I'm jolly well not going to be a go-between for you and dear, darling Eddie!'

Just at that very thrilling moment Miss Ellis put her head in at the door, looking most annoyed.

'Girls! Didn't you hear the bell? What in the world are you doing, chattering here in the cloakroom? You know that isn't allowed. Really, I do wish you fourth formers would realize that you are half-way up the school and not in the first form! I am most annoyed at having to come and fetch you.'

'Sorry, Miss Ellis,' said everyone, and hurried to go out of the cloakroom back to the classroom, where they had prep to do. Certainly they had heard the bell – but who could tear themselves away when a first-class quarrel was going on between the angelic Angela and the unpopular Eileen?

Angela felt delighted when she sat down at her desk. Now she had Eileen exactly where she wanted her – under her thumb! And if Eileen ever told tales of her again and got Matron to give her heaps of mending to do, she, Angela, would threaten to tell Matron about dear Eddie! Angela smiled a secret smile to herself, which made her look more like an angel than ever. It was extraordinary how Angela could look so innocently beautiful when she was thinking spiteful thoughts!

Eileen saw the secret smile. She pursed her lips together and ground her teeth. She hated Angela bitterly in that moment, with as deep a hatred as the love she had for Eddie. How dared Angela call Eddie common? How dared she say he was like that horrid little fishmonger's boy, with his long, greasy hair and shrill whistle?

To Eileen, her brother Edgar was the most wonderful being in the world. Their father had died when they were both very young, and their mother was a hard and stern woman. The little girl had turned to her big brother for love and companionship, and the boy had guarded and cherished his sister tenderly.

'As soon as I grow up, I'll get a fine job, and make heaps of money for you and Mother,' he told Eileen. 'Then Mother won't need to work so hard and be so tired and cross, and you shall have lots of nice presents. You'll see what wonderful things I'll do!'

And now Angela had poured scorn on darling, kind Eddie. Eileen felt as if she must burst with anger and tears. She was very anxious too. Why had Eddie left Woolaton, where he worked, and come to see her secretly? What had happened? Oh, if only that beast of an Angela would tell her!

Eileen thought of Eddie out there in the lane. She had not seen him for some weeks, and she was longing to talk to him and tell him everything. Perhaps he felt the same and had got some time off to slip along and see her. Perhaps he didn't want to come up to the school, because then he would have to see Mother too, and that would spoil the heart-to-heart talk they might have together.

Eileen looked at Angela. The girl was studying her French book, looking serene and lovely. Eileen gritted her teeth again, knowing that she would soon have to do something very difficult, something she would hate, yet which would have to be done gracefully.

I'll have to go and beg Angela's pardon and ask her to tell me what Eddie said, thought Eileen. Beast! I do hate her!

She gave a loud sigh. Miss Ellis looked up. She had already seen that Eileen was making no attempt at all to do her prep.

'Eileen, don't you feel well?' she inquired. 'As far as I can see you haven't done any work at all.'

'I'm all right, thank you, Miss Ellis,' said Eileen hurriedly. 'This – this French is a bit difficult today, that's all.'

'I should think it must be *very* difficult to learn your French out of your geography book,' said Miss Ellis in her calm voice. Eileen looked hurriedly down at her book – dash – it was her geography book she was holding! Trust the sharp eyes of Miss Ellis to spot that!

She said nothing, but got out her French book. Angela looked round and gave a scornful little smile. She knew quite well why it was that Eileen muddled her books just then – she was worried about dear darling Eddie. Well – let her worry!

Alison sat next to Eileen, and she couldn't help feeling a little sorry for her. Although she was such a little scatter-brain, Alison was sensitive to the feelings of others, and she knew that Eileen was desperately longing to know about Eddie. So, after prep was over she went to Angela and spoke to her.

'I say, Angela – hadn't you better tell Eileen her

brother's message? She's in an awful state. She sighed so hard in prep that she almost blew my papers off the desk!'

Angela was not amused at Alison's feeble little joke, neither did she like her giving her advice of any sort. She turned away, and Alison's heart sank. Now Angela was going to go all cold and sulky again. The beautiful little face was hard and haughty, and Alison knew it would be ages before she could get a smile out of her again.

She was just going after her when Eileen came up, a forced smile on her face. 'Angela! Can I speak to you for a minute? Alone, please?'

6
Angela and Eileen

'I'm busy,' said Angela, curtly.

'No, you're not,' said Eileen, trying to speak calmly and smilingly. 'It's important, Angela.'

'I hope you're going to apologize for your rudeness to me,' said Angela, haughtily. 'I certainly shan't speak to you unless you do. I'm not going to let people like you call me a hateful horrid snob.'

Eileen swallowed hard and forced herself to speak, though the words almost choked her.

'I beg your pardon, Angela. I – I just lost my temper!'

Carlotta overheard this conversation and unexpectedly came to Eileen's help. 'Well, if you ask *my* opinion I think Angela ought to apologize to *you*, Eileen, for some of *her* remarks!' said Carlotta, in her fresh, candid voice. 'I'm jolly certain I wouldn't apologize to *her* – little cat!'

Angela turned on Carlotta in a fury, her blue eyes gleaming with spite.

'You don't suppose we care what circus folk think, do you?' she said. But instead of being crushed, Carlotta gave one of her hearty laughs.

'If I wasn't in the fourth form I'd give you the biggest scolding you've ever had in your life, Angela,' she said, amiably. 'A good scolding would be the best thing you could have.'

'Nobody has ever raised their voice to me in my life,' said Angela, feeling an intense desire to smack Carlotta's vivid little face.

'I can tell that,' said Carlotta. 'You'd be a lot nicer if they had. Come on, Eileen, leave Angela to her haughty ways and come and play cards with me in the common-room.'

Eileen felt very grateful to Carlotta for her unexpected help, but she shook her head. She had simply *got* to find out about Eddie. How unfortunate it was that it should be Angela, of all people, that he had spoken to. Any of the others would have been decent about it – except Pauline perhaps.

Carlotta shrugged her shoulders and went off to find Bobby and the twins. She didn't like Eileen very much, because she thought, as the others did, that she was a tell-tale – but all the same Angela was behaving like a little cat to her, putting out those claws of hers and giving as deep a scratch as she could!

Angela turned to Eileen. 'Well,' she said, 'you've apologized and I accept your apology. What do you want to say to me?'

'Angela, *please* tell me what Eddie said,' begged Eileen. 'Did he give you a message for me?'

'Yes. He gave me a letter,' said Angela. Eileen went red with excitement and stared at Angela eagerly.

'Please give it to me,' she said.

'I don't see why I should,' said Angela. 'I don't think I

ought to take notes and deliver them, like this.'

Eileen knew that Angela was saying this to irritate her. She felt intensely angry, but she kept her temper.

'You'll never have to do it again,' she said. 'I'll tell Edgar he mustn't send in notes this way. He must post a letter. Please give me the note.'

'Now, listen,' said Angela, suddenly getting down to business, 'if I give you this note and don't tell your mother I saw her precious Eddie, you've got to promise *me* something.'

'What?' asked Eileen, in surprise. 'I'll promise you anything!'

'All right,' said Angela. 'You've jolly well got to promise me that you'll never run sneaking to your mother about *me*, see? I'm not going to have shoals of mending to do any more – I hate sewing and darning! I know you complained to Matron about me before, and that's why she presented me with stockings that had holes in *I* never made!'

'You're not to say things like that about my mother,' said Eileen.

'Well, I shall,' said Angela. 'We all know you sneak to her about us. Sneak about the others all you like – but don't you sneak about *me* any more. You'll be sorry if you do.'

There was nothing for it but to promise. So Eileen promised. 'I won't sneak about you,' she said in a trembling voice. 'I don't sneak. If Mother hands out sewing and mending, it's not my fault.'

'Hmm,' said Angela, disbelievingly, 'well, all I can say is – it's a funny thing that as soon as anyone dares to say anything about you, Matron heaps a beastly lot of mending on to them, so that they have to miss games and swimming. Anyway, Eileen, I warn you – you've got to tell your mother nice things about me, or I'll tell tales of *you*, and say I've seen Eddie and he didn't want his mother to know!'

Eileen bit her lip. It was very hard to keep her temper during this long speech. But she knew she had to, for Eddie's sake.

'I've apologized to you, Angela, and I've promised you what you want,' she said, in a low voice. 'Please give me the note now.'

Angela fished in her pocket for the note. She was a long time about it, pretending she had lost it, feeling in her blouse for it as well as in her pockets. Eileen hated her for this petty meanness, but she stood waiting patiently whilst Angela looked.

At last Angela produced the note. Eileen snatched it from her and without another word went off by herself to read it. It was very short.

Darling Sis, [said the note]
I must see you. Don't say a word to Mother. We simply must have a talk. Can you meet me outside the garden-door in the wall, any time this evening? I'll wait behind a bush till you come.
Your loving brother,
Eddie.

Eileen read the note three times and then tore it up. She was afraid her mother might find it, and then she would be angry with Eddie. Mother wasn't very sympathetic, somehow. She didn't seem to think much of Eddie, and was always telling him what a fine man his father had been and how curious it was that Eddie hadn't been much good at school, or won any scholarships, or made her really proud of him.

I'll slip down to the garden-door and see Eddie as soon as all the others are safely in the common-room, thought Eileen. Poor old Eddie – he must have been waiting a long time. He couldn't send a letter through the post, because Mother would have been sure to see it, and would have asked to read it.

The girl waited until she saw that all the fourth formers were in their common-room. She sat by the door and watched them. Doris and Carlotta were fooling about and the others were watching them, laughing. Claudine got up to join the two who were clowning, and Eileen saw that now was her chance. She slipped out.

But one person saw her go. That was Angela, who had been expecting Eileen to slip away down to the lane. It was forbidden for the girls to go out of the school grounds without permission after evening prep, and Angela smiled spitefully to herself.

If Eileen makes a habit of meeting dear brother Eddie out of hours, I shall be able to hold that over her, too, thought Angela. She went out of the room and walked into a little music-room that overlooked the school grounds. It was difficult to see anyone in the trees and bushes, but because she knew exactly where to look, Angela was able to catch a glimpse of Eileen now and again, hurrying through the trees to the little gate in the wall.

She went back to the common-room. Doris, Carlotta and Claudine were still fooling about, keeping everyone in fits of laughter. Doris was a wonderful mimic, Carlotta could do extraordinary tricks, and Claudine could imitate Mam'zelle, her aunt, to perfection.

Angela could not see anything to laugh at at all. Do they really think it's funny, to pull faces and make themselves ugly and stupid-looking? she thought to herself, as she watched Doris imitating an old charwoman, and Claudine playing up to her as a French maid. She patted her beautiful pale gold hair, comparing it with Carlotta's wild mop. A smug little smile came to her lovely face. She knew she was more beautiful than any other girl in the school! What did brains and gifts matter? Everyone stared at her in the street, everyone thought she must be a princess at least. And perhaps one day she would marry a prince and be a real princess! Angela dreamt away, not listening to the chatter around her at all.

Two people watched her, one with envy and the other with devoted admiration. The first was Pauline, who, plain and unattractive, envied Angela her beauty, and longed with all her heart to look like her. But her own perfectly straight hair, well-brushed as it was, would never shine like Angela's, nor would it curl under at the ends, as Angela's did, so prettily. Angela's eyes were a brilliant, startling blue – Pauline's were pale. Angela's cheeks were a beautiful rosy pink. Pauline's seldom had any colour. It was too bad that Angela had so much and she, Pauline, had so little in the way of looks!

The other person watching Angela, was, of course, her devoted slave, Alison. She wondered if Angela had forgiven her for offering advice about Eileen. She tried to catch Angela's eye, but Angela was lost in beautiful day-dreams.

'You do look so lovely, Angela,' whispered Alison, at last. Angela heard and smiled prettily. She had forgotten that she was offended with Alison. She spoke to her in a low voice, boasting of her conquest of Eileen.

'I ticked Eileen off properly for being a sneak,' she said to Alison. 'I forbade her ever to sneak again, and she promised she wouldn't.'

'Oh, Angela – did you really make her promise that?' said Alison. 'You're wonderful, you really are!' She looked round the common-room. 'I say – where *is* Eileen?'

'Would you like to know?' said Angela, looking at the expensive gold watch on her wrist, and seeing that there were only five minutes to go before bed-time. 'Well, come with me and I'll see if I can show you where our dear Eileen is!'

She took Alison into the little music-room. 'See the school wall, right down there?' she said. 'You know the little door let into it there, behind the tennis-courts? Well, I think Eileen has gone through there into the lane to talk to dear, darling Eddie!'

'Look – is that Eileen coming back?' said Alison. 'Golly, she'll get into a row if she's caught!'

'Yes – it's Eileen all right,' said Angela, as a figure came into view between the trees and then disappeared again. 'Let's wait outside the common-room door and catch her as she comes in!'

So the two waited there. Eileen came quickly up the passage to the room, and Angela spoke to her.

'Well – how's dear darling Eddie?'

Eileen stared at her, hardly seeming to see her. She looked pale and worried. She pushed at the shut door of the common-room, meaning to go and fetch her nightdress, which she had been mending. But Angela stopped her.

'You didn't answer my question,' she said, in a smooth little voice. 'How's dear darling Eddie?'

Eileen faced the spiteful girl. 'Eddie's all right,' she said, in a trembling voice. 'Eddie's fine. He had lots of good news to tell me. He's getting on well.'

She went into the common-room. Alison felt uncomfortable again. She didn't like this teasing, there was something spiteful in it – but how could she dare to find fault with the Honourable Angela?

7
Claudine gets her own way

'This is a jolly nice term,' said Pat to Isabel, as they dried themselves after swimming in the big swimming-pool. 'I simply adore all this open-air life – tennis and swimming and riding and gardening – and today we even had lessons out-of-doors, it was so hot!'

Isabel grinned. 'Poor old Claudine doesn't like the open air as much as we do!' she said. 'Wasn't she funny in maths?'

Claudine had indeed been funny. To begin with she had been quite horrified to hear that Miss Ellis proposed to take lessons out-of-doors under the trees. Apparently no school she had ever been to had ever thought of doing such a thing.

'Lessons out-of-doors!' said the little French girl. 'But why? What is the matter with indoors? I do not like this out-of-doors – the sun is too hot, it burns me.'

'Pity it doesn't burn you a bit more,' grinned Bobby, who was as brown as an acorn. 'Look at us, all brown and tanned – and you are like a lily, pale and white.'

Claudine looked down at her lily-white hands with great satisfaction. 'That is another thing I do not understand about you so-jolly English girls,' she said. 'It is not pretty to get burnt, it is ugly to grow freckles – and yet you try to grow as tanned as you can, all day long! Me, I like to be pale. It is more natural, more becoming. And now – what can Miss Ellis be thinking of to say lessons out-of-doors! I shall take a sunshade with me, for I will not grow one single freckle.'

But Miss Ellis did not approve of sunshades being brought out in a maths lesson. She looked at Claudine with disapproval. 'I don't know if you are merely being funny, Claudine, or if you seriously think that you need a sunshade under the trees, where there is no sun – but whatever your reason, the sunshade must go back to the school at once. I can't imagine where you got it!'

The sunshade had been used in a play, and was simply enormous. Claudine was quite lost under it. She looked at Miss Ellis pathetically.

'Please, *chère* Miss Ellis, I am not making a joke, it is because I do not wish to grow a freckle on my nose,' she said, beseechingly. 'A freckle is not for a French girl. Freckles are English, Miss Ellis, and I do not want to grow them.'

'Oh, freckles can be French as much as English!' said Miss Ellis. 'It will do your pale face good to have a few nice freckles here and there, Claudine. Take the sunshade back, please, and don't bring it out again.'

'Oh, please, Miss Ellis, couldn't Claudine and I share the sunshade?' said Angela, who also had a fear of freckles. Her face was tanned a rosy-brown, and she had no freckles at all – she was careful not to get too sunburnt, for she knew that would spoil her delicate beauty.

She gave Bobby's face a scornful glance. It was absolutely covered with little brown freckles, right to the tip of the up-turned nose. 'I couldn't bear to get freckled like poor Bobby,' went on Angela, no spite showing in her smooth little voice. 'This sun is so hot, Miss Ellis – just see how it has treated Bobby!'

'Don't you believe it,' said Bobby, not standing any nonsense of that sort. 'My face is freckled winter and summer alike. Nothing to do with the summer sun! I was born with freckles!'

The class giggled, and Bobby opened her mouth to continue. But Miss Ellis knew Bobby's speeches, and spoke first!

'That will do, Bobby. I don't want any more of the maths lesson wasted on freckles. Claudine, take the sun-shade back. Angela, don't look as if you are going to faint away – it would do both you and Claudine good to get a few freckles – Claudine because she sits too much indoors, and you because you think too much of your looks. It would be better if you thought a little more about your work. You may think it is amusing to be bottom each week, as you have been so far, but I must say I can't see the joke.'

Angela flushed. How horrid Miss Ellis could be! She caught a satisfied smile on Pauline's face. Pauline was cleverer than Angela – that was one way in which she was better than Angela, anyhow! Angela scowled and glanced at Alison for comfort. Alison gave it, smiling adoringly, and making a face at Miss Ellis.

Lessons out-of-doors were not a success at all, with Claudine in the class. She screamed whenever an insect flew near, and if a bird dared to fly suddenly out of a bush, she made everyone jump by her yells. Miss Ellis got very tired of her.

'*Now* what's the matter, Claudine?' she said, when a bee flew near the girl and hummed in her ear. Claudine had squealed, jumped up and run to the other end of the long table on which everyone was working.

'It is an animal that goes "Zzzz" and carries a sting, Miss Ellis,' said Claudine, looking genuinely frightened.

'A bee,' said Miss Ellis, in disgust. 'It won't sting you. Sit down. You are disturbing all the others.'

The next thing that upset Claudine was an ant. It crawled up her leg and she suddenly felt it. She gave such an agonized yell that everyone jumped violently.

'CLAUDINE! I shall send you indoors if you squeal again!' said Miss Ellis in exasperation. 'What's the matter now?'

Claudine was undoing her suspender with trembling hands, giving little squeals and French exclamations all the time. The ant had explored the inside of the top of her stocking. The girls went into fits of laughter, and Miss Ellis rapped angrily on her table.

'Claudine, what are you doing? Surely you are not taking off your stockings!'

Claudine was deaf to anything that Miss Ellis said. When she at last saw the ant, inside her stocking, she did not dare to touch it, and gazed round with such an agonized expression on her face that Bobby took pity on her, and flicked the ant deftly on to the grass.

'Ah!' said Claudine. '*Merci bien*, Bobbee! What a terrible thing to happen to me!'

'Much more terrible things will happen to you if I have any more disturbance,' said Miss Ellis, in such a grim tone that Claudine was much astonished. She sat down again, doing up her suspender.

'One more squeal from you and you go indoors,' said Miss Ellis. Claudine gazed at her thoughtfully. If there was one thing more than another that Claudine wanted at that moment it was to go indoors, where creatures that flew and crawled did not molest her.

She waited until Miss Ellis had bent her head to correct Hilary's book, and then she let out a piercing yell that made her neighbour, Pauline, jump so violently that she upset the ink over the table. Miss Ellis leapt to her feet, her usual calmness quite deserting her.

'Claudine! This behaviour is intolerable. Go indoors at once and find the mistress in the teachers' common-room who is free at the moment. Tell her I sent you in in disgrace and ask her to let you sit with her, whilst you do your maths. And if there is a single mistake in your paper I shall have a great deal to say about it. I am thoroughly displeased with you.'

With the greatest cheerfulness and alacrity Claudine obeyed Miss Ellis, scurrying indoors with her books before the mistress could change her mind. Doris exploded into one of her giggles. Miss Ellis glanced at her sharply, and Doris subsided. It then occurred to Miss Ellis that

Claudine, as usual, had got exactly what she wanted, in her usual unscrupulous way!

Miss Ellis wondered who the mistress was who would be in the teachers' common-room just then. She thought it would be Miss Rollins. That was good. Miss Rollins was very strict, and would make Claudine feel very small and humble before she had done with her.

But it was not Miss Rollins, much to Claudine's delight. When she knocked timidly on the mistresses' common-room door, she ran over in her mind what mistress was likely to be there. She hoped it would be the art mistress – she had a sense of fun and was very jolly.

She opened the door and went in – and she saw that it was Mam'zelle! Mam'zelle was having a cosy time by herself. She had taken off her big, flat-heeled shoes and had opened the collar of her high-necked blouse. It was such a hot day! She was half-asleep over her exercise books when the small neat figure of Claudine appeared. They stared at each other.

'Why are you here, Claudine?' asked Mam'zelle severely, in French. Claudine at once poured out a voluble and heart-rending explanation – how all the insects and winged beasts of that horrible English out-of-doors had molested her, yes, and bitten her and stung her, and altogether made life not worth living. And the sun had burnt her and she was sure she had dozens of those so-ugly freckles coming, and what would her dear mother say to that? Ah, life was very very hard at this so-sporting English school, with its love for the cold, cold water, and for striking at balls so many times a week, and for its detestable nature-walks, and . . .

Mam'zelle sympathized whole-heartedly. She too detested too much sun, and insects and reptiles of any kind filled her with fear and disgust. She forgot to inquire whether Claudine had come in of her own accord, or had been sent in in disgrace. Soon the two were talking nineteen to the dozen, going back in their thoughts to their beloved France, where girls were proper girls, and studied and did sewing and embroidery, and did not rush about in the mad way that all English girls did.

So, later on, when Miss Ellis asked Mam'zelle if she had scolded Claudine properly for being sent indoors in disgrace, Mam'zelle got a shock. She stared at Miss Ellis in dismay.

'Ah, the poor little Claudine!' she said at last. 'You must not be too hard on her, Miss Ellis. It is so difficult for a poor little French girl to learn your English ways.'

Miss Ellis snorted. 'I suppose that means that you and Claudine patted each other on the back, and that you believed everything the naughty little girl said – and I should think it is very likely that you helped her to do her maths too! She has never got all her sums right before.'

Mam'zelle felt extremely uncomfortable. She *had* helped Claudine with her work – and certainly she had believed every word she said. Would Claudine deceive her own good aunt? No, no – impossible!

But when Mam'zelle thought things over she knew that the clever little Claudine could and would deceive her if she felt inclined to. Mam'zelle loved Claudine very much, and thought the world of her – but all the same sometimes a doubt came into her mind – wasn't Claudine just a little *too* clever? Didn't she get her own way just a little *too* often? The trouble was – you never knew what Claudine wanted until she had got it, and then it was too late to do anything about it.

'My word,' said Bobby, when the maths lesson came to an end and the girls packed up their books. 'That little monkey of a Claudine can do anything she likes and get away with it! I bet she's had a perfectly lovely time indoors.'

So she had. She came beaming to meet Miss Ellis at the end of the morning, with a prettily worded apology.

'Ah, Miss Ellis! I am so, so ashamed of myself. You English, you are not frightened of anything, you keep the hairs on your head always, always you are calm – but me, I am a silly little French girl, so please excuse me and I will do better in future. My aunt was very, very angry with me, she caused me to cry bitterly, see how red my eyes are!'

Miss Ellis saw no signs of red eyes, and felt quite certain that Mam'zelle had not been angry at all. All the same, she found it difficult to hide a smile. Claudine was so very, very earnest and apologetic!

'I'll forgive you *this* time, Claudine,' she said. 'But you be careful *next* time!'

The term goes on

Although the girls knew quite well that Claudine told fibs when it suited her, borrowed without asking and still copied answers from other people's books if she wanted to, they couldn't help liking her. She was very funny, generous in her own way, and never took offence whatever was said to her.

She might easily have taken offence at things that Angela said, or Pauline. Angela looked down on her in the same way that she looked down on Eileen – because she was a pupil who was probably not paying the school fees.

'Charity girls, both of them!' she said to Alison, scornfully. 'I must say I didn't think we'd get them at schools like this.'

If Bobby, Hilary or the twins overheard things like this they ticked Angela off unmercifully.

'Look here,' Pat said once, 'we don't like Eileen any more than you do – but you've got to realize, Angela, that if Eileen's mother gets Eileen here for nothing, it's because of the work she does herself as Matron, and it doesn't matter tuppence if you pay for things in work or in money, it's good payment just the same, and Eileen isn't kept by "charity" as you call it. You're a disgusting little snob.'

Angela hated to be called a snob. She shut her book with a bang. 'Snob!' she said. 'That's a favourite word of yours for someone who happens to be out of the top drawer. Think of something more original to say.'

'Right,' said Bobby, at once. 'You think that Claudine is a charity girl too – well, instead of saying that to us, what about saying it to Mam'zelle – or even to Claudine herself? You're too cowardly to do that. You'll hit at Eileen because you've got some hold over her and she can't hit back – but you daren't hit at Claudine openly, because she's quite likely to fly at you and scratch your angelic face, or put Mam'zelle on the war-path after you!'

'Oh, you're impossible!' said Angela, angrily. 'I shall ask my mother to take me away at half-term. In fact, when she comes here and sees what kind of girls I have to live with, I'm certain she'll take me away with her, then and there!'

'Golly! If only your mother would be sensible enough to *do* that!' sighed Bobby. 'But she won't. I know mothers. She'll leave you here to be a pest to us for the rest of the term.'

Tears of anger came into Angela's eyes. In all her spoilt, petted life she had never been spoken to like this. She was angry, hurt, and miserable. She blinked back her tears, because a tear-stained face spoilt her beauty. She went to find Alison.

Alison could always put soothing ointment on Angela's wounds. In her usual feather-headed way she made herself quite blind to Angela's grave faults, and saw only the loveliness of Angela's face, and the beauty of her clothes and possessions. Poor Alison always seemed to attach herself to the wrong kind of people.

'She'll never learn!' said Hilary. 'I did think once, when she was in the second form, and was so keen on that awful drama mistress, Miss Quentin, that she had learnt a pretty sharp lesson – you remember how Miss Quentin let her down, don't you? She pretended to be awfully fond of Alison, and then laughed at her behind her back.'

The twins nodded. 'Yes,' said Pat. 'It's really a pity that Alison isn't happy unless she is worshipping someone. She's awfully bad for Angela. As soon as we get a bit of sense into Angela's head, Alison gets it out, by saying she's wonderful, too lovely for words, and all the rest of it.'

'I must say she's not a bit like you two,' said Bobby. 'You've got plenty of common sense. It's funny you should have a cousin like Alison!'

The weather went on being hot and sunny, with blue skies everyday. The girls swam and played games to their hearts' content. They all got very brown, except Claudine, who managed to remain pale as a lily in spite of everything. She worried very much one week because she felt sure she had a freckle coming on her nose. The girls teased her unmercifully.

'Golly! Isn't Claudine's freckle getting pronounced?' said Hilary, staring at Claudine's dainty little nose.

'Yes. It's going to be a real beauty,' said Pat.

'Big as a penny piece,' said Isabel.

Claudine gave a squeal of horror and fished out the

little mirror she always carried with her. She and Angela and Alison always carried small mirrors about with them, and were for ever examining their faces for something or other.

'I have no freckle,' she announced indignantly. 'You talk under your hats!'

The girls laughed. 'Claudine, you talk *through* your hat, not under it,' said Bobby. 'But if you want to keep a secret you keep it *under* your hat! See?'

Claudine sighed. 'Ah, your English sayings are so difficult. I will remember – to talk *through* your hat means to be silly – to keep something *under* your hat means to keep a secret. Ah – there goes one who keeps something under her hat!'

The girls turned to see who Claudine meant. It was Eileen Paterson.

'Yes – Eileen does seem to be all bottled up, somehow,' said Hilary, rather worried. 'As if she's got a secret and is afraid someone will get to know it. She's been looking rather miserable sometimes.'

'Well, she's got her mother here to tell anything to,' said Pat. The others made scornful noises.

'Pooh!' said Bobby. 'Would *you* tell Matron anything if she were *your* mother? I know I wouldn't. She's as hard as nails! I hope to goodness I'm never ill whilst she's here as Matron. I shouldn't fancy being looked after by her!'

The girls were all rather careful in the way they treated Eileen now, because they felt certain that any slight, intended or otherwise, that they showed Eileen was reported to Matron, and then Matron landed them with all kinds of unexpected mending to do. All except Angela. Angela could say and do what she liked to Eileen. Matron always seemed to look on Angela with a favourable eye. Eileen did not dare to tell tales of her.

'I think Eileen misses that dear brother of hers,' said Bobby. 'You know what Angela told us – how he came to see her, but didn't want to see his mother. I bet he's in some kind of trouble, and Eileen's worried about it.'

'Poor Eileen!' said Hilary. 'I'll just pump her a bit and see.'

So Hilary kindly and tactfully 'pumped' Eileen, but she learnt very little.

'How old is your brother, Eileen?' she said. 'Is he like you at all?'

Eileen fetched a snapshot and showed it to Hilary. She seemed glad of the chance of talking about Eddie.

'Eddie's eighteen,' she said. 'Two years older than I am. He's fine, Hilary. But he's never had much chance. You see, my father died when we were so little. Eddie ought to be at college now, but he's got to earn his living.'

Hilary looked at the snap of the rather weak-looking boy in the picture. He looked kind but that was about all one could say.

'What work is he doing?' she asked.

'He's in engineering works,' Eileen said. 'He's doing awfully well. He'll make a lot of money one day.'

'You're not worried about him, are you?' said Hilary, kindly, looking at the flushed face of the girl beside her.

Eileen answered at once. 'Worried about him? Of course not! Why should I be? I wish I saw him more often, that's all. You see, until this term, when Mother took this job, we all lived together. Now he's in lodgings and I do miss him a lot.'

Hilary said no more. She still thought that Eileen looked worried, and certainly she did not pay as much attention to her lessons as Miss Ellis expected – but after all, thought Hilary, it was enough to make anyone look worried if they had to listen to Matron's grumbles in their spare-time!

Eileen had to help her mother with the school linen every week, and sometimes when the girls passed Matron's room they could hear her grumbling away at Eileen. True, Eileen answered back sometimes, but usually she listened in silence. Some of the girls felt sorry for Eileen, others were glad, because they knew she was a tale-teller when it suited her to pass on things she had heard in the fourth form.

Another week or two went by, and half-term began to come near. Three or four fourth-form birthdays came along too, and there was a good deal of present-buying.

Angela had unlimited pocket-money and bought most extravagant presents. Pauline tried to vie with her and to buy marvellous gifts too. But it was impossible to spend as much as Angela did! She thought nothing of spending two pounds on a bottle of bath salts or a lace-edged handkerchief.

Eileen gave no presents at all. 'Sorry,' she said to

Hilary, whose birthday it was. 'I'd like to give you something – but I've no money at the moment. Many happy returns of the day, anyway!'

'Thanks,' said Hilary, thinking that Eileen could be very straightforward and honest, and liking her at that moment for being courageous enough to own up to having no money at all.

Angela presented Hilary with a magnificent blotter, made of real leather, and decorated very beautifully at the corners. Hilary liked it very much. Then Pauline presented her with a purse on which were Hilary's initials, H.W.W.

'Oh, Pauline – how beautiful!' said Hilary. 'But I wish you wouldn't spend so much money on me! I'm sure you can't afford it!'

This was an unfortunate remark to make to Pauline, who was very touchy about money, and was always trying to compete with Angela. She flushed and answered stiffly.

'You know that my family, the Bingham-Joneses, are wealthy,' she said, putting on the affected voice that Hilary detested. 'I have as much money as I wish. It's true I don't splash it about in the vulgar way that Angela does – I hope I am better bred than that. But I have all I ask for, Hilary, so please accept this purse with my best wishes, and don't think it cost any more than I could afford!'

'What with the Bingham-Joneses and the Honourable Favorleighs we're just overwhelmed with high-and-mightiness!' said Pat to Isabel, with a giggle. 'Well – I think I prefer Pauline of the two – Angela is really too spiteful for words, sometimes – and she says the cattiest things with the most angelic smile on her face!'

'I can't say I think a great deal of any of the four new girls, considering everything,' said Isabel, wrinkling her forehead and thinking. 'Angela's a spiteful snob. Pauline is an envious snob. Claudine is amusing but quite unscrupulous – hasn't any sense of honour at all, as far as I can see – and Eileen is a sneak and a bit of a bore!'

'Golly – you sound pretty catty yourself, Isabel!' said Pat.

'No, I'm not,' said Isabel, earnestly. 'I'm only just sizing them all up. I'm not like Alison, unable to see beyond a pretty face. And though I don't think much of any of those four, you know jolly well I'd help every one of them if they were in trouble. And if you're really catty, you don't feel like that, do you?'

'No, you don't,' said Pat. 'You're quite right, old thing – it doesn't matter seeing people for what they are, and even disliking them – so long as you're willing to help if necessary!'

Preparing for half-term

Half-term came along very shortly, and the girls were excited because their parents were coming to see them. There were to be tennis matches and swimming for the parents to watch. Hilary, Bobby, the twins and one or two others were excited about these, because they hoped to be in the teams.

'I'd like my mother to see me swim under water for the whole length of the pool,' said Bobby. 'She was a very good swimmer herself when she was young. Hope I'm chosen for the swimming competitions.'

The twins hoped to be in one of the tennis matches. They were both good at tennis, and it would be lovely for their mother to see them play together and win a match. Both girls were intensely proud of St Clare's, and badly wanted to show off their school, and their own prowess to the best advantage.

Hilary was to play in a singles match with one of the fifth formers. She had been chosen for her very graceful style, and it was to be an exhibition match more than a battle. Both girls had a beautiful natural style and the gamcs mistress was proud of them.

Mirabel was hoping to win the one-length race in the

swimming. She was very fast and very strong. Her smaller friend, the mouse-like Gladys, was also in the swimming competitions for, although she was small, she was a beautiful little swimmer. She was longing for her mother to see her. She had no father and no brother or sister, so her mother was everything to her.

'Half-term will be fun,' said Hilary. 'Is your mother coming, Angela?'

'Of course,' said Angela. 'And Daddy too. I'm longing to see their new car. It's a Rolls Royce, black with a green line, and . . .'

'I bet you're looking forward to seeing the new car more than to seeing your people!' said Bobby, with a chuckle. 'You never talk of your parents except in terms of the wealth they own, Angela. Did you know that?'

Angela looked sulky. 'I don't know what you mean,' she said. 'I guess you'd talk about cars and things if your parents had the same as mine. And you just see my mother when she comes! She will stand out above everyone else. She's absolutely beautiful – golden hair like mine – and the bluest eyes – and she wears the most marvellous clothes . . .'

'And even the safety-pins she uses are made of pure gold set with diamonds,' finished Pat.

'That's not funny,' said Angela, as the others shouted with laughter. 'I tell you, you just wait and see my mother! She's the most beautiful person you'll ever see.'

'*What* a pity you don't take after her, Angela!' said Bobby, sorrowfully. 'Isn't your mother sorry to have a daughter like you? You must be a terrible disappointment.'

Angela flushed with anger. She could never bear this kind of teasing. 'All right,' she said, in a bitter voice. 'All right. But just wait till you see my mother – and then tell me if she isn't the most wonderful person you ever saw in your lives. I hope she wears her double-string of pearls. They are worth five thousands pounds.'

'Well,' said the soft voice of Gladys, who rarely butted in on any conversation of this sort, 'well, I don't care if *my* mother wears her very oldest clothes, I don't care if she's got a ladder in her stockings, I don't care if she hasn't even powdered her nose – so long as my mother comes to see me and I can be with her for a few hours, she can be the untidiest, ugliest, poorest-dressed there – but I shall still be proud of her, and think she's the best of all!'

This was a long speech for the timid Gladys to make. Everyone was silent when she stopped. Pat found that she suddenly had tears in her eyes. There was such love in Gladys's voice – and what she said was fine. That was the way to love someone – not to care how they looked or what they did – but just to welcome them all the same!

Even Angela was taken aback. She stared at Gladys in surprise. She was about to make a sneering remark but Bobby stopped her.

'Now you shut up,' said Bobby, in a warning voice. 'Gladys has said the last word about mothers, and she's right. Good for you, Gladys.'

After that Angela said no more, but privately she rejoiced when she thought of her own beautifully dressed mother, and how the girls would have to admire her and her clothes when she came.

'Are *your* parents coming?' said Hilary to Pauline.

'Oh, yes,' said Pauline, in a bright voice, and she began to talk eagerly of them. 'My father is such a good-looking man, and Mother is sweet. I do hope she wears the dress she bought in the holidays – it's really beautiful. It makes her look so young and pretty.'

Pauline chattered away about her parents, in her way as much of a snob as Angela, though, far more than Angela, she talked of them as real people, generous, kind, amusing, instead of people cluttered up with great possessions.

'Pauline's people sound rather nice,' said Pat. 'I shall take a good look at Angela's family – I sort of feel that her father will wear diamond buttons on his coat and her mother will wear the crown jewels!'

Isabel giggled. 'Well, I'm rather glad that our mother is just ordinary,' she said, 'pretty and kind and sensible, just an ordinary nice mother!'

The girls all practised hard for half-term, swimming and playing tennis as much as they could, so that their parents might be proud of them. There was to be an exhibition of pictures too, done by the girls themselves, and a show of needlework. Here Claudine expected to shine. She had done a really beautiful cushion-cover, on which was embroidered a peacock spreading its lovely tail.

Mam'zelle was intensely proud of this. She bored everyone by talking about it. 'It is exquisite!' she said. 'Ah, the clever little Claudine! Miss Ellis, do you not think that

Claudine has done the tail most perfectly?'

'I do,' said Miss Ellis. 'Much better than she does her maths or her history, or her geography or her literature, or her . . .'

'Come, come!' said Mam'zelle, hurt. 'It is not given to us to have great gifts at everything. Now, the little Claudine, she . . .'

'I don't expect Claudine to have great gifts at anything but needlework,' said Miss Ellis. 'All I ask is a *little* attention in class, and a *little* thought in prep time! You spoil Claudine, Mam'zelle.'

'I! I spoil Claudine!' cried Mam'zelle, her glasses falling off her nose in rage. 'I have never spoilt any girl, never. Always I am strict, always I am fair, always I am . . .'

'All right, Mam'zelle,' said Miss Ellis, hastily, seeing that Mam'zelle was going to make one of her long and impassioned speeches, 'all right. I must go. You can tell it all to me when you see me next.'

Mam'zelle sought out Claudine. She fell upon her and hugged her, much to Claudine's surprise. But it had suddenly occurred to Mam'zelle that 'the poor little Claudine' would not have parents visiting her at half-term, for they were in France. So, immediately on thinking this, she had gone to comfort Claudine, who, however, was not in any need of comfort at all. She liked her parents, but as she was one of a very large family, and had only got a small share of their love and attention, she had not missed them very much.

'Ah, my little Claudine!' said Mam'zelle, flinging her

arms round the astonished Claudine. 'Do not be sad, do not be discouraged! Do not fret yourself – you shall not be alone at half-term.'

Claudine wondered if her aunt had gone mad. 'I am not sad, *ma tante,*' she said. 'What is the matter? Has anything happened?'

'No, no,' said Mam'zelle, still full of tender thoughts for her little Claudine, 'nothing has happened. It is only that I feel for you because your parents will not be with you at half-term. When everyone else has their handsome fathers and their so-beautiful mothers, you will have no one – no one but your loving Aunt Mathilde!'

'Well, that's OK,' said Claudine in English. Mam'zelle wrinkled up her nose and her glasses fell off.

'Do not use these expression!' she said. 'They are vulgar. Ah, my little Claudine, you will not have any parents to admire your so-fine cushion-case with its magnificent peacock – but I will be there, my little one, I will stand by your cushion-cover all the time, not one minute will I go away, and I will say to everyone: "See! See the beautiful cover made by the clever Claudine! Ah, it needs a French girl to do such work as this! Regard the tail, regard each feather so finely done in silk, regard the priceless cushion-cover, the most beautiful thing in this school today!'

'Oh, Aunt Mathilde, I wish you wouldn't think of saying anything like that,' said Claudine in alarm. 'The girls would laugh like anything. They would tease me terribly. Please don't. I shan't be lonely. I shan't mind not having anyone there.'

'Ah, the brave little one!' sighed Mam'zelle, wiping away a tear from her eye. 'I see your courage. You will not show others that you suffer.'

'I *shan't* suffer,' said Claudine, getting impatient. 'I shan't really, Aunt Mathilde. Please don't make a fuss like this. It would be dreadful if you stood by my cushion-cover all the afternoon and made remarks like that.'

The idea of Mam'zelle standing like a bull-dog on guard, telling surprised parents of her poor lonely little Claudine, and praising to the skies the little cushion-cover filled Claudine with horror. She began to wish that half-term was safely over.

But it hadn't even come! Four days away – three days – two days – the night before. Ah, now it really *was* near! The girls went to bed very excited that night and talked in whispers long after lights were out. Susan Howes, the head girl of the form, pretended to be asleep. She could not bear to be a spoil-sport on the night before half-term, strict as she was on all other nights.

Angela was thinking of the wonderful impression her mother would make, and how she would bask in her reflected glory. She hoped her mother would wear her famous pearls.

Eileen was thinking about her own mother. She would be there as Matron, not all dressed up and pretty as other people's mothers would be. She wished that Eddie could be there – not because she was going to do anything in the swimming or tennis matches, or had anything in the art or needlework exhibition – but because it would have been lovely to have seen him looking for her – her own darling big brother!

Alison was looking forward to seeing her own pretty mother, and also to seeing Angela's mother too. She hoped the two would be friends. It would be lovely if they liked one another, and what fun if Angela's mother asked her, Alison, to stay with them in the holidays. That *would* be fine!

Pauline was thinking of her parents too. So was Bobby. It seemed a long time since the last holidays. School was fun – but your own home and people were something very solid and real and lovely. It would be nice to get a bit of them tomorrow.

One by one the girls fell asleep. Bobby was the first to wake up. She sat up and spoke loudly. 'Wake up, you sleepy-heads! It's half-term!'

10 Half-term at last

Half-term Saturday was a perfectly beautiful day. The sun shone down from a blue sky that hadn't a single cloud in it.

'Gorgeous, isn't it, Claudine?' said Doris happily to the little French girl. 'Couldn't be better.'

Claudine groaned. 'To think we shall all have to be out-of-doors in this terrible sun!' she said. 'I know I shall get a freckle. I wish it had rained.'

'You spoil-sport!' said Bobby, grinning. 'You would like to huddle indoors even on a day like this. Come on, cheer up and smile – it's really a heavenly day.'

The art exhibition was all ready for the parents to admire. There were some really good pictures there. Miss Walker, the art mistress, was proud of them. She had a water-colour class which went out regularly to paint country scenes with her, and some of them were very good.

'Good enough to sell!' said Claudine. 'Do we sell our work? How much would you get for this so-beautiful picture, Hilary?'

Hilary laughed. 'You have got funny ideas, Claudine,' she said. 'Of course we don't sell our work. As if our proud parents would let us! No, they will take our pictures home, and our pottery, and place them in conspicuous places on the walls, or mantelpiece, so that all their friends can admire them, and say, "How clever your daughter must be, Mrs So-and-So!" '

'I bet your mother will be pleased if you send her that lovely cushion-cover of yours for her birthday,' said Pat. Claudine laughed.

'I have three sisters who do much more beautiful work than I do,' she said. 'My mother would look at my cover and say, "Ah! The little Claudine is improving! This is not bad for a beginning." '

'Mam'zelle thinks it's wonderful, anyhow,' said Bobby, grinning. 'There's one thing about you, Claudine – you're not in the least conceited. With all the fuss that everyone has made of your embroidery, you might quite well have begun to swank about it. But you don't.'

'Ah, I know that it is good compared with the sewing of you English girls,' said Claudine, seriously, 'but, you see, I know that it would be quite ordinary in France. I have a different standard to compare that so-beautiful cover with, and I cannot think it is as wonderful as you do.'

Claudine was a very funny mixture of honesty, sincerity and deceitfulness. Even her deceitfulness was odd, because she did not attempt to hide it. She often tried to deceive Miss Ellis, for instance, and if Miss Ellis saw through it, Claudine would at once admit to her attempted deceit without any shame. It was almost as if she were playing a game with the teachers, trying to get the better of them, but not trying to hide the fact that she *was* trying to get the better of them. The girls could not quite make her out.

Pat and Isabel were playing together in a school match, and they were delighted. They looked out their white skirts and blouses, their red socks and white shoes, and took the clothes to Matron for the laundry staff to iron. Everyone had to look their best when parents came!

Pauline looked a little miserable at breakfast-time, and the girls wondered why. Hilary spoke to her in her usual kindly way.

'What's up, Pauline? You're looking glum. You're not upset because you haven't been chosen to play in the school matches, are you?'

'Oh, no,' said Pauline. 'I've had a great disappointment, that's all.'

'What?' asked Hilary, and the other girls came round to hear.

'Well, you see,' said Pauline, 'it's most unfortunate – Mother is ill, and my father doesn't like to leave her – so they won't be coming today! And I was *so* looking forward to them being here and seeing everything.'

'Bad luck, Pauline!' said the twins, sympathetically. A disappointment of that kind was awful at the last minute. Everyone was very sorry.

'I hope your mother isn't really ill,' said Susan Howes.

'No, not seriously,' said Pauline. 'But she can't possibly come. Oh, dear – and I did so badly want you all to see my good-looking father and my pretty mother. I even wrote to ask her if she would wear the pretty new frock I liked so much, and she said she would.'

'Well, never mind,' said Isabel, feeling very sorry indeed. 'You can come out with us and our people, if you like, Pauline. Then you won't feel so lonely.'

'Oh, thank you,' said Pauline, and after that she seemed to cheer up a good deal, and entered into everything with enthusiasm.

Mam'zelle had displayed Claudine's beautiful cushion-cover in a very prominent place. She still seemed inclined to fall on Claudine's neck, and tell her she must not feel lonely, and the little French girl kept out of her way as much as possible, slipping deftly round the corner whenever she saw her aunt approaching.

'Sort of hide-and-seek you're playing, Claudine!' said Bobby. 'You'll have to have a word with Mam'zelle soon, or she'll burst. She's longing to show you how beautifully she has arranged your so-marvellous cushion-cover!'

Lunch was a very scrappy affair that day because the cooks were concerned with the strawberry tea that the parents were to have in the afternoon, and scores of pounds of strawberries were being prepared in big glass dishes. The cooks had made the most lovely cakes and biscuits, and there were sandwiches of every kind. The girls kept peeping into the big dining-room, where the dishes were all set out.

Claudine slipped in and sampled some of the strawberries. She was the only one who dared to do this.

'You'll get into a row if anyone catches you,' said Bobby.

'You go and taste them,' said Claudine, running her

little pink tongue round her crimson lips. 'They are so sweet and juicy!'

'No,' said Bobby. 'We've been put on our honour not to sample this afternoon's tea, and I wouldn't dream of breaking my honour.'

'This honour of yours, it is a funny thing,' said Claudine. 'It is a most uncomfortable thing. It stops you from doing what you want to do. I have no honour to worry me. I will never have this honour of yours. I do not like it.'

'You're awful, Claudine,' said Angela, screwing up her nose. 'You do exactly as you like. I'm glad I'm not as dishonourable as you are.'

The tone was very unpleasant, but Claudine only laughed. She hardly ever took offence. 'Ah, Angela,' she said, 'you think it is worse to take a few strawberries than to tell untruths about another girl behind her back? Me, I think it is really dishonourable to speak lies against another girl as you do. To me you are dishonourable, a worth-nothing girl, not because of a few strawberries but because of your evil tongue!'

The listening girls laughed at this. It was said in a pleasant voice, but there was such truth in it, and the tables had been turned so cleverly on Angela that the girls couldn't help being amused. Only Angela was angry. But there was little time to quarrel on half-term day. There were so many jobs to do, and everyone had her own allotted task.

Some had to do the flowers all over the school, and this

took a long time. The vases had to be washed, old flowers thrown away, new ones picked, and then arranged to the best advantage in all kinds of bowls, jars and vases. The twins were especially good at this, and were very busy all the morning.

After lunch everyone changed into either sports clothes or school uniform. The summer uniform was a brightly coloured tunic. The girls could choose any colour they liked, so every girl was able to wear the one that suited her best. Dark girls, like Carlotta, chose reds and oranges, fair girls like Angela chose pale colours, blues and pinks. They looked like flowers, moving about against the green lawns of the school grounds, on that hot summer day.

'The parents are arriving!' squealed Alison, as she heard the sound of wheels coming up the drive. 'The first lot are here. Who are they?'

The fourth formers looked out of their windows, but nobody knew the people in the car. 'They must belong to some of the lower school,' said Bobby. 'Here come some more!'

'They're mine!' cried Janet. 'Oh, goody-goody! I hoped they'd come early. I say, doesn't my mother look nice and tanned. I'm going to greet them.'

She sped off happily. More and more cars drove up the drive, and soon the lawns were crowded with fathers and mothers and aunts, and with younger or older brothers and sisters. How Eileen wished that Eddie could be there!

Eileen's mother was very trim and starched in her

Matron's uniform and white apron. Some of the parents went to talk to her about the health of their children. Eileen was glad that her mother was sought out by so many parents – but she could not help wishing that she had on a pretty frock and looked as sweet and attractive as many of the other girls' mothers.

Mother ought to smile more, thought Eileen. She looks so strict and hard. Look at the twins' mother over there – she's really sweet. And I do like the way she's got her arm round both Pat and Isabel. Mother never puts her arm round me or Eddie.

An enormous car rolled up the drive, with a smartly uniformed chauffeur in front. It was a beautiful new Rolls Royce, black with a small green line. It came to a stop and the chauffeur got out. Angela gave a loud squeal.

'That's our new car! Look, everyone, isn't it a beauty! And do you like the chauffeur's uniform, black with green piping to match the car? The cushions are black too, with green edges and green monograms.'

'I should have thought you would have been so excited to see your parents that you wouldn't even have noticed the car!' said Janet's cool voice. But Angela took no notice. She was very pleased indeed that so many of the fourth formers were near when her grand new car drove up!

The chauffeur opened the car door. Angela's mother stepped out. Certainly she was a vision of beauty! She looked very young, was extraordinarily like Angela, and she was dressed in a most exquisite fashion.

The girls stared at her. She looked round with brilliant

blue eyes, also very like Angela's. After her came her husband, a tall, military-looking man, with rather a serious face. Angela gave another squeal.

She ran to her parents and flung her arms round her mother as she had seen the others do, purposely exaggerating everything because she knew they were watching.

'Angela dear! Be careful of my dress!' said her mother. 'Let me see how you are looking.'

Her father gave Angela a good hug, and then pushed her a little way away so that he could have a good look at her.

'She looks very well indeed,' said her father.

'But this awful school uniform spoils her,' said her mother. 'I do think it is most unbecoming. And I can't bear those terrible school shoes, with their flat heels.'

'Well, all the girls wear the same,' said Angela's father, reasonably. 'I think Angela looks very nice.'

'If only the school had a prettier uniform!' said Angela's mother, in a complaining voice. 'That was one reason why I didn't want to send her here – the dress was *so* ugly!'

Angela's 'wonderful' mother

The complaining voice of Angela's mother could be heard very often indeed that afternoon. Beautiful as she was, attractive and exquisite in her dress and looks, the lovely face was spoilt by an expression of discontent and boredom.

She complained of so many things, and her voice was unfortunately harsh and too loud! She complained of the hard bench that she had to sit on to watch the tennis matches. She found fault with the cup of tea that Angela brought her. 'What terrible tea! They might at least provide China tea. You know I can't drink Indian tea, Angela.'

She complained of the cake she took. 'Awfully dry,' she said. 'I can hardly eat it.'

'Leave it then,' said Angela's father. And to Angela's horror her mother dropped the cake on the ground, where it could be trodden underfoot. The sharp eyes of the other girls noted all these things, and Angela began to feel rather uncomfortable.

'Isn't my mother lovely?' she whispered to Alison. 'Don't you think those pearls are marvellous? Hasn't she got beautiful hair?'

Alison agreed. Privately she thought that Angela's mother acted like a spoilt child, complaining and grumbling all the time. She did not praise the pictures in the art exhibition, neither did she show any enthusiasm for the pottery work. She was forced to express a good opinion on Claudine's cushion-cover, because Mam'zelle stood there like a dragon, looking so fierce that everyone felt they must praise her niece's handiwork.

'Ah! So this is your mother, Angela?' said Mam'zelle, in a most amiable voice. 'We will show her the work of the little Claudine! Is it not beautiful? See the exquisite stitches! Regard the fine tail, spreading so well over the cover!'

Angela's mother looked as if she was going to pass the cover by without saying anything, but Mam'zelle was certainly not going to let that happen. She took hold of the visitor's arm and almost forced her to bend over Claudine's cushion-cover. 'You have not seen it! It is a work of art! It is the finest thing in the exhibition!' said Mam'zelle, getting excited.

'Very nice,' said Angela's mother, in a tone that seemed to say 'Very nasty!' She took her arm away from Mam'zelle's hand, brushed her sleeve as if it had some dust left on it, and turned away impatiently.

'Who is that awful old woman?' she asked Angela, in much too loud a voice. 'Surely *she* doesn't teach you, my dear? Did you ever see anyone look so dowdy?'

The girls were very fond of Mam'zelle, and they were angry to hear this remark. Bobby felt certain that Mam'zelle herself had caught some of it. The Frenchwoman was standing looking after Angela and her parents with a puzzled and hurt expression in her eyes.

'Well – I always thought Angela was pretty beastly,' said Bobby to Pat, in a low tone, 'and now I see where she gets her cattiness from! How ashamed I'd be of *my* mother if she walked round like that, criticizing things and people at the top of her voice. Poor old Mam'zelle! It's a shame to hurt her.'

Claudine had overheard the remarks made by Angela's mother, and she too was hurt and angry. She was fond of her Aunt Mathilde, and though she was cross with her for standing by her cushion-cover and behaving in such an exaggerated way about it, she saw that it was the intense love and pride she had for Claudine herself that made her do it.

She looked at Angela's beautiful mother. She noted her discontented face, and the petulant droop of the mouth that at times quite spoilt its loveliness. She thought of all the hurts and insults that that beautiful mouth must have uttered through the years. And Claudine longed to punish Angela's mother in some dramatic way for the cruel words she had spoken about her Aunt Mathilde!

Angela took her parents to the swimming-pool. St Clare's was proud of this, for it was one of the finest and biggest swimming-pools owned by any school in the kingdom. The water lapped against the sides, a beautiful blue-green colour.

But even here Angela's mother had fault to find. 'I suppose they change the water every day, Angela?' she said.

'No, Mother, twice a week, sometimes three times,' said Angela. Her mother gave a little disgusted squeal.

'Good gracious! To think they can't even change the water every day! What a school! I really must make a complaint about it. Angela, you are not to bathe in the pool unless the water has just been changed. I forbid it.'

'But, Mother,' began Angela, uncomfortably, 'I have to do what the others do – and really, the water *is* quite clean, even when it's two days old, or three.'

'I shall complain,' said Angela's mother. 'I never did like the idea of sending you here. It's a second-rate school, I think. I wanted to send you to High Towers School. *Such* a nice school! I can't think why your father wanted to send you here. Perhaps now he has seen it he will think again.'

'Pamela, don't talk so loudly,' said Angela's father. 'People here don't like to listen to what you are saying. You are in a minority – it is plain that all the other parents here think as *I* do – that St Clare's is splendid in every way!'

'Oh, *you*,' said Angela's mother, as if what her husband thought was of simply no account at all. She shut up her scarlet lips, and looked just as sulky as Angela always did when anybody ticked her off.

No – Angela's mother was certainly not a success! Beautiful she might be, expensive she certainly was – but she had none of the graciousness of the twins' mother, or the common sense of Bobby's jolly-looking mother, or the affection of Gladys's plainly dressed but sweet-faced mother.

'I'm jolly glad I haven't got a mother like Angela's!' said Janet to Alison. 'Isn't she perfectly awful?'

Loyal though Alison wanted to be to Angela, she

couldn't help nodding her head. She had overheard many of Angela's mother's rude remarks, and she had not liked them, because even feather-headed Alison felt a deep sense of loyalty to St Clare's and all it stood for. She was not at all eager to be introduced to Angela's mother now – but the time came when she had to be, for Angela sought her out and took her off.

'Mother, this is Alison, the friend I told you about in my letters,' said Angela. Her mother looked at the pretty, dainty girl with approval. Alison was like Angela, and could wear the school uniform well.

'Oh, so this is Alison,' said Angela's mother. 'How do you do? I must say you look a little more attractive than some of the girls here. One or two that Angela has introduced me to have been perfect frights!'

Bobby had been introduced to Angela's mother and was presumably one of the 'frights'. Her frank freckled face was not at all attractive to anyone as exquisite as Angela's mother.

'Where is your mother?' asked Angela. 'We must introduce her to mine. Mother wants to ask if you can spend some of the summer hols with me.'

But, rather to Alison's relief, when the introduction had been made, and the two mothers had greeted one another, the invitation was quite firmly declined by Alison's own mother!

'Thank you,' she said, 'but I am afraid I have other plans for Alison.'

She did not explain what these were. She did not say

that she had watched Angela's mother, and had heard some of her insolent remarks and detested them. She did not say that Angela's mother was the sort of person she would hate Alison to spend even a day with! But Alison knew what her mother was thinking, and silly girl as she was, she knew that her mother was right.

Angela's mother sensed that the other mother was snubbing her, and she was surprised and annoyed. She was about to say something more, when a bell rang loudly.

'Oh! Must they ring bells like that!' said Angela's mother, putting her hands to her ears. 'How crude!'

'But sensible, don't you think so?' said Alison's mother drily, and left her.

'That's the bell to tell us to go and watch the swimming,' said Alison, slipping her hand into her mother's arm. 'Come on, Mummy. You'll see Bobby swimming there – you know, the freckled girl you liked. And Mirabel too – she's awfully fast.'

The hot sun blazed down as the company took its place round the swimming-pool. The parents sat at the edge of the baths, but the girls were in the big gallery above, watching eagerly.

Many of them were not taking part in the swimming, but they were all keen to see the performers diving, somersaulting and swimming. It was fun to hear the continual splashes, and to see the rippling of the blue water.

'Isn't it a gorgeous afternoon?' said Janet, happily. 'I *am* enjoying myself! I feel so glad that it's a fine day so that we can show off St Clare's at its very best.'

'All our parents seem to think it's a great success,' said Bobby. 'Well – except *one* parent!'

She meant Angela's mother. Angela heard this remark and flushed. She had been so pleased to show off her beautiful mother – but somehow everything had been spoilt now. She couldn't help wishing that her mother had made nice remarks like the others had made. But then, Mother wasn't usually very pleased with things, no matter what they were.

Claudine, Alison, Angela and many others not in the swimming got front places in the big gallery above the water. Claudine leant over rather far, not so much to look at the swimmers, in their navy-blue swim-suits, but to see the rows of parents.

'Look out, Claudine, you'll fall in!' said Alison, in alarm, trying to pull her back.

'I shall not fall,' said Claudine. 'I am just looking at that so-discontented person below, with the voice that makes loud and rude remarks!'

'Sh,' said Alison. 'Angela will hear you.'

'I do not care,' said Claudine. 'Why should Angela expect us to praise a mother who is beautiful only in appearance, and whose character is ugly?'

'Do be quiet,' said Alison, afraid that Angela would hear. 'I'm sorry Angela's mother said that about your aunt, Claudine. I heard it, and I'm sure poor Mam'zelle was hurt.'

The swimming began. Angela's mother looked disgusted when a drop of water splashed on to her beautiful dress. She shook it daintily and tried to move backwards a little – but other people were behind her and she couldn't.

It was an exciting hour, for the swimmers were fast and good, and the divers graceful and plucky. But the most exciting bit of the whole afternoon was not the swimming or the diving, or the backward somersaulting done so cleverly by Bobby.

It was an unexpected and highly dramatic performance, quite unrehearsed, given by Claudine!

She was leaning well over the gallery balcony. She suddenly gave a piercing shriek that made everyone jump in alarm – and then to the horror of all the lookers-on, the little French girl fell headlong from the gallery into the water below!

A happy time

She made a most terrific splash. The water rose up and fell all over Angela's mother, soaking her from head to foot!

'Good gracious!' said Miss Theobald, the head mistress, startled out of her usual calm dignity. 'Who has fallen into the water? Get her out, quickly!'

Claudine could not swim. She sank under the water, and then rose to the surface, gasping. Bobby and Mirabel, who were in the water, too, at once swam over to her. They got hold of her and helped her to the steps.

'Claudine! Whatever happened?' said Bobby. 'You *are* an idiot!'

Claudine was gasping and spluttering. She cast an eye towards Angela's mother, and saw, to her delight, that she was drenched. Miss Theobald was by her, apologizing, and saying that she must come at once to the school, and allow her, Miss Theobald, to lend her some clothes whilst hers were drying.

Angrily Angela's mother followed the head mistress from the swimming-pool. She looked a dreadful sight, with her dress soaked and clinging tightly to her, and her beautiful hat dripping with water. Angela looked very distressed.

'You too, Claudine, you must go with Matron and get into dry clothes,' said Miss Ellis to the soaking wet fourth former. 'Get into another tunic, quickly, or you'll catch cold. Hurry, now.'

Claudine, out of the tail of her eye, saw Mam'zelle bearing down upon her, alarm and anxiety written all over her. The little French girl at once fled off up to the school. She felt she could not bear to be enwrapped in Mam'zelle's overwhelming affection just then.

'Wait, wait, Claudine,' called Matron, who was annoyed that Claudine had caused her to leave the company and go back to the school. But Claudine did not wait. Better to face Matron's annoyance than Mam'zelle's loud exclamations of dismay and sympathy!

'How exactly like Claudine to cause such a disturbance!' said Pat to Isabel. 'Oh, Isabel – I can't help feeling delighted that the person who got soaked was Angela's tiresome mother!'

'I suppose Claudine couldn't possibly have done it on purpose, could she?' said Isabel, doubtfully. 'You know, she doesn't care in the least what she does, if she wants to get a result she has set her heart on. I bet she wanted to punish Angela's mother for her rudeness to Mam'zelle!'

'But Claudine simply hates and detests the water!' said Pat. 'Nothing will make her undress and have a swim. And to let herself fall from the gallery into the water would be a very brave thing to do, considering she can't swim.'

Claudine soon returned, in dry clothes, looking

demure and innocent. She could look just as innocent as Angela when she liked – and now that the girls knew her better, they were certain that the more innocent Claudine looked, the worse mischief she had done or was about to do!

Angela's mother also returned, after a while – dressed in Miss Theobald's clothes! Miss Theobald was about the same size as Angela's mother, but a little taller, and although she always looked nice, her clothes were very simple, plain and dignified.

They did not suit Angela's mother at all. In fact she looked very extraordinary in them and she knew it. She was angry and she showed it. It was bad enough to be drenched like that by some silly, careless girl, but much worse to be made to wear clothes too long for her, and so dowdy and frumpish after her own!

But somehow Angela's mother could not be rude to Miss Theobald. The head mistress was extremely kind and apologetic, but she was also calm and dignified, and she acted as if she expected Angela's mother to be calm and dignified also. And, much to her surprise, the spoilt woman found herself guarding her tongue and behaving quite well, whilst she changed into Miss Theobald's clothes.

The rest of the time went quickly. The matches and competitions were all over. Parents went off with their children, taking them out to dinner in the various hotels round about, for a treat.

Pauline went with Mrs O'Sullivan, the twins' mother. The twins had told their mother about the girl's great disappointment, and she had at once said that Pauline must come with them.

Alison's mother spoke to Alison. 'Is there anyone you would like to bring with you this evening? I hope you don't want to go with Angela and her people, because your father and I would rather be on our own with you.'

Alison understood that her mother had no wish to become at all friendly with Angela's mother. If she could choose someone to go with her, it would be easy to refuse Angela, if she asked for the two families to have dinner together. Alison wondered whom she could ask.

She took a look round at the girls. Most of them were clustered around their parents, chattering gaily, waiting for the various cars to come along. Eileen stood alone, watching. Her mother had disappeared – gone to see to some of the younger children, probably. The girl had such a forlorn look on her face that Alison was touched.

'I'll ask Eileen, Mother,' she said. 'I don't like her much – or her mother, who is Matron – but she would so enjoy coming! And oh, Mother – could I ask someone else too?'

'Who?' said her mother, in surprise.

'Could I ask Claudine, the little French girl who fell into the water?' said Alison. 'Her parents are in France. She's only got her aunt here, Mam'zelle. I know she would simply love to come! She adores going out.'

'All right, dear. Ask them both,' said her mother, pleased. Anything rather than having that spoilt little Angela and her equally spoilt mother with them!

Alison tore off to Eileen. 'Eileen. Go and ask your

mother if you can come out to dinner with my people. Hurry up.'

'Oh!' said Eileen, her eyes suddenly shining like stars. 'Oh, Alison – do you really mean it? You *are* decent!'

She rushed off to find her mother. Alison went up to Claudine. 'Claudine, will you come out with me and my people? Mother said I could ask you. Eileen is coming too.'

'Thank you,' said Claudine, all her pretty manners coming into play. 'It is indeed very kind of you, Alison, and of your mother too. I will go to ask my aunt.'

Mam'zelle was delighted. She liked Alison, although she despaired over her French. 'Yes, you go, my little Claudine,' she beamed. 'You need a treat after your so-terrible shock this afternoon. Poor little one – to fall into the water like that, to be nearly drowned, to . . .'

'Well, I wasn't nearly drowned really, you know,' said Claudine, a twinkle coming into her eye. 'I knew I *shouldn't* be drowned, Aunt Mathilde, because Bobby and Mirabel were both in the water – and oh, wasn't it grand when I splashed that hateful woman from head to foot? I never guessed I would drench her like that!'

Mam'zelle's mouth fell open, and she stared at Claudine as if she could not believe what she heard.

'Claudine! Claudine! What is this that you are saying? Surely, no it is not possible – you could not have fallen on purpose! You would not be such a bad girl!' Poor Mam'zelle could hardly get the words out.

Claudine answered demurely. 'On purpose, Aunt Mathilde! Why, how could you think of such a thing? Do you suppose that your niece could do a so-shocking thing as that? But how wonderful that it should happen just by Angela's mother! Ah, truly, that was a miracle!'

With a wicked twinkle in her eye, the unscrupulous Claudine walked off to get herself ready for going out. Mam'zelle stared after her. Ah, this Claudine – she was a bad, bad girl – and yet what a good, good girl she was too, to throw herself into the water in order to splash and punish an unkind woman, someone who had hurt and puzzled her aunt! Mam'zelle sat down on a hall-seat, feeling quite breathless. Which *was* Claudine – a bad girl or a good one? For the life of her Mam'zelle could not decide.

Meanwhile all the girls and their parents had gone off in their different cars. Angela had rolled away in her magnificent car – but a very quiet and subdued Angela. Somehow things had not turned out quite as she had planned. She hadn't shone in the reflected glory of her beautiful mother. She had only felt the scorn of the other girls because her mother had criticized their school in loud and complaining tones.

Angela looked out of the car window and saw the happy faces of the twins, and saw Pauline walking with Mr and Mrs O'Sullivan. They were all going off together, chattering gaily.

'You all did *mar*vellously!' she heard Mrs O'Sullivan say, in clear, happy tones.

Then she saw her friend Alison – and to Angela's enormous surprise, Eileen and Claudine were with her, all getting into a car together! Oh! How mean of Alison! Why hadn't she asked Angela to join up with her and her people? Fancy asking that common little sneak, Eileen, and that awful outspoken niece of Mam'zelle's, Claudine! How *could* Alison do such a thing!

Angela did not think of what the real reason might be – a real feeling of kindness on Alison's part. She was angry and annoyed. She would show Alison exactly what she thought of her when she saw her next! If Alison wanted to make friends with charity girls, let her – but she wouldn't have Angela Favorleigh, the Honourable Angela Favorleigh, for her friend too!

There were two or three fairly big towns within easy reach of the school by car, and the different families chose their own town and hotel, and drove off. To Eileen's intense joy, Alison's mother chose to go to the town where Eddie lived!

'Oh,' she said, as the car slid into the town. 'This is where my brother lives. I wonder if I shall see him.'

'Would you like to ask him to come and have dinner with us?' said Alison's mother.

Eileen shook her head. 'Oh, no, thank you. It's kind enough of you to ask *me* without asking *him* as well! But – if you wouldn't mind – I would love to slip along and see him after we've had dinner. His lodgings aren't very far from the hotel. He'd love to see me.'

'Just as you like, dear,' said Alison's mother. So they had their dinner, and a very good one it was, and then Eileen slipped off to see Edgar.

Claudine proved a great success with Alison's people.

The French girl had naturally good manners, she was vivacious and amusing, and she was extremely pleased to have such a treat. Alison's parents really enjoyed the girl's company.

'Alison, I wish that French girl was your friend, and not Angela,' said her mother. 'She really is nice. Don't you like her?'

'Yes, Mother, I do,' said Alison. 'She's quite different from us English girls, though – I mean, she hasn't our sense of honour – and honestly, she simply doesn't care *what* she does. But she's fun, quite sincere, and awfully kind.'

'Here comes Eileen back again,' said Alison's mother. 'She must be very fond of her brother. She really looks happy now!'

Eileen did. Eddie had been delighted to see her. She beamed at Alison and Claudine in an unusually friendly manner. What a lovely day it had been!

13
Janet and the 'stink balls'

After the excitements of half-term the girls felt flat and dull. There didn't seem anything to look forward to now. Lessons were boring. The weather was too hot. It seemed a long time till the summer holidays.

'Janet! Bobby! Can't you think up some trick or other?' said Pat, with a yawn. 'I wish you would. I shall die of boredom this week if something doesn't happen.'

Janet grinned. 'I've got rather an awful trick from my brother,' she said. 'I don't really know if we ought to play it, now we're fourth formers.'

'Oh, don't be an idiot!' said Doris. 'Why can't we have a few jokes, even if we *are* fourth formers! What's the trick?'

'Well – it's a perfectly frightful smell,' said Janet. 'Wait a bit – I'll get the things.'

She went up to her dormitory, rummaged about in one of her drawers and then came down again with a small box.

The others crowded round her. The box was full of what looked like tiny round glass balls, full of some sort of clear liquid.

'What are they?' said Pat, puzzled. 'I've never seen them before.'

'They are smell balls,' said Janet. 'Stink balls my brother calls them. When you break one and let out the liquid, it dries up at once – but leaves the most frightful smell behind.'

'What sort of smell?' asked Doris, with great interest. 'Like drains or something?'

'Well – like very bad eggs,' said Janet. 'My brother – he's simply awful, you know – he broke one of these balls at a very solemn meeting once, in our sitting-room at home – and in less than a minute the room was empty! You simply can't imagine what it was like!'

Bobby chuckled. 'Let's break one in French class tomorrow,' she said. 'It's going to be terribly dull – translating pages and pages of that book Mam'zelle is so keen on – that French play. This trick is absolutely *sent* for things like that. Will you break one of these balls tomorrow, Janet, or shall I?'

'Well, you take one and I'll take one,' said Janet. 'Then if mine doesn't work – my brother says they are sometimes disappointing – you can use yours. See?'

The whole class were thrilled about the 'stink balls'. Everyone but Eileen knew about them. The girls were afraid of telling Eileen in case she sneaked to Matron, and the secret was found out. So Eileen was not told a word. She was astonished to find that so many of the girls hurriedly stopped talking when she came up, and then began chattering very loudly about quite silly things. She was sure they had been talking about her, and she felt hurt.

If they're going to be beastly to me, I shall tell Mother, and they'll all get dozens of stockings to mend! thought Eileen, spitefully.

Janet and Bobby went into the French class the next day with the little 'stink balls' in their pockets. The lesson was just before break.

'We'd better not choose any lesson except one just before break,' Janet had said, 'because if the smell goes on too long, it might still be there in Miss Ellis's class, and I bet she'd smell a rat.'

'She'd smell much worse than a rat once she sniffs one of your "stink balls",' said Bobby, with a grin.

'You see, we can open all the windows and doors and let the smell out well during break,' said Pat. 'There won't be anything of it left by the time maths lesson comes afterwards with Miss Ellis.'

The class were standing politely and silently when Mam'zelle came in. She beamed at the girls.

'Sit! Now today we will go on with this play of ours. I will allot the parts. You, Janet, can take the part of the old servant; you, Alison . . .'

The girls opened their books, hiding their grins as best they could. A trick performed by Janet or Bobby was always fun, great fun! The girls remembered the many other tricks the two had played, and chuckled. This would liven up a dull French lesson very considerably.

'Janet, will you please begin?' said Mam'zelle, aimiably. She liked this fourth form. They were good, hard-working girls – and her dear little Claudine was there too, her face buried in her book – the good, good little girl!

Janet began reading in French. Her hand stole to her pocket. The girls behind her saw it, and tried to choke back their giggles. That was the worst of playing a trick – you always wanted to begin giggling far too soon, and it was terribly difficult to stop real giggles. Doris gave one of her sudden snorts, and Mam'zelle looked up in surprise.

Doris turned it into a long cough, which set Mirabel off into giggles too. Mam'zelle glared at Mirabel.

'Is it so funny that the poor Doris has a bad cough?' she enquired.

This seemed funnier still to Mirabel and she went off into more helpless giggles which began to infect the others. Janet turned round and frowned. She didn't want Mam'zelle to suspect too soon that she was playing a trick. The others caught her warning look, and became as serious as they could again.

The lesson went on. Janet slid the little glass ball out of her pocket. Her hand was behind her, and the girls saw her press firmly on the tiny glass ball. The thin glass covering broke, and the liquid ran out, drying almost as soon as the air touched it. The liquid disappeared, and the tiny fragments of thin glass dropped unheeded to the floor.

After a few moments a curious smell drifted all round. Doris coughed. Alison sniffed loudly and said 'Pooh!'

It was a horrid smell, there was no doubt about that. It smelt of bad eggs, drains, dead rats, old cats' meat . . . all that was horrid!

Mam'zelle did not smell the smell at first. She was

astonished at the sudden outburst of sniffing and coughing. She looked up. She saw expressions of disgust on everyone's face, mixed with the desire to giggle.

'What is the matter?' demanded Mam'zelle, suspiciously. 'Why do you pull these faces? Alison, stop saying, "Pooh!" Janet, why do you look so disgusted?'

'Oh, Mam'zelle – can't you smell it?' said Janet, an agonized expression on her face.

'Smell *what*?' said Mam'zelle, exasperated. The smell had not drifted her way as yet.

'Oh, Mam'zelle – the *smell*!' chorused half a dozen voices.

Mam'zelle looked puzzled and angry. She took a few enormous sniffs of the air, which made Doris explode into laughter.

'I smell no smell,' said Mam'zelle. 'This is a silly trick, yes. Stop sniffing, Janet. If you say "Pooh" again, Alison, I will send you out of the room. Claudine, do not look like a duck that is dying.'

'But, Aunt Mathilde, the smell, the smell! *C'est abominable*!' cried Claudine, who detested bad smells, and looked as if she was about to faint.

'Claudine! You too!' rapped out Mam'zelle, who, safely away at the end of the room, had not even got so much as a sniff of the evil smell yet. 'Now listen, *mes enfants* – one more mention of a smell, and I fetch Miss Theobald herself here to smell it! It is all pretence. You are bad children.'

This was a truly terrible threat! Miss Theobald would certainly be able to smell the smell as soon as she got into the room, and then there would be a big row. The girls looked at one another in dismay. They put their handkerchiefs to their noses and tried not to sniff up the ghastly odour.

Mam'zelle began to read out loud from the French play. After a few lines, she stopped. Strange! She felt as if she too now could smell something. She took a cautious sniff. Was it a smell, or was it not? Nonsense! Strange and horrible smells do not invade classrooms all of a sudden. Mam'zelle took another breath and went on reading.

The smell stole round her. Mam'zelle could smell it quite distinctly now. She stopped reading again and sniffed wildly. Yes, there was no doubt about it, a perfectly horrible smell was in the room! The poor, poor girls – they had smelt it first – and she had not believed them.

Mam'zelle gave a gulp and a choke as the smell really took hold of her. She fished about for her handkerchief. The girls, divided between disgust at the smell and an intense desire to giggle at Mam'zelle's horrified face, stuffed their hankies into their mouths, making all kinds of most peculiar noises.

'Girls,' said Mam'zelle, in a choking kind of voice, 'girls, you are right. There is a terrible smell in here. What can it be?'

'A dead rat under the floorboards?' said Doris, obligingly, removing her hanky from her mouth for a moment.

Mam'zelle gave a small shriek. Rats, dead or alive, gave her shivers all down her back.

'Perhaps a drain has burst outside the window,' said Pat, speaking in a muffled voice. 'I'll look.'

She went to the open window and leant out, taking in deep breaths of the pure air there. One or two others joined her, thinking it was a very good idea.

'Perhaps it will go away,' said Mam'zelle, hopefully.

'Open the door, Janet, and maybe it will help to clear the room of this evil odour.'

Janet thankfully opened the door. This was an amusing trick to play – but it had its drawbacks!

The draught of air took a good strong dose of the smell over to Mam'zelle's desk. She gave a loud exclamation. '*Tiens*! This is terrible! We shall all be ill. Pick up your books quickly and we will finish our lesson in the garden. I will tell Miss Theobald and maybe she will have the boards up to seek for a rat that is quite dead.'

All but Claudine were delighted to go out into the garden. Claudine did not know which was worse – the smell in the classroom, or the insects out-of-doors. She thought there was very little to choose between them!

Soon the girls were sitting in a nice shady part of the garden, giggling whenever they thought of the awful smell drifting round their classroom. The lesson was no longer boring or dull! The smell had made it a great success.

Mam'zelle kept her word and reported the smell to Miss Theobald. 'Ah, Miss Theobald,' she said, 'it is a smell truly unbelievable! Of dead rats and mice, of eggs that are bad, of drains that are broken! It came into our classroom whilst the girls were reciting their French lesson, and it spoilt the whole hour. We had to leave the room and go into the garden.'

Miss Theobald was surprised to hear of such a very strong and disgusting smell. In all her experience of schools, she had never yet come across a smell that had driven a class from the room.

'I will go and smell it,' she said to Mam'zelle. 'If it is a dead rat, or bad drains, then, of course, we must have the smell seen to at once, this very afternoon. The smell will remain there, if those are the causes.'

But, to Mam'zelle's great astonishment and to Miss Theobald's mild astonishment, not a trace of the smell remained. The two of them sniffed all round the room, but it smelt fresh and clean.

'Extraordinary,' said Miss Theobald, gazing at Mam'zelle. 'You are quite sure, Mam'zelle, that it *was* a strong smell, a really bad one?'

Mam'zelle was most indignant. What, the head mistress was doubting her word? Mam'zelle at once began to describe the smell all over again, this time making it a smell ten times worse than before. Miss Theobald smiled to herself. She knew Mam'zelle's indignant exaggerations by this time.

'Well,' she said, 'I won't have the floorboards up, or the drains inspected today – maybe the smell will not return. If it does, Mam'zelle, kindly report it to me at once, please, so that I may smell it myself before it goes away.'

'Yes, Miss Theobald,' said Mam'zelle, and went to the mistresses' common-room, full of the smell and of its power in sending her class into the garden. Everyone listened in astonishment. It didn't occur to anyone but the first-form mistress, Miss Roberts, that it might be a trick. But Miss Roberts had had much experience of Janet's jokes, and it did cross her mind to wonder if this could be one of them.

'Let me see, Mam'zelle,' she said, thoughtfully, 'Janet is in the fourth form, isn't she?'

'Yes,' said Mam'zelle, 'but what has that got to do with my smell?'

'Oh – nothing I expect,' said Miss Roberts. 'But – if I were you, Mam'zelle, if that smell appears again, you trot down to Miss Theobald *at once*. I think she may be able to find the cause of it without taking up any floorboards and examining any drains!'

'Of course I shall report to the head at once,' said Mam'zelle, with dignity.

And the time came when she did!

14

Miss Ellis plays a trick too

The girls had been really delighted with the success of Janet's 'stink ball'. Whenever Eileen had not been in the room, they had chattered and laughed about Mam'zelle's disgust and astonishment.

'All the same, we'd better not do it again,' said Janet. 'I have a sort of feeling that once would be a success, but that twice would be a failure! You can pull Mam'zelle's leg beautifully once in a while, but not all the time.'

'If you do the smell again, I shall be sick and go out of the room,' said Claudine. 'It is the worst smell I have ever sniffed.'

'We won't do the smell again,' promised Bobby. 'But I tell you what we *will* do – we'll pre*tend* there is a smell, shall we – and get old Mam'zelle all hot and bothered expecting one – she'll sniff and snuff, and we shall die of laughing!'

'Oh, yes – that's a good idea,' said Janet. 'Doris, you can start off about the smell again in tomorrow's French grammar class.'

Doris grinned. She could act that kind of thing very well. So the next day, when Mam'zelle was ensconced safely at her desk at the end of the room, Doris began her act.

There was a very nice smell in the room, for Alison, the

girl doing the flowers for the classroom that week, had filled a big vase with white pinks, and they scented the room beautifully. The girls could smell them as they worked.

Doris began to sniff. At first she gave very little sniffs. Then she gave two or three bigger ones.

'Doris! Have you a cold?' said Mam'zelle, impatiently. 'Are you a first former, come to class without a handkerchief?'

'I've got a hanky, thank you, Mam'zelle,' said Doris, humbly, and took it out.

Then Janet began to sniff. She screwed up her nose, sniffed, and looked all round. Bobby gave a chuckle and turned it into a long cough. Mam'zelle frowned. She did not like behaviour of this sort! It made her angry.

Then Pat began to sniff, and pulled out her hanky too. Soon the whole class, all except Eileen, who was not in the joke, were sniffing as if they had bad colds.

Mam'zelle gazed at the sniffing girls, exasperated. 'What is all this noise? Sniff-sniff-sniff! I cannot bear it.'

Doris put on an expression of disgust. Mam'zelle saw it, and an alarming thought came into her head. Could it be that terrible smell again?

'Doris,' she said, urgently, 'what is the matter?'

'I can smell something,' murmured Doris. 'Distinctly. It's very strong just here. Can't you smell anything, Mam'zelle?'

Mam'zelle couldn't, which was not at all surprising. But she remembered that before she could not smell the smell until after the girls. She looked anxiously at the class. They all seemed to be smelling it.

'I will report it at once,' said Mam'zelle, and she left the room in a hurry.

'Crumbs!' said Bobby. 'I don't know that we wanted her to go to the head about it! I say – she shot off so quickly we couldn't stop her!'

Unluckily for Mam'zelle the head was out. Mam'zelle was annoyed and upset. Here was the smell again, and no Miss Theobald to smell it, and to know that she, Mam'zelle, had not exaggerated last time!

Mam'zelle popped her head in at the mistresses' common-room as she hurried back to the classroom. Miss Ellis was there, correcting exercise books belonging to the fourth form.

'Miss Ellis – I regret to say that that terrible smell is back again,' said Mam'zelle. 'It is abominable! I do not think you will be able to take the fourth form in your room next lesson.'

She withdrew her head and hurried back to the fourth form. She went in, expecting to be greeted by a wave of the terrible smell. But there seemed to be no smell at all. Very strange!

'Miss Theobald is out,' said Mam'zelle. 'Alas, she cannot smell our smell. Neither do I smell it yet!'

It was good news that Miss Theobald was out! The girls felt cheerful about that. Doris spoke up at once.

'Don't worry, Mam'zelle. We know what the smell was this time – quite different from last time. It was only these pinks!'

Doris picked up the big bowl of pinks, walked jauntily to Mam'zelle and thrust them under her big nose. Mam'zelle took a sniff and the strong and delicious scent went up her nose.

'So!' she said to Doris. 'It was the pinks you smelt. Well, it is a good thing Miss Theobald was not in. She would have come to smell for nothing!'

There were a few giggles – and then, as the door opened, the girls fell silent, and looked to see if it was Miss Theobald coming in after all.

But it wasn't. It was Miss Ellis, who, curious to smell this extraordinary smell that Mam'zelle seemed continually to get excited about, had come to smell it herself. She stood at the door, sniffing.

'I can't smell anything, Mam'zelle,' she said, surprised. Mam'zelle hastened to explain.

'I smelt nothing, either, Miss Ellis. It was the pinks the girls smelt. Doris has just told me.'

Miss Ellis was surprised and most disbelieving. 'I don't see how the girls could mistake a smell of pinks for the kind of awful smell you described to me last time,' she said. 'I am not at all sure I believe in that smell at all.'

She gave her form a glare, and went out.

Mam'zelle was indignant. Had she not smelt the smell herself last time? For the rest of the lesson the class had a very peaceful time, discussing smells, past and present, with their indignant French mistress.

After break came geography, taught by Miss Ellis. She came into the room looking rather stern.

'I just want to say,' she said, 'that I shall regard any mention of smells, bad or good, as a sign that you want a little extra work given to you.'

The class knew what that meant. 'A little extra work' from Miss Ellis meant a good two hours extra prep. So everyone immediately made up their minds not to mention the word smell at all.

But a terrible thing happened in ten minutes' time. Bobby had quite forgotten that she still had her 'stink ball' in her pocket, left over from the day before. And, in sitting down rather violently, after going with her book to Miss Ellis, she broke the thin glass surrounding the liquid. Then, in a trice, the perfectly awful smell came creeping round the classroom once more!

Doris smelt it. Janet smelt it. Bobby smelt it and put her hand at once into her pocket, desperately feeling about to see if she had accidentally broken the little 'stink ball'. When she found she had, she gazed round, winking and nodding at the others, to tell them of the awful accident. Miss Ellis's sharp eyes caught Bobby's signs. So she was not really very surprised when she smelt the smell coming towards her. What a terrible smell it was!

Miss Ellis thought things out quietly. Evidently yesterday's smell had been this same horrible one – and the one Mam'zelle had reported today, and which Doris had said was pinks after all, was nothing to do with the real smell – just a silly joke played on Mam'zelle.

But this awful smell is the real thing again, thought Miss Ellis. And, judging by Bobby's signs to the others, was a mistake. I don't think the girls would dare to play a trick like this on me. Well – I will just play a little trick on *them*!

Quietly Miss Ellis wrote a few directions on the board. Then she turned and left the room, closing the door after her. The girls stared at the board.

'Page 72. Write down the answers.

'Page 73. Read the first two paragraphs and then rewrite them in your own words.

'Page 74. Copy the map there.'

'I say!' exploded Doris. 'She's gone – and we've got to stay here in this awful smell and do that work. Bobby, you absolute idiot, why did you break that stink ball?'

'It was an accident,' said Bobby, most apologetically. 'I sat on it. I quite forgot it was there. Isn't this frightful? Miss Ellis has smelt it, of course, guesses it's a trick, and for punishment we've got to sit through the smell and work at our geography – and we simply daren't complain!'

'I am not going to sit in the smell,' announced Claudine, emphatically. She got up. 'I feel sick. I go to be sick.'

She went off, and she made such wonderful sick-noises as she passed Miss Ellis in the passage outside, that Miss Ellis said nothing, but let her go to the bathroom. Trust Claudine to do what she wanted! Not one of the others dared to leave the room.

They sat there, choking into their handkerchiefs, moaning over their fate, but not daring to scamp their work. At the end of the hour, when the smell had somewhat lessened, Miss Ellis opened the door.

She left it open. 'You may go for a short run round the

garden and back,' she said. 'Bobby, remain behind, please.'

With a wry face Bobby remained behind whilst the others fled out gladly into the fresh air.

'I was the one who caused that terrible smell this time,' said Bobby, at once. It was never any good beating round the bush with Miss Ellis – not that Bobby was given to that, anyway. She was a straightforward and truthful girl. 'But it was an accident, Miss Ellis, really it was. Please believe me.'

'I do,' said Miss Ellis. 'But it is an accident that is on no account to happen again. You have all had your punishment, so I shall say no more about it. But I want you to warn the fourth formers that any future smells will result in quite a lot of punishment!'

A birthday – and a grand idea!

'Isn't it gorgeous weather?' said Isabel to Pat. 'Day after day we get nothing but sun and blue sky. I wish we could have lessons sitting in the swimming-pool!'

'The coolest part of the day is the night!' said Doris. 'I should like to sleep all day and work all night in the cool night breeze.'

'Last night I woke up and saw the moon shining in at the window,' said Hilary. 'I got up and looked out – I simply can't tell you how beautiful the country looked, all lit up by moonlight. I wished I could go for a walk – have a moonlight picnic all by myself!'

'I *say*!' said Bobby, at once. 'A moonlight picnic! What an absolutely marvellous idea! Let's!'

'Oooh,' said the others, staring at Bobby, really impressed by the unusual idea. 'Golly – what fun!'

'Yes, it would be,' said Hilary, 'but – now that we're fourth formers, do you think we *ought* to?'

'Oh, Hilary – don't be so pious!' said Janet.

'I'm *not*,' said Hilary, indignantly. 'That's a thing I've never been. Well – perhaps it wouldn't matter. We could picnic in the school grounds. Oh, I *say* – let's picnic by the swimming-pool, and have a moonlight swim!'

'Better and better!' said Bobby, giving a whoop of delight. 'Golly – that would be super! Look here – let's wait till full-moon night – that's two nights from now – and have it then. The pool would be brilliantly lit and we could have a gorgeous time.'

'It's my birthday then,' said Mirabel. 'That very day. Oh, let's make it then, and I'd feel it was a birthday treat too!'

'Right,' said Janet. 'Now we'd better make plans quickly, because we haven't much time to get anything.' She turned to the quiet and responsible head girl of the form, Susan Howes. 'Susan, you'll come, won't you?'

Susan nodded. She was a good and trustworthy girl, but she loved a bit of fun, and she could not see that there was any harm in a moonlight picnic.

'I'll go down to the town today with Hilary, and buy a few things,' she said. 'I'll leave word at the grocer's and the baker's that you will all go in at different times and fetch one or two things. Then no one will suspect anything – we shall just quietly return to school with small parcels!'

'Shall we tell Eileen or not?' said Janet.

'No, of course not,' said Bobby. 'I bet she'd split on us and tell her mother – and then we'd all get caught and everything would be spoilt.'

'Well – it's a pity to leave Eileen out of everything like this really,' said Pat, 'but we can't risk being found out. And these midnight affairs *are* such fun!'

Mirabel was thrilled that it was her birthday that day!

It would make it all the nicer. She and Gladys, her quiet little friend, talked and talked about it.

'I'll take my birthday cake, of course,' said Mirabel. 'I'll save it up till then. Mother said she would send sixteen candles separately, and we'll stick them on the cake in their holders, and light them in the moonlight!'

Eileen was by now used to the others planning things without her. She knew that the tricks they whispered about together were not told her beforehand because she was known as a sneak. So she did not prick up her ears at all when she saw the girls talking together in low tones.

What do I care for their silly tricks? she thought. If they want to act like that, let them!

So she did not try to overhear or find out their fresh secret. She went her own way, looking rather pale and unhappy. She rarely smiled now, kept herself quite to herself, and did not try to make friends with anyone. She had been nice to Alison after the half-term treat, and Alison had benefited from her kindness by having no mending of her own at all to do ever since! But she still struggled with Angela's darning, though Angela was never very grateful.

Mirabel's birthday came. As usual her form gave presents. Some were small presents, if the girls had little money left, some were extravagant, like Angela's.

Angela gave Mirabel a book of very expensive music that she wanted. It cost five pounds and Mirabel was really quite overcome. 'You shouldn't spend so much money on a birthday!'

'Why not?' said Angela. 'My grandfather sent me ten pounds last week. What's the good of having money if you don't spend it?'

Pauline, not to be outdone, gave Mirabel a music-case of fine leather. Mirabel was amazed. It was not usual to have such beautiful presents for a school birthday. She had not even known that Pauline had noticed that her own old music-case had a broken strap and was almost worn out.

'Oh, Pauline – this is beautiful!' said Mirabel, red with surprise and delight. 'But you shouldn't do it. It's bad enough for Angela to do it – and for you to give me something so extravagant too, well really, I feel quite overwhelmed!'

'If Angela can do it, I can as well,' said Pauline, a little stiffly. That took the pleasure out of the gift somehow, thought Mirabel. If Pauline only gave her something fine just because she didn't want to be outdone by Angela, well, there wasn't much kindness or affection behind the gift!

Claudine surprisingly gave Mirabel a very pretty bag. Claudine was one of the girls who had very little money, and said so – so Mirabel was really touched to have such a nice gift from her.

'Oh, thank you, Claudine,' she said. 'It is really lovely. But it's too extravagant of you! I know you don't have much pocket-money.'

But Claudine seemed to have plenty that week! She bought eight pounds of cherries as her share of the picnic's goodies, and they came to three pounds. Everyone thought it was decent of her.

'Ah, when I have a little money, I like to spend it,' said Claudine. 'It is nice to spend. I wish I could spend always. That would be fine, to be like Angela and to say, "I will have this, I will have that!"'

'Yes – but it does mean you don't have many treats, real *treats,*' said Gladys. 'I mean – if Mother and I save up for ages to go on a good holiday together, it means much more to us and is a greater treat than any holiday could possibly be to Angela – who can have expensive holidays whenever she likes. To have a lot of money doesn't mean that you get more enjoyment than those who haven't much.'

'Quite right as usual,' said Isabel, giving the quiet Gladys a little pat. 'Well, I wish I and Pat could buy more for this picnic, but it was our granny's birthday last week and we spent most of our money on that mauve silk scarf we sent her. So we're cleaned out for a bit. I hope you won't turn up your nose at our birthday offering, Mirabel – it's only two drawing pencils with your name on!'

'That's very decent of you,' said Mirabel, who really did not mind whether gifts cost ten pounds or ten pence. 'I think you're all decent to me, everyone of you. Everybody has given me a present.'

Even Eileen had, though with many apologies for the poorness of her gift. 'It's only a little hanky,' she said to Mirabel. 'And I'm afraid it's not even new. It's one of my own, but please take it, Mirabel, with my birthday wishes. I don't want to be the only one not giving you anything!

You know I have hardly any pocket-money, and it's Eddie's birthday soon and I'm saving every penny for that.'

Everyone knew that Eileen had less money than any girl in the school. Her mother was mean over pocket-money. Certainly she had to work hard for her own money, but she seemed to think that the sixteen-year-old Eileen could manage on a penny or two a week, just as she had managed when she was a small six-year-old.

'I wish we could ask Eileen to go with us tonight,' said Mirabel. She was usually a thick-skinned girl, who had little feeling for anyone else, except for her friend Gladys – but she had been touched by Eileen's little gift, and her honest confession of having no money.

'Well, we can't,' said Bobby, decidedly. 'I know she told her mother that Janet said that there seemed to be more torn sheets in the fourth-form dormitories than in the whole of the rest of the school put together – and poor Janet has done oceans of mending this week. But who can help thinking our sheets are torn on purpose? On purpose to give us work to do! They were never torn like this before. Why, I could go a whole term without having to mend a pillow-case or sheet at all when our old Matron was here!'

'All right. We won't ask Eileen,' said Mirabel. 'I don't really care. She *is* a dreadful sneak, I suppose.'

Everything was prepared in readiness for the moonlight picnic and swim. The sky was clear when the girls went to bed that night. They went to bed in the daylight, for the evenings were very long just then.

'There won't be any darkness at all, I should think,' said Bobby, looking out of the window. 'When daylight begins to go, the full moon will come swimming up the sky, and then everything will be almost as bright as day again. Golly, isn't it hot? I shall adore being in the water at midnight!'

Luckily for the girls, Eileen was a very sound sleeper. Once she was asleep, nothing ever seemed to wake her, and even when the fire-practice alarm had gone once in the middle of the night, she had not awakened. So the girls felt sure she would know nothing.

It was too hot to sleep! Some of the girls dozed off, and Eileen and Mirabel slept soundly. But the others tossed and turned, half-asleep and half-awake. So, when the big clock in one of the towers struck half-past eleven, there was only Mirabel to wake!

Eileen slept in a bed by the door of one of the fourth-form dormitories, and the girls had to tip-toe past her. But she did not stir. She had looked rather pale and tired lately, and now she slept very deeply. The girls had on swimming-costumes under their dressing-gowns, and rubber shoes on their feet. They made no sound as they stole down the corridors, went down the stairs, and came to the big cupboard where they had hidden their food and drink.

With giggles and whispers they loaded themselves with the goodies, and then undid the garden door as quietly as they could. They left it a little open so that they could get in easily when they returned. There was no wind to bang it shut.

Keeping in the cover of the trees, the line of excited girls made their way towards the swimming-pool. How gorgeous the still water looked, lying calm and deep in the brilliant moonlight. The moon was now up, and was flooding the grounds with cold, silver light. Everything could be plainly seen. Only the warm colours of daylight were missing.

'We mustn't make too much noise,' said Janet. 'Our voices would carry a good way on a still night like this. I only hope no one will hear the splashing of the water when we go in! Let's go in first, before we eat. I'm so hot.'

Off came the dressing-gowns. Bare long legs gleamed in the moonlight. One after another the girls dived in or jumped in – all but Claudine, who had steadfastly refused to come in a swimming-costume, but had on her night-gown under her dressing-gown. The little French girl liked the excitement of the midnight picnic but, hot though it was, nothing would persuade her to go in the water! She would throw herself in to punish a spiteful-tongued woman – but she certainly would not go in for pleasure!

She stood and watched the girls, laughing. She glanced away from the pool – and suddenly saw a figure slipping silently between the trees. Whoever could it be?

Claudine deals with Matron

Claudine ran quietly in her rubber shoes to see who was out in the grounds that night, besides the fourth formers. It was Eileen! Eileen, whom the girls had left sound asleep in bed.

'The sneak!' said Claudine to herself. 'She comes to peep and pry at us, and then she goes back to her so-severe mother to tell a tale! I will follow her back.'

But somehow she missed Eileen, and could not see where she had gone. Claudine rushed back to the pool and almost fell into the water in her excitement at telling the others what she had seen.

'Oh, blow!' said Bobby, climbing out, the moonlight shining on the silvery drops running down her legs. 'I suppose that sneak of an Eileen will go straight off to Matron – and before we can have anything to eat, she'll be here scolding us and rowing us and sending us back in disgrace.'

'I will go back to the school, and keep watch,' said Claudine, eagerly. 'I know where Matron sleeps. I will go outside her door and stand there till I know for certain that either she is coming here, or that Eileen has not told tales after all.'

'Right,' said Bobby. 'Hurry! And be sure to race back and warn us if you hear Matron dressing or wandering about. We simply mustn't be caught. But oh, what a shame if we can't have the moonlight picnic. And I bet Matron will confiscate Mirabel's lovely cake!'

Claudine sped off in her rubber shoes. She did not see Eileen at all. She went in at the open garden door and ran quietly up the stairs to the corridor at the end of which Matron slept.

She stood outside Matron's door and listened. There was not a single sound from inside. She could not hear either Eileen's voice or Matron's. On the other hand, she could not hear slight snores or heavy breathing. Claudine stood there, wondering what to do. *Had* Eileen seen the picnickers? *Did* she mean to tell tales? Where had she gone?

Then Claudine's quick ears caught a sound from inside Matron's room. The bed was creaking! Plainly Matron was awake. The bed creaked a little more, and then there came the sound of someone shuffling into slippers.

'Now she puts on a dressing-gown,' thought Claudine. 'Now she ties the belt. But why is she getting up just now, if Eileen has not been to tell her?'

The little French girl squeezed herself into a dark corner as Matron's door suddenly opened. The thin narrow-shouldered figure appeared framed in the doorway, full in the moonlight. Matron looked rather grim.

She set off silently down the passage and turned off in the direction of the dormitory belonging to the fourth formers. Claudine followed her like a moving black shadow, keeping cleverly in the dark corners. Matron went into the dormitory where Eileen always slept.

'Eileen!' said Matron, in a whisper. But there was no answer. Then Matron evidently patted the bed and found no one there. There came an exclamation, and Matron switched on the light. In a moment she saw the empty beds!

She went into the next dormitory, where the fourth formers also slept, and again switched on the light. No girls there!

'Where are they?' said Matron, angrily. 'I will not have this sort of thing! Why didn't Eileen warn me of this? She ought to know better than to join in tricks of this sort!'

Claudine heard these muttered words, and was surprised. So Eileen *hadn't* warned her mother! She had followed the others out, and must be hiding somewhere in the grounds, watching the fun.

And now Matron was going to spoil everything. Why should she? Claudine felt a sudden and intense dislike for the severe and spiteful Matron. There was no harm in a moonlight swim and picnic! Quite likely if the girls had asked Miss Theobald's permission, she would have aughed and granted it, just for once! And now Matron was going to interfere.

Matron went down the stairs. She came to the cupboard where the girls had stored their picnic food and drink. They had left the door open. Matron gave an angry exclamation and went to shut it.

And it was then that the Great Idea came to Claudine!

It was an idea that might have occurred to any angry girl, but only Claudine would have carried it out.

Matron suddenly got the shock of her life! Someone gave her a violent push so that she landed inside the cupboard, among old lacrosse sticks and tennis-rackets. Then the door was shut – and locked!

Matron was a prisoner! Claudine took the key out of the cupboard and put it into her dressing-gown pocket. Choking with laughter she ran out of the garden door and made her way to the swimming-pool. She could hear Matron hammering on the door. But the little back-hall beyond the garden-door, near the cupboard, was seldom used, and far from any sleeping-quarters. It was quite likely that no one would hear Matron at all.

Now we are safe! thought Claudine, triumphantly. What a fine joke! But will these English girls think it is a joke?

For the first time a doubt came into her mind. She, Claudine, knew it to be a grand, grand joke to lock that so-detestable Matron up in a dark cupboard, to stop her from spoiling the fun – but would the others think like Claudine? Might not this curious 'honour' they were always talking about prevent them from thinking it a joke? Might not Susan Howes, fourth-form head girl, think it her duty to go and rescue Matron? One could never tell what the English would think right or wrong!

Then I shall not tell them what I have done! thought Claudine, as she sped along to the pool. If they do not know, they cannot worry. Now I will only tell them that it is all right, Eileen has not told tales, and that Matron is quite, quite safe.

The girls climbed out of the pool and surrounded Claudine when she came running back.

'It's all right,' said Claudine. 'Very much OK. Eileen has not told tales. She is not back at the school. And Matron is quite, quite safe!'

'Oh, *good*!' said all the girls, and shook the water from themselves. 'What about some eats now?'

'Where's Eileen then, if she isn't in bed and didn't go back to school?' said Bobby, puzzled.

But nobody knew and nobody cared. Let Eileen wander where she liked so long as she didn't spoil their fun. And how good that Matron was safe too!

The girls were very hungry after their swim. They sat down to enjoy the food. There was bread, butter, potted meat, tins of sardines, marmalade, apricot jam, cherries, biscuits and Mirabel's big birthday cake. The candles did not show up very well in the bright moonlight, but still, it was fun to light them.

The girls had their picnic by the edge of the water, dangling their legs in the pool. The water was lukewarm, for the sun had warmed it thoroughly. It was simply lovely. There had never been such midnight fun as this!

'This cake is gorgeous,' said Bobby, eating an enormous slice. 'My word – I don't ever remember feeling so hungry. Are those sardine sandwiches? Pass them along, Susan.'

Claudine enjoyed her meal more than anyone. True, she was not so hungry as the others, for she had not been in for a swim – but she could not help thinking of Matron shut up in the dark cupboard, quite unable to spoil the fun of the fourth formers! And that gave a very keen edge to her enjoyment of the picnic. She felt no anxiety as to what would happen when Matron was let out. Claudine never let things like that worry her at all!

The meal was over at last. Every scrap was finished. Even Angela said she had enjoyed it. Alison had not enjoyed it quite so much as the others because she had fallen into the water in her dressing-gown, and was worried as to how to dry it before Matron saw it. Mirabel said she had never enjoyed a birthday so much in all her life.

'It's been a great success,' said Janet, pleased. 'Now we'd better go back. Hark – there's one o'clock striking – Dong! Golly, I'm tired now.'

Everyone was tired. The swim had been rather strenuous, for there had been a lot of good-humoured racing and teasing. The girls cleared up crumbs, cartons and paper-bags, and put empty ginger-beer bottles into a locker up in the gallery, meaning to collect them when it was safe.

'That's all, I think,' said Susan, looking round. 'Isn't the water lovely, gleaming in the moonlight. I just hate to leave it!'

But they had to leave the gleaming pool. They made their way back through the trees, whispering together. They came to the garden door, which was still open.

And then they heard a most peculiar noise. Bang, bang, bang, knock, knock, knock!

'Crumbs! What's that?' said Susan, startled.

'Let me out, let me out!' cried a muffled voice, and somebody kicked against a wooden door.

Alison and Angela were terrified. 'It's a burglar!' said Alison, and tore up the stairs as fast as ever she could. Angela followed her, trembling.

Claudine pushed the others towards the stairs quickly. 'Don't stop,' she whispered. 'Get back to the dormitories as quickly as you can. Don't stop. I will explain everything.'

In the greatest astonishment the girls went upstairs to their dormitories. They crowded into the one in which Claudine slept, and demanded to know what the explanation of the curious noises was.

'It's Matron,' said Claudine. 'She's locked in that cupboard.'

There was an amazed silence.

'*Who* locked her in?' said Bobby at last.

'I did,' said Claudine. 'She came into our dormitories and saw we weren't there. I did not want her to spoil your fun – so I pushed her into the cupboard and locked her in. Was I not quick and clever?'

17
An infuriated Matron

For a minute or two no one said anything at all. The girls found it simply unbelievable that Claudine should have done such a thing. Locked Matron into a games cupboard! Left her there, shouting and hammering! Really, the French girl must be completely mad.

'No, I am not mad,' said Claudine, reading their thoughts. 'It was the only thing to do, wasn't it? She would have spoilt your fun, and I could stop her. So I stopped her.'

'But Claudine – you'll get into the most fearful row!' said Janet at last.

'That matters nothing,' replied Claudine, and certainly she acted as if she did not mind what happened! She was not in the least excited or upset. The girls went on staring at her, hardly able to take in the fact that Matron had been, and still was, a prisoner downstairs.

Then an awful thought came to Bobby. 'Who's going to let her out?'

Nobody said anything. Not even Claudine wanted to set free a woman who would be sure to be violently and spitefully angry. But certainly she could not be left in the cupboard till the morning.

'Where's the key?' said Janet. Claudine produced it

from her dressing-gown pocket. It was a large key. Claudine put her finger in the hole at the top of it and swung it thoughtfully to and fro.

'As I was the one who locked her in, I will also be the one to let her out,' she said at last. 'But I shall unlock the door very, very quietly, then open it a tiny way, and then I shall fly up the stairs, taking my heels with me.'

The girls couldn't help smiling. 'You mean, you will take to your heels and fly upstairs!' said Bobby. 'You do say ridiculous things, Claudine. Honestly, I can't imagine how you dared to do such a thing – locking Matron into a cupboard – golly, it's unheard of! Why didn't you tell us what you had done, when you came back to the pool and joined the picnic?'

'I thought you would say, "Ah, it is not honourable to do such a thing,"' explained Claudine. 'I thought maybe Susan would feel she ought to go and set Matron free. So I said nothing.'

'I never met anyone quite like you before,' said Pat. 'You do the most awful things for perfectly good reasons! I mean – you throw yourself into the pool when you *hate* the water, just to punish someone who's been unkind to your aunt – and you go and lock Matron up in a cupboard just so that we shan't have our picnic spoilt! I must say you do the most dramatic things – we never know what you're going to do next!'

'Well – what are we going to do about Matron?' demanded Susan, who was getting worried. 'Shall we let Claudine let her out?'

'I go,' said Claudine, and got up with much dignity. She loved moments like this, when she took the stage and everyone looked at her. She was not at all conceited, but there was to her a very satisfying feeling in doing something unusual and dramatic.

She went. The girls scrambled into bed, feeling that very shortly Matron would come bursting into the dormitories like an angry bull!

Claudine crept downstairs to the little back-hall by the garden-door. Matron was still shouting and hammering. Claudine slipped along to the door and put the key quietly into the key-hole – but just as she was about to turn it and unlock the door, she heard the sound of quiet footsteps on the gravel path outside!

She darted up the stairs at once, without turning the key. Let whoever it was coming by unlock the door! They would be sure to hear Matron, and set her free. Then she, Claudine, could get away in safety!

The footsteps came to the garden-door, and then someone slipped inside. It was Eileen! She stood still in the greatest astonishment as she heard the muffled cries and the banging on the door of the games cupboard.

'Why – it's Mother's voice!' said Eileen out loud, in the very greatest amazement. 'Where is she? She can't be in that cupboard!'

But she was, as Eileen very soon realized. The girl turned the key at once and opened the door. Matron stumbled out, almost beside herself with rage. She caught hold of Eileen in a fierce grip, not seeing which girl it was. Eileen cried out in pain.

'Mother! Don't! It's me, Eileen. However did you get into that cupboard?'

'*You*!' cried Matron, and let go Eileen's arm. 'What are *you* doing here? Where have you been? How dare you go out at night like this? Tell me what you have been doing, at once!'

Eileen said nothing at all. Her mother gave her a shake. 'You've been out somewhere with the fourth form. They are all out of their beds! What have you been doing? I shall report you all to Miss Theobald. Why didn't you tell me what was happening?'

'I can't say anything, Mother,' said Eileen, in a frightened voice. It was news to her that the fourth form had been out that night. She had not noticed any empty beds when she had slipped out herself. She had not heard any noise from the swimming-pool either. She had been out to meet her brother Eddie in the lane, and she was not going to tell her mother this. She no longer dared to meet him in the daytime, for she felt that anyone might see her, and report her. So she had been meeting him once a week in the middle of the night, when all her dormitory was sound asleep.

Nobody knew this. And certainly she must not let her mother know, or Eddie would get into trouble too. What had the fourth formers been doing? How mean of them to go off on a spree at night and leave her out! Somehow or other she must make her mother think she had been with them.

'You won't say anything?' said her mother in a threatening voice. 'Well, tell me this – who locked me in here? I can't imagine that *you* would dare to!'

'Of course I didn't,' said Eileen. 'And I don't know who did, either. Carlotta might have. It's the kind of thing she would do. I really don't know, Mother. Please let me go back to bed!'

But Matron was far too angry and humiliated to let the matter drop. She swept up the stairs to the fourth-form dormitories, and switched on the lights. The girls all pretended to be asleep. Matron walked into the dormitory where Eileen slept, and spoke in a loud and angry voice.

'It's no good your pretending to be asleep. I know you're not. I've come to find out who locked me into that cupboard! I insist on knowing, here and now. That girl will be expelled from St Clare's!'

Susan Howes sat up and looked at the angry Matron. 'We all take the blame for that,' she said, quietly. 'We are very sorry, Matron, and we hope you will accept our apologies.'

Matron made a fierce explosive noise. 'Accept your apologies! Of course I don't! You won't get out of this as easily as that! I insist on knowing who locked me in. Otherwise I shall go straight to Miss Theobald, here and now, in the middle of the night.'

Claudine sat up in bed, ready to speak. She did not in the least mind owning up. But Bobby laid a warning hand on her shoulder, and pulled her over towards her, to whisper into her ear.

'Don't own up to Matron! She will go to your aunt too, and make a fearful fuss, and there's no reason why Mam'zelle should be brought into this. You can tell Miss Theobald yourself tomorrow if you want to.'

'*Bien*!' said Claudine, snuggling down into bed again. 'Very good! I do as you say, Bobbee.'

Matron stood glaring round the room. Then she stamped heavily with her foot and almost shouted. 'All right! I shall go to Miss Theobald. You will all have to explain what you were doing in the middle of the night, leaving your beds like that – and I warn you, I shall show no mercy to the person who has not owned up to locking me in. Eileen, get into bed. I am absolutely ashamed to think that a daughter of mine should have joined in midnight wrong-doing, and should refuse to tell me anything about it!'

She went off down the corridor, walking angrily. The girls sat up.

'Whew!' said Bobby. 'What a volcano! I say, Eileen, where were you? Does your mother really think you were with us?'

'Yes,' said Eileen, in a low voice. 'Please don't give me away. I was only meeting Eddie, my brother. I was afraid to tell my mother that, so I let her think I was with you. I didn't know what you had been doing, so I couldn't possibly tell her, of course, and that has made her very wild with me. We're all going to get into a most fearful row.'

'I bet Miss Theobald won't be too pleased at being

wakened up at this time of night,' said Janet, looking at her watch. 'It's half-past one! We'd better try and get some sleep – though I expect the next thing will be Miss Theobald coming in and demanding explanations too!'

The girls tried to settle down and go to sleep. Mirabel fell asleep first, and then one by one the others did . . . all except Eileen, who lay awake, staring into the dark, worried and unhappy. Everything was going wrong! Everything was getting worse! Oh dear, she did hope the girls wouldn't give her away and say she had not been with them that night. They might quite well sneak about her. She had done plenty of sneaking that term, and it would not be at all surprising if they got a bit of their own back!

Matron walked down the corridor and made her way to the separate wing in which the head mistress, Miss Theobald, had her set of rooms. She knocked loudly on the bedroom door.

'Come in!' said a startled voice, and there was the sound of a light being switched on. Matron opened the door. Miss Theobald was sitting up in bed, eyes heavy with sleep.

'What is the matter?' she said anxiously. 'Is someone ill, Matron?'

'No,' said Matron, her thin face still purple with rage. 'Something much worse than that!'

'Good gracious, what?' asked Miss Theobald, hurriedly getting out of bed and reaching for her dressing-gown. 'Quick, tell me!'

'It's the fourth form,' said Matron, in a grim voice. 'All out of their beds, every one. Even my Eileen. Goodness knows what they were doing!'

Miss Theobald sat down on her bed in relief. 'Oh,' she said, 'a midnight feast, I suppose? I thought you had come to report something really serious! Couldn't this have waited till the morning, Matron?'

'Indeed it couldn't,' said Matron, 'and for a very good reason, too. Somebody locked me for hours into the games cupboard in the back-hall by the garden-door!'

Miss Theobald stared at Matron as if she really could not believe her ears. 'Locked you into the cupboard?' she said at last. 'Are you quite sure? I mean – I really cannot imagine any of the fourth formers doing that.'

'You don't know half that goes on in the school,' answered Matron in a grim and righteous tone. 'Not half! My Eileen tells me most things, and you'd be surprised if I told you some of them.'

'I don't think I want to hear,' said Miss Theobald, 'and I can't help thinking it is a mistake, Matron, to encourage Eileen to tell tales to you. Also I think you need not worry whether I know all that goes on or not. That is my concern.'

Matron sensed the rebuke in Miss Theobald's words, and she began to feel angry that the head had not expressed more anger and concern over her imprisonment in the cupboard. She looked grimmer than ever.

'Eileen set me free,' she said. 'Otherwise I might have been in the cupboard till the morning. A fine thing to happen to the Matron of a school like this! I went up to the fourth-form dormitories at once, and there were all the girls pretending to be asleep. Little hypocrites!'

'Oh, Matron, don't be quite so vindictive!' said Miss Theobald, feeling rather shocked at the Matron's tone. 'You have never been Matron in a girls' school before, and you are not yet used to the mischievous ways of the various forms. But as a rule there is little harm in them. Who locked you in?'

'The girls won't say,' said Matron, angrily. 'But I demand that whoever locked me in should be expelled, Miss Theobald. A girl that does a thing like that is a very bad influence on the others!'

'Well, I expect they were all in it,' said Miss Theobald. 'I should never expel a girl without a much stronger reason than mere mischief, Matron. I am certain that the whole form shared in the fun, and you would not expect me to expel the whole lot, would you? Do try and see things in a reasonable light. You are angry and annoyed now – you will not be so inclined to want girls expelled in the morning.'

'Aren't you coming back to the dormitories with me to demand who it was that locked me in?' demanded Matron, furiously, as she saw Miss Theobald taking off her dressing-gown and slippers.

'The girls will, I hope, be asleep by now,' said the head, getting into bed. 'I see no reason for waking them all up again. This can easily wait till the morning.'

Matron was infuriated. She had planned a most

dramatic return to the dormitories with Miss Theobald, and had gone so far as to hope that the head would demand to know the culprit and announce her expulsion there and then. She bit her thin lips and glared at Miss Theobald so angrily that the headmistress began to feel annoyed.

'Please go now, Matron,' she said. 'We will continue this rather complicated conversation in the morning.'

Matron took a step forward, and her face took on a malicious look. 'Well,' she said, 'I wasn't going to tell you till I'd found out the thief – but there's somebody in the fourth form who's been stealing, Miss Theobald! I've missed money – yes, and stamps too – and all kinds of things like notepaper and envelopes. You've got a nasty little thief in the fourth form, and I shall want *that* matter cleared up too! Otherwise, I am afraid – I shall go to the police!'

Claudine scores again

Miss Theobald disliked Matron intensely at that moment. It was quite plain that she took a real pleasure in saying these poisonous things.

'I think all these things must wait till the morning, Matron,' said the head. 'I will go into them thoroughly then. We can do nothing satisfactory tonight. Good night.'

Matron walked out of the room without answering. She hoped she had given Miss Theobald a shock. She had not meant to talk about her missing money, for she was taking a great pleasure in trying to track down the thief herself – and then she had meant to take her by the shoulder and lead her triumphantly to Miss Theobald. Matron hoped that the thief and the one who had locked her into the cupboard were one and the same. She felt certain they were. Surely only a very bad character could lock her into a cupboard!

'We shall perhaps get to the bottom of things tomorrow!' she thought, as she got into bed. 'I'll make Eileen tell me all that the fourth form did. I shan't say anything about my missing money to her, though, in case she warns the fourth form and the thief isn't caught.'

The fourth-form girls woke up tired and sleepy and

rather fearful the next morning. Had Matron been to Miss Theobald? What was going to happen?

Matron appeared at breakfast, grim and stern. Eileen had tear-stained eyes. Her mother had scolded her and demanded to know what the fourth form had been doing the night before. But Eileen had not told.

Bobby had spoken seriously to her. 'Look here, Eileen – we didn't ask you to our picnic last night because we were afraid you'd sneak to your mother, as you often do. But we'll make a bargain with you. We will say nothing at all about your not being with us – Matron can go on thinking you *were* with us – but you in your turn aren't to give us away any more at all. See? And if you do, the bargain is automatically broken, and we shall tell on you. It's the only way to teach you that sneaking doesn't pay.'

Eileen, looking pale and unhappy, had nodded. 'Thank you,' she said. 'I couldn't bear Mother to know I go and meet Eddie. She would be so angry with him. I won't split on any of you any more. I've sneaked, I know – but it's so difficult not to answer Mother's questions sometimes.'

Bobby guessed it was. Eileen had her own problems – but they wouldn't be solved by being weak and telling-tales! She had to find that out sooner or later.

But this morning Eileen had been determined and strong, for once, and had not answered Matron's insistent questions. Her mother had been very angry, and had scolded her severely. Matron had a fierce temper when she let herself go, and poor Eileen had had to bear the brunt of it.

'Claudine,' said Susan, in a low voice at breakfast-time, 'if you want to own up to Miss Theobald about locking Matron up, you'd better go immediately after breakfast. But if you don't want to own up, you needn't. We'll all stick by you, and ask Miss Theobald to hand out a punishment to the whole form. After all, we had a good time, because of you, and we none of us want you to be punished for something we would all dearly like to have done ourselves.'

'Thank you, Susan,' said Claudine, thinking that these English girls could be very nice and fair and generous. 'But I shall go to Miss Theobald. I am not ashamed of what I did. She is a nasty woman, the Matron, and I shall tell Miss Theobald that it filled me with pleasure to punish her for some of the unkind things she has done this term.'

'Well – do and say what you like,' said Susan, thinking that Claudine would, all her life, quite probably do and say exactly what she liked! 'And good luck to you!'

So Claudine went to the head, knocked firmly at the door and went in.

She began without any beating about the bush. 'Please, Miss Theobald, I have come to say that it was I who locked Matron in last night. I suppose it is not a thing that any English girl would have done, with their so-fine sense of honour, but I am French, and I did not like Matron, and I wanted the fourth form to have a good time. We went for a moonlight picnic, Miss Theobald, and swam in the pool. At least, I did not swim, but the others did, and they said it was magnificent.'

Miss Theobald found it difficult not to smile at the frank confession. Claudine always had such a very disarming and innocent air, even when she was doing or owning up to the most extraordinary things. The head looked keenly at the intelligent French girl.

'Why do you dislike Matron?'

'You wish me to say the truth to you?' asked Claudine. 'Well, then, I will say this. Matron can find out, through Eileen, all the little stupidities and mischiefs of the fourth formers, and then, see what happens! Miraculously our sheets get torn and we spend hours mending them. Suddenly stockings are full of holes, blouses are without buttons. Alas, Miss Theobald, we do not all like Eileen, and if we show it, then these unhappy things happen, and we sit indoors mending, whilst others play games.'

'I see,' said Miss Theobald. She had suspected this. 'Claudine, you cannot go about locking people into cupboards. I am certain that even French school girls do not do this!'

'Ah, Miss Theobald, I do not go about always locking people up!' said Claudine, beginning to launch herself on one of her long and involved speeches. 'No, no – only those people who deserve it should be imprisoned into cupboards. Me, I would never . . .'

Miss Theobald thought that Claudine had many of Mam'zelle's own ways. She smiled to herself and stopped the voluble explanation.

'That will do, Claudine. You will please apologize to Matron this morning, and you will accept what punishment she gives you. There is one thing more . . .'

She stopped and looked keenly at Claudine. The little French girl listened intently, for she had a great liking and respect for the wise and kindly head mistress.

'That one thing more is about the English sense of honour,' said Miss Theobald. 'You speak lightly of it, even mockingly – but I think, Claudine, in your heart of hearts you see it for the good and fine thing it really is. When you go back to France, Claudine, take one thing with you – the English sense of honour.'

Claudine looked solemn. She was very much moved.

'Miss Theobald,' she said, 'believe me when I say that I do not really mock at it. First I did not understand it. Then I thought it was tiresome in others and even more tiresome to have oneself. But now I begin to learn it, and it is good, very good.'

There came a knock at the door and Matron came in, looking grimmer than ever. She meant to have things out with Miss Theobald at once. Claudine was simply delighted to see her. 'Now,' thought the clever girl, 'now I will apologize to Matron in front of Miss Theobald, and she will not dare to be too spiteful to me nor to give me too great a punishment!'

So Claudine went meekly up to Matron, cast her eyes down to the ground, and spoke in a very timid voice.

'Matron, it was I who locked you in last night. I apologize to you and beg your forgiveness. I will gladly bear what punishment you give me!'

Miss Theobald looked on with much amusement. She

knew that Claudine was acting a part, and had cleverly taken advantage of Matron's coming, to apologize at once, in front of the headmistress herself.

Matron went purple in the face. She glared at Claudine and scolded her severely.

'You're a very naughty girl! You deserve to be expelled! And what is more, I *would* have you expelled if it was not that your aunt is the French mistress here, and it would break her heart to have a thing like that happen.'

Actually Matron was afraid of Mam'zelle, who was apt to fly off into even more violent tempers than Matron herself. Matron even felt that Mam'zelle might come and scratch her face and pull her hair out if she dared to try and get Claudine expelled.

'It is good of you to consider my kind aunt,' replied Claudine, still in a very meek voice. 'What is my punishment to be?'

'You will spend every hour of your spare-time this week helping me to mend the school linen,' said Matron. She did not see the flash of joy in Claudine's downcast eyes. Ah, now she would be able to get out of games and walks for a whole week! 'Very well, Matron,' she said, putting on a most miserable voice, that did not deceive the listening Miss Theobald in the least. She turned to the head.

'I will return now to my class,' she said, and gave Miss Theobald a brilliant and grateful smile. She went out of the room, shutting the door quietly. Miss Theobald thought that no one could help liking the naughty little girl, clever as she was at always getting her own way!

'Well, Miss Theobald,' said Matron, in a war-like tone, 'can we get down to this business of stealing? I can't have it happening any longer. It's got beyond me. Day after day it happens. And what's more, some more of my money has gone since last night! Only two pounds, it is true – but stealing two pounds is as bad as stealing ten pounds. It's thieving, right down bad thieving. And I think the girl who does it ought to be expelled. You wouldn't agree to expelling the girl who locked me in last night – but maybe you'll have to, Miss Theobald! Yes, maybe you'll have to!'

'What do you mean?' asked Miss Theobald in surprise.

'I mean this,' said Matron, 'I think it's that little French girl who's taking things! She's always in and out of my room with mending – and I hear she's been throwing a lot of money about lately – and *I* know she hasn't much, because Mam'zelle herself told me. So maybe, Miss Theobald, you will find that it's best to get rid of a girl of that sort, and will agree with me that it would be a good thing to expel her!'

19

Pauline's mother

Before Miss Theobald could make up her mind that day what would be the best way to tackle the Matron and her accusations, a nasty accident happened in the gym.

It happened to Pauline. She was climbing one of the ropes, and somehow slipped and fell to the ground. She fell with one leg doubled up under her, and there was a sickening crack.

Pauline crumpled up on the floor, went very white, and then quietly fainted. The games mistress hurried to her in alarm, and Matron was at once called and the doctor telephoned for.

'Broken her leg,' he said. 'Clean break. Nothing to worry about.'

He set it, and Pauline was put to bed, still white from the shock. Miss Theobald went to see her, and Pauline looked beseechingly up at her.

'Don't tell my mother,' she said. 'I don't want to worry her. Please don't tell her.'

'My dear child, I have already telephoned her,' said Miss Theobald in surprise. 'Why shouldn't she be told?'

'I don't want to worry her,' said Pauline, faintly. 'Please ring her up again, Miss Theobald, and say she is not to worry, and of course she is not to bother to come and see me. Say I will write to her today.'

'You can't write today,' said Miss Theobald gently. 'You must keep absolutely quiet today. I will ring your mother up again this evening, and tell her not to bother to come and see you if she cannot do so.'

'Tell her *not* to,' said Pauline. 'She – she hasn't been well, you see. I don't want her to be worried.'

Everyone was sorry about Pauline. The girls were not allowed to go and see her that day, but they sent her in little gifts of flowers and fruit and books.

'Everything seems to be happening at once,' said Bobby. 'I say – wasn't that a perfectly awful talk that Miss Theobald had with us this morning?'

It had been a very serious and solemn talk indeed, and had happened just before dinner that morning. All the fourth formers, except Pauline, who was in the sickbay, under Matron's care, had been called to Miss Theobald's sitting-room.

The head had lightly touched on the night before, telling them that Claudine had confessed, and had apologized to Matron and received a punishment for her extraordinary behaviour. She said that she would have given permission herself for a moonlight picnic and swim if she had been asked, but she realized that girls as young as the fourth still thought it was more fun to do things with*out* permission, than with.

This made the more responsible ones squirm a bit. They did not like being considered young and silly. Then

Miss Theobald passed on to Matron's other complaint. This was very much more serious, of course, and the fourth form listened in great discomfort as the head told them that a thief was in their midst, and must be found out, or must come and confess.

'You must realize that what would be a small thing, comparatively speaking, in the lower school, among the younger children, is a much more serious thing among you older girls,' said the head, 'and Matron is quite rightly concerned about the matter. Whoever is taking things from her room is doing it deliberately and continually – it is not something done in a moment of urgency and perhaps regretted bitterly afterwards – it is, apparently, quite cold-blooded, frequent and deliberate.'

The girls talked about it all afterwards, the affair of Matron being locked up in the cupboard taking second place to this much more serious accusation. Who in the wide world could it be?

'Matron is certain it's someone in the fourth form because our common-room is the only one near to her room,' said Bobby. 'It would be easy for someone to slip out now and then, see if the coast was clear, and then pop into Matron's room and sneak something.'

'Such peculiar things have been stolen besides money,' said Janet, puzzled. 'Stamps – and notepaper and envelopes. Why those? Matron says that biscuits and sweets have been taken too. It almost looks as if somebody has been taking anything they could, just out of spite.'

'Well, we none of us loves Matron!' said Bobby,

grinning. 'If it was just a question of paying her out for her meannesses, any one of us might be the culprit!'

'I am glad such things happen to her,' said Claudine. 'She deserves to have unhappiness, because she gives so much sadness to others. The poor Eileen has red eyes all day long today!'

'Yes, I can't help feeling sorry for her,' said Doris. 'It's bad enough to have Matron as Matron, but to have her as mother as well must be pretty awful!'

Pat, Isabel, Janet, Bobby and Hilary discussed the matter between themselves on the tennis-court that day.

'Who *could* it be?' said Bobby.

'Has anyone suddenly been having more money than usual?' wondered Pat. The same thought at once came into everyone's mind.

'Yes – Claudine has! She's been splashing it about like anything!'

'And she has plenty of chance of going into Matron's room because she is always taking mending there!'

'But it *can't* be Claudine! It's true she hasn't our sense of honour – but she wouldn't do a thing like that!'

'You know she doesn't care *what* she does when she dislikes somebody or wants to get even with them. She wouldn't think it was wrong, even.'

The five looked at one another, suddenly feeling extremely uncomfortable. They knew Claudine had very little money indeed – and yet she had given Angela that lovely bag – and had spent three whole pounds on cherries for the picnic. It did really seem as if it might be Claudine.

The bell rang for tea-time and the girls sped into the school. After tea Angela and Alison went off together down to the town to get something they wanted. On the way back they overtook an elderly woman, dressed in sober black clothes, sensible flat-heeled shoes, and a plain hat. She wore glasses, and her face was thin and worn, but kindly.

'I bet that's a cook come after the job at St Clare's,' said Angela to Alison. The girls passed her and she turned and spoke to them.

'Could you tell me if I am on the right road for St Clare's? You are St Clare girls, aren't you?'

'Yes,' said Alison. 'Keep straight on.'

The girls made as if to go on, but the woman stopped them with a question that astonished them very much.

'How is my girl Pauline now? The head mistress telephoned me to say she had broken her leg this morning, and I caught the first train I could. I'm Mrs Jones.'

Angela and Alison stopped dead in the road and stared open-mouthed at the little elderly woman. They remembered Pauline's wonderful stories of Mrs Bingham-Jones, her beautiful and wealthy mother. They simply could not understand this plain, tired-looking woman, almost old, being Pauline's supposedly wonderful mother.

Scorn welled up at once in Angela's heart. So Pauline, who was always trying to out-do and out-boast Angela herself, had, for a mother, a woman who looked like a worn-out cook. She tried to pull Alison up the road quickly.

But something in Mrs Jones's tired face had touched

Alison. Alison had many faults, but she was sensitive to other people's feelings, and she could sense Mrs Jones's worry and anxiety. She shook her arm away from Angela's.

'Pauline is all right,' she said, kindly. 'We couldn't see her today but we've all sent her something – you know, flowers and books and things – just to cheer her up. Are you better now? Pauline was *so* disappointed that you and her father couldn't come and see her at half-term, because you were ill.'

Mrs Jones looked extremely surprised. 'I haven't been ill,' she said. 'I wanted to come at half-term, but Pauline wrote to say there was a case of scarlet fever at the school, and the half-term matches had been put off, so would I not come.'

Alison was horrified. In a flash she saw that Pauline, afraid that her mother would not shine among the other mothers, knowing that she had told all kinds of lies that would be found out when the girls saw her elderly, tired mother, had actually made up the lie about scarlet fever to stop her people from coming at half-term – and had pretended to be bitterly disappointed because they weren't coming!

Angela, of course, heard what was said, and an expression of scorn and contempt came over her face.

'*Well*!' she said. 'There was no case of . . .' But Alison was not going to let Angela interfere in the matter. She gave her friend a sharp nudge that made her squeal in surprise. Then she gave her such a fierce look that Angela said no more, but thought in surprise that Alison must be mad to treat her, Angela, like that.

'I hope Pauline is happy at St Clare's?' said Mrs Jones. 'She has always wanted to go there, ever since she heard about it. I didn't see that I could afford to send her, but I managed to scrape enough together. Her poor father is an invalid, you know – has been for years – but I expect she's told you all that. We haven't a lot of money, but I did want Pauline to have a good time at a nice school. I said to her, "Well, my dear, you won't have as much pocket-money as the others, and you won't have as many treats, but there you are, if you like to go under those conditions, I won't stop you."'

Mrs Jones talked to Alison, not to Angela. She liked Alison's pretty, kindly little face, and was glad to have someone to talk to. Angela gave a snort of contempt, and went quickly on, up the hill towards St Clare's.

'It's quite a way, isn't it?' said Mrs Jones, beginning to pant. 'I didn't take a taxi, because taxis are expensive and I thought I could easily walk. Poor little Pauline – it is terribly bad luck to have broken her leg like this. I thought she would be so pleased to see me, if I can hurry along at once.'

Alison didn't feel so certain. She thought that if Pauline had kept her mother away by lies at half-term she would certainly not want her at St Clare's now, with all her lies exposed for what they were.

'Pauline is disgusting,' thought Alison. 'She really is. She takes everything from this poor little mother of hers, who probably goes without a lot of things she wants in order to pay for Pauline here – and then keeps her away from the school because she is ashamed of her! Beast!'

Alison took Mrs Jones to the school door and left her there in charge of a teacher. She went to take off her hat and blazer and joined the rest of her form in the common-room.

'I hope Angela doesn't go and hold forth about Pauline's poor old mother,' thought Alison uncomfortably. 'I feel sorry for the old thing. She looked so tired and worn.'

She heard Angela's voice as she opened the common-room door.

'And, my dear, *I* know who it was that took Matron's beastly money and everything! There's not a doubt of it. It was Pauline!'

'Pauline! What do you mean? Why do you say that?' came Janet's voice at once.

'I'll tell you why,' said Angela, and paused dramatically. 'I and Alison walked up the road with Pauline's mother today – and from what she said to us it's pretty certain that our dear Pauline is a frightful story-teller and quite likely a horrid little thief!'

Angela – and Claudine

'You'll have to tell us why you say all this,' said Bobby. The whole of the fourth form crowded round to hear. Only Claudine was not there, and neither, of course, was Pauline.

'Well, listen,' said Angela, spitefully, 'I and Alison were walking up the road and we saw an ugly little elderly woman, awfully plain, dressed in black, in front of us. I thought she must be a cook coming to try for the job going here. And it turned out to be Mrs Jones, Pauline's mother – not Mrs *Bingham*-Jones, if you please, but just plain Mrs Jones.'

'She's a nice little woman,' said Alison, not liking the contempt in Angela's voice.

'*Nice* little woman!' said Angela, rounding on Alison scornfully. 'Common as dirt, you mean! And when I think of Pauline's airs and graces – trying to make out her mother was as good as mine – trying to pretend that her family were as grand as mine really are – swanking about her cars and things – and they're as poor as church mice, and can only just afford to send Pauline here! Golly, won't I tell Pauline what I think of her when I see her! *I'll* tell her what I think of dear Mrs Jones, dressed up like a cook, moaning about her poor little Pauline.'

Before anyone else could speak, Alison stood up. She was rather white, and there was a strange look on her face.

'You won't tell Pauline anything of the sort,' she said. 'You won't tell Pauline *any*thing that's going to make her ashamed of that poor old mother of hers. Don't you realize how you'll make her hate her mother, if she knows you saw her and are saying this kind of thing about her? I think Pauline has behaved disgustingly about things, but I'm not going to have you making matters worse for Mrs Jones by saying horrible things about her to Pauline.'

Angela was amazed. Could this be her friend Alison talking to her like this? She stared at her, unable to say a word. Then she found her tongue.

'Well, if you stick up for people like Pauline's awful mother, I'm jolly glad you're not coming to stay with me for the holidays,' she said, spitefully. 'I'm going! I shan't stay here to be insulted by somebody I thought was my best friend.'

Poor Alison was now trembling, for she hated rows. Angela moved towards the door. But to her intense surprise and annoyance, two girls caught firmly hold of her arms and sat her down violently, almost jerking the breath out of her body.

'You may not want to listen to Alison, but you're jolly well going to listen to *us*!' said Carlotta, her eyes flashing fire. 'Now *we* will say a few things!'

'Let me go, you beasts,' said Angela, between her teeth.

'You seem to be talking a lot about mothers,' said Carlotta, bending over the angry Angela, and talking in such a fierce tone that Angela drew back, afraid. 'Well, we *will* talk about mothers – *your* mother! We would not talk about her if it was not necessary – but it is very necessary now, in order to get some sense into your thick head!'

'I'll scream if you don't let me go,' said Angela, in a rage.

'Every time you scream I shall pinch you hard, like that,' said Carlotta, and gave Angela such a pinch on her plump shoulder that she squealed in pain.

'Shut up, Carlotta,' said Bobby. 'You can't act like that.'

'Yes, I can,' said Carlotta, coolly. And Angela knew she could, so she made no further sound.

'Pauline's mother may be tired and old and plain and poor,' said Carlotta, 'but that's no reason to despise her. Now there *is* reason to despise *your* mother, Angela! She is a spoilt, rude, discontented, horrible little snob – just like you are! And will you please tell her on no account to come here again, turning up her nose at everything, because we don't want to see her, we dislike her and despise her, and we want her to take you away as soon as ever she will!'

'Hear hear!' said Bobby, Janet and the twins. Angela went very pale. These were terrible things to hear, but she had brought them on herself. She, too, had been ashamed of her spoilt mother when she had come at half-term – but she had not guessed how bitterly the girls had resented her contemptuous attitude towards the school and all it stood for.

'That's enough, Carlotta,' said Susan Howes, uncomfortably. And it was enough. Angela looked as if she was about to faint. She wanted to sink through the floor. She, who had boasted and bragged of herself and her family, who had set herself up as better than any of them, was being spoken to as if she were dirt. She gave an enormous sob, and fled from the room.

'Well, thank goodness she's gone,' said Pat. 'Cheer up, Alison. I was proud of you when you spoke up like that. Perhaps now you will see Angela as clearly as *we* see her.'

'Yes – I do,' said poor Alison, really distressed. 'I think she's awful. I did feel so sorry for that poor Mrs Jones – and Angela had nothing but scorn for her. There's no kindness in her!'

'None at all,' said Janet. 'Well – she's got to learn that kindness breeds kindness, and spite breeds spite. She'll have an awful time if she doesn't.'

'Do you think it's right, what Angela said, that Pauline might be the thief?' said Doris. 'She *has* splashed money about very much lately – and if she's really poor – where did it come from?'

'We half thought it might be Claudine,' said Isabel. 'You know, she's poor too – hardly ever has a penny – and then, quite suddenly, she had lots of money. And you know how unscrupulous Claudine is! I like her – but she simply has no sense of honour at all! We did wonder if it could be her.'

'Sh! Sh!' said someone. But too late – for Claudine, who had come in unnoticed, had heard what Isabel had said!

The little French girl at once pushed her way to the front of the crowd of girls. Isabel saw her coming, and was horrified. Not for the world would she have had Claudine hear what she had said!

'Claudine!' she said. 'I'm sorry you heard. Don't be angry. We only thought it because you seem so different from us in your ideas of honour. And it did seem to us that if you disliked Matron, you might pay her out in that way.'

Claudine looked round the little group, intense anger in her small face. She saw Isabel's earnest face, Pat's scared one, Bobby's watchful one – and then, to the enormous astonishment of the listening girls, the anger in her face melted away – and Claudine threw back her head and laughed!

The girls stared at her in surprise. Honestly, thought Doris, you simply never know what Claudine will do!

Bobby thought how like Mam'zelle she was, in her swift changes from anger to laughter. But what a blessing that Claudine could see some humour in Isabel's words!

'I am not angry,' said Claudine, at last, wiping away the tears of laughter. 'No, I am not angry. You English girls, you are so serious and solemn and so very, very honourable. I too have my own honour, and although it is not quite like yours yet, perhaps, one day it will be. The good Miss Theobald, she said to me this morning that one thing I must take back to France with me, one only – the English sense of honour.'

'Just like Miss Theobald to say a thing like that,' said Janet. 'But why did you laugh just now, Claudine?'

'I laugh because I was thinking so suddenly of the

reason why I have so much money now to spend,' said Claudine, smiling her infectious smile. 'But first, if I tell you, you must promise, on your English honour, that never, never will you tell my Aunt Mathilde what I have done!'

'Oh, Claudine – *what* have you done?' said Pat, imagining the most awful things.

'You remember my so-beautiful cushion-cover that my aunt loved so much?' said Claudine. 'Well, I sold it to one of your mothers for quite a lot of money! You see, I needed money – there were birthdays coming, and I do not like to have so little. And one of your mothers, she was so nice to me, and she bought my so-beautiful cover, and I sent it to her by post. I explained to her that it was my own, and I lacked for money, and she was so, so kind to me.'

'Was that *my* mother?' asked Alison, suspiciously. 'I saw you talking nineteen to the dozen to her at half-term. Mother *would* do a nice thing like that, and never say a word about it. I hope she puts the cushion-cover in my bedroom, that's all!'

'Well,' said Claudine, grinning all over her little monkey-face, 'it *might* have been your so-nice mother, Alison. My sense of honour forbids me to say. And now I appeal to *your* sense of honour also, not to tell my aunt what has happened to my cushion-cover. I told her I had sent it to my mother.'

'You *are* an awful story-teller, Claudine,' said Gladys, shocked. 'You deceive people right and left! I just can't understand you. Why couldn't you tell Mam'zelle you had sold the cover, instead of telling lies and keeping it a secret?'

'Ah, me, I adore secrets!' said Claudine, her eyes dancing. 'And Aunt Mathilde would have written to the so-kind mother and got the cover back and repaid the money, and I should have been so, so sad, for it is nice to earn money, do you not think so?'

'I think you're a puzzle,' said Janet. 'I'll never make you out, Claudine. You go and tell lies in order to sell your cushion-cover and get money for somebody's birthday – you shut Matron up to give us a good time – you . . .'

'Ah, say no more of my badness,' said Claudine, earnestly. 'One day I may become good. Yes, certainly I shall become good if I stay at this so-fine school for another term!'

'Well, you're jolly decent not to have taken offence at what I said,' said Isabel, warmly. 'I'm glad you told us where you got the money from. I'm afraid now it means that Pauline must have taken it. She's had such a lot of money lately. Blow! I wish beastly things like this wouldn't happen! What do you think we ought to do about it?'

'Hilary and I will go to Miss Theobald and tell her everything,' said Susan. 'We can't tackle Pauline now, she won't be fit enough. But Miss Theobald ought to know what we think and why. Come on, Hilary. Let's get it over!'

Alison is a good friend

Hilary and Susan went to Miss Theobald's room and knocked on the door. She called out to them to come in. Fortunately she was alone. She looked up with a pleasant smile as the two girls came in.

'Well,' she said, 'what do you fourth formers want? You haven't been getting into any more trouble I hope?'

'No, Miss Theobald,' said Susan. 'But we are rather worried about this stealing business – and we have an idea who it is.'

'Why doesn't the girl herself come to me, then?' said Miss Theobald, looking very serious.

'Well – she can't,' said Susan. 'You see – we think it's Pauline – and you know she's in the sickbay with a broken leg.'

'*Pauline*!' said Miss Theobald, astonishment showing in her face. 'I can't think it is Pauline. She isn't the type. No – surely it cannot be Pauline.'

'We thought it might be Claudine at first,' said Hilary. 'But it isn't.'

'Ah, I am glad of that,' said Miss Theobald. 'I still cannot think it is Pauline. She is not altogether sensible in some ways – but she did not seem to be at all a dishonest girl.'

'Well, Miss Theobald, we have something else to tell you about Pauline, which will show you that she is really peculiar in some ways, and not at all truthful,' said Susan, gravely. 'We are not, of course, telling tales to you – but we know we can't deal with this ourselves, so we have come to you.'

'Quite rightly,' said Miss Theobald, also very gravely. 'Well – what is there to say about Pauline? Her mother is with her now, and possibly I might be able to have a talk with her about Pauline before she goes.'

Hilary and Susan together told Miss Theobald of Pauline's ridiculous boasting and lying – of how she had put off her mother coming at half-term by telling an absurd story about a scarlet-fever case – how she had pretended to be bitterly disappointed – how she had always seemed to have plenty of money, and yet her mother had told Alison she was afraid that Pauline would always be short of pocket-money.

'So, you see,' said Hilary, 'putting everything together, and knowing what an awful fibber Pauline was, we felt it was probably she who stole from Matron.'

'I see,' said Miss Theobald. 'Curiously enough, people who tell lies for the reason that Pauline tells them, are rarely dishonest in other ways. You see, Pauline lies because she longs to be thought better than she is – that is the *only* reason she lies. Now, if she stole, she would know herself to be despicable, and that others would despise her too. So she would not steal. But from all you tell me I am afraid that she does steal. Having so much money when it is clear that her mother cannot supply her with much is very curious.'

'Yes, it is,' said Susan. 'Well, Miss Theobald, we have told you all we know and think. We would all like this stealing business to be cleared up – the fourth form hate it, as you can imagine – and we are glad to leave it in your hands to settle.'

There came a knock at the door. Miss Theobald called, 'Come in.' Before anyone entered she nodded to the two fourth formers to dismiss them.

'I will see to everything,' she said. 'I will talk to Pauline – possibly tomorrow or the day after – as soon as she has recovered from the shock of her broken leg. The doctor is to put it in plaster, and then she will return to school to do lessons, whilst it is healing. It is essential that I should have this matter cleared up before she returns to the fourth form.'

A staff member had entered the room and waited until Miss Theobald had finished speaking. 'Mrs Jones would like a word with you before she goes.'

'Tell her to come in,' said Miss Theobald. Mrs Jones came in. Hilary and Susan glanced at her curiously as they went out. So this poor, tired, worried-looking little woman, so plainly dressed, was Pauline's marvellous, pretty, beautifully dressed, wealthy mother! What an idiot Pauline was!

Mrs Jones plunged into her worries as soon as the door shut. 'Oh, Miss Theobald, I'm really bothered about Pauline. She didn't seem at all pleased to see me. She cried her heart out when I told her I'd met some of her school-fellows on the way up, and had talked to them. I just can't understand her. I thought she'd be so pleased to see me. She even blamed me for coming – said I was making a fuss – and after all she's my only child, and very precious to me.'

Miss Theobald looked at the distressed woman and was very sorry for her. She wondered whether or not to say anything about Pauline's stupid boasting, and to explain that Pauline's unkindness was because she was ashamed of having her lies exposed for what they were – she was ashamed of her mother, ashamed of not having enough money, ashamed of everything, so that she had forced herself to make up a whole new family and home of her own.

Then she decided not to say anything. It would only hurt and worry the poor little woman even more. She must have a serious talk with Pauline first, and perhaps she could persuade Pauline herself to put matters right.

So she listened, and tried to comfort Mrs Jones as best she could. 'Don't worry,' she said. 'Pauline has had a shock, through falling like that. Don't take any notice of what she says.'

Mrs Jones went at last, only half comforted, feeling puzzled and hurt. Miss Theobald sighed. There suddenly seemed to be quite a lot of difficult problems to solve. How upset poor Mrs Jones would be if she had to be told that her only child was a thief, as well as a stupid boaster!

'I will have a talk to Pauline tomorrow or the next day,'

thought Miss Theobald. 'I only hope Matron does not make any more fuss – really, she is a most unpleasant woman.'

Matron did make plenty more fuss! She went storming into Miss Theobald's room the next morning, with another complaint.

'Five pounds gone this time! A five-pound note! Out of my purse too. And I had hidden it for safety in my mending-basket. But it's gone all the same. Miss Theobald, that girl has got to be found and expelled!'

Miss Theobald listened in astonishment. How could *Pauline* be the thief if she was in the sickbay with a broken leg? But, as Matron went on complaining, it appeared that her mending-basket had been in the sickbay. She had taken it there to do her mending, as she had to sit with Pauline.

So Pauline *might* have been able to take the note from the purse. Other girls had popped in and out too, as Pauline was allowed to see her form that day. It was all very tiresome. Miss Theobald got rid of Matron as soon as she could, thinking that a lot of trouble was coming out of the fourth form that term!

The fourth formers had been very cool towards Angela since the row. Angela looked pinched and unhappy but nobody felt sorry for her, not even Alison. At half-past twelve Alison saw Angela putting on her hat to go out.

'Where are you going?' she asked. 'You know we mustn't go down to the town alone – do you want me to come with you?'

'No,' said Angela, sulkily. 'If you want to know what I'm going to do, I'll tell you. I'm going down to the nearest telephone box to telephone my mother and tell her all the beastly things you've said about her, and ask her to come today and take me away!'

'No, don't do that,' said Alison, distressed. 'We only said those things because you were so horrid about poor old Mrs Jones, Angela.'

But Angela's mind was made up and off she went. Alison waited about miserably, not liking to tell the others. She pictured Angela's mother sweeping down in her Rolls Royce, spiteful and malicious, ready to say all kinds of horrible things about St Clare's and its girls. It was not a pleasant thought.

Presently, about five minutes before the dinner-bell, she saw Angela coming back. But what a miserable, tear-stained Angela! Alison went to meet her, unexpectedly liking this humble, unhappy Angela far more than she had liked the bright and boastful one.

'What's the matter?' she said. Angela turned to Alison, and began to weep bitterly.

'Oh, Alison! Mother's away – and I got on to Daddy instead. But instead of listening to me and comforting me, he was very angry. And oh, he said Mother hadn't any right to talk as she did at half-term – and he was going to see *I* didn't grow up thinking I could say hurtful things to people – and he's coming today to see Miss Theobald about me!'

'Oh, Angela!' said Alison, in dismay. 'How simply

awful! He *must* have been angry. Miss Theobald won't be at all pleased when she hears you've been telephoning to your people and complaining. You'll get into a row from everyone!'

'Oh, I know, I know,' wept Angela. 'I don't know what to do. Oh, Alison, I know I've been beastly. But please don't desert me now. I was awful yesterday about Pauline's mother. I'm ashamed of it now. Do, do be my friend again.'

'Angela,' said Alison, looking very serious all of a sudden, 'I've been a very bad sort of friend to you. I've praised you and flattered you and thought the world of you, when all the time it would have been better to have laughed at you and teased you, like the others do. Bobby would have made you a much better friend, or the twins. They would have been sensible with you. I've spoilt you and been silly.'

'Well, never mind, go on being my friend,' begged Angela, who, now that things were looking black, felt that she simply *must* have someone who liked her. 'Please do, Alison. I'll try and be nicer, I really will. But oh, what shall I say to Daddy when he comes this afternoon? I'm so afraid of him when he gets really angry.'

'Listen,' said Alison, 'immediately after lunch we'll go down to the telephone box again. You get on to your father, and then say that you've been thinking things over, and you've come to the conclusion you've been an idiot but you'd like another chance. Then let me have a word with him, and maybe between us we can stop him coming.'

'Oh, Alison, you're a brick!' said Angela, drying her

eyes, and sniffing. 'Daddy liked you. He'll listen to you. Oh, thank you for your help.'

The dinner-bell had long since gone. The two girls were late. Miss Ellis, taking a look at Angela's swollen eyes, contented herself with a few sharp words and then said no more.

Immediately after dinner the girls went off to the telephone box. Angela got through to her annoyed father, and made her little speech. 'I've been an idiot. I see it now. Don't come down, Daddy. I'm going to try and do better. Here's my friend Alison to talk to you.'

The telephone receiver was passed to Alison who, rather nervous, spoke the little speech she herself had prepared.

'Good afternoon! This is Alison speaking, Angela's friend. Angela is all right now. She was upset before, and rather silly. But I am sure she is going to settle down now and be a sport. So I don't think you need to leave your work and come to St Clare's.'

'Oh,' said Angela's father, in a grim voice. 'Well, as I'm very busy, I won't today. But any more nonsense from Angela and I shall come down and make a Big Row. I put Angela into St Clare's because it's the finest school I know. And there she is going to stay until she, too, thinks it's the finest school *she* knows. If you really are her friend, you'll help her to realize this. You've been there some time, I know.'

'Yes, I have,' said Alison, earnestly. 'And it is the very finest school in the kingdom! I'll teach Angela that, really I will, and so will the others.'

'Well, don't spoil her,' said the far-off voice, not sounding quite so grim. 'Shake her up a bit! She may look like a golden princess, or an angel, but she's not a bit like one inside. And I'd like her to be. Tell her to speak to me again.'

Angela took the receiver. What she heard comforted her. 'Thank you, Daddy,' she said. 'I'll try. I really will. Goodbye.'

She put the receiver back, looking much happier. 'Daddy said that although he is often angry with me, he will always love me,' she said to Alison. 'And he said if I loved him, I'd try to be a bit more like he wants me to be. So I shall try now. Thanks, Alison, for your advice!'

She squeezed her friend's arm. Alison took Angela's arm in hers and they walked back to the school. Alison was talking sternly to herself as they went.

'Now, no more telling Angela she is lovely! No more flattering her! No more praising her up to the skies because she looks like an angel! It's no good looking like one if you're just the opposite inside. Tease her and laugh at her and scold her and point out her faults – that's what I've got to do if I'm to be a real friend to Angela.'

And, to the astonishment of all the fourth form, things between the two friends appeared now to be quite changed! Angela was now the docile one, accepting teasing criticism, and Alison was the leader!

'Good for both of them!' said Bobby, with a grin. 'This will make Angela a nicer person altogether, and will end in giving Alison quite a lot of common sense!'

22

Matron has a shock

'I wonder whether Miss Theobald has tackled Pauline about taking Matron's money and other things yet,' said Hilary to Susan, after tea that day.

Eileen looked up, startled. She had not been there the day before when the matter had been discussed and Hilary and Susan had gone off to see Miss Theobald. She had been cross-examined continually by her mother, who had tried to find out exactly what the fourth formers had done on Mirabel's birthday night – but Eileen had kept her word, and had not told her anything.

'Pauline – taking Mother's money?' said Eileen, amazed. 'What's all this? I haven't heard a word about it.'

'*Haven't* you?' said Janet, surprised. 'Oh, no – you were with Matron when we discussed it yesterday – and today we haven't had a minute to say anything about it. Not that there's anything much to say, really, except that we all think it's Pauline who has taken the things belonging to your mother. You see, we know now that her people can hardly afford to send her here and that she hasn't much pocket-money – so, as she has been splashing money about lately, we felt sure she was the thief. She's such a fibber, she could quite well go a bit further and be a thief as well!'

'And Miss Theobald is going to tackle her about it,' said Susan. 'Hilary and I went and told her everything yesterday. I'm sorry Pauline broke her leg – but really, if she's a thief as well as a story-teller, I think it's a good punishment for her.'

Eileen sat and stared at the chattering girls. Bobby thought she looked rather strange.

'Do you feel all right?' she asked. 'You look a bit funny.'

'Of course I'm all right,' said Eileen. She got up and went out. To the girls' astonishment they saw her, a minute later, flying down the drive at top speed.

'What's up with Eileen?' said Hilary, in amazement. 'Has she forgotten we've got prep to do tonight?'

She apparently had. She did not turn up for prep at all, and Miss Ellis sent to ask Matron if she had kept Eileen with her for any reason. Matron appeared at the classroom door, looking annoyed.

'I can't imagine where Eileen is,' she said. 'I hope you will punish her, Miss Ellis. She has been such an obstinate, stubborn girl lately.'

Eileen did not even return for supper, and it was only when the fourth formers were getting undressed that they saw her again. Doris looked out of her dormitory window and saw Eileen coming up one of the school-paths. With her was somebody else.

'It's Eddie!' said Alison. 'Gracious, won't Eileen get into a row! She must have shot off to see Eddie, and now he's come back with her.'

Eileen looked strung-up and tearful. Eddie looked

much the same. They disappeared into the school. Instead of going up to their mother's room, they went straight to Miss Theobald's room.

'Cheer up!' whispered Eddie. 'I'm here! I'll take care of you, Eileen.'

The two went into Miss Theobald's room. The head mistress looked surprised to see Eileen with a boy. Eileen told her who Eddie was.

'This is my brother Edgar,' she said, and then she broke down, and began to sob bitterly and piteously. Miss Theobald was distressed. Eddie put his arm protectively round his sister.

'Don't cry,' he said. 'I'll tell about everything.' Then he turned to Miss Theobald.

'Miss Theobald,' he said, 'today Eileen heard that another girl, Pauline, was going to be accused of stealing from Matron, our mother. Well – it was Eileen that took all the money and other things, not Pauline or anyone else!'

'*Well*!' said Miss Theobald, thinking that surprises were coming thick and fast in the last few days. 'But why? What made her do such an extraordinary thing?'

'It was because of me,' said Eddie. 'You see, I got a job in an engineering works at the beginning of this term, and Mother was very pleased. Well, I hadn't been there long before I had an accident with a car, and they sacked me. I – I didn't dare to tell my mother, Miss Theobald.'

Miss Theobald looked at the weak, thin face of the lad in front of her, and was not surprised that he feared his bad-tempered, spiteful-tongued mother. How she would tear him and rend him with her tongue if she knew he had failed in his job!

'Well,' went on Eddie, swallowing hard, and still holding his arm round Eileen, 'well, I thought maybe I'd be able to get another job fairly soon, and then Mother need only be told that I'd changed jobs. But, you see, I'd no money, and I had my lodgings and food to pay for – so I managed to hitch-hike over here one day and see Eileen without Mother knowing. And I asked her to give me what money she had.'

'I see,' said Miss Theobald, very grave. 'And Eileen stole from her mother to give to you.'

'I didn't know she was taking Mother's money,' said Eddie. 'I thought it was her own – out of her money-box or out of the post office savings. I knew she'd got a little. And she brought me biscuits too, and some notepaper and stamps to apply for other jobs. She's – she's been such a brick to me, Miss Theobald.'

'Oh, Eddie, I'd do anything for you, you know that,' sobbed poor Eileen. 'But Miss Theobald, when I knew Pauline was going to be accused of something *I'd* done – then I rushed out and went to Eddie, and told him everything. And he came back with me to tell you. Oh, Miss Theobald, we don't dare to tell Mother!'

'What a mix-up!' said Miss Theobald, looking at the two scared, unhappy young faces before her. She could not help in her heart blaming Matron very much for all this. If she had been a kindly, loving mother, helping her children instead of expecting far too much of them, this would never have happened. They would have gone running to her for comfort and help, instead of hiding things from her, and stealing from her, too frightened to do anything else.

'You see,' said Eileen, drying her eyes, 'as Eddie is Mother's son, I didn't really think it was wrong to take her money and other things to help him.'

'I see,' said Miss Theobald. 'But it *was* wrong all the same. Eileen, I am glad to think that you had the courage to realize that you could not let another girl bear the blame for your own wrong-doing. That is a great point in your favour.'

There was a pause. Then Eddie spoke, rather nervously. 'Miss Theobald – do you think you could see Mother for us? Please do. She might not be so terribly angry if you spoke to her first.'

Miss Theobald felt a little grim. 'Yes,' she said, 'I *will* see her. You two can wait in the next room until I have spoken to her.'

Eddie and Eileen retired to the next room, looking forlorn and frightened. Miss Theobald sent a message asking Matron to come and speak to her.

Matron soon appeared, crackling in starched apron and uniform.

'Sit down, Matron,' said Miss Theobald. 'I have found out who has taken your money and I wanted to tell you about it.'

'I hope you will expel the girl,' said Matron, in a severe voice. 'After all, Miss Theobald, I've got a girl here myself, in the fourth form. It's not a very good influence for her, is it, to have a thief living side by side with her?'

'Well, Matron,' said Miss Theobald, 'I have made up my mind that I myself will not decide whether to expel this poor little thief or not. You shall decide, and you alone.'

Matron's eyes sparkled. 'Thank you,' she said. 'You may consider that my decision is taken. The girl will go – and go tomorrow!'

'Very well,' said Miss Theobald. 'Now listen to my story, please. This girl did not steal for herself, but for someone she loved, who was in trouble.'

'Stealing is always stealing,' said Matron, in a righteous voice.

'She was afraid to go to her mother for help, afraid to go to her for advice,' continued Miss Theobald.

'Then the mother is as much to blame as the girl,' said Matron. 'Mothers who have children so scared of them that they will steal have done a very bad job as mothers.'

'I thoroughly agree with you,' said Miss Theobald. 'Nevertheless, this girl had the courage to come and tell me, and she asked me to tell you.'

'Where *is* the little thief?' said Matron, fiercely. '*I* shall have a few words to say to her, I promise you! Out she goes tomorrow!'

Miss Theobald stood up and opened the door connecting her sitting-room with her study. 'You will find the little thief in here,' she said. 'With her brother.'

Matron walked firmly into the study, ready to lash out at the thief. She saw there her two children, Eileen and Eddie. They stared at her nervously.

'What's this?' said Matron, in a faint voice. 'Why is Eileen here – and Eddie?'

'Eileen is the thief, Matron – and Eddie is the one she stole for – and you are the hard mother they were too scared to come to for advice and help,' said Miss Theobald, in a grave and serious voice. 'And I think, knowing you as I do – that Eileen is not the one who should leave St Clare's – but you!'

Matron's face suddenly crumpled up and her mouth began to tremble. She stared unbelievingly at Eileen and Eddie. Eileen was crying again.

'You are a hard and spiteful woman,' went on Miss Theobald's solemn voice. 'This boy and girl need help and comfort, but they would never get it from you!'

'I've got another job, got it today, Mother!' said Eddie. 'I shall pay back every penny Eileen took. You're not to scold her. She did it for me because she loved me. Soon I shall earn enough money to let her live with me and keep house for me. Then you won't be bothered by either of us. We've always disappointed you. We weren't clever or gifted, though we did our best. But I'll look after Eileen now.'

'Don't, Eddie, don't,' said his mother, in a choking voice. 'Don't talk like that. What have I done? Oh, what have I done to have this punishment on my shoulders?'

Miss Theobald shut the door. They must sort things out for themselves. Matron had made her own bed and must lie on it. Those two children would probably be all right because they loved each other and would always stick together. They were weak-willed and not very attractive characters – but their love for each other would give them strength and courage.

Miss Theobald took up the telephone receiver. She got through to the old Matron, who was now almost recovered from her illness.

'Matron?' said Miss Theobald. 'Can you come back tomorrow? You can have as easy a time as you want to – but we can't do without you any longer! Yes – I have a feeling that the present Matron will be gone by tomorrow! Good – we *shall* be pleased to see you back!'

Things settle down at last

And now still one more thing remained to be done. Pauline must be seen, and her affairs put right too. So accordingly next day Pauline was astonished to see Miss Theobald coming into the sickbay looking much more serious than usual.

It was the second surprise Pauline had had that day. The first was when quite a new Matron had appeared, plump and jolly and twinkling. Pauline had stared at her in astonishment, delighted not to see the other Matron.

'Hallo!' said this new Matron. 'So you've broken your leg! Very careless of you. Don't make a habit of it, will you?'

'Where's the other Matron?' asked Pauline.

'She's had to leave in a hurry,' said Matron, putting Pauline's bedclothes straight. 'So I've come back. And let me warn you I'm a Real Old Bear! I've been here for years and years, I'm probably a hundred years old, and I've scolded most of the girls' mothers as well as the girls themselves!'

'Oh, you're the old Matron the girls have told me about,' said Pauline, pleased. 'That's good! Why did Matron leave in such a hurry? Has Eileen gone too?'

'Yes,' said Matron. 'They both had to leave in a hurry.

Not our business why, is it? Now then – what about those pillows?'

Pauline had hardly got over her astonishment at seeing a different Matron, when Miss Theobald came in. As usual the head went straight to the point, and soon the horrified Pauline was realizing that Miss Theobald, and the girls too, all knew what a stupid, untruthful boaster she had been.

She lay back in bed, feeling ashamed and miserable. Miss Theobald went relentlessly on, and finished by telling her how unhappy and puzzled she had made her mother.

'She came rushing to see you,' said Miss Theobald. 'She panted up from the station because she could not afford a taxi – and you know what sort of a welcome you gave her!'

Pauline turned her face to the wall and a tear trickled down her cheek.

'And there is yet another thing,' said Miss Theobald, remembering. 'Someone has stolen money – and because you seemed to have plenty, though the girls heard this week you were supposed to have very little pocket-money, *you* were suspected of being the thief! So you see, Pauline, to what big and terrible suspicions bragging and story-telling can lead us!'

'Oh! I've never stolen a thing in my life!' cried Pauline. 'I had some money in the savings bank – and without Mother knowing I took my savings book here with me – and when I wanted money I took some out. That's how I had plenty of pocket-money, Miss Theobald. Please believe me!'

'I do believe you,' said Miss Theobald. 'But you must hand over your book to me and not withdraw any more money without your mother's permission. And, if you stay here at St Clare's, you will have to do what some of the other girls do who have very little money – say so quite honestly! Nobody minds. We should never judge people by the amount of money or possessions they have, but by what they *are*. You must learn that, Pauline, or you will never know what real happiness is.'

'I feel very miserable,' muttered Pauline, anxious for a kind word. 'I – I don't know how I shall face all the girls after this!'

'Tell Susan or Hilary or the twins that you have been foolish,' said Miss Theobald, getting up. 'They are all sorry you have broken your leg, and I think they will see that you are treated kindly – but you will have to *earn* their kindness and friendship now, Pauline – not try to buy it with tales of wealth and great possessions! Earn their friendship by being sincere and natural and kindly. As for feeling very miserable – well, that is part of the punishment you have brought on yourself, isn't it, and you will have to bear it as bravely as you can!'

Miss Theobald turned to go. She smiled down at Pauline, her smile kinder than her words, and the girl felt a little comforted.

She did as Miss Theobald had advised and confided in Hilary when she came to see her. Hilary was outspoken but helpful.

'You're a frightful idiot, really frightful. And I shall only help you, and make the others decent to you, on one condition, Pauline.'

'What?' asked Pauline.

'That you write to your mother, and say you are sorry for being such a beast to her when she came to see you, and tell her you'll give her a great welcome next time she comes,' said Hilary. 'I'm not going round putting everything right for you, my girl, unless you first do a little putting-right yourself! And don't you dare to brag about a single thing more this term, or we'll all sit on you good and hard!'

And with that piece of advice, Hilary went off to tell the others that Pauline had come to her senses at last, and, as she had broken her leg, and was feeling pretty miserable, what about giving her a chance when she came back to class?

'Well, what with Eileen gone, and Angela reforming herself fast, and Pauline getting a little sense knocked into her, and Matron disappeared for good, we seem to be getting on nicely!' said Bobby, with one of her grins.

'It only remains for Claudine to get the English sense of honour,' put in Pat. 'Then we shall indeed be a form of saints!'

Alison had a letter from Eileen the following week. She read it to the others.

Dear Alison,

I don't know whether you were ever told, but I was the thief. You see, Eddie was out of a job (he's got a good one now) and hadn't any money, so he asked me to help him and I did. But I hadn't much money myself, so I took Mother's, and some other things too.

Well, it was a most frightful shock to Mother, and she said she couldn't bear to stay at St Clare's another day. So we packed and went. Miss Theobald was frightfully decent to Eddie and me. I simply can't tell you how decent. She even offered to keep me on at St Clare's when Mother went. But I couldn't face you all, and anyway I don't fit in there. I know I don't.

So I am going to study shorthand and typing, and then I am going to get a job in the office where Eddie works, and we shall be together. Mother is quite different now. I think it was an awful shock to her to find out how bad I was – but it was for Eddie, and I couldn't help it. Mother has been kinder and gentler. Really, you would hardly know her. Eddie and I think that when we are both earning money Mother won't need to work, and then she can take a rest and perhaps feel happier.

I thought I had better let you know what happened to me, because I left so suddenly. I left my silver thimble behind, in the school work-box – the one in the fourth-form cupboard. Will you please have it yourself in gratitude for taking me out at half-term, as I can never repay that?

I hope Pauline's leg is better. Please, Alison, don't always think unkindly of me, will you? I know I was a sneak, but you can't imagine how difficult things were for me sometimes.

Yours with gratitude,

Eileen Paterson.

The girls were all rather touched by this letter. Alison at once found the thimble and said she would wear it and not think too badly of Eileen.

'It was mostly her mother's fault she was such a little sneak and beast,' said Bobby. 'Golly, we're lucky to have decent mothers, aren't we?'

Angela went red at this remark but said nothing. She had been so much nicer lately – and she had determined that when she went home for the holidays, she was going to praise St Clare's night and day, and not allow her mother to say a single word against it! Mothers could make bad or good children – but, thought Angela, maybe children could alter mothers sometimes too. She was going to have a good try to make her mother change her mind about quite a lot of things. Miss Theobald would have been very delighted if she had known some of the thoughts that went through Angela's golden head those days.

'Hols will soon be here now,' said Pat to Isabel.

'It's been an exciting term, hasn't it – and aren't you glad our old Matron is back? Hi, Bobby – what about a really good trick to round off the term? Can't you and Janet think of one?'

'I dare say we can,' grinned Bobby, her good-natured face looking tanned and even more freckled than usual.

'We could put a frog in Claudine's desk, or fill her pencil-box with earwigs,' suggested Janet with a wicked look at the horrified Claudine.

'If you do such a thing I take the train and the boat to France at once,' declared the French girl.

'She would too,' said Janet. 'Well – perhaps we'd better not try out anything of that sort on Claudine. It would be a pity if she went back to France before she had had time to get that "sense of honour" she is always talking about!'

Claudine threw a cushion at Janet's head. It knocked over Doris's work-basket. Doris leapt up and threw a heap of mending at Claudine. It scattered itself over Mirabel who was just coming into the room. The girls shrieked with laughter to see Mirabel standing in surprise with somebody's blouse over her head.

In no time, there was a finc fight going on, with squeals and yells. Arms, legs, and heads stuck out in all directions.

The door opened again and Miss Theobald looked in with a visitor.

'And this,' she said, 'is the fourth-form common-room. Girls, girls, what *are* you doing? What *will* you be like as six formers, if you behave like kindergarten children now?'

What will they be like? Not very different I expect! We'll wait and see.

FIFTH
FORMERS
of
St CLARE'S

Contents

1 Back for the winter term

St Clare's had stood silent and empty during eight weeks of the summer holiday. Except for the sound of mops and brushes, and a tradesman ringing at the bell, the place had been very quiet. The school cat missed the girls and wandered about miserably for the first week or two.

But now everything was different. The school coaches were rolling up the hill, full of chattering, laughing children – St Clare's was beginning a new winter term!

'Who would think this was a winter term?' said Pat O'Sullivan, to her twin, Isabel. 'The sun is as hot as it was in the summer. We might be able to have a few games of tennis still.'

'I shall certainly have a swim in the pool,' said Bobby Ellis, whose face seemed even more freckled than usual. 'I hope there's fresh water in today – I might have a swim after tea.'

'Ah, you Bobbee! Always you must play tennis or swim or run or jump!' said Claudine, the little French girl. 'And your freckles! Never did I see so many on one face. I have been careful in the hot sun these holidays – not one freckle did I catch!'

The girls laughed. Claudine was always terrified of

getting freckles – but never did one appear on her pale face and white hands.

The girls poured into the school, running up the familiar steps, shouting to one another, dumping their lacrosse sticks everywhere.

'Hallo, Hilary! Hallo, Janet! Oh, there's Carlotta, looking more like a gypsy than ever. Hey, Carlotta, where did you go for your holidays? You look so tanned.'

'I have been to Spain,' said Carlotta. 'Some of my people live there, you know. I had a grand time.'

'There's Mirabel – golly, she's awfully tall now!' said Isabel. 'Gladys looks more like a mouse than ever beside her.'

'Hallo!' said the big, strapping Mirabel, coming up. 'How's everyone?'

'Hallo, Mirabel. Hallo, Gladys,' said the girls. 'You've been spending the hols together, haven't you? I bet you played tennis and swam all the time!'

Both Mirabel and Gladys were fond of games, and this term Mirabel was anxious to be sports captain at St Clare's. She had been in the fifth form for two terms, and Annie Thomas, the sports captain, had let Mirabel help her. Now Annie had left, and there was a chance that Mirabel might be captain, for there was no one in the sixth form really fitted to have that post.

'Let's go and look at our classroom,' said Bobby Ellis. 'It was going to be re-decorated in the hols, I know. Let's see what it's like.'

They all trooped upstairs to the big fifth-form room.

Certainly it looked very nice, painted a pale banana yellow. The light was clean and clear in the room, and the view from the windows a lovely one.

'We've only got this term here – and then we go up into the sixth form!' said Hilary. 'Fancy being at the top of the school! I remember when I first came to St Clare's, I thought the fifth and sixth formers were almost grown-up. I hardly dared to speak to them.'

'I expect the young ones think the same thing of us,' said Janet. 'I know most of them scuttle out of my way when I come along – like frightened rabbits!'

'I have a young sister in the second form this term,' said Claudine, the French girl. 'She came over with me from France. Look – there she is, the little Antoinette.'

The girls looked out of the window. They saw a girl of about fourteen, very like the pale-faced, dark-haired Claudine, standing watching the others. She looked very self-possessed.

'Don't you want to go down and show Antoinette round a bit?' said Pat. 'I bet she feels lonely and new.'

'Ah, Antoinette would never feel so,' said Claudine. 'She can stand on her own toes, like me.'

'Stand on her own feet, you mean,' said Bobby, with a chuckle. 'You'll never get those English sayings right, Claudine. Ah – there's old Mam'zelle!'

The girls watched Mam'zelle going out into the garden, an anxious look on her face.

'She is looking for the little Antoinette,' said Claudine. 'She has not seen her for two years. Ah, Antoinette will now be swamped in love and affection! My aunt will think her little niece Antoinette is as wonderful as me, her niece Claudine!'

Mam'zelle was Claudine's aunt, and this fact was at times useful to Claudine, and at other times embarrassing. For Antoinette just then it was most embarrassing. The little French girl had been enjoying herself, watching the excited English girls catching hold of one another's arms, swinging each other round, chasing one another, and generally behaving in the usual schoolgirl way – a way, however, that the demure Antoinette had not been used to.

Then, quite suddenly, an avalanche descended upon her, two plump arms almost strangled her, and a loud and excited voice poured out French endearments in first one ear and then the other. Loud kisses were smacked on each cheek, and then another hug came which made Antoinette gasp for breath.

'Ah, *la petite Antoinette, mon petit chou,*' cried Mam'zelle at the top of her voice. All the girls stopped playing and stared at Antoinette and Mam'zelle. They giggled. It was plain that Antoinette was not at all pleased to be greeted in public in this way. She disentangled herself as best she could.

She caught sight of her elder sister, Claudine, leaning out of a high window, grinning in delight. She pointed up to her at once.

'Dear *tante* Mathilde, there is my sister Claudine who looks for you. Now that she has seen you greet me, she will wish you to greet her too.'

Mam'zelle glanced up and saw Claudine. Still holding Antoinette, she waved frantically and blew kisses. 'Ah, there is the little Claudine too! Claudine, I come to embrace you.'

Antoinette wriggled away and lost herself in the nearby crowd of girls. Mam'zelle turned her steps towards the door that led to the stairs. 'I come, I come!' she called to Claudine.

'And I go,' said Claudine, pushing away the giggling girls. 'Mam'zelle will be quite overcome this term with *two* nieces here.'

So, when poor Mam'zelle panted into the fifth-form classroom to embrace her second niece, Claudine was not to be found. 'I have missed her, but I will find her!' cried Mam'zelle, and she beamed round at the fifth formers there.

'Ah, Bobbee, you have come back – and you Angela – and Alison – all of you, the dear girls! And you are going to work hard for me this term, so hard – for is it not next term that you go up into the top form, the sixth form? That is indeed a solemn thought!'

The French teacher went out of the room, hunting for her dear Claudine. The girls laughed. 'Dear old Mam'zelle,' said Hilary, 'I shall never forget her, if I live to be a hundred! The tricks we've played on her – do you remember those awful stink balls you had, Janet, when we were in the fourth form? I laughed till I cried then, when I saw Mam'zelle's face as the smell reached her.'

'There's only one new girl this term,' said Janet, 'in our form, I mean. I saw her name on the list downstairs. She's called Anne-Marie Longden. And Felicity Ray has come up from the fourth form.'

'About time too,' said Mirabel. 'She's older than most of the fifth already. I think she's a bit batty.'

'No, she's not – it's only that she's a real musical genius,' said Gladys. 'You've said yourself heaps of times that she is, Mirabel. She doesn't seem to care about anything but music – other lessons just roll off her, like water off a duck's back. She's always bottom of everything except music.'

'Well, Miss Cornwallis won't be very thrilled if Felicity takes no notice of anything but music,' said Bobby, who had reason to know that the fifth-form mistress was what the girls called among themselves 'a real slave-driver'. 'I bet Felicity will know more geography, history and maths this term than she has ever known all the time she has been at school!'

'Any other girls?' said Mirabel.

'Well, it's funny, Alma Pudden's name was down on the list of fifth formers,' said Janet. 'But she's sixth form, isn't she? I mean, when she came last term, she was put into the sixth form – but now her name is down for our form. Perhaps she's been put back into the fifth for some reason.'

'Well, I wish she wasn't,' said Bobby. 'I can't say she thrills me. She's so like her name – puddeny! She's a bit like a suet pudding, fat and stodgy and dull.'

'She's got a beastly temper,' said Hilary. 'I guess she won't be too pleased at coming down into the fifth form!'

Matron appeared at the door of the classroom with a

tall, slender, dark-eyed girl, whose pale blonde hair made her eyes seem very black indeed.

'Hallo, fifth formers!' she said, her cheerful smile beaming at everyone. 'All back? Good girls. Now don't any of you dare to go down with mumps or measles, chickenpox or anything else! I've brought you the only new girl for your form – Anne-Marie Longden.'

Anne-Marie smiled nervously. She was not pretty, but her golden hair and dark eyes made her rather striking. 'Hallo,' she said, awkwardly, 'are you all fifth formers? What are your names?'

Hilary, who was head of the form, introduced everyone quickly.

'These are the O'Sullivan twins, Pat and Isabel. You'll probably know t'other from which in a few terms! This is Janet, and this is Roberta, commonly called Bobby. You'll always know her by her freckles! Look out for these two, for they know more tricks than anyone else.'

Anne-Marie smiled politely. Hilary went on, dragging first one girl forward and then another.

'This is Doris – she can mimic anyone under the sun. She'll be mimicking *you* before long, Anne-Marie!'

Anne-Marie did not look as if this thrilled her very much. She thought Doris looked a rather clumsy, stupid girl. She did not see the intelligent eyes and humorous mouth of the born actress that Doris was.

'Here's Carlotta, sun tanned as ever!' went on Hilary. Carlotta gave her usual cheeky grin.

'And please let me tell you, Anne-Marie, that I was

once a circus girl, and rode horses in a circus-ring,' said Carlotta. 'Angela is sure to tell you that sooner or later, so I may as well tell you now!'

The golden-haired beautiful girl called Angela flushed with annoyance. It was quite true that she looked down on Carlotta and always had – but she had hoped that Carlotta had not thought of it the last term or two. Carlotta had a very sharp tongue, and lashed out unmercifully at anyone she disliked.

Hilary hurried on, hoping to avert a quarrel between the hot-tempered Carlotta and the annoyed Angela. 'This is Angela,' she said. 'Our dream of beauty!'

'You've forgotten the Honourable,' said a malicious voice – Carlotta's. 'The *Honourable* Angela Favorleigh! Angela must have her label.'

'Shut up, Carlotta,' said Hilary. Angela scowled, making her lovely face quite ugly for a moment. Then she tossed her head and went out of the room. She had learnt by now that beauty and wealth were no match for a sharp wit like Carlotta's. Angela might be the most beautiful girl in the school and the richest, but Carlotta could always defeat her in a squabble.

'This is Pam, the brains of the form,' said Hilary, pulling a plain, undergrown girl forward, with great big glasses in front of her short-sighted eyes. 'She works much too hard, but nobody can stop her!'

Someone peeped in at the door. It was Claudine, come to see if her aunt was still there.

'It's all right. Mam'zelle is still looking for you, but not here,' said Carlotta. 'Anne-Marie, this is Claudine, the Bad Girl of the form – she only works at what she likes, she always gets what she wants – and she doesn't care how she does it. She has been here quite a long time already, trying to learn what she calls "the English sense of honour" – but she hasn't even smelt it yet!'

'Ah, you bad Carlotta,' said the good-humoured Claudine. 'Always you make fun of me. I am not so bad, and not so good.'

Mirabel and Gladys were pulled forward, and the plain, quiet Pauline, who had once been as big a boaster as Angela, but had learnt a bitter lesson, and was now a much nicer girl.

'There you are – that's the lot,' said Hilary, 'except Felicity, our musical genius, who is coming up from the fourth form, and hasn't arrived yet – and Alma Pudden who comes down from the sixth. I haven't seen her about yet, either.'

'I hope *you* don't do anything wonderful!' said Bobby, to Anne-Marie. 'What with Pam's brilliant brains, and Angela's film-star beauty, and Felicity's musical genius, the fifth form has got enough wonderful people in it! I hope you're a nice ordinary person, Anne-Marie.'

'Well – I'm not,' said Anne-Marie, flushing red. 'I'm – I'm a poet.'

There was a deep silence after this. A poet! What exactly did Anne-Marie mean by that?

'What do you mean – you write poetry, or something?' said Bobby. 'Oh, help!'

'You can't help being a poet, if you are one,' said Anne-Marie. 'You're born a poet. My grandfather was a famous poet, and my great-aunt was a great writer. It's in the family – and it's come out in me, I suppose. I'm always writing poetry. Mostly in the middle of the night.'

'Help!' said Bobby, again. 'We've had many odd things at St Clare's – but not a poet, as far as I remember. You and Felicity will make a pair! She gets up in the middle of the night to write a tune – you get up to write poems! Well – you'll be able to keep each other company!'

Another girl put her head in at the door and the twins yelled to her. 'Alison! Where have you been? Come and be introduced to our poet.'

A pretty, dainty girl came into the room, smiling. It was the twins' cousin, Alison.

'This is Alison,' said Pat. 'Our little feather-head. Thinks of nothing but her hair and her complexion and whether she has a shiny nose, and . . .'

Alison would have scowled, or burst into tears, a few terms before at this candid introduction, but she was thicker-skinned now. She merely lunged out at Pat, and nodded amiably at Anne-Marie.

'You'd better look out, Claudine,' she said, 'your aunt is coming along the passage.'

'You can't escape now,' said Hilary. 'You've got to go through with it – go on, it pleases old Mam'zelle. She really is fond of you, goodness knows why!'

Mam'zelle swept into the room, saw Claudine and flung herself on her. '*Ma petite Claudine*! How are you?

How are your dear father and mother, and all the family? I have seen the little Antoinette – ah, how lonely and shy the poor child looked. I have cakes and biscuits for you both in my room – you will come now, this very minute, and eat them with me!'

Claudine let herself be taken off. The others laughed. 'Funny to think of Claudine being a fifth former! Perhaps she will turn over a new leaf now she's so high up in the school.'

But that was the last thing Claudine meant to do. She went her own way, saying what she pleased, doing what she pleased, and always would. It was surprising that so many people liked her!

Studies of their own

It was the rule at St Clare's that as soon as any girl had been in the fifth form for two terms she should be allowed to have a small study of her own, which she shared with one other girl. These studies were tiny places, and the girls could, if they wished, furnish them themselves, though the school provided such things as a table, chairs and a carpet and shelves.

Most girls contented themselves with putting up a picture or two, bringing their own vases for flowers, a tablecloth or so, and a clock. A few were more ambitious and got a carpet from home, and maybe even an arm-chair.

The girls themselves chose the companion with whom they wanted to share a study. This was not usually difficult, because by the time they reached the top forms the girls had all more or less made their own friends, and, when they were in the fourth form, had planned with whom they were going to share the study.

It was fun arranging about the studies. The pairs had to go to Matron and tell her they were going to share a study, and then Matron would allot one to them.

'Fancy *you* having a study!' she would say. 'Dear me – it seems no time at all since you were in the first form and

I nearly gave you a scolding for not reporting your sore throats to me!'

Pat and Isabel O'Sullivan were to share a study, of course. Mirabel and Gladys wanted to as well. Angela had asked Alison to share with her – both girls had the same dainty tastes.

'I bet there will be nothing but mirrors all the way round the walls of your study!' said Bobby to Alison. It was a standing joke that Alison always looked into any mirror she passed, or even in the glass of pictures, to see if her hair was all right.

Bobby and Janet were to share a study. Both were tomboys, with a love for practical jokes. What tricks would be hatched out in their study!

One odd pair was Pam Boardman, the brainy one of the form, and Doris Edward, who was always near the bottom. For all her brilliance at mimicry and acting, Doris could not do ordinary lessons well, and admired Pam's brains deeply. Pam had tried to help the bigger girl at times, and a warm friendship had sprung up between them, which made Doris suggest sharing a study. Pam had left St Clare's once, but had missed it so much that her parents had sent her back again some time later.

The lonely little Pam, who had never had a real friend, at once welcomed the idea of sharing a study with Doris. Doris made her laugh, she teased her and put on her big glasses and mimicked her. She was good for Pam.

'Whom is Carlotta going with?' wondered Pat. 'Hilary, perhaps. They like one another very much.'

But no – Hilary, as head girl of the form, had the honour of a study all to herself. So Carlotta could not share with her. She chose Claudine!

Matron was openly doubtful about this.

'You'll have a mighty bad effect on each other,' she said. 'You're both as cheeky and don't-carish as can be. What you'll be like if you share a study, I can't think. But mind – any broken furniture or reports of rowdiness, and you'll go down to the common-room of the fourth formers.'

'Oh, Matron – how can you think that we should be rowdy?' said Claudine, putting on her most innocent look. 'I shall keep our study beautifully, so beautifully. Did I not in the holidays embroider two tablecloths, and three cushion-covers for our study?'

Anne-Marie and Felicity were to share a study, although Felicity had not been two terms in the fifth form, and Anne-Marie was new. Matron did not want them to be the only two without a study.

'Two geniuses together,' said Bobby, with a laugh. 'They ought to use up the midnight oil all right, writing poems and tunes!'

No one had asked Pauline to share a study with them, and she had no friend to ask. She was not a girl that anyone liked much, for she was envious, and had been very boastful till the others had found out that all her wonderful tales were made up. She had gone into her shell, and no one knew quite what the real Pauline was like.

'You had better share with Alma Pudden,' said Matron, ticking them off on the list. 'You're the only two left.'

'Oh,' said Pauline, dismally. She didn't like Alma very much. Nobody did. She was so fat and unwieldy and bad-tempered. But there was no one else to share with, so that was that.

'Well – that's the lot of you,' said Matron, shutting her book. 'You all know the study-rules, don't you? You can have your teas there by yourselves, if you don't want to go to the dining-room. You can get in someone from the first or second form to do any little job you want done. You can do your prep there in the evenings, and you can go up to bed when you want to, providing it is not after ten o'clock.'

The girls felt free and independent, having little rooms of their own. The studies were cosy corners, dens, bits of home – they could be arranged how the girls liked, and the tiny fire-places could burn cosy fires to sit by.

Angela, of course, furnished hers like a miniature palace. She bundled out every bit of the school furniture there, and got her mother to send down things from her own bedroom. She went down to the town with Alison, and the two had a wonderful time choosing curtain material, cushion-covers and rugs.

They cost a lot of money. Alison hadn't very much, but Angela had had magnificent tips from wealthy uncles and aunts in the holidays, and had saved them up for her study. She spent lavishly, and would let no one into their room till it was finished.

Then she and Alison gave a 'house-warming' as they called it. They had ordered in cakes and sandwiches from the local baker, and had bought lemonade and ginger beer.

The table was loaded with eatables, and a bright fire burnt in the grate, though the day was far too hot.

The girls crowded in curiously. They gasped at the polished furniture, beautiful mirrors and pictures, the two arm-chairs, and the lovely rugs. They fingered the silk curtains and looked at the brilliant chrysanthemums in the vases.

'*Well*!' said Bobby. 'Just wait till Matron sees all this! She'll tell Miss Theobald you have too much money to spend, Angela!'

'I don't see that it's anything to do with Matron,' said Angela, stiffly. 'Alison and I don't consider there is enough beauty or comfort at St Clare's – not as much as *we* are used to at home, anyway – and now that we have a study of our own, we don't see why we can't fill it with our own ideas. Don't you like it, Bobby?'

'Well – it's a bit too showy for me,' said Bobby. 'You know my simple tastes! But you certainly have made a marvellous job of it, Angela – and this tea is super!'

The other girls added what they wanted to their studies. Claudine put out her embroidered tablecloths and cushion-covers. Carlotta added a few things she had brought from Spain, one thing especially giving the little study colour and character – a deep red embroidered shawl from Seville.

The only study that was quite plain and without character was the one shared by Pauline and Alma. Neither of them had any taste or much money, and except for a blue vase contributed by Pauline and a tea-cosy as plump as Alma herself given by Alma, the little study was as bare as in the holidays.

Alma Pudden had a most unfortunate name. It would not have mattered a bit if she hadn't been so like a suet pudding to look at, but she was. Her school tunic always looked like a sack tied round in the middle. Her eyes were almost hidden in her round, pasty face.

It was the fifth formers who nicknamed her Pudding, and she hated it, which was not to be wondered at. If she had laughed, and said, 'Yes, I *am* rather puddingy – but I shall thin out soon!' the others would probably have liked her, and called her Pudding more in affection than in derision. But Alma flew into one of her bad rages when she was teased.

She had peculiar tempers – not hot ones, quickly flaring up and down, like Carlotta's or Janet's – but cold, spiteful rages. Try as they would, the others could not like anything about poor Alma.

Poor Pauline found sharing a study with Alma very dull indeed. Alma seldom had any intelligent remark to make, and though she pored over her prep she rarely got good marks. She was selfish too, and always took the more comfortable chair, and helped herself to more cakes than Pauline.

Felicity and Anne-Marie found it rather trying to live together in the same study. Felicity thought there was nothing in the world but music, and she was always singing or trying out tunes on her violin, when Anne-Marie wanted to work or to write.

'Felicity! *Must* you play that awful, gloomy tune again?' Anne-Marie would say. 'I'm trying to get the last verse of this poem right.'

'What poem? Is it the one you were doing last week?' Felicity would say. 'Well, it's a dreadful poem – all words and no meaning. You are no poet, Anne-Marie. Why should I stop my music in order that you should write third-rate poetry?'

Felicity did not mean to be rude or even hurtful. She was, as Bobby said, quite 'batty' about her music. She was working for a stiff exam, the L.R.A.M. and was very young indeed to take it. Miss Theobald, the head mistress, did not want her to work for it, and had already told Felicity's people that the girl must live an ordinary life, and take more interest in ordinary things.

'She is growing one-sided,' Miss Theobald explained to Felicity's parents, who came to see her one day. 'Sometimes I think she doesn't live in this world at all! That is bad for a young girl. She is already far too old for the fourth form, and yet is not fit to do the work of the fifth. But I think I had better put her up into the fifth, where the girls there of her own age will wake her up a bit. I wish you would say that Felicity must put off working for this difficult music exam for a year or two. She has plenty of time before her!'

But Felicity's people were too proud of their brilliant daughter to put off any exam. It would be wonderful to have a girl who was the youngest to pass such an exam!

'Put her up in the fifth form if you wish, Miss

Theobald,' said Felicity's father. 'But don't let her slacken in any way in her music studies. We have been told she is a genius, and a genius must be helped and encouraged in every way.'

'Of course,' said the head mistress, 'but we must be sure that our ways of encouragement are the *right* ones, surely. I don't like all this hard, musical work for so young a girl, when it means that other, quite necessary work has to be scamped.'

But it was no use talking like that to Felicity's parents. Their girl was brilliant, and she must go on being even more brilliant! And so it was that Felicity was put up into the fifth form, to be with girls of her own age even though her work was far below the form's standard – and yet had to work even harder at her music than before.

She did not like or dislike Anne-Marie. She was there and had to be put up with, but so long as she did not interfere too much with her music, Felicity did not really notice her study companion.

But Anne-Marie was jealous of Felicity and her undoubted genius. Anne-Marie was convinced that she too was a genius. Her people were sure she was, as well. They had her best poems framed, they recited them to visitors, who were too polite to say what they really thought, and they tried to get publishers to print them.

It was most annoying that the girls at St Clare's didn't seem to think anything of her loveliest poems. There was that one beginning:

Down the long lanes of the Future
My tear-bedimmed eyes are peering.

Only Angela and Alma had been impressed with it. Neither of them had enough brains to know a good poem from a bad one, and they could not see the would-be cleverness and insincerity of the long and ostentatious poem.

'What's it *mean*?' said Carlotta. 'I may be very stupid, but I don't understand a word of it. Why are your eyes tear-bedimmed, Anne-Marie? Are you so afraid of your future? Well, I'm not surprised, if that's the way you're going to earn your living! You won't get much money.'

'It's tosh,' said Bobby. 'You write something you really *feel*, Anne-Marie, and maybe you'll get something good out of your mind. This is all pretence – just trying to be awfully grown-up when you're not.'

So Anne-Marie was bitterly disappointed that *her* genius was not recognized, whilst everyone apparently agreed that Felicity really was gifted.

Still, on the whole, the study companions got on fairly well, some of them much better than others, of course. The twins rarely quarrelled, and had so much the same tastes and likings that sharing a study was, for them, a thing of delight. Bobby and Janet too were very happy together, and so were Mirabel and Gladys.

It was strange at first to get used to sending for the younger ones to do odd jobs. But on the whole that was quite a good idea too. Many of the first formers, for instance, had been head girls, or at least in the top forms of their prep schools, and it did them good to be at the bottom of another school, having, at times, to rush off to do the bidding of the older girls. The twins remembered how they had hated it at first.

'We thought it was beneath our dignity to light someone's fire, do you remember?' said Pat to Isabel, as she poked up the fire that a first former had just been in to light for her. 'It was jolly good for us. We were so stuck up – thought such a lot of ourselves too! We got our corners rubbed off all right.'

'We get to know the younger ones too,' said Isabel. 'They chatter away to us when they come to do their jobs. I'm getting to like some of the little first formers very much. One or two of them will be very good at games – they are awfully keen.'

'Angela sends for the young ones far too much, though,' said Pat, frowning. 'She and Alison make them do too many jobs. They've got a bit of power, and they are using it badly.'

'Better get Hilary to tick them off,' said Isabel, yawning. 'Golly, it's five to ten. Come on, we'd better pack up and go to bed. Isn't it fun to go when we like?'

'So long as it's not after ten o'clock!' said Pat, imitating Matron's crisp voice. 'Hurry – or it *will* be after ten!'

3 The new English teacher

That term there were a great many more girls at St Clare's in the younger forms, and Miss Theobald decided to engage an extra mistress, to take some of the work off the shoulders of the class-mistresses.

So, to the interest of all the girls, Miss Willcox appeared. She was present at Assembly the second day and looked round with vague, rather soulful eyes.

'Her name's Miss Willcox,' the girls whispered to one another. 'She's awfully clever. She's going to take English. She writes! She has had a book of poetry published.'

The girls all gazed at Miss Willcox with awe. They thought that anyone must indeed be clever to have written a book. Miss Willcox gazed back at the girls, her eyes dreamy and far away. What could she be thinking of? Another book, perhaps?

It was always exciting to have a new teacher. What would she be like in class? Strict? Humorous? Lenient? Dull? Would she be a good one to play a few tricks on?

'I think she looks most interesting,' said Alison. 'I do really. I think she looks as if all kinds of beautiful thoughts are passing through her mind.'

'She's probably wondering what there will be for

lunch,' said Bobby. 'I always suspect those people that look dreamily into the distance. Anne-Marie does it sometimes, and I know jolly well that half the time she's wondering if Felicity has remembered to get the cakes for tea, or something like that, and the other half she's thinking of nothing at all.'

Anne-Marie wished she could think of something smart to say back, but she never could. Well – poets were always misunderstood, she knew that. People laughed at them, and jeered at their work – but then, years after they were dead, people said how wonderful they were.

'Perhaps Miss Willcox will know that I am a real poet,' she thought. 'It would be nice to have someone on my side. I dare say if Miss Willcox reads my poems and likes them she will make the others change their minds. I'll work awfully hard in her classes, and get on her good side.'

Miss Willcox's lessons were certainly interesting. They were filled with plays and poetry, and the girls were allowed to debate anything they liked, so long as it had to do with literature.

There was no doubt that Miss Willcox 'knew her stuff' as Bobby put it. She was very widely read, had an excellent memory, and really did know how to pick out things that would interest the girls, and make them think.

She was a strange woman to look at, though – untidy, vague and given to 'bits and pieces' as Janet said. A scarf wound round her neck, a brilliant belt, a very striking handkerchief. She wore gold-headed pins in her black hair, and her dresses all had a drapy look about them. They did not really fit her.

She had an affected voice which rather spoilt her reading of poetry, for she pitched it deep and low, when really it should have been quite ordinary. She had graceful, dramatic gestures, which filled Alison's romantic soul with delight.

Alison copied one or two of the gestures. She flung out her hand dramatically when she was telling Pat and Isabel something, and hit Bobby with the back of her fingers.

'Hey!' said Bobby. 'Our feather-head is copying Miss Willcox! Alison, you're not going to lose your heart to *her*, are you?'

Alison went red. She always blushed very easily, which annoyed her. 'I don't know what you mean,' she said. 'I admire Miss Willcox, I must say. Her knowledge of English literature is marvellous.'

'Oh, Alison!' groaned Bobby. 'Don't say you're going to worship Miss Willcox. Haven't you got over that silly habit yet? You never choose the right people to worship, either!'

'Why isn't Miss Willcox the right person?' said Alison, trying to speak coldly, though she felt very hot and cross. 'She's clever – she's written a book of most marvellous poetry – she's got a lovely deep voice, and I think she's most picturesque-looking.'

'Untidy and messy, you mean,' said Bobby, in disgust. 'Picturesque-looking, indeed! What an idiot you are, Alison. I think Miss Willcox wants smartening up and making tidy. Gold-topped pins in her hair – gosh, it nearly made me sick to see them.'

Bobby was going to extremes and did not mean all she said. She was such a downright, boyish person, she so much hated nonsense and show, that people like Miss Willcox made her 'go off the deep end' and say more than she meant.

'Oh, Miss Willcox is not so bad as you make out, Bobby,' said Pat, seeing that Alison looked as if she was about to burst into tears. 'And she's not so wonderful as *you* make out, either, Alison. Anyway – for goodness' sake don't put on a worshipping act this term. You've been fairly sensible the last two terms or so.'

Alison turned away. 'Remember Miss Quentin,' said Bobby, warningly. 'Don't make the same mistake again!'

Miss Quentin had been worshipped by Alison when she was in a lower form, and Alison had been bitterly hurt by her, because she had found out that the mistress was laughing at her behind her back. She had learnt a hard lesson then and had been more careful about whom she gave her heart to. But now it looked as if she was going to start all over again!

'It's no good trying to stop her,' said Pat, watching her cousin as she left the room, her head high in the air, and her cheeks burning. 'You only make her worse, Bobby. She goes all loyal and intense.'

'Well, I've said my say,' said Bobby. 'It wouldn't matter a bit if only Alison would choose somebody decent, but she never does.'

'If Miss Willcox was sensible she'd nip Alison in the bud,' said Pat. 'Miss Cornwallis soon nips any silliness in the bud! So do the other mistresses. I can see that Miss Willcox is going to encourage that awful Anne-Marie too.'

'Well – let her!' said Bobby. 'If she wants the Alisons and Anne-Maries of the world sitting at her feet, she's welcome to them. Come on – let's go and see if the court is hard enough for tennis.'

They passed Alma Pudden on the way out. The girl looked rather dull and miserable. Pat felt sorry for her.

'Come and have a game!' she called. 'Make up a four.'

'I can't run,' said Alma, in her usual dull voice. 'I'm too fat.'

'Well, it will get your fat down a bit,' said Isabel. 'Come on!'

But no – Alma was almost as obstinate at refusing any exercise as Claudine was. Claudine got out of all games if she could, and even out of the nature-walks. At first she had arranged matters so that Matron piled mending on her, which had to be done in games time – but Matron had got wise to this little trick after a time, and Claudine suddenly found that she had not enough mending to make an excuse for missing out-door life.

But Claudine was not to be defeated in anything. If she did have to put on games clothes and shoes, and appear on the field or court, she would be taken with violent cramps, or would feel sick, and have to go off. It was simply amazing how she managed to slide out of the things she disliked.

She and Carlotta were a real pair in their study. Carlotta would not do things she disliked either, if she could get out of them, but she used open and direct methods, whereas Claudine really enjoyed getting her way secretly, putting on an innocent face all the time.

They both made war against Mirabel, who, to her intense delight, had been made sports captain for the school that term, as she had hoped. Gladys had been made vice-captain, and this pleased them both. Gladys was small, but very quick and deft on the playing-field or tennis-court, and a fine little swimmer. Also, she was very good at dealing with some of the shy, younger girls, who were a bit afraid of Mirabel's heartiness and drive.

Mirabel was a typical sports captain, loud-voiced, hearty in manner, strapping in figure, and not very sensitive to the feelings of others. She was always trying to make Alison, Claudine, Angela and Carlotta take more interest in games, and they were just as determined not to. It annoyed her intensely when they would not turn up at practices she had arranged, or got bored on the field and talked.

'This Mirabel, she is a pest,' complained Claudine to her aunt, Mam'zelle. 'Always she wants me to go to the field and make myself hot and dirty and untidy. Can you not tell her my heart is weak, *ma tante*?'

'Claudine! Have you a weak heart, my child? This you have never told me before!' cried Mam'zelle, in alarm. 'Have you a pain? You must go to Matron.'

This was the last thing that Claudine wanted to do. Matron was the one person who consistently disbelieved all that Claudine said.

'No, I have no pain,' said Claudine, demurely. 'Only

just a little flutter here – now and again when I run or go up the stairs.'

Mam'zelle looked at Claudine hard. She loved her dearly, but it did sometimes cross her mind that her niece might deceive her in order to gain her own ends. Claudine had pressed her hand over the place where she thought her heart was, to show where the flutter came – but unfortunately she wasn't indicating the right place.

'*Tiens*!' said Mam'zelle, half-alarmed still but a little angry. 'That is not your heart. That is your stomach. Maybe you need a dose of good medicine.'

Claudine disappeared at once. She was not going to have any of Matron's good medicine. She made up her mind to find out exactly where her heart was, so that another time she would not make a mistake.

After a few days the fifth form settled down into their usual familiar routine. They tackled their new work, grumbled and groused, laughed and talked, played games and went to bed tired out. It was a good life, an interesting, full and friendly one. Sometimes the fifth formers felt a little sad when they thought that they had only one more form to go into – and then St Clare's would be left behind for ever.

There was to be a stiff exam half-way through the term, which everyone was to take, even Doris and Alma and Felicity, who felt absolutely certain they would not be able to pass it.

'But it won't do you any harm to work for it,' said Miss Cornwallis, in her crisp voice. 'If you could just get a Pass

I should feel you had achieved something! I shall allow you to relax, all of you, after the exam is over, but I must insist that you do your very best for the first half of the term, and really study hard.'

So there was some very hard work done in the little studies that term. Carlotta groaned over her maths and Claudine puzzled over grammar. Felicity tried to learn her English literature and to write essays which usually ended abruptly because she had suddenly thought of a new tune. Anne-Marie rushed through all her prep except the English and then spent laborious hours over that, hoping to win approval from Miss Willcox.

Even Doris and Angela worked, though neither of them liked it. School was fun – but it *was* hard work too!

4
Angela loses her temper

The little first formers came and went at the bidding of the fifth. They ran errands, they made toast for tea and they chattered about their affairs to anyone who would listen.

Mirabel was always kindest to those who were good at games. She encouraged them to practise well at catching and running for lacrosse, she made up the teams for the school, and coached them well in her spare time. The younger girls thought she was wonderful.

'You know, that little Molly Williams is awfully good,' said Mirabel to Gladys, when she was making up the teams one day. 'I've a good mind to let her play in the third team, Gladys. And Jane Teal is good too, if she would practise running a bit more. She could be quite fast.'

'Little Antoinette is just as bad as Claudine,' said Gladys. 'I can't get her to practise at all, or to take any interest in games. Claudine doesn't back us up there, either. She is always telling Antoinette good excuses to make.'

'I'm tired of Claudine and her silly ways,' said Mirabel, impatiently. 'She's cunning. She'll get herself expelled one day!'

'Oh, no – she isn't as bad as that,' said Gladys, quite

shocked. 'She's just different from us, that's all. She's better than she was.'

'I should hope so, after all this time at St Clare's,' said Mirabel, writing the list of girls for the third team. 'Well – I've put Molly Williams down – she'll be thrilled.'

'It's a pity Angela and Alison order the young ones about so much,' said Gladys. 'They have always got one or other of them in their study, doing something for them. Angela even got Jane Teal in to do some mending for her, and that's not allowed.'

'I'll speak to Jane about it,' said Mirabel, in her direct way. 'I'll tell her she's not supposed to do Angela's mending, and she must use that time to get out on the practice field.'

'Well – wouldn't it be better to tell Angela that, not Jane?' said Gladys. 'It would come better from Angela, if she told Jane to stop doing her mending, than it would from you.'

'I'll deal with Jane myself,' said Mirabel, very much the sports captain, rather overbearing and arrogant that morning.

'Jane's fond of Angela,' said Gladys, as Mirabel went out of the roon. Mirabel snorted.

'She looks up to *me* no end,' she said. 'I'm pretty certain she'll do what *I* want, and not what Angela says. You really can leave these things to me, Gladys.'

Mirabel found Jane Teal and called to her. 'Hi, Jane! Come here a minute!'

The fourteen-year-old Jane, small, slight and quick,

went to Mirabel, her face flushing. She wondered if Mirabel was going to tell her she was to play in the third team with Molly. What a thrill that would be!

'Jane,' said Mirabel, in her direct way, 'I want you to do a bit more practising in the field the next few weeks. You'll be good if you really do practise. You ought to have been out this week. I hear you've been doing Angela's mending instead, and you know you don't need to do that.'

'I like to,' said Jane, flushing again. 'I'm good at sewing and Angela isn't. I like doing things for her.'

'Well, you give that up and pay more attention to games,' said Mirabel. 'I'm in charge of games and I want the good players doing their best.'

'I will do my best,' said Jane, proud to hear the great Mirabel say that she was one of the good players. 'But I did promise Angela to do all her mending this term – at least I offered to, Mirabel.'

'Well, you must tell her you can't,' said Mirabel, who quite failed to see that anything mattered except what she wanted herself.

'But – she'll be very cross and upset – and I do like doing things for her,' said Jane, half-frightened, but obstinate. 'I – I think she's beautiful, Mirabel. Don't you?'

'I don't see what that's got to do with it,' said Mirabel, impatiently. 'Anyway, I'm your sports captain and you've got to do as you're told. If you don't, I shan't let you play in even the fourth team, let alone the third.'

Mirabel's tone was sharp. She turned on her heel and went off. Jane looked after her, and tears smarted in her eyes. She admired Mirabel so much – and she did like Angela so much too. Angela had such a lovely smile and she said such nice things. The other girl she shared her study with was nice too – Alison.

Jane went to find her friend, Sally. She told her all that Mirabel had said and Sally listened.

'Well,' said Sally, 'you'll have to do what Mirabel tells you if you want to play in the third team and have some good matches. Why don't you go to Angela and tell her what Mirabel has said? You know quite well that if she is as sweet and kind as you say she is, she'll say at once that of course you mustn't do her mending any more.'

'Oh – that's a good idea,' said Jane, looking happier. 'I couldn't bear to upset Angela, Sally. I do really think she's wonderful. I should be miserable if she was angry with me.'

'Tell her when you go and make toast for her tea today,' said Sally. So that afternoon, rather tremblingly, Jane began to tell Angela what Mirabel had said.

'Angela,' she began, putting a piece of bread on to the toasting-fork, 'Angela, I've brought your mending back. I've done everything, even that stocking that had a ladder all the way down the back of the leg.'

'Thanks, Jane,' said Angela and gave Jane a smile that thrilled her.

'But – I don't believe I'll be able to do it much more,' went on Jane.

'Why ever not?' demanded Angela. 'You promised you would. I hate people who back out of things when they have promised to do them.'

'Well, you see – Mirabel spoke to me about it today,' said Jane, rather desperately. 'She said – she said – '

'Oh, I can guess what she said,' said Angela sneeringly. 'She said you were a wonderful player – and you must practise more – and you mustn't do odd jobs for that horrid Angela. And you meekly said you wouldn't. Little turncoat.'

'Oh, Angela, don't talk like that,' said poor Jane. 'It's not fair. Of course Mirabel didn't speak against you. But I have to do what she says, don't I? She's sports captain.'

'I don't see why *any*one has to do what dear, hearty, loud-voiced Mirabel says!' said Angela. 'I don't see why because *she's* mad on something she should expect everyone else to be mad on it too. This passion for games, games, games! I agree with Claudine that it's silly.'

'Oh, but Angela,' said Jane, shocked, 'games are lovely. And they make you get the team-spirit too, and play for your side instead of yourself – and – '

'Don't preach at *me*,' said Angela, angrily. 'You're only a half-baked first former. I don't care what you do, anyway. Go and practise running and catching morning, noon, and night if you want to. I shall certainly not allow you to do anything for me in future. I don't like turn-coats. Leave that toast and go and find Violet Hill and send her to me. She can do my jobs instead of you.'

Jane was horrified at this outburst. She had given her heart to the beautiful, radiant Angela, and now it was treated as rubbish! Angela didn't want her any more. She would have that silly Violet Hill, who adored Angela from afar and would do anything for a smile from her.

Jane gave a sob and rushed out of the room. In a few minutes Violet Hill came in, thrilled to be sent for. Angela gave her orders in a lazy voice, amused to see how the little first former almost trembled with excitement as she tidied up the room, and hung on Angela's lightest word.

Alison came in after a while and looked surprised to see Violet there instead of Jane. 'Where's our devoted Jane?' she asked.

Angela told her in a few words what had happened. Violet Hill listened eagerly. She was glad that Jane was in disgrace. She would show Angela how much nicer she, Violet, was!

When Violet went out Alison spoke rather shortly to Angela. 'You shouldn't have said all that in front of Violet. You know how keen Jane was on you – she'll have a fit if she knows all this will be passed round her form.'

'Serves her right,' said Angela, viciously.

'Angela, you make these kids awfully silly,' said Alison, after a pause. 'I don't really think you treat them properly. You oughtn't to let them think you're so wonderful. I bet poor Jane is crying her eyes out. You know Miss Theobald dislikes that kind of thing.'

Angela went pale with rage. She always hated being found fault with. She glared at Alison and tried to think of something really cutting. She found what she wanted at last.

'Really, Alison,' she said, in her lightest, most jeering voice, 'really, Alison – who are *you* to talk of thinking people wonderful? You're a perfect ninny over that wonderful Miss Willcox of yours, aren't you? Why, you're even trying to copy that deep voice of hers. It just makes me laugh.'

Alison was deeply hurt. When she was fond of anyone she could not bear to hear a single word said against them.

'Miss Willcox is an absolutely sincere person,' she said, with dignity. 'That's why I like her. You've no interest in English literature, or anything at all really, except yourself, Angela – so you can't understand my admiring anyone with such an interesting character as Miss Willcox.'

'Tosh,' said Angela, rudely.

The two girls said no more to each other that evening. Angela fumed in silence and Alison wrote a long and, as she fondly hoped, intelligent essay for Miss Willcox. It was not a very happy evening.

Angela had her knife into Mirabel after that. She did not dare to go and tackle Mirabel openly about Jane, because she was afraid of Mirabel's rudeness. Mirabel was tasting power for the first time as sports captain, and she was rather arrogant and blunt in her speech. Also she was very thick-skinned and Angela despaired of being able to say anything that would hurt her.

So she had to content herself with looking at her sneeringly, and saying mocking things behind her back. But as sneering glances and words were typical of Angela when she was upset about something, no one took much notice, Mirabel least of all.

Angela made things up with Alison, not so much

because she wanted to, but because she simply had to have someone to talk to and air her views to. Also, Alison genuinely admired her looks and her clothes, and it was always pleasant to bask in admiration of that sort.

Alison was not foolish with Angela as she had been when she first came. She no longer spoilt her and praised her and agreed with everything. But she could not hide her real admiration of the lovely girl with her shining golden hair, and brilliant blue eyes.

She was glad to make up the quarrel with Angela, for she wanted to talk about Miss Willcox – how wonderful she was in class, what beautiful poetry she wrote, how well she recited in that soulful voice of hers.

So, in return for admiration, Angela listened, rather bored, to all that Alison wanted to say. They were friends again – but it would not take much to turn them into enemies once more!

5

Hard work – and a little fun

The fifth form were certainly working very hard. Miss Cornwallis kept their noses to the grindstone, as Pat said, and piled prep on to them. Miss Willcox expected a great deal of them too. Miss Theobald, the head, took the form for one or two lessons and although she did not give them a great deal of prep, the girls felt that what she did give them must be specially well done.

When Mam'zelle piled prep on them too, the girls grew indignant. 'Gracious! What with all that maths to do, and that map to draw, and those French poems to memorize, and that essay for Miss Willcox, we'll all have nervous breakdowns!' groaned Bobby.

Only Pam Boardman did not seem to mind. She had an amazing memory, and had only to look at a page once to know it by heart. Doris envied her this gift from the bottom of her heart.

'I've no memory at all for lessons,' she sighed. 'What I learn in the morning I've forgotten in the evening.'

'Well, if you're going to be an actress, you'll have parts to learn, won't you?' said Pam.

'The funny thing is, when I act a part and say the words out loud, I can remember them quite easily,' said

Doris. 'I never forget them then. It's sitting hunched up over a book, reading and re-reading the words that gets me down.'

'Well, Doris, stand up and recite the words out loud, and act them if you want to,' said Pam, a gleam of fun coming into her solemn eyes. 'Here – take this French poem – it's all about the so-beautiful country-side, as Mam'zelle would say. Recite it out loud, act the cows and the sheep, frisk when you come to the part where the little lambs play, and waddle like a duck when you get to them. You'll soon learn it.'

So, to the amazement of Pat and Isabel, who looked in at Pam's study to borrow a book, Doris threw herself heart, soul and body into the French pastoral poem.

She declaimed the poem loudly, with gestures of all kinds. She frisked like a lamb, she chewed cud like a cow, she waddled like a duck. It was perfect.

The girls shrieked with laughter. Doris had turned the solemn and rather heavy French poem into a real comedy.

'Now – do you know it?' said Pam, when Doris finished, and sat down panting in a chair.

Doris screwed up her nose and thought hard. 'Let me see,' she said, 'it begins like this . . .'

But until she got up and acted the poem as she had done before, she could not remember a word. It was evidently the acting that brought the words to her mind.

'Well – you do know the poem,' said Pam, pleased. 'You won't forget it now. Mam'zelle will be pleased with her *chère* Doris tomorrow!'

Doris, however, was not in Mam'zelle's good books the next day. Her French exercise was nothing but mistakes and was slashed right across with Mam'zelle's thick blue pencil. Mam'zelle never spared her blue pencil when she was annoyed, and a page disapproved of by her was always a terrible sight.

'Ah, you Doris!' began Mam'zelle, when she was going through the work with her class. 'You! Have I had you on my thumb . . .'

'*Under* my thumb,' said Bobby, with a grin. Mam'zelle glared at her and resumed.

'Have I had you on my thumb for all these terms and still you do not know that a table is she not he. Why are you not in the kindergarten? Why can you still not pronounce the French R? All the others can. You are a great big stupid girl.'

'Yes, Mam'zelle,' said poor Doris, meekly. When Mam'zelle flew into a rage, it was best to be meek. But for some reason Doris's meekness irritated Mam'zelle even more.

'Ah – you mock at me now! "Yes, Mam'zelle" you say, with your tongue in your mouth and butter melting in your cheek!' cried Mam'zelle, getting things mixed up as usual.

The girls giggled. 'You mean, with your tongue in your cheek, and butter that won't melt in your mouth,' suggested Bobby again.

'Do not tell me what I mean, Bobbee,' said Mam'zelle, exasperated. 'Always you interrupt. Doris, stand up.'

Doris stood up, her humorous mouth twitching. She would act this scene afterwards for the benefit of the girls. How they would laugh!

'Your written work is very bad. Now let me hear your oral work,' demanded Mam'zelle. 'You have learnt the French poem? Yes – then let me hear it. Begin!'

Doris couldn't think of a single word. She stared into the distance, racking her brains. She knew there were all kinds of animals in it – but how did the words go?

'She did learn it, Mam'zelle,' said Pam's voice, earnestly. 'I heard her say it all through without looking at the book once.'

'Then I too will hear it now,' said Mam'zelle. 'Begin, Doris.'

Pam sat just behind Doris. She whispered the first line to her. Doris began – and then she suddenly knew that if only she could act the poem, she could say every word – but not one line would come unless she acted it! Oh, dear – she couldn't possibly act it in front of Mam'zelle, who loved French poetry, and would think she was making fun of it.

'Well, Doris, I wait. I wait patiently,' said Mam'zelle, who was anything but patient at that moment. 'Can you or can you not say the poem to me?'

'Yes. I can,' said Doris. 'But – but only if I act it.'

'Then act it,' said Mam'zelle, losing the last of her patience. 'But if you are not telling me the truth, *ma chère* Doris, I complain to Miss Theobald. Act it – but say the poem through without mistake.'

So, in despair, Doris acted the French poem in her usual exaggerated, ridiculous manner, waggling herself, chewing the cud, waddling, frisking – and, of course, as soon as she acted the poem, she knew it all the way through without a single mistake. She certainly had a peculiar memory.

The girls were thrilled and amused at Doris's rendering of the solemn poem, but they felt certain that Mam'zelle would be exceedingly angry. It was Claudine who saved the situation.

She clapped her hands in delight. She threw back her head and laughed her infectious laugh. She held her sides and almost doubled herself up.

'Oh, *ma tante, ma tante*!' she cried to her aunt. 'The clever Doris, the marvellous Doris! Such a poem she makes of it – and not one single mistake. Ah, never never shall I forget this poem now!'

Mam'zelle pushed her glasses on to her nose more firmly. Her face changed. She let out a roar of delighted laughter, and the class breathed loudly in relief. So long as Mam'zelle saw the joke it was all right.

Mam'zelle took off her glasses and wiped her streaming eyes. 'It is clever, very clever, Doris,' she said. 'It is not the right way to recite such a poem, no. But it is very clever and very amusing. I will forgive you this time for your bad work. It is true that you know the poem, and you have made it very funny. Is it not so, Claudine?'

Claudine agreed. 'We too will say the poem like that,' she suggested, her eyes gleaming with fun. But Mam'zelle was not going so far as that.

'*Ah, non*!' she said. 'Doris has a gift that way. One girl is funny, but fourteen, fifteen girls would not be funny. *Tiens*! Look at the clock. We have wasted half the lesson on this bad, clever Doris. Get out your books, please.'

Doris found that she could learn anything if only she said it out loud and put ridiculous actions to the words. But so often she could not repeat what she had learnt unless she accompanied it with the absurd actions. Miss Willcox did not think this was funny. She called it 'playing the fool' and said it was very bad taste.

As for doing such a thing in Miss Cornwallis's class or Miss Theobald's, it was quite unthinkable. However much the girls begged Doris to recite the latest maths rules with appropriate – or inappropriate – actions she would not.

'I'm not going to get expelled just to make you laugh,' she said. 'I must go on plodding away, and get Pam's help as much as I can. I'll never be any good at lessons.'

'But you'll always be able to make people laugh!' said Isabel. 'I'd almost rather do that than anything, but I'm not much good at it.'

'I'd rather write a book or paint a beautiful picture,' said Alison.

'So would I,' said Anne-Marie. 'Much rather. To leave something of oneself behind, something one has made or created – now that's really worthwhile.'

'Deirdre fans!' said Carlotta, mockingly.

Alison had found out that Miss Willcox's first initial was D and had asked her what it stood for.

'Deirdre,' said Miss Willcox, and Alison had thought it

a most beautiful name, almost picturesque enough for her darling Miss Willcox. Deirdre Willcox – a lovely name for a poet!

She had told Angela and Angela had told everyone else. Both Anne-Marie and Alison were always round Miss Willcox, and the girls now called them 'Deirdre fans'. It annoyed them very much. Alison was sorry now that she had told anyone Miss Willcox's name – she would have liked to be the only one who knew it.

She and Anne-Marie both vied with each other for Miss Willcox's attentions. Alison was jealous of Anne-Marie because she could write poetry, and Miss Willcox encouraged her to bring her her poems. Anne-Marie was jealous of Alison because she felt sure that Miss Willcox liked Alison the better of the two, which was quite true. A little of Anne-Marie and her intenseness went a very long way.

'You're both silly,' said Bobby, who never could understand what she called 'sloppiness'. 'Can't you see that anyone who encourages a couple of idiots like you can't be worth sucking up to?'

But this kind of remark only made Alison and Anne-Marie more devoted. It even brought them together a little in their common indignation, which amused the girls very much. The 'Deirdre fans' were the cause of a lot of fun that half-term!

6

Angela and the younger girls

Little Jane Teal turned up on the lacrosse field and practised zealously, much to Mirabel's satisfaction.

'There you are,' she said to Gladys, triumphantly. 'You see, a little plain talking has done Jane Teal a lot of good. I shall make her a very good player in no time.'

Gladys had noticed that Jane had done exactly what Mirabel had told her, but she had also noticed too that Jane looked rather miserable.

'She doesn't seem very happy about it,' she said. 'And it doesn't seem to me that she puts much heart into all her practising. I bet Angela made things very unpleasant for her when she told her she couldn't do her mending any more.'

'Oh, well – it's a good thing if Jane gets that sort of nonsense knocked out of her,' said Mirabel. 'I can't bear these kids who go round worshipping people.'

'Well, a lot of them think no end of *you*,' said Gladys, 'and you like them to.'

'That's different,' said Mirabel at once. 'They look up to me because I'm sports captain, because I make them work hard, and because I don't stand any nonsense. I should tick them off if they got sloppy over me.'

'Well – all the same I think little Jane looks miserable,' said Gladys. 'Don't frown like that at me, Mirabel. After all, I'm your vice-captain, and I have a right to say what I think to you.'

Mirabel looked in surprise at Gladys, who was often called the Mouse, because she said so little and was so quiet. Mirabel was fond of Gladys – in fact she was the only girl in the school that she had any real affection for at all. All the same, she didn't think she could allow Gladys to find fault with her decisions – what was the sense of being captain if you didn't make your own decisions and stick to them? A little power had gone to Mirabel's head!

'You can say what you like to me, of course,' said Mirabel, stiffly, 'but that doesn't mean I shall pay attention to your suggestions, I'm afraid, Gladys. I shall *listen* to them, of course – but I am the one to decide everything.'

Gladys said no more. Mirabel was not going to be a very easy person to live with that term! Gladys wished she was bold like Carlotta, or forthright like Bobby, or a strong character like Hilary – they always seemed able to cope with others in the right way, but Gladys was afraid of hurting them, or of making them angry.

Angela made a fuss of Violet Hill, in order to punish poor Jane. She gave her one of her best hair-slides and a book, which sent the foolish Violet into transports of delight. Violet showed them to Jane and Sally.

'Look,' she said, 'isn't Angela a dear? She's so generous. I think she's wonderful. I do think you were silly to quarrel with her, Jane. I think Angela is worth three of Mirabel!'

Jane looked miserably at the book and the hair-slide. Angela had never given *her* a present. She wished she could dislike Angela, but she couldn't. Every time she saw the golden-haired girl, with her starry eyes set in her oval face, she thought how wonderful she was.

Sally was sorry for Jane. 'Cheer up,' she said. 'Angela isn't worth worrying about. I believe she's only making up to Violet just to make you jealous. I think she's being beastly.'

But Jane would not hear a word against Angela, however much she had been hurt by her. Violet too was cross at Sally's remarks.

'As if Angela would give me presents just to make Jane jealous!' she said, sharply. 'If you ask *me*, I think she gave me them because I mended her blue jumper so neatly. It took me hours.'

'Do you do her mending then?' said Jane, jealously.

'Of course,' said Violet. 'I don't care what Mirabel says to *me* – if I prefer to do things for Angela, I shall do them.'

Violet told Angela how upset Jane was, and Angela was glad. She could be very spiteful when anything upset her. She was especially sweet to Violet and to the other first former who came when Violet could not come. The two of them thought she was the nicest girl in the whole school.

Antoinette, Claudine's little sister, also at times had to do jobs for the fifth and sixth formers. She did not like Angela, and always found excuses not to go to her study, even when an urgent message was sent.

'That young sister of yours is a perfect nuisance,' Angela complained to Claudine. 'Can't you knock some sense into her, Claudine? When I sent for her yesterday, she sent back to say that she was doing her practising – and now I hear that she doesn't even *learn* music!'

'She might have been practising something else,' suggested Claudine, politely. 'Maybe lacrosse.'

Angela snorted. 'Don't be silly! Antoinette gets out of games just like you do – the very idea of thinking she might put in a bit of practice is absurd. I believe you encourage her in these bad ways – slipping out of anything she doesn't like.'

Claudine looked shocked. 'Ah, but surely the little Antoinette loves everything at this so-English school?'

'Don't pretend to me,' said Angela, exasperated. 'I should have thought that in all the time you have been here, Claudine, you would have got more English – you're just as French as ever you were!'

Claudine would not lose her temper at this ungracious speech. 'It is good to be French,' she said, in her light, amiable voice. 'If I were English I might have been *you*, Angela – and that I could not have borne. Better a hundred times to be a French Claudine than an English Angela!'

Angela could not think of any really good retort to this, and by the time she had found her tongue Claudine had gone over to speak to Mam'zelle. Angela knew she had gone to Mam'zelle on purpose – no one would dare to attack Claudine with Mam'zelle standing by! Mam'zelle was intensely loyal to her two nieces.

'All right,' thought Angela, spitefully. 'I'll just get that slippery sister of hers and make her do all kinds of things for me! I'll speak to Hilary about it, and she'll tell Antoinette she's jolly well got to come when I or Alison send for her.'

Hilary knew that Antoinette was being very naughty about coming when she was sent for – but she knew too that Angela used the younger girls far too much. She used her prettiness and charm to make them into little slaves. So she was not very helpful to Angela when the girl told her about Antoinette.

'I'll tell her she must obey the fifth and sixth formers,' she said. 'But Angela, don't go too far, please. Most of us know that you are using your power too much in that direction.'

'What about Mirabel?' said Angela, at once. 'Doesn't she throw *her* weight about too much? She's unbearable this term, just because she's sports captain!'

'There's no need to discuss Mirabel,' said Hilary. 'What we've all got to realize this term, the term before we go up into the sixth, is that this is the form where we first shoulder responsibilities, and first have a little power over others. You're not given power to play about with and get pleasure from, Angela, as *you* seem to think. You're given it to use in the right way.'

'Don't be so preachy,' said Angela. 'Really, are we never going to have any fun or good times again at St Clare's? Everyone looks so serious and solemn nowadays.

Bobby and Janet never play tricks in class. We never have a midnight feast. We never . . .'

'Remember that we are all working jolly hard,' said Hilary, walking off. 'You can't work hard and play the fool too. Wait till the exam is over and then maybe we can have a bit of fun.'

Hilary spoke to Antoinette and the small, dark-eyed French girl listened with the utmost politeness.

'Yes, Hilary, I will go to Angela when she sends for me,' said Antoinette. 'But always she sends for me at so – busy a time!'

'Well, make your excuses to me, not to Angela,' said Hilary, firmly. Antoinette looked at Hilary and sighed. She knew that Hilary would not believe in her excuses, and would insist, in that firm, polite way of hers, that Antoinette should do as she was told.

Angela saw Hilary speaking to Antoinette and was pleased. She decided to give Antoinette a bad time – she would teach her to 'toe the mark' properly.

'Violet, I shan't want you for a few days,' she told the adoring Violet. 'Send me Antoinette instead.'

'Oh, but Angela – don't I do your jobs well enough for you?' said Violet in dismay. 'Antoinette is such a mutt – she can't do a thing! Really she can't. Let *me* do everything.'

'Antoinette can sew and darn beautifully,' said Angela, taking pleasure in hurting Violet, who had been very silly that week. 'You made an awful darn in one of my tennis socks.'

Violet's eyes filled with tears and she went out of the

room. Alison looked up from her work.

'Angela, stop it,' she said. 'I think you're beastly – making the kids adore you and then being unkind to them. Anyway – you'll have a hard nut to crack in Antoinette! *She* won't adore you. She's got her head screwed on all right.'

'She would adore me if I wanted her to,' boasted Angela, who knew the power of her prettiness and smiles, and who could turn on charm like water out of a tap.

'She wouldn't,' said Alison. 'She's like Claudine – sees through everyone at once, and sizes them up and then goes her own way entirely, liking or disliking just as she pleases.'

'I bet I'll make Antoinette like me as much as any of those silly kids,' said Angela. 'You watch and see. You'll be surprised, Alison.'

'I'll watch – but I shan't be surprised,' said Alison. 'I know little Antoinette better than you do!'

Antoinette defeats Angela

The next time she was sent for, Antoinette arrived promptly, all smiles. She was just as neat and chic as Claudine, quick-witted and most innocent looking. Miss Jenks, the second-form mistress, had already learnt that Antoinette's innocent look was not to be trusted. The more innocent she looked, the more likely it was that she had misbehaved or was going to misbehave!

'You sent for me, Angela?' said Antoinette.

'Yes,' said Angela, putting on one of her flashing smiles. 'I did. Antoinette, will you clean those brown shoes over there, please? I'm sure you'll do it beautifully.'

Antoinette stared at Angela's beaming smile and smiled back. Angela felt sure she could see intense admiration in her eyes.

'The polish, please?' said Antoinette, politely.

'You'll find it in the cupboard, top shelf,' said Angela. 'How chic and smart you always look, Antoinette – just like Claudine.'

'Ah, Claudine, is she not wonderful?' said Antoinette. 'Angela, I have five sisters, and I like them all, but Claudine is my favourite. Ah, Claudine – I could tell you things about Claudine that would make you marvel, that would make you wish that you too had such a sister, and . . .'

But Angela was not in the least interested to hear what a wonderful sister Claudine was, and she was certain she would never wish she had one like her. Angela preferred being a spoilt only child. You had to share things with sisters!

'Er – the polish is in the cupboard, top shelf,' she said, her bright smile fading a little.

'The polish – ah, yes,' said Antoinette, taking a step towards the cupboard, but only a step. 'Now, Claudine is not the only wonderful sister I have – there is Louise. Ah, I wish I could tell you what Louise is like. Louise can do every embroidery stitch there is, and when she was nine, she won . . .'

'Better get on with my shoes, Antoinette,' said Angela, beginning to lose patience. A hurt look came into Antoinette's eyes, and Angela made haste to bestow her brilliant smile on her again. Antoinette at once cheered up and took another step towards the cupboard.

She opened her mouth, plainly to go on with her praise of Louise or some other sister, but Angela picked up a book and pretended to be absorbed in it.

'Don't talk for a bit,' she said to Antoinette. 'I've got to learn something.'

Antoinette went to the cupboard. She took a chair and stood on it to get the polish. Then she stepped down with a small pot in her hand, and a little secret smile on her mouth – the kind of smile that Claudine sometimes wore. Angela did not see it.

Antoinette found a brush and duster and set herself to her task. She squeezed cream on to the shoes and smeared it on well. Then she brushed it in and then rubbed hard with the soft duster. She held the pair of shoes away from her and looked at them with pride.

'Done?' said Angela, still not looking up in case Antoinette began talking again.

'They are finished,' said Antoinette. 'Shall I clean yet another pair, Angela? It is a pleasure to work for you.'

Angela was delighted to hear this. Aha – Alison would soon see that she could win the heart of Antoinette as easily as anyone else's.

'Yes, Antoinette – clean all the shoes you like,' she said, smiling sweetly. 'How beautiful that pair look!'

'Do they not?' said Antoinette. 'Such beautiful shoes they are too! Ah, no girl in the school wears such fine clothes as you, Angela – so beautifully made, so carefully finished. You have more chic than any English girl – you might be a Parisian!'

'I've been to Paris and bought clothes there two or three times,' said Angela, and was just about to describe all the clothes when Antoinette started off again.

'Ah, clothes – now you should see my sister Jeanne! Such marvellous clothes she has, like those in the shops at Paris – but all of them she makes herself with her clever fingers. Such style, such chic, such . . .'

'You seem to have got a whole lot of very clever sisters,' said Angela, sarcastically, but Antoinette did not seem to realize that Angela was being cutting.

'It is true,' she said. 'I have not yet told you about Marie. Now Marie . . .'

'Antoinette, finish the shoes and let me get on with my work,' said Angela, who felt that she could not bear to hear about another sister of Antoinette's. 'There's a good girl!'

She used her most charming tone, and Antoinette beamed. 'Yes, Angela, yes. I am too much of a chatter-tin, am I not?'

'Box, not tin,' said Angela. 'Now, do get on, Antoinette. It's lovely to hear your chatter, but I really have got work to do.'

Antoinette said no more but busied herself with three more pairs of shoes. She stood them in the corner and put the empty pot of cream into the waste-paper basket. 'I have finished, Angela,' she said. 'I go now. Tomorrow you will want me, is it not so?'

'Yes, come tomorrow at the same time,' said Angela, switching on a charming smile again and shaking back her gleaming hair. 'You've done my shoes beautifully. Thank you.'

Antoinette slipped out of the room like a mouse. She met Claudine at the end of the passage and her sister raised her eyebrows. 'Where have you been, Antoinette? You are not supposed to be in the fifth-form studies unless you have been sent for.'

'I have been cleaning all Angela's shoes,' said Antoinette, demurely. Then she glanced swiftly up and down the corridor to see that no one else was in sight, and shot out a few sentences in rapid French. Claudine laughed her infectious laugh, and pretended to box her sister's ears.

'*Tiens! Quelle méchante fille*! What will Angela say?'

Antoinette shrugged her shoulders, grinned and disappeared. Claudine went on her way, and paused outside Angela's study. She heard voices. Alison was there now too. Claudine opened the door.

'Hallo,' said Alison. 'Come for that book I promised you? Wait a minute – I've put it out for you somewhere.'

She caught sight of all Angela's shoes standing gleaming in a corner. 'I say! Did young Violet clean them like that for you? She doesn't usually get such a polish on!'

'No – Antoinette did them,' said Angela. 'She was telling me all about your sisters and hers, Claudine.'

'Ah, yes,' said Claudine, 'there is my sister Louise, and my sister Marie and my sister . . .'

'Oh, don't *you* start on them, for goodness' sake,' said Angela. 'What's the matter, Alison, what are you staring at?'

'Have you used up all that lovely face-cream al*ready*?' said Alison, in a surprised voice, and she picked an empty pot out of the waste-paper basket. 'Angela, how extravagant of you! Why, there was hardly any out of it yesterday – and now it's all gone. What *have* you done with it?'

'Nothing,' said Angela, startled. 'I hardly ever use that, it's so terribly expensive and difficult to get. I keep it for very special occasions. Whatever can have happened to it? It really is empty!'

The two girls stared at each other, puzzled. Claudine sat on the side of the table, swinging her foot, her face quite impassive. Then Angela slapped the table hard and exclaimed in anger.

'It's that fool of an Antoinette! She's cleaned my shoes with my best face-cream! Oh, the idiot! All that lovely cream gone – gone on my shoes too!'

'But your shoes, they look so beautiful!' remarked Claudine. 'Maybe the little Antoinette thought that ordinary shoe-polish was not good enough for such fine shoes.'

'She's an idiot,' said Angela. 'I won't have her do any jobs again.'

'Perhaps that's why she did this,' said Alison, dryly. 'It's the kind of thing our dear Claudine would do, for the same kind of reason, isn't it, Claudine?'

'Shall I tell Antoinette you will not need her again because you are very angry at her foolishness?' said Claudine. 'Ah, she will be so sad, the poor child!'

Angela debated. She felt sure that Antoinette had made a real mistake. She was certain the girl liked her too much to play such a trick on her. How thrilled Antoinette had seemed when she had smiled at her! No – the girl had made a genuine mistake. Angela would give her another chance.

'I'll try her again,' she said. 'I'll forgive her this time. We all make mistakes sometimes.'

'How true!' said Claudine. 'Now, my sister Marie, hardly ever does she make a mistake, but once . . .'

'Oh, get out,' said Angela, rudely. 'It's bad enough to

have you and Antoinette here without having to hear about your dozens of sisters!'

Claudine removed herself gracefully and went to find Antoinette to report the success of her trick. Antoinette grinned. '*C'est bien,*' she said. 'Very good! Another time I will again be foolish, oh, so foolish!'

Angela sent for her again the next day. Antoinette entered with drooping head and downcast eyes.

'Oh, Angela,' she said, in a low, meek voice, 'my sister Claudine has told me what a terrible mistake I made yesterday. How could I have been so foolish? I pray you to forgive me.'

'All right,' said Angela. 'Don't look so miserable, Antoinette. By the way, I think I'll call you Toni – it's so much friendlier than Antoinette, isn't it?'

Antoinette appeared to greet this idea with rapture. Angela beamed. How easy it was to get round these young ones! Well – she would get all the work she could out of this silly French girl, she would wind her round her little finger – and then she would send her packing and teach her a good sharp lesson!

'What would you have me do today?' Antoinette asked, in her meek voice. 'More shoes?'

'No,' said Angela. 'No more shoes. Make me some anchovy toast, Toni.'

'Please?' said Antoinette, not understanding.

'Oh, dear – don't you know what anchovy toast is?' sighed Angela. 'Well, you make ordinary buttered toast – and for goodness' sake toast the bread before you put the butter on – then you spread it with anchovy paste. You'll find it in the cupboard. Make enough for three people. Anne-Marie is coming to tea, to read us her new poem.'

'Ah, the wonderful Anne-Marie!' said Antoinette, getting out the bread. 'Now one of my sisters, the one called Louise, once she wrote a poem and . . .'

'Toni, I've got to go and see someone,' said Angela, getting up hurriedly. 'Get on with the toast, and do it really carefully, to make up for your silly mistake yesterday.'

'Angela, believe me, your little Toni will give you such toast as never you have had before!' said Antoinette with fervour. She held a piece of bread to the fire.

Angela went out, determined not to come back till Antoinette had made the toast and was safely out of the way. Talk about a chatterbox! She seemed to have a never-ending flow of conversation about her family. She might start on her brothers next – if she had any!

As soon as Angela had gone out of the room, Antoinette put aside her artless ways and concentrated on her job. She made six pieces of toast very rapidly and spread them with butter. Then she got a pot down from the cupboard shelf – but it was not anchovy. It was the pot of brown shoe polish that she should have used the day before!

It looked exactly like anchovy as she spread it on the toast. Carefully the little monkey spread the brown paste, piled the slices on a plate and set them beside the fire to keep warm. Then she slipped out of the room and made her way to the noisy common-room of her own form.

Soon Alison came in and sat down by the fire. Then

Angela popped her head round the door and saw to her relief that Antoinette was gone.

'I simply couldn't stay in the room with that awful chatterbox, drivelling on about her sisters,' said Angela. 'Ah, she's made a nice lot of toast, hasn't she? Hallo – here's Anne-Marie.'

Anne-Marie came in, her big eyes dark in her pale face. 'You look tired,' said Angela. 'Been burning the midnight oil? I wish *I* could write poems like you, Anne-Marie.'

'I worked on a poem till past twelve,' said Anne-Marie, in her intense voice. 'It's a good thing no one saw the light in my study. Ah – tea's ready, how lovely! Let's tuck in, and then I'll read my latest poem.'

Three disgusted girls

Angela lifted the toast on to the table. 'I got Antoinette to make anchovy toast for us,' she said. 'It looks good, doesn't it? Take a slice, Anne-Marie.'

Anne-Marie took the top slice. It seemed to have rather a peculiar smell. Anne-Marie looked rather doubtfully at it.

'It's all right,' said Alison, seeing her look. 'Anchovy always smells a bit funny, I think.'

She and Anne-Marie took a good bite out of their toast at the same second. The shoe-cream tasted abominable. Anne-Marie spat her mouthful out at once, all over the table. Alison, with better manners, spat hers into her handkerchief. Angela took a bite before she realized what the others were doing.

Then she too spat out at once, and clutched her mouth with her hands. 'Oh! Oh! What is it? I'm poisoned!'

She rushed to the nearest bathroom and the others followed, their tongues hanging out. Anne-Marie was promptly sick when she reached the bathroom. Tears poured from her eyes and she had to sit down.

'Angela! What filthy paste! How *could* you buy such stuff?' she said.

'Horrible!' said Alison, rinsing her mouth out over and

over again. 'All that toast wasted too. It's wicked. Angela, whatever possessed you to get paste like that? I've never tasted anchovy like that before, and I hope I never shall again. Ugh!'

Angela was feeling ill and very angry. What in the world had that idiot Antoinette done? They went back to the study and Angela opened the door of the little cupboard. She took down the pot of anchovy. It was untouched. So Antoinette couldn't have used it. Then what *had* she used? There was only jam besides the paste.

Alison picked up the pot of brown shoe-cream and opened that. It was practically empty. 'Look,' said Alison, angrily. 'She used the shoe-cream – plastered all the toast with it! She deserves a good scolding.'

Angela was white with anger. She put her head out of the door and saw a first former passing. 'Hey, Molly,' she called, 'go and find Antoinette and tell her to come here at once.'

'Yes, Angela,' said Molly, and went off. Very soon Antoinette appeared, her dark eyes wide with alarm, and her lips trembling as if with emotion.

'Antoinette! How *dare* you put shoe-cream on our toast?' almost screamed Angela. 'You might have poisoned us all. Can't you tell the difference between anchovy paste and shoe-polish, you absolute idiot? You've made us all ill. Matron will probably hear about it. You ought to be reported to Miss Jenks, you ought to . . .'

'Ah, ah, do not scold your little Toni so,' said Antoinette. 'You have been so kind to me, Angela, you have smiled, you have called me Toni! Do not scold me so! I will give up my tea-time, I will make you more toast, and this time I will spread it with the anchovy, there shall be no mistake this time.'

'If you think I'm ever going to trust you to do a single thing for me again, you're mistaken,' said Angela, still tasting the awful taste of shoe-cream in her mouth. 'I might have known a French girl would play the fool like this. I tell you, you've made us all ill. Anne-Marie was sick.'

'I am desolated,' wailed Antoinette. 'Ah, Angela, I pray you to let me come again tomorrow. Tomorrow I will be good, so good. Tomorrow you will call me Toni and smile at me again, tomorrow . . .'

'Tomorrow I'll get Violet Hill,' said Angela. 'Clear out, Antoinette, you're a perfect menace.'

Antoinette cleared out and there was peace. 'Well,' said Angela, 'she'll wish she'd been more sensible tomorrow. Serves her right! I was nice to her, and she thought the world of me – but I can't put up with idiots. She'll be jolly sorry when she sees I don't mean to give her another chance!'

'I don't feel like any tea now,' said Alison, looking at the remains of the toast with dislike. 'Do you, Anne-Marie?'

'No.' said Anne-Marie, and shuddered. 'I still feel sick. I don't even know if I can read my poem. It doesn't go very well with shoe-polish.'

'Oh, do read it, Anne-Marie,' begged Angela, who really did admire her poems. 'What's it about?'

'It's all about the sadness of spring,' said Anne-Marie, reaching for her poem. 'It's a very sad poem, really.'

'All your poems are sad,' said Alison. 'Why are they, Anne-Marie? I like poems that make me feel happy.'

'I am not a very happy person,' said Anne-Marie, very solemnly, and looked intense. 'Poets aren't, you know.'

'But some must have been,' objected Alison. 'I know lots of very cheerful poems.'

'Shut up, Alison,' said Angela. 'Read your poem, Anne-Marie.'

Anne-Marie began her poem. It was very doleful, full of impressive words, and rather dull. Neither Alison nor Angela liked it very much, but they couldn't help feeling impressed. However could Anne-Marie write like that? She must indeed be a genius!

'It must be nice for you, sharing a study with Felicity, who thinks as much of music as you do of poetry,' said Alison. 'You ought to get Felicity to set some of your poems to music. That would be wonderful.'

'I've asked her. She won't,' said Anne-Marie, shortly. The truth was that Felicity would not admit that Anne-Marie's poems were worth tuppence. It was very humiliating to Anne-Marie.

'Write something real, and I'll put a tune to it,' Felicity had said. 'I'm not going to waste my music on second-rate stuff.'

The door opened suddenly and Matron looked in. 'I hear you poor girls have had a nasty dose of shoe-polish,' she said. 'I hope it wasn't anything very serious.'

Angela thought she would take the chance of getting Antoinette into trouble, so she exaggerated at once.

'Oh, Matron, it was awful! We had our mouths absolutely full of the beastly stuff. Anne-Marie must have swallowed a lot, because she was sick. I shouldn't be surprised if we are ill, seriously ill, tonight,' said Angela.

'I'm sure I swallowed some,' said Anne-Marie, looking solemn. 'I expect we all did.'

'Then you must come and have a dose at once,' said Matron. 'That shoe-cream contains a poisonous ingredient which may irritate your insides for a week or more, unless I give you a dose to get rid of it. Come along with me straight away.'

The three girls stared at her in alarm. They simply could not bear Matron's medicines. They were really so very nasty! Angela wished fervently that she had not exaggerated so much.

She tried to take back what she had said. 'Oh, well, Matron,' she said, with a little laugh, 'it wasn't as bad as all that, you know. We spat out practically all of it – and we rinsed our mouths out at once. We're *per*fectly all right now.'

'I dare say,' said Matron. 'But I'd rather be on the safe side. I don't want you in bed for a week with a tummy upset of some sort. Come along. I've got something that will stop any trouble immediately.'

'But Matron,' began Alison.

It was no good. Nobody could reason with Matron once she had really decided to give anyone a dose. The three girls had to get up and follow her. They looked very blue, and felt most humiliated. As a rule Matron left the fifth and sixth formers to look after themselves, and seldom came after them, suggesting medicine. They felt like first or second formers, trooping after her for a dose.

Matron took them to her room, and measured out the medicine into tablespoons, one for each of them. It tasted almost as nasty as the shoe-polish toast!

'Pooh!' said Alison, trying to get the taste out of her mouth. 'Why don't you get some nice-tasting medicines, Matron? I've never tasted any so beastly as yours.'

'Well, I've got a much worse one here,' said Matron. 'Would you just like to try it?'

'Of course not!' said Alison. Then a thought struck her. 'Matron – how did you know we'd had shoe-polish on our toast today? We hadn't told a soul. Who told you?'

'Why, the poor little Antoinette told me,' said Matron, corking up the bottle. 'Poor child, she came to me in a terrible state, saying she had poisoned you all by mistake, and what was she to do if you died in the night, and couldn't I do something about it?'

The three girls listened to this with mixed feelings. So it was Antoinette who not only provided them with shoe-polish toast, but also with medicine from Matron! The little horror!

'You've no idea how upset she was,' went on Matron, briskly. 'Poor little soul, I felt really sorry for her. An English girl might have been amused at the mistake she had made, but Antoinette was so upset I had to comfort her and give her some chocolate. It's wonderful what chocolate will do to soothe the nerves of a first or second former! Nothing but babies, really.'

The thought of Antoinette eating Matron's chocolate was too much for Angela, Alison and Anne-Marie. They felt that they simply *must* get hold of Antoinette and tell her what they thought of her.

'Where is Antoinette, do you know, Matron?' asked Angela, wishing she could get the combined tastes of shoepolish and medicine out of her mouth.

'I sent her to her aunt, Mam'zelle,' said Matron. 'I'm sure she would cheer her up and make her think she hadn't done such a dreadful thing after all! Fancy thinking she really had poisoned you!'

The three fifth-formers went back to the study. It wouldn't be a bit of good going to fetch Antoinette now. She would probably be having a nice cosy tea with Mam'zelle, who would be fussing her up and telling her everything was all right, a mistake was a mistake, and not to worry, *pauvre petite* Antoinette!

'I'll send for her tomorrow and jolly well keep her nose to the grindstone,' said Angela, angrily. 'I told her she needn't do anything more for me – but I'll make her now. I'll make her sorry she ever played those tricks. Clever little beast – going off to Matron and play-acting like that. She's worse than Claudine!'

Alison was alarmed to hear that Angela was going to make Antoinette do some more jobs for them.

'For goodness' sake, don't be silly!' she said to

Angela. 'Antoinette is far too clever for us to get even with. She'll only do something even worse than she has already done. I told you she wouldn't be like the others, silly and worshipping. I told you she would size you up! I told you . . .'

'Shut up, Alison,' said Angela. 'I hate people who say "I told you, I told you!" I won't have Antoinette if you think she'll play worse tricks. She'd end in poisoning us, I should think. I wish I could pay her out, though.'

'It's partly your own fault, all this,' said Alison. 'If only you'd treat the younger ones like the others do, sensibly and properly, we shouldn't have all these upsets.'

Anne-Marie thought it was time to go. She always said that quarrels upset her poetic feelings. So she went, taking her mournful poem with her.

'We'd better not say a word about this to anyone,' said Angela. 'Else the whole school will be laughing at us. We won't let it go any further.'

But alas for their plans – Antoinette told the story to everyone, and soon the whole school was enjoying the joke. It made Angela furious, for she hated being laughed at. It humiliated Alison too, for even Miss Willcox got to hear of it and teased her and Anne-Marie.

'What about a little essay on "Anchovy Sauce"?' she said. 'Poor Alison, poor Anne-Marie, what a shame!'

Miss Willcox is in a bad temper

Miss Willcox was in a bad temper. She had just had back from her publishers her second book of poems, with a polite note to say that they were not as good as the first ones, and they regretted they did not see their way to put them into book form.

Miss Willcox had an excellent opinion of her own writings, just as Anne-Marie had of hers. Also she had boasted in advance of her second book of poems – and now it would not be published. She was disappointed, and, like many rather weak characters, her disappointment turned to resentment instead of to a determination to go on and do better.

So she went to her English class looking rather grim, and feeling that she could not stand any nonsense or bad work that morning.

As a whole, the class had been working really very well, for Miss Willcox's lessons were interesting. Alma Pudden had not been able to keep up with the class very well, and Doris could not learn by heart with any success unless she was allowed to act what she said. Felicity too was only really interested if the poems or plays aroused her sense of rhythm and music.

The girls were rather tired that morning. They had had a strenuous half-hour with the gym mistress, who, feeling rather brisk, had put them through a great many vigorous exercises. Then had come a very hard three-quarters of an hour over maths and then the English lesson. The girls were feeling that they wanted to relax a little – but here was Miss Willcox demanding intense concentration and attention.

Carlotta let out an enormous yawn which drew Miss Willcox's wrath upon her. Then Claudine said she felt sick and please could she go out of the room?

'It is astonishing how many times you manage to feel sick when you want to miss some part of a lesson,' said Miss Willcox, irritated. 'Go straight to Matron, please, and tell her.'

'I would rather not,' said Claudine, politely. 'I do not feel sick enough for that. I can be sick in here if you would rather I stayed for the lesson.'

It looked as if Miss Willcox was going to overwhelm Claudine with her wrath, when Felicity made them all jump. She began to tattoo on her desk, swaying to and fro in ecstasy.

'La-di-la-di-la!' she sang, 'oh, la-la-la-di-la!'

'Felicity! What in the world are you doing?' cried Miss Willcox, incensed with rage. Felicity took not the slightest notice. With eyes still closed, she continued her swaying, and her singing, at times thumping the desk to accent the rhythm.

'*Felicity*!' almost shouted Miss Willcox, one of her

gold-topped pins falling out of her hair on to the desk. She didn't notice it. 'Do you hear what I say? What has come over this class this morning?'

Bobby gave Felicity a bang on the shoulder. Felicity opened her eyes with a start, and gazed round the room. She did not in the least seem to take in the fact that she was in class and that Miss Willcox was furious with her. She shut her eyes again and began swaying.

'She's music-mad,' said Bobby. 'She's in a kind of music-dream, Miss Willcox. I don't believe she can help it. Hi, Felicity!'

'She goes like this in our study at night, very often,' said Anne-Marie. 'I often think she does it on purpose. She always does it when I want to read one of my poems out loud.'

'Jolly sensible of her,' remarked Pat.

'La-di-la-di-la!' hummed Felicity. Miss Willcox stared at her very hard. She simply could not make out if the girl's actions were genuine or put on.

'Boom-di-boom, di-boom,' finished Felicity and banged the desk hard. 'Ah, I've got it at last!'

The girls laughed. Acting or not, it was very funny. Felicity beamed round. 'I have it!' she said. 'The melody I've had in my mind for the last two weeks. It goes like this – la-di-la-di-la . . .'

Now it was Miss Willcox's turn to bang on the desk. It was seldom that she really did lose her temper, for she considered that meant a loss of dignity, and Miss Willcox always liked to appear dignified and self-controlled.

But really, Felicity was too much for anyone!

'Leave the room,' commanded Miss Willcox, her voice trembling with anger. 'I won't have anyone in my class playing the fool like this. You shouldn't have come up into the fifth form – you should have gone down into the third!'

'Go out of the room?' said Felicity, puzzled. 'Why must I? I didn't mean to interrupt the lesson – I didn't do it on purpose. It came over me suddenly. Now I am quite all right.'

'Leave the room,' ordered Miss Willcox again. The girls were silent. It was almost unheard of for a fifth-form girl to be sent from the room. If Miss Theobald heard of it there would be serious trouble for Felicity.

Felicity got up and walked out of the room as if she was in a dream. She looked puzzled and shocked. She stood outside the door and leant against the wall. Her head ached. Then the new melody came back again into it and she began to sing it quietly. The sound came into the silent classroom.

'Anne-Marie, tell Felicity to go to her study, and to write out the whole of the act of the play she is now missing,' said Miss Willcox. 'I will not have this behaviour.'

'Felicity thinks she's a genius,' said Anne-Marie. 'She's always acting like this.'

'I didn't ask for any comment,' said Miss Willcox. She always forgot to put on her deep, rather drawling voice, when she was in a temper, and her voice now sounded rather harsh and unpleasant.

Almost everyone got into trouble that morning. Doris

was scolded for not knowing her part in the play they were reading. Alma was hauled up for eating sweets, 'like any silly little first former,' said Miss Willcox in disgust, taking the bag away from the unhappy Alma.

'Poor old Pudding!' whispered Pat to Isabel. 'I believe eating is her only pleasure in life!'

'Pat! What did you say?' demanded Miss Willcox. Pat went red.

'Well – I can't very well tell you,' she said, not wishing to repeat what she had said and hurt Alma.

Miss Willcox at once felt certain that Pat had been saying something rude about *her*. 'Miss games this afternoon and write out your part in the play instead,' she snapped. Pat looked upset, but did not dare to argue with Miss Willcox in her present mood.

The girls grew nervous. Pauline dropped her books on the floor and made Miss Willcox jump. She got a few sharp words that made her squirm and look at the mistress with resentment. Bobby debated whether or not to cheer things up by making Miss Willcox and the class laugh but decided that nothing on earth would get a smile out of the mistress that morning. Whatever could be wrong with her? She was not usually like this.

Only Alison and Anne-Marie gazed at her with admiration that morning. They both thought that their beloved Miss Willcox looked lovely with her dark soulful eyes flashing. A bit of Miss Willcox's hair came down and hung by her ear. Alison saw her feeling about for the pin that usually kept it up, and walked from her seat.

She picked up the pin that had dropped and put it on Miss Willcox's desk with one of her rather sweet smiles. Somehow the action and the smile soothed Miss Willcox.

'Thank you, Alison,' she said, using the deep voice that always thrilled Anne-Marie and Alison. 'You are always on hand to help!'

Anne-Marie felt jealous. She never liked it when Miss Willcox praised Alison in any way. She sat looking gloomy. The class was amused to see this little by-play.

After the reading of the play was finished, there were five minutes left. 'Has anyone found anything interesting to read?' asked Miss Willcox, who always encouraged the class to bring any poem they liked or to quote any prose lines they came across which pleased them.

Apparently no one had. 'We've been working too hard this week to read much,' said Hilary. 'We haven't time for anything till this awful exam is over.'

'Miss Willcox,' said Anne-Marie, nervously smiling. 'Could I read the class a poem of mine, please? I would so like to know if you like it.'

Miss Willcox was not really in the mood to hear poems by anyone, since her own had been sent back. But the class, thinking that they could sit back and have a little rest for five minutes, applauded Anne-Marie's suggestion loudly. Anne-Marie flushed with pleasure. She thought they were welcoming her poem. It didn't enter her silly little head that the girls wanted a rest, and wouldn't listen to a word of it.

'Well,' said Miss Willcox, rather ungraciously, 'you can read it if you like, Anne-Marie.'

Anne-Marie got a piece of paper out of her desk, covered with her sprawling hand-writing, which was always far too big. She cleared her throat, and began, putting on a deep voice that was supposed to be a flattering imitation of Miss Willcox's own style.

'THE LONELY MILL

Lost in the wreathing mists of time,
Silent as years that are lost,
Brooding . . .'

Nobody but Angela listened. The whole class was bored to tears by Anne-Marie's pretentious, solemn and insincere poetry. Anne-Marie let herself go, and her voice rang quite sonorously through the classroom.

But she was not allowed to finish it. Miss Willcox had listened in a state of irritation, and stopped her half-way through. The poem was plainly an imitation of one of her own poems, in the book she had had published, a copy of which the adoring Anne-Marie had bought.

Her poem was called 'The Deserted Farm', and the whole plan of it was much the same as Anne-Marie's, even to the ideas in the different verses. As an imitation it was very clever – but Anne-Marie had not meant it to be an imitation. She had thought she was writing a most original poem, and had not even realized that she had drawn on her memories of Miss Willcox's own poem.

'Stop,' said the mistress, and Anne-Marie stopped, puzzled. She glanced at Miss Willcox, who was frowning.

'When you write something *really* original, something out of your own mind, something which isn't copied from *my* work or anyone else's, I'll listen to it, Anne-Marie,' said Miss Willcox, putting on her deep, drawling voice again.

'But Miss Willcox – I didn't copy it from anywhere,' stammered Anne-Marie, horrified. 'I – I only tried to model it on your own style, which I admire very much. I – I –'

Even if Anne-Marie's poem had been as good as one by Shakespeare, Miss Willcox would not have admired it that morning, when she was still smarting from the sending back of her own precious collection of poems.

'Don't make excuses,' she said coldly. 'If I were you I should tear the poem up. Now – there's the bell. Put your books together and go out for break. Alison, you can stay and help me for a few moments. I want these papers put in order.'

In tears poor Anne-Marie went out of the room – and with smiles Alison helped Miss Willcox. The other girls hurried out thankfully – what a nerve-racking English lesson it had been!

10 About geniuses, sport, and mending

'You weren't sick after all, Claudine,' said Angela, rather maliciously, as they went out.

'It passed,' said Claudine, airily. 'Happily Felicity took Miss Willcox's attention, or I might have had to go to Matron.'

'We'd better go and get Felicity out of her study,' said Isabel to Pat. 'I wonder if she's written out the act of that play. It's an awfully long one.'

They went to Felicity's study. Anne-Marie was there, crying. She scowled at the others when they came in.

'Cheer up, silly,' said Pat. 'What does it matter what dear Deirdre says about your poem? I bet she's jealous, that's all!'

'You don't know anything about poetry,' sniffled Anne-Marie. 'I don't believe you heard a word of my poem, anyway.'

'Quite right, I didn't,' said Pat. 'I'd listen if I understood what you were trying to say in your poems, Anne-Marie, but it always seems to me as if you haven't got anything to *say*.'

'You're all unkind to me,' sobbed Anne-Marie,

thoroughly upset by two things – the fact that her precious poem had been scoffed at, and that her adored Miss Willcox had snubbed her.

'Oh, don't be such a baby,' said Pat, and turned to look at Felicity, who was writing feverishly in a corner, copying out the play in nervous, very small hand-writing.

'Bad luck, Felicity,' said Pat. 'Come on out now, though. Do you good to get a blow in the air this morning. You look awful.'

'I don't know what happened to me in class today,' said Felicity, raising her head for a minute. 'You see, I've been working so hard on my music, and the tune I've been groping for suddenly came to me – and my mind just went after it, and I forgot everything else.'

'It's because you're a genius,' said Pat, kindly, for she liked Felicity, who put on no airs at all, and was not in the least conceited. 'Geniuses always do funny unusual things, you know. They can't help it. They like working in the middle of the night, they go without food for days sometimes, they walk in their sleep, they are absent-minded – oh, they're not like ordinary people at all. So cheer up – you can't help being a genius. Personally, I think you're working too hard.'

Anne-Marie listened to this sympathetic speech with sniffles and a discontented look. She thought herself just as much a genius as Felicity – but nobody ever talked to *her* like that! Nobody ever called her a genius, except Angela – and Angela really didn't know the difference between a nursery rhyme and a great poem! Life seemed very hard to poor Anne-Marie just then.

'Perhaps,' thought Anne-Marie, suddenly, 'perhaps if I do some odd things, like Felicity does, the girls will realize I'm a genius too. It's worth trying, anyway – so long as I don't get myself into a row. It's no good doing anything in Miss Willcox's class – after Felicity's performance it would be silly.'

She cheered up a little and went out for break. Felicity would not go out. She was intent on finishing the writing out of the play, so that she could once more give her mind freely to the music that seemed always all around her. Felicity was finding things very hard that term. The work in the fifth form was more difficult than in the fourth, and there was the strain of the exam to face. She was also working even harder at her music, and very often could not sleep at night.

Mirabel also was working very hard at the sports standard of the whole school. She wanted to raise the standard of the lacrosse so that even the fourth and third teams would win all their matches. What a feather it would be in her cap, if she did!

Gladys did not approve of all this intense drive for high efficiency in games and gym and running practice. 'You're trying to do too much too quickly,' she said to Mirabel. 'You'll get much better results if you go more slowly, Mirabel. Look at this practice list of yours for the first form. You'll make them all fed up with games if you insist on so much time being given to them.'

'Do them good,' said Mirabel, intent on the second-form list. 'These kids ought to be very grateful for the interest I take in them. That Jane Teal, for instance – she is ten times better since she did what I told her and put in more practice. She's the best catcher in the first form.'

'Well, you can drive people like Jane Teal, who always want to do the best they can for anyone they like,' said Gladys, 'but you can't drive everyone. Some just get obstinate. I think you're not at all sensible with some of the fourth formers – and you really ought to know better than to go after people like Carlotta and Angela and Claudine.'

'I wish you wouldn't always find fault with me, Gladys,' said Mirabel, impatiently. 'You're quite different from what you used to be. You used to like being guided by me, you said I was the strong one, and you quite looked up to me.'

'I know,' said Gladys, 'and I do now. I only wish I had half your strength of will and purpose, Mirabel. But as I accepted the post of vice-captain, which does bring with it the responsibility of sharing with you most of your decisions, I can't sit back and not say things I ought to say. I don't *want* to say them – I know you won't like some of them – but I'd be a very poor thing if I *didn't* say them.'

Mirabel really was surprised at Gladys. Always she had been the leader of the two and Gladys had followed meekly and willingly. It was something new for Mirabel to find Gladys sticking up for her own ideas, and actually going against her sometimes! Mirabel should have admired her quiet friend for this, but instead, glorying in her position of sports captain, she only felt resentful.

'I mean to make St Clare's the best sports school in the country,' she said obstinately. 'I shan't listen to any excuses of overwork or tiredness from anyone. They'll just have to put as much into their games as they do into their school work.'

'Everyone is not as big and strong as you are,' said Gladys, looking at the huge, strapping girl. 'I don't wonder you are going to train as a games mistress. You're just cut out for it! You could take gym and games the whole day long and then go for a ten-mile walk in the evening! But do, do remember, Mirabel, old thing, that youngsters like Jane Teal really haven't the strength to do all *you* do!'

Jane Teal had most conscientiously done all that Mirabel had asked her, for she was a loyal and hard-working girl. She felt proud when Mirabel told her that she was now the best at ball-catching in lacrosse in the whole of her big form.

But she had never stopped worrying about Angela, and she longed to make up the quarrel with her, and do things for her again. She sat in prep and debated things in her mind. How could she become friends with Angela again? How could she do her jobs instead of Violet, who, after the upset with Antoinette, had been taken back into favour again. She could not for the life of her think how to get back into Angela's good books.

'You seem to be lost in dreams, Jane,' said Miss Roberts's voice. 'I can't think you are doing your maths, with that faraway expression on your face.'

'I – I was just thinking of something,' said Jane,

embarrassed, and bent her head to her work.

The next day Violet went down with a very bad cold, and was taken off to the sick-bay by Matron, sniffling and feeling very sorry for herself. She called to Jane as she went.

'Find that school story for me, and my new jigsaw puzzle and bring them in some time to me,' she said, and Jane promised she would. Accordingly she went to Violet's locker after morning school, and looked for the things she wanted.

She found them – and she also found two pairs of Angela's stockings, and two blouses, all wanting quite a lot of mending. She stared at them.

Violet would be away from school for three or four days. Should she, Jane, do the mending, and take it back to Angela, and ask if she might take Violet's place till she came back? It would be lovely to go to her study again, and tidy up the beautiful place, look at the pictures on the wall, fill the vases with water – do all the things she loved doing. Angela would smile at her again, and everything would be all right.

Jane mended everything beautifully, spending all her free time on the stockings and the blouses. Some of her free time should have been spent in learning a part in a play the first form were doing. How could she learn it, when she had to go to bed early, like all the other first formers?

'I'll take my torch to bed with me, and when the others are asleep, I'll switch it on under the bedclothes and learn my part then,' thought Jane. She was pleased at having thought of such a good way out. No one would know. She did not think of how tired she would feel the next day!

She took the things to Angela that afternoon when Angela sent for Violet. She went in timidly, her heart beating fast, for she was afraid of Angela's sneers and snubs.

Alison was there alone. She was surprised to see Jane. 'Hallo, kid,' she said. 'Where's Violet?'

'In the sick-bay with a cold,' said Jane. 'I mended Angela's things instead. Where is she, Alison?'

'Having a talk with Mirabel,' said Alison. Mirabel had been having serious talks with all the fifth form that day, asking them to help her in making the sports standard for St Clare's much higher. She would certainly not have much success with Angela, who detested getting hot and untidy!

'Oh,' said Jane, disappointed, and put the mended stockings and blouses down. Then her face brightened, for Angela came into the room and shut the door violently. She looked cross.

'That idiot of a Mirabel!' she said to Alison, not seeing Jane at first. 'She wants to turn us all into tomboys like herself, great strapping creatures, striding along instead of walking, shouting instead of speaking, playing . . .'

'Jane is here,' said Alison, warningly. Angela turned and saw her. She still looked cross, and Jane hastened to explain why she was there.

'Violet's ill, please Angela,' she said. 'So I have done your mending myself. I hope you don't mind. I – I – would like to do it for you again, if you'll let me.'

Angela stared at Jane unsmilingly. 'But what about dear

Mirabel, and her anxiety to make you into a wonderful little sportswoman?' she said in a mocking voice.

'I can do both,' said Jane, anxiously. 'I can make time for my work, and my games and for anything you'd like me to do too.'

Angela knew it would annoy Mirabel if she heard that she was making Jane spend her time on all kinds of jobs for her. So she nodded her head and gave the girl a slight smile, which was Heaven to Jane.

'All right,' she said. 'I'll have you again. I'm tired of that silly Violet anyway, with her big cow's eyes. You can come instead.'

Filled with delight Jane sped off. Everything was all right again! The wonderful Angela had smiled at her! She didn't mind if she had to work in bed every night so long as Angela went on being nice to her.

Mirabel makes herself a nuisance

Mirabel was really making herself a nuisance just then, especially with the fifth form, who were working very hard indeed for the exam. She was trying to get them interested in the younger ones, to make them go and take practice games with them. They objected to this very much.

'It's a silly idea,' said Pat. 'Those babies much prefer to practise on their own. They don't like being chivvied about by us big ones.'

'Besides, we've got to *work,*' said Hilary, exasperated. 'I can't imagine when you do any extra work for the exam, Mirabel – I'm sure you spend all your evenings in your study, preparing your sports lists and lists for matches, and goodness knows what.'

It was true that Mirabel was doing very little extra work. She was trusting to scrape through the exam, but she did not care whether she got good marks or not. Her whole soul was in the running of the school games, and she often annoyed the games mistress intensely. But Mirabel's thick skin made her quite invulnerable to cutting remarks or snubs.

'She just drives on like a tank,' said Bobby. 'Nobody can stop her. She'll have us all trailing after her helping her in her sports ideas just because we're so tired of arguing with her.'

'You can't argue with Mirabel,' said Doris. 'She never listens to a word anyone says. I doubt if she even listens to Gladys now. It's a pity Gladys isn't a stronger character. She might have some influence over our headstrong Mirabel!'

'Gladys *used* to have influence over her,' said Pat. 'Do you remember when Mirabel first came to St Clare's and was rude and defiant, and said she wouldn't stay longer than half-term, whatever happened?'

'Yes,' said Isabel, remembering. 'She was simply unbearable – quite unreasonable. And it was the little Mouse, Gladys, who got her round, and made her stay on, and become quite a decent member of St Clare's.'

'But Mirabel has got a swelled-head now she's sports captain,' said Bobby. 'Gladys can't do anything with her. I heard her arguing with Mirabel the other day, and all that happened was that Mirabel got angry and shut her up.'

'I have never liked this Mirabel of yours,' remarked Claudine, who had consistently got out of games and gym whenever she could, all the time she had been at St Clare's. 'She is always hunting me here, there and everywhere, calling upon me to do this and that.'

The girls smiled. Claudine usually found it quite easy to evade people who wanted her to do something she disliked, but few people were so persistent as Mirabel. No matter where Claudine hid herself, Mirabel would run her to earth, produce a list of games and try to pin Claudine down to a practice.

'Yesterday, in my great despair, I went to speak to Miss Theobald,' said Claudine, raising her eyebrows and her shoulders in an amusing way. 'There was Mirabel close behind me, waving a great list, and there was I, taking to my toes.'

'Heels,' said Bobby, laughing.

'I run fast,' said Claudine, 'and I find myself outside Miss Theobald's door. What shall I do to get away from this dreadful Mirabel? I knock at the door. I go in!'

The girls were amused and wondered what Claudine could have found so suddenly to say to Miss Theobald.

'What excuse did you make?' asked Janet.

'I held a long conversation with Miss Theobald,' said Claudine, solemnly. 'Ah, we talked, and we talked, whilst the poor Mirabel, she waited patiently outside the door!'

'What on earth did you talk about?' said Bobby, curiously.

Claudine looked mischievous. 'There was no Miss Theobald there!' she said. 'I talked to myself, and then I talked again as if I was answering. The door was shut. How could the good, patient Mirabel know that only I, Claudine, was in the room?'

'Was Mirabel outside the door when you went out?' said Bobby.

'Alas – Miss Theobald herself came to the door when Mirabel was still standing there,' said Claudine. 'The poor Mirabel! She must have been so surprised to see Miss

Theobald, as surprised as I was suddenly to hear her voice outside the door. Me, I did not stay in the room any longer. I jumped out of the window. The gardener was there, and he too jumped – how do you say it – he jumped out of his skin.'

The girls yelled at the thought of Claudine jumping out of Miss Theobald's window in order to avoid both Mirabel and Miss Theobald. None of the others, except perhaps Carlotta, would have thought of doing such a thing.

'You really are the limit,' said Bobby.

'What is this "limit" that you are always talking of?' inquired Claudine.

'Never mind. What happened next?' said Hilary, who always enjoyed Claudine's pranks.

'Ah, well – I went in at the side-door,' said Claudine, 'and I heard Miss Theobald and Mirabel being most surprised at each other. Miss Theobald said, "My dear Mirabel, how can Claudine be talking to me in the sitting-room if I am here, outside the door? Do not be foolish."'

The girls giggled. 'Didn't Miss Theobald open the door?' asked Janet.

'Yes,' said Claudine, 'and there was no one in the room. Ah, it was good to see poor Mirabel's face then! So surprised it was, so puzzled. And Miss Theobald, she was quite cross.'

'Did Mirabel ask you what had happened?' said Pat, grinning.

'Ah, yes – she asks me so many times,' said Claudine. And I say, 'I do not understand, Mirabel. Speak to me in

French. But the poor Mirabel, her French is so bad I do not understand that either!'

'Sh – here *is* Mirabel,' said Pauline, as the sports captain came into the room. You always knew when Mirabel was coming – she walked heavily, she flung doors open, and her voice was loud and confident. She came towards the girls.

'I say,' she said, 'I've just got Miss Theobald's permission to call a big sports meeting tomorrow night in the assembly hall. Seven o'clock. It's to discuss all the matches this term – and there are some jolly important ones. Seven o'clock, don't forget. And I shall expect every member of the fifth form to be there. The younger girls are all coming, of course, and it wouldn't do to let them see any of us slacking or not attending the meeting.'

'Yes, but Mirabel – it's Saturday night, and you know we were going to have a dance,' protested Angela. 'You *know* that. It was all arranged. The third and fourth form were coming too. It was to be real fun.'

'Well, I put the meeting tomorrow night because the dance isn't a bit important and the meeting *is*,' said Mirabel. 'We can have a dance any other Saturday. But I've got quite a lot of new ideas to put before the school. I've been working them all out.'

'You might ask *us* if we would agree to exchanging a dance for your silly meeting,' said Alison. 'You're so jolly high-handed! I shan't come to the meeting. I've got better things to do.'

Mirabel looked shocked. How could there be better

things to do than attend a sports meeting, and discuss the ins and outs of matches? She stared at Alison and frowned.

'You've got to come,' she said. 'Miss Theobald said I could arrange the meeting, and tell everyone to attend. It won't take long.'

'You always say that – but your meetings take hours,' said Carlotta. 'You stand up and talk and talk and talk. I shan't come.'

'I shall report anyone who doesn't,' said Mirabel, beginning to look angry.

'Mirabel – put the meeting another time,' said Hilary. 'You're only getting everyone's back up. You really are. We want a little fun tomorrow night. We've all worked hard this week.'

'I'm sorry,' said Mirabel, stiffly. 'The meeting will be held tomorrow night, and nothing will prevent it, not even *your* wish, my dear Hilary. You may be head of the form, but I am head of the whole school for sports.'

She went out and shut the door loudly. She knew the girls would say hard things about her, but she didn't care. She meant to have her way. The girls would thank her all right when every single match against other schools was won! She would put St Clare's at the top.

'She has a wasp in her hat, that girl,' said Claudine, disgusted.

'A bee in her bonnet, you mean,' said Pat. 'How you do get things mixed up, Claudine! Yes, old Mirabel certainly has got a bee in her bonnet – its sports, sports, sports with her all the time, and everyone else has got to be dragged into it too. I love games – but honestly, I find myself not wanting to turn out on the field now, simply because I know Mirabel will be there, ready to check all shirkers and late-comers!'

'Shall we *have* to go to this beastly boring meeting?' said Felicity. 'I wanted to work at my music.'

'And I wanted to finish my new poem,' said Anne-Marie at once.

'We'll have to go, if Miss Theobald has agreed to let Mirabel call the meeting,' said Hilary, reluctantly. 'I suppose she told Miss Theobald that we were all keen on the meeting. It's a nuisance – but we'll have to turn up.'

'Maybe the meeting will not be held after all,' said Claudine.

'Not a hope,' said Bobby. 'I know Mirabel. Once she makes up her mind about something, that something happens. She's a born dictator. She'll be appalling in the sixth form!'

'I think maybe the meeting will not happen after all,' said Claudine, looking dreamily into space.

'What do you mean?' said Bobby.

'I have a feeling here,' said Claudine, pressing a hand to her tummy. 'It tells me, this feeling, that something will stop the meeting tomorrow night. What can it be?'

Hilary looked suspiciously at Claudine, who was wearing one of her most innocent and angelic expressions. Claudine returned her look with candid wide-open eyes.

'Are you planning anything?' said Hilary. 'Because if so, don't. You can't meddle with things like school meetings once you're a fifth former.'

'How true!' said Claudine, with a sigh, and went off to her study with Carlotta.

That night, when everyone in Claudine's room was asleep, the little French girl slipped out of bed and went along the corridor. She went down the stairs and soon returned with something that shone brightly each time she passed under a dimmed light. She deposited it in an unused chest outside the dormitory door, covered it with an old rug, and then slipped along another corridor to the dormitory in which her sister Antoinette slept.

She awoke Antoinette by a light touch, and knelt by her sister's bed to whisper.

'*Oui, oui,*' whispered back Antoinette. 'Yes! Yes, Claudine, I will do as you say. Do not fear. It will be done!'

Claudine slipped back to bed like a little white ghost. She climbed between the sheets, grinning to herself. Dear Mirabel, it will be difficult for you to hold your meeting tomorrow, poor Mirabel, you will be disappointed, foolish Mirabel, you cannot get the better of the little French Claudine! With these pleasant thoughts Claudine fell fast asleep.

The meeting is spoilt

The third, fourth, and fifth forms were very much annoyed and upset by Mirabel's command to attend the sports meeting on Saturday night. They had looked forward to the dance so much – it was just like Mirabel to spoil everything!

'She walks about with those long strides of hers as if she owns the whole school,' said Belinda of the fourth form.

'I used to like games but now I'm getting fed up with them,' complained Rita of the third form. 'Mirabel ticks me off in public on the field as if I were one of the first form. I won't stand it!'

But she did stand it because Mirabel was a very strong personality determined to get her own way. She was using her power to the utmost and beyond.

The fifth formers all put away their various occupations that Saturday night as seven o'clock drew near. They grumbled as they shut their books, rolled up their knitting, put away their letters. But not one of them refused to go when the time came, for they knew that, as fifth formers, they must turn up even if only as a good example to the younger ones.

Mirabel was standing on the platform of the assembly

hall, running through the list of things she meant to say. She glanced up as the girls came filing in, her quick eyes watching to see that everyone turned up. Woe betide any unlucky first or second former who did not arrive! Mirabel would be after them the next day!

Antoinette came up to Mirabel. The sports captain glanced up impatiently. 'What is it, Antoinette?'

'Please, Mirabel, may the second form have a new ball to practise with?' said Antoinette. 'It seems that we have lost the one we had, and we are oh, so keen to practise hard for you.'

'Hm,' said Mirabel, rather disbelievingly, for Antoinette could not by any means have been called keen on games. 'Why didn't Violet come to me about it?'

'Violet is in the sick-bay,' said Antoinette.

'Well, come to me on Monday about the ball. I can't possibly deal with matters like that now,' said Mirabel. 'You ought to know better than to come just before an important meeting like this.'

'Yes, Mirabel,' said Antoinette, and sidled away. Mirabel thought of her with exasperation. She was a slacker, just like Claudine – but she would pin her down and make her play games properly if it took her three terms to do it!

The girls all filed in. Mirabel caught sight of Jane Teal in the first-form benches, looking rather pale. Jane was gazing at Angela, who was looking very beautiful that evening. She had had her hair washed, and it glistened like finest gold. Mirabel frowned. She wished that Jane and the other first formers would stop raving about that foolish Angela!

She ran her eyes over the fifth form. They all seemed to be there – but wait a minute, where was Felicity?

Mirabel spoke to Anne-Marie, who was passing by the platform at that moment. 'Where's Felicity?'

'She's coming, Mirabel,' said Anne-Marie, shortly, for she, like everyone else, resented giving up a jolly dance for a dull meeting. 'She had some music to finish copying out. She said she was just coming.'

'Well, I shall begin without her,' said Mirabel. 'She's always unpunctual. Such a bad example for the younger ones! It's a minute past seven already.'

Everyone was now in their seats. There was a great shuffling of feet, and an outbreak of coughing from the second form, who were a very lively lot this term.

Mirabel went to the front of the platform. She looked enormous there. She began very self-confidently, for she was seldom at a loss for words when her beloved games were the subject.

'Good evening, girls,' she began, in her loud, determined voice. 'I have called this important meeting here tonight for a very special reason. I want to make St Clare's the head of all the schools in the kingdom in their proficiency at games of all kinds. I want us to have hockey as well, I want us to . . .'

There came an interruption. A first-form girl stood up and stopped Mirabel.

'Jane isn't well. She says she won't leave the meeting,

but she must, mustn't she?'

It was Sally, Jane Teal's friend. Everyone turned to look at poor Jane, who, white in the face, felt quite faint with embarrassment.

'Take her out, Sally,' said Mirabel, rather impatiently. She did not like being interrupted in her opening speech. Sally helped Jane out. 'Are you going to be sick?' she asked in a loud whisper, which embarrassed poor Jane even more. She was terribly upset at holding up Mirabel's meeting, but she really did feel strange.

The two went out, and Mirabel resumed her speech, which went on for three or four minutes. 'I want us to win all our lacrosse matches, I want us to form a hockey team that is unbeatable, I want us to . . .'

But what else Mirabel wanted nobody ever knew. There came a sudden and unusual noise that made everyone jump violently. It was the loud clanging of the school fire-bell!

Clang! Clang! Clang! Clang!

Mirabel stopped and listened, startled. Fire! This was not just a practice alarm she was sure – Miss Theobald would never choose a time like this for an unexpected fire-practice; she knew there was an important meeting being held.

The first and second formers looked uneasily at one another, and then looked for a lead from the older ones. There were no mistresses present.

Hilary stood up, her face quite calm. 'Help me to get the first and seconds out quietly,' she said to the twins and to Janet and Bobby. 'We'll march them into the grounds, out by the side door.'

Mirabel also took quick command. Her strong voice rang out reassuringly.

'That's the school fire-bell. You all know what to do. Stand, please.'

The girls stood, glad to have a leader. Mirabel saw that Hilary, the twins, Bobby and Janet had moved across to the younger girls, and she saw that she could expect the utmost help from them. Some of the first formers looked rather scared.

'Right turn!' roared Mirabel. 'Follow Hilary Wentworth. *March*!'

In perfect order, without any panic at all, the first and second forms marched out, led by Hilary, who undid the garden door and went into the grounds. It was a dark night, but the girls knew the grounds well.

Pat and Isabel took out the second form. Bobby and Janet, and the head girl of the third form then marched off with that form. The fourth formers followed with the fifth, sniffing the air eagerly to see if they could smell smoke.

'Where's the fire?' cried Belinda. 'I can't see a sign anywhere!'

Mirabel went out of the hall last, pleased to find that she could handle an emergency so efficiently. Her loud confident voice had at once instilled trust into every girl. She wondered where the fire was.

The first of the mistresses to arrive on the scene was

Mam'zelle. Miss Theobald was out, and the French Mistress had been left in charge for that evening. The loud, distressed voice of Mam'zelle was heard long before she appeared in the doorway.

'Ah! Where are the girls? Yes, yes – in the assembly hall. To think that a fire should come when Miss Theobald is out! Girls, where are you? Claudine, Antoinette, show yourselves to me, I pray you! Are you safe?'

'Quite safe!' came Claudine's amused voice, and then Antoinette left the darkness of the grounds and went to where Mam'zelle stood in the doorway. 'I too am safe,' she said in her demure voice.

Mam'zelle threw her arms round Antoinette as if she had rescued her from flames. 'Ah, my little Antoinette! Do not be afraid. I am here, your strong Aunt Mathilde!'

'Where's the fire, Mam'zelle?' called a voice.

'Ah, the fire! Where is it?' repeated Mam'zelle, still feeling rather dazed.

Then Matron appeared on the scene, and took command at once. She had sped round the school immediately she had heard the fire-bell, to see where the fire could be. She had been to the place where the fire-bell was kept to see who was ringing it – but the fire-bell was standing in its place, and no one was near it!

She was puzzled, but as her nose, eyes and ears told her that certainly there was no fire raging anywhere near she felt sure that someone had been playing a joke. Matron had been long enough at St Clare's to smell a joke a mile away by now.

'Girls, come in at once!' she said, in her crisp, cool voice. 'There is no fire. But I must congratulate you on responding to the bell so quickly and quietly, and going out of doors in this sensible way.'

'Well, we were all at a meeting,' said Hilary, who was near the door. 'It was easy. We just marched out. But Matron – who rang the bell then?'

'We shall no doubt find that out later,' said Matron, drily. 'In the meantime, please march indoors again.'

The girls all marched in. Some of them were shivering, for it was a cold night. Matron saw this and hoped the sick-bay would not be inundated with people having colds the following week!

She looked at her watch and made up her mind quickly. 'You will all go to your common-rooms and your studies at once,' she said. 'Head girls, make up the fires in the common-rooms, please, and see that the rooms are warm. In ten minutes' time come to the kitchen, two girls from each form, and there will be jugs of hot cocoa ready, which I want you all to drink as soon as possible.'

This was pleasant news. The girls hurried in, glad to think of warm fires and hot cocoa. But Mirabel was annoyed. She spoke to Matron.

'Matron, I'm sorry, but I'm afraid the girls must go back to the hall. We were just beginning a most important meeting. Shall I tell them or will you?'

Matron looked hard at the self-confident Mirabel. 'We shall neither of us tell them,' she said. 'You heard what I said to them. They've had a spell out there in the cold and I don't want them to get chills. There will be no meeting tonight.'

'Hurrah!' said one or two low voices, as the girls hurrying in heard this welcome news. 'Good old Matron.'

Mirabel ought to have known that one person she could never flout was Matron. She began to argue. 'But, Matron – this is a most important meeting. I shall have to go to Miss Theobald, I'm afraid, and ask her for her authority to continue my meeting, if you won't give the girls permission.'

'Very well. Go and ask her,' said Matron, who knew quite well that Miss Theobald was out. So off went Mirabel, angry and determined, bitterly disappointed that her wonderful meeting was spoilt.

But Miss Theobald was not in her sitting-room. It was most annoying. Mirabel hardly dared to go back and take up the matter with Matron again. She had not at all liked the tone of Matron's voice. Her spirits sank and she felt rather miserable.

Then her face grew grim. 'Well, I shall find out who rang that bell and spoilt my meeting, anyway! And won't I give them a dressing-down – in front of the whole school, too!'

Who rang the fire-bell?

Mirabel went storming to her study. Gladys was there, warming herself in front of a cheerful little fire.

'Pity the meeting was spoilt,' she said, thinking that Mirabel would be in need of a little comfort about it. 'You were making a very good speech, Mirabel.'

'Gladys, who do you think rang that fire-bell?' said Mirabel, grimly. 'Is that cocoa in the jug? I'll have a cup. Not that I'm cold, but I do feel a bit upset at having the meeting completely spoilt by some silly idiot who thinks it clever to play a practical joke like that.'

Gladys said nothing. She had no idea at all who the culprit could be. Mirabel stirred her cocoa violently, and went on talking.

'Who wasn't there? Well, Felicity wasn't, of course! Gladys, could it have been Felicity?'

'Of course not,' said Gladys. 'I don't suppose Felicity even knows there is a fire-bell, let alone where it is!'

'Well – I shall certainly find out where she was all the time,' said Mirabel. 'This is really the sort of idiotic joke Claudine would play – but she was there all the time. I saw her myself – and Antoinette was there too, because she came up and spoke to me at the beginning of the meeting.'

'And she was out in the grounds with the others,' said Gladys, remembering. 'Didn't you see her go up to Mam'zelle and speak to her when Mam'zelle yelled out for Claudine and Antoinette?'

'Yes,' said Mirabel, frowning. 'Well, who else wasn't there? Violet is in the sick-bay. Everyone else was there as far as I can remember. I ticked people off as they came in, because I wasn't going to let anyone get out of the meeting if I could help it.'

Gladys offered no suggestion. Mirabel suddenly slapped the table hard and made Gladys jump. 'Don't, Mirabel,' she said. 'Don't be so violent.'

Mirabel took no notice. 'Of course – Jane Teal went out, didn't she – and Sally. Do you think either of them would have done it?'

'I shouldn't think so for a moment,' said Gladys. 'Why, Jane is very fond of you, and Sally is far too sensible to do a thing like that.'

'I shall find out,' said Mirabel, her face hard. Gladys looked rather distressed.

'Don't go about it too angrily,' she said. 'You'll only put people's backs up.'

'I don't care if I do,' said Mirabel, and she didn't. Gladys sighed. If only Mirabel did care a little more about other people's feelings, she would find them easier to tackle. She was always complaining that people would not co-operate with her or help her.

Mirabel gulped down her cocoa. 'I'm going off to Felicity's study first,' she said. 'See you later.'

She went out of the room. Gladys took up some knitting. She was making a jumper for her mother, and she had very little spare time for it, with all her exam work, sports work, and Mirabel's incessant demands to cope with. She couldn't help feeling rather glad that she had an unexpected hour to get on with her knitting!

Mirabel went into Felicity's study. Felicity was there, trying her violin softly, whilst Anne-Marie sat over the fire, a pencil and notebook on her knee, trying to compose a wonderful new poem. She kept frowning at Felicity's soft playing, but Felicity was quite unaware of Anne-Marie's frowns or even of Anne-Marie herself. She jumped violently when Mirabel came into the room.

Then, thinking she had come to see Anne-Marie, she went on with her soft playing. Mirabel spoke to her roughly.

'Felicity, why weren't you at the sports meeting this evening?'

Felicity looked startled. 'Oh, Mirabel – I'm so sorry. I really did mean to come, and I forgot all about it! I was playing my violin, and somehow forgot I had said I would go! How awful of me!'

'Where were you when the fire-bell went?' said Mirabel.

'Fire-bell?' said Felicity, looking astonished. 'What fire-bell?'

'She never hears anything but her music when she's really wrapped up in it,' said Anne-Marie. 'You know how she behaved in class the other day, Mirabel. I don't expect she heard the bell at all.'

'I didn't,' said Felicity, looking really bewildered now.

'Did it ring? Was there a fire? What happened?'

'Oh, you're hopeless,' said Mirabel, and went out of the study. Felicity stared at Anne-Marie, who made an impatient noise, stuffed her fingers in her ears, and tried to go on with her poem.

Mirabel went to find Jane Teal and Sally. They were in the first-form common-room, Jane still looking rather pale, but better. She flushed when Mirabel came in, quite thinking that the sports captain had come to see how she was.

But Mirabel hadn't. She came straight to the point. 'Jane and Sally – did either of you ring the fire-bell when you left the meeting?'

The girls stared at her in surprise. It would not have occurred to either of them to spoil such an important meeting! Jane felt very hurt to think that Mirabel should imagine her to be capable of such a thing.

'Well – haven't either of you tongues?' said Mirabel. The whole of the first form had now gathered round the three, and were listening with the greatest interest.

'Of *course* we didn't,' said Sally, indignantly. 'As if we'd do a thing like that! Anyway, poor Jane was feeling awfully ill. She had a terrible headache. She's always having headaches.'

'Shut up, Sally,' said Jane, who knew that Mirabel did not look very kindly on such things as headaches.

'Did you leave Jane alone at all?' said Mirabel to Sally. 'Yes – you came back to the meeting without her, didn't you? Then she could easily have slipped out of your common-room and rung the bell, couldn't she?'

'*Oh*!' said Sally, really indignant. 'As if Jane would do a mean thing like that! Yes, I did leave her here as she seemed a bit better and I went back to the meeting – and as soon as I sat down, the bell rang. But it wasn't Jane ringing it.'

Jane was terribly upset to think that Mirabel should even think she could spoil a meeting of hers. Her lips trembled, and she could not trust herself to speak.

'Now don't burst into tears like a baby,' said Mirabel to Jane. 'I'm not saying you *did* do it – I'm only saying that you had the *chance* to do it. It just puzzles me to know who could have done it, because everybody was at the meeting, except you and Felicity – and I'm pretty certain that Felicity didn't even know St Clare's possessed such a thing as a fire-bell!'

'Well, it looks as if I must have done the deed then,' said Jane, bitterly, trying to keep the tears out of her eyes. 'Think it was me, if you like. I don't care!'

'Now that's not the way to talk to your sports captain,' said Mirabel. 'I'm surprised at you, Jane. Well, I suppose I shall find out one day who rang that bell.'

She went out of the room and shut the door unnecessarily loudly. The first formers looked at one another.

'Beast,' said Sally. 'I shan't do one single minute's more lacrosse practice than I can help!'

'Nor shall I,' said Hilda, and the others all agreed, Jane mopped her eyes, and the others comforted her.

'Never mind, Jane. Don't you worry about it. We all know you didn't do it!'

'I wish I knew who *had* done it,' said Sally, her eyes sparkling. 'I'd go and pat her on the back and say, "Jolly good show!" '

The others laughed and agreed. It was strange how in a few short weeks Mirabel had changed from an object of great admiration into one of detestation.

Miss Theobald had to be told about the strange ringing of the fire-bell, apparently done by nobody at all. She was rather inclined to take a serious view of it and Mirabel was pleased.

'I am glad you too think it is a serious matter to have an important, pre-arranged meeting completely spoilt by somebody's stupid ragging,' said Mirabel.

'Oh, dear me, I was not thinking of your meeting,' was Miss Theobald's rather damping reply. 'I was thinking that I cannot have the fire-bell rung without proper cause. If it is, then the girls will not take warning when the bell is rung for a real fire. That is a very serious matter – not the interruption of your meeting.'

'Oh,' said Mirabel, rather crest-fallen. 'Well, could I have the meeting next Saturday night instead, Miss Theobald?'

'I'm afraid not,' said the head mistress. 'The heads of the third, fourth and fifth forms have already been to me to ask me if they may have the postponed dance then, Mirabel. I don't think we can possibly expect them to postpone it again. These forms are working very hard this term, and very well. I want them to relax when they can.'

Mirabel left Miss Theobald, angry and depressed.

She went into her study and sat down at the table to do some work. 'What's the matter?' said Gladys.

'Hilary and the head girls of the third and fourth have been to Miss Theobald behind my back and got her to say they could have their dance this coming Saturday,' said Mirabel, gloomily. 'It's absolutely the only chance I have of getting the whole school together on Saturday evenings, and they know it. Deceitful beasts!'

'Don't be silly,' said Gladys, feeling a wave of anger. 'They probably never even *imagined* you'd actually want them to give up *another* Saturday evening. Do be sensible, Mirabel. And look here – why have you left little Jane Teal out of next week's matches? She's very good and you know it. It will break her heart to be left out, when you've as good as told her she might play.'

'I'm not satisfied that she didn't have something to do with the ringing of that bell,' said Mirabel.

'*Well*!' said Gladys, exasperated. 'You might at least wait till you *are* sure, before you punish her like this. I think she's a very decent little kid, I must say, and I'm dead certain she wouldn't do a thing like that.'

'Look here, *I'm* captain, not you!' said Mirabel, losing her temper. 'I keep *on* having to remind you of that. I won't have you preaching at me and interfering.'

Gladys went rather white. She hated rows of any sort, and always found it difficult to stand up to Mirabel for any length of time. She took up a book and said no more. Mirabel took up a book too, and looked at it frowning. But she did not see a word that was printed there. She was turning over and over in her mind the same question – WHO rang that fire-bell?

She would have been interested in a little conversation between Claudine and Antoinette if she could have heard it.

'Very good, *ma petite*,' Claudine remarked to Antoinette. 'It was good to show yourself so well to Mirabel at the beginning of the meeting, and to appear out in the grounds when *tante* Mathilde called us. There is no one who thinks of you, no one at all.'

'Clang, clang, clang!' said Antoinette, her dark eyes gleaming with mischief. 'I felt like the old town crier at home. Clang, clang, clang, the meeting will not be held, clang, clang, clang! Ah, it is a good bell to ring!'

'Sh. Here come the others,' said Claudine. 'Slip away, Antoinette. Be sure *I* will help *you* if you want me to, since you have done this thing for me.'

Some of the fifth formers came up. 'What mischief are you thinking of?' said Bobby to Claudine. 'You look pleased.'

'I was remembering how I said, "I feel as if there will be no sports meeting,"' said Claudine. 'And I was right, was I not, Bobbee?'

The term goes on

The girls soon forgot about the strange ringing of the fire-bell – all except Mirabel, who felt sure Jane must have done it. In fact, she went even further in her thoughts and suspected Angela of having put Jane up to doing it! She took no notice at all of poor Jane, left her out of the matches, and altogether made her life miserable.

Angela tried to make things up to Jane, delighted at the chance of making a fuss of somebody neglected by Mirabel. Poor Jane was in a great state of mind, upset because Mirabel was unkind to her, thrilled because Angela was sweet to her, and overtired with all her learning in bed at night with the light of her torch.

She had headaches, felt terribly sleepy all the day, and could not see properly, for she was spoiling her eyesight by reading in bed by the dim light of the torch.

She was not the only one with headaches just then. Felicity, always more or less afflicted with them, was having them almost continuously. Also, to Anne-Marie's alarm, Felicity had begun to walk in her sleep at night!

This was something that Felicity had done as a child, when her mind was over-taxed, and now she had begun to do it again. Anne-Marie slept in the bed next to

Felicity's, and was awakened one night to see a dim white figure stealing out of the door. She sat up and switched on her torch. Felicity's bed was empty!

Has she gone to the study to do some more work? thought Anne-Marie. What an idiot she is! I'd better go and get her. She'll get into an awful row if Miss Cornwallis finds out.

Anne-Marie flung her dressing-gown round her shoulders and went after Felicity. To her surprise Felicity did not go in the direction of their study. Instead she went down the stairs and into the assembly room. She climbed up the platform steps, and stood in the middle of the platform.

'Felicity!' whispered Anne-Marie, astonished. 'What are you doing? Felicity!'

Felicity took absolutely no notice at all. She bowed gracefully, took a step backwards and then raised her arms as if she was playing a violin. It was strange to see her in the light of the moon that shone through a nearby window.

Up and down went Felicity's right arm, as the girl played an imaginary tune on an imaginary violin. Her eyes were wide open, fixed and staring. Anne-Marie shivered to see them.

She went up the steps and touched Felicity on the arm. The girl made no response. She went on with her tuneless playing, and then bowed as if she had finished. Anne-Marie took her by the arm. To her surprise Felicity came quite readily with her.

'Are you awake or asleep, Felicity?' said Anne-Marie, fearfully, as they went up the stairs. There was no reply. Felicity was fast asleep, though her eyes were wide open.

Anne-Marie took her safely to her bed and got her in. Felicity cuddled down, shut her eyes and breathed deeply. Anne-Marie got into bed too, but lay awake a long time puzzling over Felicity's sleep-walking.

'It must be because she's a genius,' thought the jealous Anne-Marie. 'She does odd things, as all geniuses seem to do. Sleep-walking must be a sign of genius, I suppose. I wish I did unusual things too. Then maybe everyone would think I was a genius – as I am! Suppose I start a little sleep-walking of my own? If only the girls would wake up and see it, it would be a good way of showing them I'm a genius too. But they all sleep so soundly!'

Still, it was an idea, and Anne-Marie pondered over it a good deal, making up her mind that when a suitable chance came she too would sleep-walk!

Felicity did not remember anything about her sleep-walking the next day and was half inclined to disbelieve Anne-Marie's account of it. She shrugged her shoulders, and went off to her music lesson. She could not find interest in anything but her beloved music these days.

Anne-Marie was still trying her best to win back Miss Willcox's smiles – but as the only way she knew was by pestering her to read her poems, she was not very successful. She so badly wanted praise and admiration for her talents that she did not see that Miss Willcox only had time for those who gave praise and admiration to *her*!

Miss Willcox was in many ways a grown-up Anne-Marie, posing and posturing, soaking up adulation and flattery from anyone who would give it to her. She had no time for people like Anne-Marie, who also demanded it.

For this reason Alison was very much her favourite. Alison had a real gift for making herself a willing slave to people of Miss Willcox's type. Like Jane for Angela, Alison was pleased to do all kinds of jobs at all kinds of hours, if she could please her idol. Miss Willcox took advantage of this, and kept the devoted Alison quite busy.

'It's a pity,' said her cousins. 'She's even beginning to dress like Miss Willcox – rather untidy and bitty!'

So she was. She would appear in class with a startling belt round her slim waist, or a scarf round her neck, and had even managed to get some pins rather like Miss Willcox wore in her hair – only Alison's were gilt-topped, not gold!

'Dear little Deirdre fan!' said Bobby, mockingly, when she saw the pins holding back Alison's pretty, curly hair. 'Golly, you and Anne-Marie really are a pair! Look at Anne-Marie, she's got on a brooch just like the big ones our Deirdre wears!'

It was really funny to see the way the two girls vied with each other to imitate Miss Willcox. But Miss Cornwallis was not pleased. She eyed the two girls each day, and said nothing at first, for the fifth formers were allowed more freedom with their clothes than the forms below.

But, when Alison appeared with two scarves of different colours twined round her neck, and Anne-Marie came with an out-size pewter brooch that had a brilliant orange stone in the middle, Miss Cornwallis could bear it no longer.

'Have you a sore throat, Alison?' she inquired politely. Alison looked surprised.

'No, Miss Cornwallis,' she said.

'Then why *two* scarves, Alison?' said Miss Cornwallis, still in a tone of great politeness, which rang a warning in the ears of the class. How well they knew that extra-polite tone! It always spelt Danger!

'I – I thought they looked nice,' stammered Alison, also hearing the warning in that cold, polite voice.

'Well, Alison, I had thought till this term that you had good taste,' said Miss Cornwallis. 'You always looked tidy and neat and dainty – well-turned out, in fact. But this term you look like a third-rate imitation of some little shop-girl who thinks the more colours and scarves and pins and brooches she wears, the better she looks.'

'Oh,' said poor Alison, scarlet in the face.

'And Anne-Marie seems to be going the same way,' said Miss Cornwallis, looking at the would-be poet in a way that made her squirm and long to take off the enormous brooch. '*What* is that dinner-plate you are wearing, Anne-Marie? Do you really think it becomes you?'

Anne-Marie removed the brooch with trembling fingers. She could not bear to have any faults pointed out in public.

'That's better,' said Miss Cornwallis. 'I don't know if you are imitating anyone, either of you – but let me tell you this – imitation is *not* always the sincerest form of flattery when you make yourselves look such silly little sights!'

'Poor little Deirdre fans!' whispered Bobby to Janet. 'That was a crack at dear Miss Willcox! I bet Corny knows all about what sillies they are over her!'

That was the end of Alison and Anne-Marie trying to dress like Miss Willcox – but they still went on trying to imitate her deep, drawling voice, her graceful gestures, and her rather round-shouldered walk. The girls got very tired of it, and tried to tease them out of it.

But Alison, thrilled because her dear Deirdre was making such a friend of her, was not in a state to listen to anything the others said, and Anne-Marie was too obstinate. If Alison could imitate Miss Willcox and please her by doing so, then Anne-Marie meant to as well!

Tempers began to be rather short as the exam drew near. Hard work and worrying about the exam made most of the fifth form feel harassed and worn. Only Bobby kept cheerful, and Claudine, of course, did not turn a hair. Even Carlotta worried a little, for she wanted to please her father, who had said he would be proud if she passed this rather stiff exam well.

Pauline worried a lot too. She was not brainless and could do quite well if she tried, but she did not like her study-companion, Alma.

'She's strange,' she told Alison. 'She doesn't seem to work at all, just sits and stares at her book and eats and eats, like a cow chewing cud. She's always grumbling too – says the food isn't enough here, and she wants more sweets and isn't allowed them. It's awful to swot over your work when a person like that sits opposite, glowering and grumbling and chewing!'

'Poor old Pudding!' said Alison, thinking of the fat, dull Alma, who was always at the bottom of the form. The mistresses did not seem to be unduly upset at Alma's position. In fact, they rather seemed to take it for granted, which was odd. Miss Cornwallis always had a few sharp words to say to any of the others who stayed too long at the bottom of the form! But she rarely spoke sarcastically to Alma about her work.

'It's awful to live with somebody like Alma all the time,' sighed poor Pauline. Carlotta heard her and made a suggestion.

'Come in and share our study with me and Claudine when you get too fed up,' she said, generously, for she did not really like Pauline very much. 'It's a bit bigger than most people's, so there'll be a corner for you if you like. But don't do it too often or you'll get Alma's back up.'

'Oh, thank you,' said Pauline, gratefully. 'It will make such a difference if I can sometimes pop in next door to your study, Carlotta. You will be cheerful company after Alma. She really *is* a pudding!'

Carlotta and Claudine got on very well together. The younger girls who came to do jobs for them liked them very much. Antoinette often came, and strangely enough, never made the kind of extraordinary mistakes she had made in Angela's study!

One day Antoinette found her sister alone and spoke to her with dancing eyes.

'Claudine! Our form is to have a midnight feast! Do you remember telling me of the fine feast you had when you were in the fourth form – you had a midnight picnic by the swimming-pool.'

'Yes, I remember,' said Claudine, and she sighed. 'It is a pity to be in the fifth form. We are so good now. We do not have midnight feasts, we do not play tricks. You will enjoy your feast, my little Antoinette.'

'Claudine, could you tell us a good place to keep our cakes and tins and ginger beer in?' asked Antoinette. 'We can't keep them in the common-room, and we daren't hide them in our dormitory. Tell me where we can keep them in safety.'

Claudine thought hard. 'There is a big cupboard just outside my study,' she said at last. 'It has a key. You shall put your things there, Antoinette, and I will take the key! Then everything will be safe and I can give you the key when you wish for it. You have only to put your head into my study and wink at me – and I will come out with the key!'

'Oh, thank you, a million times!' said Antoinette. 'The second form will be so pleased. What a fine sister you are!'

She disappeared, and in due time the cupboard was piled full of eatables and drinks. Claudine removed the key. 'Now no one will find them,' she said, and hung the key on a nail in her study.

But somebody did find them, which was very unfortunate!

Alma and the store cupboard

Alma did not at all like the way Pauline deserted the study they both shared in the evenings. Pauline would sit for a little while, trying to study, then, exasperated by Alma's continual chewing of chocolate, gum or toffee, she would gather up her books and disappear.

'Where are you going?' Alma would call after her. But Pauline did not bother to reply.

So Alma decided to see where Pauline went to. She popped her head out of her study door in time to see Pauline go into the next study, which was Claudine's and Carlotta's. She stood and frowned.

Pauline was not really friendly with either of them – so why, thought Alma, should she keep popping into their study? She sat and brooded over the matter. The next time that Pauline disappeared she made up her mind to follow her into the next study, after a while, and see exactly what she was doing there.

It so happened that Carlotta had had a big box of sugared candies sent to her by her grandmother, and, in her usual generous way, she opened it and laid it on the table in front of Claudine and Pauline.

'Help yourselves whilst you work,' she said. Claudine

looked longingly at the delicious candied sweets. There were bits of lemon and orange and nut, all candied round beautifully. Claudine, however, thought a great deal of her complexion, which was very good, and she took only one sweet, meaning to make it last all the evening. But Pauline helped herself liberally. She had very little pocket-money to buy herself luxuries, and sweets of this kind did not often come her way.

Just as she was choosing her fourth sweet, the door opened and Alma came in. 'Could you lend me a maths book?' she asked, rather self-consciously. 'Oh, *you're* here, Pauline! I say, what gorgeous sweets! You never told me you had a lovely box like that, Pauline.'

She thought it was Pauline's box because the girl was helping herself to them. Carlotta gave Pauline no time to reply, nor did Claudine. They both disliked Alma, and were afraid that, seeing Pauline there, she might sit down and stay for the whole evening. Then there would be no sweets left!

'Here's the maths book, Alma,' said Carlotta, and threw her one.

'Shut the door after you,' added Claudine.

Alma glared. She thought them very rude, as indeed they were. But who could bear to have Alma sitting there all the evening? Pauline looked uncomfortable as Alma went out and banged the door after her, almost shaking the pictures from the wall.

'She'll be simply beastly to me now,' she said. 'I suppose she spied after me and saw where I went. What's the matter with her? She's so terribly fat and pasty-looking.'

'Just over-eating, I should think,' said Carlotta, beginning to write an essay. 'Now shut up for a bit, both of you. I want to think.'

Alma was very angry that the three girls in the study had not asked her to have even one sweet. She did no work at all that evening. She sat and brooded over that enormous box of sweets. Alma had a craving for that kind of thing.

They're mean pigs, she thought. Really mean. I shall get even with them, though. I'll wait till Carlotta and Claudine are out, and I'll slip in and help myself to a few sweets. I suppose they're Pauline's, and she took them in there to share with the others, instead of sharing them with me.

So Alma kept a watch to see when Carlotta and Claudine went out. There was a little alcove some way up the passage, over which a curtain hung. If she stood there quite quietly she could see when the two girls left their study.

Two evenings later her patience was rewarded. Pauline had gone to a debate. Alma slipped into the alcove and waited to see if Carlotta and Claudine would go to it at half-time, as she had heard them say they would.

Sure enough, in a short while, the study door opened, and Carlotta and Claudine came out. They went down the corridor, talking. Alma waited till their footsteps had died away. She was just going to slip out of the alcove and into the study, when she heard footsteps returning. She peeped out to see who it was.

It was Claudine hurrying back. She had just met Antoinette, who had given her a tin of sugar biscuits to hide in the cupboard with the other things. Claudine ran into her study, took down the key of the cupboard, went outside and unlocked it, pushed in the tin, then locked the door again and hung the key on its nail. Alma watched in the greatest amazement.

Claudine hurried off to join the debate downstairs. Alma stepped out of the alcove, her little eyes gleaming. So that was where the fifth form kept their stores. They must be going to have a party of some kind, and they hadn't told her a word about it! Alma was trembling with rage.

How mean everyone was! It had been bad enough in the starchy sixth form the last term, but really, the fifth form were even worse, the way they left her out of things. Alma walked into her own study and sat down heavily. She looked across at the cupboard there. There was absolutely nothing to eat, nothing – and it was ages till supper-time – and even then there wouldn't be much to eat.

She wondered where Claudine kept the key of that store cupboard. It would be fun just to have a peep inside and see what was there – not to *eat* any of it, of course – oh, no, thought Alma, she wouldn't do that, mean though the others had been not to ask her to share. But she would dearly like to *look*.

There was no one about at all. She tiptoed to Claudine's study and pushed open the door. She looked round for the key. Could that be the one, hanging on the nail by the fire-place? She took it off and went to the cupboard in the passage outside.

With trembling fingers she slipped the key into the lock. It turned easily! It *was* the key. Alma opened the cupboard and looked inside.

The things that were there! It seemed as if every single thing she liked was there – sardines and tinned milk, strawberry jam and pineapple in tins, ginger beer and a box of sweets, biscuits and chocolate.

It was quite impossible for Alma to resist the temptation to pilfer the cupboard. Just one of those chocolates – just a biscuit to go with it – just a sweet or two! Guiltily the girl helped herself, then, hearing footsteps, hurriedly shut the door, turned the key, and slipped back into her own study.

She waited till the footsteps had gone by, then ran into Claudine's study next door, and returned the key to its nail.

For quite a long time Alma sat and brooded over her discovery. She felt certain that the fifth form were going to have a party. She hadn't heard a word about it – but then, nobody ever told her anything!

Alma badly wanted the things in the cupboard. Her continual craving for food made her find excuses for the wrong thing she wanted to do. 'It's only right I should share! Even if they don't ask me, I'm a fifth former and I ought to share in their treats. Well, I *shall* share – but in secret, instead of with them at the party! That will punish them for their meanness. It will give them a shock to find a lot of the things gone.'

It was a curious secret to have, but Alma found great pleasure in thinking about that store cupboard in bed at night, and in class the next day. She hugged the secret to herself, and gave Claudine many triumphant glances, which the French girl was quite at a loss to understand.

Alma began to go to the store cupboard whenever Claudine's study was empty. She was very artful, for she was careful not to take things whose absence would be very noticeable. She did not take much of the barley sugar in the bottle there, for instance, because she knew it might catch Claudine's eye. But she carefully took all the bottom row of the box of chocolates, which would not be noticed till the first row was eaten. She took a few biscuits from each row in the big tin, not one whole row. She drank half of each ginger beer bottle, but filled each one up with water so that it would seem as if the bottles had not been tampered with.

She enjoyed being cunning like this. Poor Alma – her whole interest seemed to lie in food, more food and yet more food. Fat, unwieldy and pasty-faced, with no friends, few brains, and a sly, suspicious nature, she was not a happy person.

She had a wonderful time pilfering the store cupboard. Claudine added a few more things to it, never suspecting that many had already gone. Alma was very clever at getting the key, and taking food when no one was about. If she had only used half as much brain in class as she did in stealing from the cupboard, she would not have been so far down at the bottom of the form.

Then one evening something happened. Pauline, Claudine, and Carlotta had gone down to the common-room of the fourth form to discuss something with the girls there, and Alma, alone in her study, planned to take some biscuits and some chocolate – perhaps she might even take a tin of sardines, as there were now five or six of them. She could open them when she was alone in her own study.

She stole out and got the key from the study next door. She had just put it into the lock of the cupboard and turned it, when she heard someone coming. In a panic she fled to her own study next door, only just disappearing in time. But the key fell out of the lock with a clang and lay on the floor.

It was Alison coming. She heard the key fall, and was surprised. She picked it up when she came to it, and put it into the cupboard lock. The door swung open – and to Alison's surprise she saw the stores there! She was still staring in amazement when Claudine came along, gave an exclamation and slammed the door shut.

She glared at Alison. 'Did you get the key from my study? Well, really, Alison, I did not think it of you! What business is it of yours?'

Alison was puzzled. 'From your study?' she said. 'Of course not! Someone must have been at the cupboard and opened it when I came along, because I heard footsteps scurrying away, and then heard the key fall out of the lock. I put it back, the door swung open – and I saw the things. I don't want to know anything at all about the food, Claudine, and I certainly shan't tell anyone – but it's obvious that somebody knows about the cupboard, isn't it?'

Claudine believed Alison at once. Alison might be weak and silly in many ways, but she was honest and truthful. Claudine swung the door open and looked into the cupboard very thoughtfully. So someone knew of the stores – someone knew where the key was kept – someone knew the secret!

It wasn't long before Claudine discovered that the someone had also taken various things from the stores. She shut the door and locked it, angry and puzzled.

'Someone's been at the things,' she said to Alison, 'but as far as I know only I and my little sister Antoinette knew the hiding-place. The second form are to have a midnight feast, and I have kept their food under lock and key for them. Who could have found out the hiding-place – and who could be dishonest enough to steal the things?'

'I can't imagine,' said Alison, amazed. 'It is such a mean, low-down thing to do. Whoever did it is absolutely despicable. It's unbelievable! Anyway, Claudine, if I were you I'd keep the key somewhere about your person. Then the thief, whoever it is, won't be able to get it!'

16
Alma – Alison – and Anne-Marie

Alma heard all this conversation quite clearly. She felt a wave of anger against Alison. Interfering little busybody! Now she, Alma, would not be able to feast herself on the hidden goodies any more. She sat perfectly still, hoping that neither of the girls would come into her study and see her there. She felt guilty, and was sure her guilt would show in her face.

But they did not come. It did not occur to either of them that the thief would be anywhere near. They felt sure she had run away. Maybe it was a second former – but how disgusting, whoever it was!

The next time Alma had a chance of tip-toeing into the study next to hers, the key was missing. She had feared it would be. She supposed that Claudine had it round her neck in safety. Now Alma would not be able to enjoy those delicious, deceitful little feasts any more!

The girl made a curiously big thing out of the whole happening, and for a few days thought of nothing else. She hated Alison for being the unwitting cause of depriving her of the food she craved for.

I'll pay her out, she thought. Spoiling things for me like this! I'll get even with her.

Alma was strangely clever in underhand ways. Stupid people can often be cunning, and Alma was no exception. She set her wits to work, and Alison began to go through an unpleasant and most annoying time.

Things kept disappearing out of her study. Never Angela's things, but always Alison's.

'*Where's* my hair-slide?' wailed Alison. 'It's gone, and I only *saw* it on the window-sill this morning. Have you borrowed it, Angela?'

'Of course not,' said Angela. 'You've dropped it somewhere.'

Then it was Alison's hair brush that disappeared from her dressing-table in the dormitory. She hunted all over for it, and then had to report the loss to Matron, who was not very pleased.

'How can you possibly mislay a *hair* brush?' she said to Alison. 'I suppose you've been using it in a bedroom battle or something, and it's flown out of the window!'

'We fifth formers don't have bedroom battles,' said Alison, with much dignity.

Then her geometry outfit went. It completely and utterly vanished, and no amount of hunting brought it to light. Bobby had two and lent her one.

'But for goodness' sake don't lose it,' she said. 'You seem to be losing everything this term!'

The same day Alison's knitting-needles disappeared out of the scarf she was knitting, and the stitches all pulled out loose when she took the work out of her bag.

'Now this is very strange,' said Alison, and she held it up

to show Angela. 'Look – the needles are gone – and all the stiches are dropped. Angela – what do you think of that?'

'Well,' said Angela, 'I think someone's doing beastly things to you, Alison. I do really. And I bet I know who it is, too!'

'Who?' said Alison, feeling shocked and hurt.

'Someone who is awfully jealous of you,' said Angela.

'You don't mean – Anne-Marie?' said Alison, still more shocked. 'Oh, *Angela* – surely she wouldn't do mean things like this! Do you think that she's been taking all those things of mine that disappeared too? Oh, *no* – she couldn't be as low down as that.'

'People say that when anyone is jealous they don't mind what they do,' said Angela. 'And you know Anne-Marie is awfully jealous because you are so well in with your dear Deirdre, and at the moment she isn't in Deirdre's good books. Why she can't see that her dear idol is bored stiff with her poems I really don't know!'

'She's a beast if she is really taking my things, and spoiling my knitting,' said Alison, almost in tears. The girl always loved to be liked by everyone, and it hurt her very much to think that one of her own form could be so unkind. 'I shan't listen to a single one of her silly poems now.'

So, much to Anne-Marie's surprise, neither Angela nor Alison evinced the slightest interest in a long new poem, called 'The Weary Heart', which she went along to their study to read out loud that evening.

'We're busy,' said Alison, shortly.

'And you ought to be, too,' said Angela, virtuously. 'The exam is coming jolly near.'

'It won't take long to read my poem to you,' said Anne-Marie, crestfallen. 'This is how it begins . . .'

'Do get out,' said Angela. 'I'm doing maths and they don't go with poetry, even if the poem *is* called "The Weary Heart", which is very descriptive of mine at the moment.'

'Why don't you write a poem called "The Missing Knitting-Needles"?' said Alison, unexpectedly. Anne-Marie stared at her, puzzled.

'Why knitting-needles?' she inquired at last.

'Well, you ought to know, oughtn't you?' said Alison. But Anne-Marie didn't. Thinking that Alison and Angela were rude and unkind, and a little mad, she went away, carrying her precious poem with her. She bumped into Miss Willcox on her way, and gave a gasp.

'Oh – Miss Willcox – please would you read this? I spent hours over it last night.'

Miss Willcox took the poem and glanced at it. It was the same kind as usual, pretentious, full of long words, solemn, sad and far too long. Miss Willcox felt impatient. She determined to be candid with Anne-Marie, now that she had her alone.

'Look here, Anne-Marie,' she said, in her deep voice. 'I want to give you a little advice – and I want you to listen to it carefully, and follow it.'

'Oh, *yes*, Miss Willcox,' said Anne-Marie, fervently. 'I will, indeed I will.'

'Well,' said Miss Willcox, 'you can't write poetry, and

you may as well know it. You can rhyme and get the metre right – but your ideas are rubbish. *Real* poetry has ideas in it, beautiful pictures, great feelings. Tear up all your poems, Anne-Marie, and set your mind on the coming exam. That is my advice to you. You think you're a genius. Well, you're not! You are just an ordinary little school girl who has got a swelled head, and thinks she can write. It is my opinion that unless your character changes considerably, you never *will* write a really good poem!'

Miss Willcox swept off, glad to have relieved her mind of the irritation that Anne-Marie and her never-ending poems always aroused in her. Anne-Marie, struck absolutely dumb, gazed after her, too hurt even for tears.

Her knees felt rather weak. She went to her study and sat down. Felicity was there, conning over some music theory, humming softly to herself. She did not even see Anne-Marie come in.

It took a little time for all that Miss Willcox had said to sink in. Poor Anne-Marie had had the greatest shock of her life. All her great ideas about herself began to totter and waver. *Wasn't* she a genius? *Couldn't* she write marvellously? She began to feel as if she wasn't Anne-Marie any more – she was nobody, nobody at all. She gave a sudden loud sob that entered even Felicity's ears.

'What's up?' said Felicity, looking round.

'Oh, *you* wouldn't understand!' said Anne-Marie, bitterly. 'You're a genius, you don't seem to live in this world, you don't notice anything that goes on at all. You don't even know I'm here half the time. Well, what does it matter? I'm nobody, not even Anne-Marie. I've had everything stripped away from me, everything I cared about.'

'Don't exaggerate so,' said Felicity, mildly surprised at this curious outburst. 'Can't you find the right rhyme for one of your poems? Is that what has upset you?'

'Oh, you're im*possible*!' said Anne-Marie, and threw a book at Felicity, which surprised her even more. Anne-Marie went out of the room. Felicity was at once absorbed in her work again, little creases between her eyes, her headache bothering her as usual.

Anne-Marie was hurt, shocked and resentful. She wondered if Miss Willcox could possibly be right. After all, she knew about poetry, so she ought to know if Anne-Marie's was good or bad. Anne-Marie thought a great deal about Miss Willcox that evening, and what she had said.

Her resentment made her begin to see the English mistress rather more clearly than usual. She remembered how the girls laughed at her posing and pretence, her vague ways and soulful looks. Almost in a flash her adoration turned to detestation. Poor Anne-Marie – all the things she cared for had indeed been reft from her suddenly. Her pride in herself and in her genius was gone, her hopes for the future, her confidence that Miss Willcox liked and admired her, even her poems now seemed worthless.

She half thought she would do as Miss Willcox had so coldly advised her, and tear them up. But a doubt still persisted in her mind about the teacher's ability to know, really *know*, whether her, Anne-Marie's, poems were good. Suppose she tore them up, and wrote no more – and suppose after all Miss Willcox was wrong, and her poems *were* good – what a loss to the world they might be!

If only I could find out whether or not Miss Willcox is as good a judge as she always sets out to be! thought Anne-Marie, quite obsessed by the subject. But how could I? I don't see *how* I could.

Then a way came to her, and she thought so deeply about it that she didn't even hear Alison speaking to her as she passed. I'll do it! thought Anne-Marie, exultantly. I'll do it! I'll find some little-known poem of one of the very great poets – Matthew Arnold perhaps, or Browning – and I'll write it out in my own hand-writing – and next time we have to write a poem for Miss Willcox, I'll send in not a poem of my own, but a classic!'

She got up to go to the school library to look through the books of poets there.

If Miss Willcox praises the poem, I shall know she genuinely appreciates good poetry – if she sneers at it, thinking it is mine, I shall know she doesn't! Ah, Miss Willcox, we shall see!

Anne-Marie was soon busy turning over the pages of Matthew Arnold, Tennyson and Browning. She felt as if her whole happiness, her whole future depended on this. She must be careful not to choose a poem at all well known, or certainly Miss Willcox would recognize it. She must choose one as like her own style as possible – something yearning and soulful and rather high-brow. Ah, Anne-Marie meant to test Miss Willcox, no matter whether she cheated or not in doing so!

Now that her liking for Miss Willcox had so suddenly vanished, Anne-Marie's jealously of Alison disappeared too. Silly little Alison, she thought, pityingly, as she shut one book of poems and opened another.

But Alison, not knowing anything about Miss Willcox's unkindness to Anne-Marie, and its result, still thought that the other girl was jealous of her, and put down the annoying disappearances of her things to spite on Anne-Marie's part.

Alma knew this and rejoiced. It made things much easier for her if Alison so clearly suspected someone else! She took a few more things, enjoying poor Alison's exasperation and annoyance. To Alma the loss of the hidden food in the cupboard was as great a blow as Miss Willcox's words had been to Anne-Marie!

Mirabel is very high-handed

The second formers decided to have their feast in their own dormitory, which was conveniently far from any mistresses' quarters. They asked the first form to join them and there was great rejoicing among the younger ones at this.

'Jolly decent of them,' said Sally. 'I vote we get in a spot of food ourselves. Don't you think so, Jane?'

Jane was not as thrilled as the others. She had been very quiet and subdued lately, hurt at Mirabel's neglect of her, and at her unjust suspicion regarding the ringing of the fire-bell, which mystery still had not been cleared up. She worked hard for Angela, finding comfort in the older girl's liking and praise, and still did a good deal of her work at night under the sheets.

'Cheer up, Jane!' Sally kept saying. 'You look like a hen caught in the rain. *Do* cheer up!'

Jane tried to smile. She had been very afraid of suddenly bursting into tears lately, a most unusual thing for her to do. 'It will be fun having a midnight feast,' she said, trying to think it *would* be fun. But somehow nothing seemed fun lately. It was so awful to be left out of matches, when she knew she was better than the others. What was the use of practising hard every spare minute she had, when Mirabel kept treating her like this? It wasn't fair, thought Jane, resentfully. It really wasn't.

Claudine had told Antoinette of the pilfering of the cupboard, and the second formers were annoyed and puzzled, for Antoinette had told no one of the hiding-place. Still there was plenty of food left, so never mind!

Antoinette went to Claudine. 'Claudine, we are to have our feast tomorrow night. Can I have the key of the cupboard please? I and one of the others will come up here very quietly just before midnight, and get the things.'

'Here is the key,' said Claudine, taking it off a thin string she wore round her neck. 'Now don't make a noise tomorrow night, whatever you do. Have a good time! I wish I was coming too!'

Antoinette grinned. She was enjoying this first term at St Clare's. Like Claudine, she had slipped out of things she did not like, had played many undetected pranks, and had enjoyed the fun and the jolly companionship. She took the key and went off. She hadn't gone far before she retraced her footsteps.

How many bottles of ginger beer were there? Would there be enough, now that the first form was coming? She slipped the key in the lock and turned it.

Alma, in her study, heard the click of the lock. How well she knew it! She peeped out of the door. Why, it was Antoinette at the cupboard, not Claudine. She went out of the door. Antoinette jumped violently and shut the door.

'What have you got in that cupboard?' said Alma, in a smooth voice. 'Let me see.'

Before Antoinette could object she grabbed the key from her and opened the cupboard. Then she pretended to be very surprised at the contents. 'Good gracious! What is all this? Does it belong to you, Antoinette?'

Antoinette hesitated. She disliked Alma and did not trust her. But what could she do? If she was rude, Alma might be most unpleasant.

'I see it is a secret,' said Alma, longing to take one of the tins of pineapple. 'Give me one of those tins, Antoinette, and I will not tell anyone of this at all. I suppose you are going to have a midnight feast?'

'Yes, tomorrow,' said Antoinette, disliking Alma even more. 'I'm sorry I can't give you a tin, Alma. I should have to ask the others first. It is not a nice thing for you to ask, anyway – I do not like a bargain of this sort!'

Antoinette shut the door firmly and locked it again, before Alma had made up her mind what to do. She took the key from the lock and stuffed it into her pocket, eyeing Alma defiantly. 'I will ask the others if you *may* have a tin of pineapple, if you wish me to, Alma,' she said. 'But – surely you do not wish me to?'

Alma scowled. Of course she could not have Antoinette telling the second form that she wanted a tin of pineapple. She tried to laugh it off.

'Don't be silly! I didn't really mean it. I don't like pineapple. Well – I hope you enjoy your feast!'

'You won't tell tales of us, will you?' said Antoinette, distrusting Alma more and more. 'You promise that, won't you? The second form would think you were terrible to tell such a tale, Alma. You have the English sense of honour, have you not, this honour that always you English girls are talking of?'

'Of course,' said Alma, walking off with what dignity she could muster. She went into her study. She thought of the food in that cupboard. She thought of Antoinette's half-veiled insolence. Probably she *would* tell the second formers about the tin of pineapple she had asked for – and they would nudge each other when she passed, and giggle.

Alma wished she *could* tell tales, and get the feast stopped! But who would listen to her? She would not dare to carry tales to Miss Theobald or Miss Cornwallis, nor was she certain that Hilary, the head girl of the form, would even listen to her!

Then a thought struck her. What about Mirabel? Mirabel was so keen on sports – and there was a match the day after next! She would not be at all pleased if she knew that the first and second form were going to have a midnight feast just before the match. Mirabel should be told about it, and maybe, in her blunt, overbearing way, she would stop it. That would punish Antoinette all right!

Alma did not dare to go to Mirabel dircct. She printed a note, so that her handwriting would not be recognized, and did not sign her name at the end.

'DO NOT EXPECT THE THIRD TEAM TO WIN ITS MATCH ON FRIDAY,' said the note. 'THEY WILL ALL BE UP AT MIDNIGHT!'

Mirabel found the note on her table in the study that evening. She picked it up in curiosity and read it.

'Gladys,' she said, tossing the note over to her, 'what in the world does this mean?'

Gladys read it distastefully. 'It's a wretched anonymous letter,' she said, 'sent by someone who wants to tell tales and doesn't dare to do it openly. Beastly. Tear it up and put it in the waste-paper basket. Don't take any notice of it. That's the way to treat letters of that sort.'

'Yes, but Gladys – the third lacrosse team *won't* win their match if they are up at midnight,' argued Mirabel. 'And I do want them to. I've set my heart on it. I suppose they're going to have a midnight feast or something, silly kids. They'll be tired out next day.'

'Well, didn't *you* enjoy midnight feasts when you were in the lower forms?' said Gladys. 'Have you forgotten what fun they were?'

'We didn't have them just before an important match,' said Mirabel. 'We didn't, Gladys.'

'For goodness' sake don't think of stopping the feast, or whatever it is,' said Gladys, alarmed. 'You can't interfere like that, Mirabel, and be such a spoilsport.'

Mirabel thought for a few moments. 'I know what to do. I'll send a note to Katie, who's head of the second form, and inform her that I have heard there is to be something going on at midnight tomorrow, and I would like her to see that it is put off till after the match. They will respect my wishes I am sure – then they can play the match properly without being tired, and have their feast afterwards.'

'Well, I shouldn't even do that,' said Gladys. 'I don't think the feast will really make much difference to the match – and anyway, only about a quarter of the girls are playing in it – hardly that!'

'You never back me up in anything now,' said Mirabel, frowning. She said no more, but busied herself in writing a short note to the head girl of the second form.

Katie got it that day and read it in surprise. She showed it to Antoinette. 'However did Mirabel get wind of our plans?' she said. 'Have you told anyone, Antoinette?'

'Well – only Alma,' said the French girl, and she told Katie what had happened at the store cupboard.

'How awful!' said Katie, shocked at the tale and at Alma's behaviour. 'I say – I wonder if she was the one who pilfered our stores!'

'Perhaps,' said Antoinette. 'She is not a nice girl, that one.'

Katie called a meeting of the second formers in the common-room and read them Mirabel's note. It was, as might be expected, rather arrogant and peremptory. Evidently Mirabel expected to be obeyed, and that was that.

'I vote we have the feast tomorrow night as planned,' said Yolande. 'Mirabel has been throwing her weight about too much lately. I call that a most uncivil note. Anyway, what business is it of hers? She's always interfering now.'

Everyone followed Yolande's lead. It was curious how unpopular Mirabel had become. She had tried to drive everyone too fast, and now they were digging their toes in and refusing to budge!

'I'd better not answer this note of Mirabel's today, had I?' said Katie. 'I'll answer it *after* we've had the feast, then she can't stop it!'

Mirabel was surprised to have no answer from Katie, giving an undertaking to postpone the feast till after the match, but it did not occur to her at all that the first and second formers would dare to defy her. She felt puzzled and thought that Katie was not very mannerly – surely she knew that an answer should always be sent at once to any request from one of the top form girls?

The first and second form were getting excited. It was the first time they had had a feast at night, and to them it seemed a terribly exciting thing. Every single girl was going. Violet was back from the sick-bay now after a bout of flu, and was looking forward to it too.

Jane tried to look forward to it, but she was feeling very unhappy. Then a dreadful quarrel blew up between her and Violet, and Jane felt as if she couldn't bear things any more!

Violet had come back from the sick-bay expecting to do Angela's jobs as usual. She had been disappointed because Angela had not even sent a kindly message to her when she was ill. Never mind – Angela would be very glad to see her back, doing her cleaning and mending as before, thought Violet.

But Angela didn't want Violet mooning round again. She had got used to the quiet and efficient little Jane, who, so long as she got a smile and a word of praise now and again, seemed to be quite content. Violet was too talkative, and always liked to recount all her thoughts and doings, which was very boring to the self-centred Angela.

So, to Violet's enormous dismay, Angela did not greet

her warmly, and merely informed her that perhaps she would like to go and see to Pauline's jobs, as Jane was doing everything necessary. Violet did not dare to argue with Angela, but rushed off to Jane at once.

'You underhand thing!' she said, her eyes sparkling with anger. 'You go behind my back when I'm ill – and worm yourself into Angela's good graces again – and do all the things she was letting me do. Jane Teal, I shall never speak to you again, and neither will half the first form!'

Jane tried to defend herself, but Violet had a ready tongue, and could say some bitter, cutting things. Jane was tired out and unhappy, and she burst into tears.

'Just like you!' said Violet, scornfully. 'You think you'll get sympathy just because you cry. Well – you just burst into tears with Angela, and see what *she* says! She can't stand anything of *that* sort!'

Jane could not help feeling that perhaps she *had* done a mean trick to Violet. She hardly slept at all that night, and in the morning she awoke with a sore throat and a headache, which made her feel more miserable than ever. It's a good thing I'm not playing in the match tomorrow! she thought and wondered if Mirabel would ever put her name down for a match again.

Jane felt rather odd that day. She had a high temperature and didn't know it. She did badly on the lacrosse field and Mirabel ticked her off. She could not concentrate in class and Miss Roberts was not pleased. Violet avoided her and some of the other first formers, who were friends of Violet's, did not speak to her either.

'I wish I was at home,' thought Jane, longingly. 'If I could just tell Mother all about it I'd feel better. I can't write it in a letter. I wish I could go home.'

The idea grew and grew in her worried mind and at last Jane made a plan she would never have made if she had been quite well. Instead of going to the feast she would go home! Luckily for her, her home was actually in the next village, four miles away. Jane felt sure she could easily walk there in the middle of the night! Then she would see her mother, tell her everything, and things would be all right again.

She did not know she was beginning to have flu and had a temperature, she had no idea she was not normal just then. Sally could not get a word out of her and was worried. Poor Jane – she was not having an easy time just then. But never mind, she thought, I'll be home tonight!

18

A surprising night

That Friday night was to be a most astonishing one for Mam'zelle, though she did not know it. She never forgot it, and, whenever she took a holiday in her beloved France, she would often recount the happenings of that night, to show her enraptured listeners how odd were the English girls!

It was the night of the Feast, and the first and second formers were to have it at twelve o'clock sharp in one of their dormitories. Antoinette had already secreted some of the things on the top of a high cupboard in her dormitory, and meant to fetch the rest just before midnight.

Mirabel, unfortunately, had seen Antoinette hurrying along the corridor outside her study, carrying various suspicious parcels. She had called after Antoinette, but Antoinette had thought it advisable not to hear, and had scurried fast round the corner, almost knocking over Miss Willcox.

Mirabel stared after the disappearing Antoinette in exasperation. Really, these kids were getting too uncivil for words. She went back into her own study and frowned. *Could* those kids be going to have their feast that night after all – when she had asked them not to? Could they flout her request in that way – surely not!

All the same a doubt persisted in Mirabel's mind, and she could not get rid of it. She said nothing to Gladys, but she made up her mind to keep awake that night, and to go along to the first- or second-form dormitories about midnight, to see if anything was happening.

And if there is – won't I give them a talking to! thought Mirabel, grimly. I'll report them too. I'll make them see they can't disregard *my* orders!

Now Anne-Marie had planned to stage a sleep-walking act that night. She had thought of quite a lot of things to do which were extraordinary, and might make people say 'Ah, she does those because she's a genius,' as so often was said of the absent-minded Felicity. But she rather doubted her ability to carry them off in front of the sharp-eyed, quick-minded members of the fifth form.

It would never do to put on some sort of genius act, and have the others roar with laughter, disbelieve in it, and tell her it was all put on. It was getting to be quite imperative to Anne-Marie to be thought really clever. She had to do something to cancel out the damping effect of Miss Willcox's words.

Who would be taken in most easily? She thought for a while, and then decided on Mam'zelle. She had heard of the many tricks the girls had played on the French mistress through the years, and she felt sure she would take in Mam'zelle. Mam'zelle would exclaim, and waggle her hands, and tell everyone. She would say, 'Ah, *la petite* Anne-Marie, she walks in her sleep, she recites poetry as she walks, she is a genius! We must be careful of her, we must cherish this talented girl! One day she will be famous!'

Yes, certainly Mam'zelle would be the best one to impress. The middle of the night would be the best time. She would find some means of waking Mam'zelle, and bring her out in the passage, and then she would let her see her, apparently walking in her sleep, reciting lines and lines of poetry. Mam'zelle would be most impressed, and perhaps even Miss Theobald would think that Anne-Marie was a genius, and ask to see some of her poems.

Anne-Marie was really very pleased with her idea. She quite looked forward to putting it into practice that night. About half-past twelve or so, she thought. That would be the best time. Everyone will be asleep by then.

She had, of course, chosen a most unfortunate night for her sleep-walking, for quite a number of people were going to be wide awake! All the first and second formers would be revelling in their feast. Jane Teal would be stealing through the school, meaning to run off home. Mirabel would be on the prowl to find out if the younger girls were really having their feast. Alma would be snooping about to see if there was likely to be any food left in the cupboard. Antoinette and one or two others would be fetching the rest of the food.

And Felicity was to choose that night for sleep-walking too – but genuine sleep-walking, in her case. So there would be quite a number of people wandering about, though Anne-Marie hadn't the remotest idea of this.

All the girls went off to bed as usual at their ordinary times. The first and second formers went first, giggling with excitement, vowing that they wouldn't sleep a wink till midnight. Antoinette and Sally were to be responsible for rousing anyone who *did* go to sleep. It was thrilling to look forward to such an escapade.

The third and fourth formers went off to bed later.

The fifth and sixth could stay up till ten o'clock, and usually did. They all retired as usual, even Felicity, who often did not go till much later, lost as usual in her music. It was astonishing that no mistress had discovered her light burning so late in her study, but so far no one had.

Then the mistresses went to bed, yawning, having a last word together before they parted. Mam'zelle was the last to go. She had a pile of French essays from the sixth form to go through, and had left them rather late.

I will correct these, and then go, she thought, glancing at the clock. Half-past eleven already! How slow I have been tonight!

At just about five minutes to twelve Mam'zelle went into her bedroom. At twelve o'clock she was getting into bed, and the bed was about to creak under her rather heavy weight, when some sound caught her ears.

It sounded as if something hard had been dropped on the floor immediately above her head. Mam'zelle sat on the side of the bed and pondered over the various possible causes of the noise.

It was not the cat. It was not the unexpected groan or creak that furniture sometimes gave at night. It was not any mistress on the prowl, because all had gone to bed. Then what could it be? Mam'zelle thought hard. She knew that the fifth-form studies were above her bedroom, stretching in a long couple of rows down and around two corridors. Surely no one could possibly be up still? The fifth form must all be in bed!

Another small sound decided Mam'zelle. She had better go and investigate. It might be a burglar. Mam'zelle had a horror of burglars, but she felt it her duty to find out whether there was one in the school or not. Feeling extremely brave, and arming herself with a hair brush, she put on her dressing-gown and slippers, tied the belt tightly round her plump waist, and opened her bedroom door.

All the passages and corridors of St Clare's were lighted throughout the night, but with specially dimmed lights. It was possible to see a figure, but not to make out who it was. The corridors looked rather eerie to Mam'zelle as she set out on her journey of investigation.

The first thing that Mam'zelle did was to fall over the school's big black cat, much given to wandering around at night. Seeing Mam'zelle perfectly clearly, though she could not see him at all, he advanced upon her, and tried to rub against her ankles, delighted to see a fellow-wanderer in the night.

Mam'zelle gave a muffled shriek, and almost over-balanced. One of her big feet caught the cat on its side, and it gave one of its yowls. Mam'zelle recognized the cat's voice, and was relieved to find that it was not a burglar lying on the floor to catch her foot, but only the cat.

'Sssst!' she said, in a piercing, sibilant whisper, and the cat fled, grieved at Mam'zelle's lack of friendliness.

Mam'zelle went up the stairs to the next floor, where she had heard the noise. Antoinette was up there, on her third journey to collect the eatables with Sally. To her horror she suddenly heard Mam'zelle's piercing 'Ssssst!' noise from the floor below. She clutched Sally.

'Somebody's about! Did you hear that? Oh, how tiresome, Sally! What shall we do?'

'There's an alcove near here,' whispered Sally. 'Look – where that curtain is. We'll get behind there with our tins and bottles. Quick! Maybe whoever it is will pass by. Don't sneeze or anything!'

The two girls pressed themselves behind the curtain, their hearts beating fast. They heard Mam'zelle's footsteps coming along, making a soft swishing noise in her big bedroom slippers. They stood quite still.

Mam'zelle came to the alcove. She thought the curtain bulged suspiciously, and she put out a trembling hand. She distinctly felt some soft body behind it! She gave a gasp. Antoinette and Sally decided to make a bolt for it, and suddenly shot out from the alcove, dropping a ginger beer bottle on poor Mam'zelle's toes. She gave an anguished groan, lifted her foot, and did a few heavy hops over to the opposite wall, putting out a hand to steady herself when she got there.

She caught sight of two figures racing down the dim passage, and round the corner. She had no idea whether they were burglars or girls. As she felt her corns tenderly, wrath swept over her. How dared people drop things on her feet in the middle of the night, and then run away without apologizing? Mam'zelle determined to chase the scamps, whoever they were, and run them to earth.

She did not see the ginger beer bottle lying at her feet, and she fell over it as she went swiftly down the passage, stubbing her other foot this time. The bottle went rolling off and hit the wall. Mam'zelle stopped again and groaned.

She ran down the passage and came to the corner. There was no one to be seen there. The passage went completely round the third floor of the building, and came back again where it began, and Mam'zelle thought it would be a good idea to go the whole way and see if anyone was about on that floor. So off she set, determined to run to earth whoever was up so late at night.

Pad-pad-pad, went her feet, and every now and again Mam'zelle set her pince-nez firmly on her nose, for they had an irritating way of jumping off when she ran. Pad-pad-pad – the chase was on!

19

Mam'zelle on the war-path

Alma was the next one to be dimly seen by Mam'zelle. She had been certain that Antoinette would go to the store cupboard that night, and would probably make two or three visits. Probably in between she would leave the door open. Then, thought greedy Alma, she might be able to pop in and take something for herself. A tin of pineapple for instance. She seemed to crave a tin of pineapple!

So, making sure that the rest of her dormitory were asleep, Alma rose quietly from her bed, and went up the stairs to the third floor. She made her way to the cupboard just at the same moment as Mam'zelle, panting, came round the last of the four corners of the corridor, back again to where the alcove was. The store cupboard was quite near.

Mam'zelle saw a figure in the passage. Ah – there was *one* of the midnight wanderers, at least! Mam'zelle would teach them to drop things on her poor toes! She crept up behind the unsuspecting Alma, who was half in the cupboard, groping about for a tin of some kind.

Alma had the shock of her life when she felt a hand on her shoulder. She lunged out in fright and struck poor Mam'zelle square in the middle. Mam'zelle doubled up at once, and gave such a deep groan that Alma was horrified. She could not move an inch, but stood there, trembling.

Mam'zelle recovered rapidly. She felt certain that this must be a burglar rifling cupboards. He was dangerous! He had given her a terrible blow, the big coward! Mam'zelle was not going to come to grips with him. Giving Alma a sudden push, which landed her among the tins, bottles and old rugs, she shut the door firmly, locked it, and took the key.

'Ha!' said Mam'zelle, addressing the alarmed Alma in the cupboard. 'Now I have you under key and lock! I go for the police!'

With this terrifying threat she padded off to telephone to the police. She went downstairs, congratulating herself heartily on her smartness and bravery, and feeling her middle tenderly to see if she was bruised.

As soon as she got downstairs she saw Jane Teal, who had chosen that moment to creep away from the others, put on her hat and coat and go to find a side-door she could open quietly. But poor little Jane was now feeling very ill. The flu was sending her temperature high, and she felt as if she was in a dream. All she wanted was to get to her mother, and to do that she knew she must get out of St Clare's and walk and walk.

So, hardly knowing what she was doing, she felt with a feverish hand along the wall to find the side-door. She muttered to herself as she went. 'I must find the door. That's the first thing. I must find the door.'

Mam'zelle heard the muttering and stopped in

amazement and alarm. Could this be yet another burglar? Who was this person groping along the wall – with a hat on too! Mam'zelle could not see in the dim light what kind of a person it was, but having got the idea of burglars firmly in her mind, she felt certain this must be another – probably the second of the two she had first seen racing down the upstairs passage. She began to tiptoe cautiously after Jane.

Jane felt along the wall till she came to a door. 'Here is a door,' she muttered. 'I must open it and go out. I've found a door.'

But it was not the side-door, leading into the garden. It was the door of the second-form games cupboard, full of lacrosse sticks, old goal-nets, a few discarded raincoats and such things as this. Jane opened the door and went into the cupboard. Mam'zelle, triumphant, saw a chance of repeating her recent brilliance, and of locking this second burglar into a cupboard too.

She darted forward, shut the door and locked it, leaving poor Jane in the darkness among things that felt most extraordinary to her hot little fingers.

'I want to go home,' said Jane and suddenly sank down on to a pile of sticks and nets, for her legs felt as if they would no longer carry her. She lay there, feverish and half dreaming, not knowing or caring in the least where she was.

Mam'zelle could not help feeling very proud of herself. What other mistress at St Clare's could catch and imprison two burglars in one night like this? Mam'zelle began to think she was wasted as a French mistress. She should have been in the police force.

'Now I go to the telephone,' she said to herself, thinking with delight of the astonishment of the police when they heard her news. But she was not yet to broadcast her news, for, even as she went into the hall, she saw somebody else!

This time it was Felicity, walking in her sleep, trying to find the assembly room, so that she might once again mount the platform, and play her imaginary violin. She walked solemnly, her eyes wide open, humming a melody in a low, soft voice. She had on her white night-gown, and Mam'zelle was absolutely petrified to see this figure walking towards her, making a strange low humming.

'*Tiens*!' said Mam'zelle, and took a step backwards. For the first time she began to wonder whether the night's happenings were real or whether she might be dreaming. It seemed astonishing that so many people were about in the middle of the night.

This could not be a burglar. It looked like something unearthly – a spirit wandering about, lost and lone! Mam'zelle shivered. Burglars she had been able to deal with – but spirits were different. They faded away, they disappeared into thin air if they were touched, and Mam'zelle did not like things of that sort.

She decided not to go to the telephone just then, as she would have to meet this wandering spirit face to face. She would retire to her bedroom for a little while till the spirit had returned to wherever it had come from. So Mam'zelle turned tail and fled.

But for some reason Felicity, fast asleep as she was, seemed to perceive Mam'zelle as she disappeared towards the stairs. Into her dreaming mind came the idea that this person might take her to the platform, so that she might play her wonderful compositions, and she followed Mam'zelle up the stairs, her eyes glassy and wide open, her hands outstretched.

Mam'zelle glanced behind and was most alarmed to find the white spirit following her. She had not bargained for this at all. She almost ran to get to her bedroom on the second floor.

Felicity followed, seeming almost to float up the stairs, for she was tall and thin, and much too light for her age. Mam'zelle bolted into her bedroom and sat down on her bed, out of breath.

The door opened and Felicity came in, her eyes still wide open. As Mam'zelle had her light on, she saw at once that what she had thought was a frightening apparition was only Felicity.

'*Tiens*!' said Mam'zelle, putting her hand up to her forehead. '*Tiens*! What kind of a night is this, when burglars and children walk around? Felicity, my child, are you awake?'

There was something rather terrifying about Felicity's white, unawakened face. Mam'zelle saw that she was sound asleep, and was afraid to wake her. She was more than relieved when Felicity, feeling the bed, drew back the covers, got into it and shut her eyes. In a minute or two she was apparently sleeping quite peacefully.

Mam'zelle stared down at the pale face on her pillow. To have two burglars shut into two separate cupboards and a sleep-walking girl in her bed was rather bewildering. She could not make up her mind whether to telephone to the police or to go and call Miss Theobald and show her Felicity. Mam'zelle had had enough experience of girls to know that sleep-walking was not a good thing – something had happened to make Felicity act in this way, and that something must be investigated.

There was a noise upstairs again. Antoinette and Sally had returned to the cupboard for eatables, and had found the door locked, the key gone, and a prisoner in the cupboard! In amazement and fear they fled back to their dormitory to tell the others. Mam'zelle, disturbed by the noise they made, went out of her bedroom, and, as an afterthought, turned the key in the lock, in case Felicity should try a little more sleep-walking.

She was just in time to see Antoinette and Sally, two vague figures in the distance, running back to their dormitory.

'*Tiens*!' said Mam'zelle again, thunderstruck to find yet more people abroad that night. 'Do I sleep or wake? Everywhere I go I see people fleeing in the night!'

The next person Mam'zelle saw was Mirabel, who was creeping down the stairs to see if the second formers were holding their feast after all. Mam'zelle could not believe her eyes. Was the whole school wandering about that night – or was this yet another burglar?

Mirabel was a tall, strapping girl, and she wore

pyjamas. In the dim passage she looked as big as a man, and Mam'zelle felt certain this must be another of the gang of burglars that appeared to be infesting St Clare's that night. She followed her, trying to make no noise at all. It was becoming quite a common-place for Mam'zelle to lock people up that night, and she fondly imagined she could somehow imprison this burglar also.

Mirabel went towards the second-form dormitories. Mam'zelle, afraid that the burglar might scare the girls there, hurried her steps. The school cat reappeared at this moment, and tripped poor Mam'zelle up, so that she made a noise. Mirabel looked round, and slipped quickly into one of the bathrooms that ran opposite the dormitories. She did not want any of the second formers to know she was snooping round, in case by any chance they were *not* holding the feast after all.

Mam'zelle saw with great pleasure that once again she could lock somebody into somewhere. She began to think that burglar-catching was the easiest thing in the world – merely a matter of turning a key in a lock. She turned the key in the shut bathroom door – and there was yet another burglar accounted for!

Mam'zelle thought with delight of the surprise and admiration of the other mistresses when they heard of her exploits. She felt ready to imprison half a dozen more burglars into cupboards and bathrooms if necessary.

Mirabel was horrified at being locked in. She had no idea who had turned the key, but thought it was some silly trick of one of the younger girls. So she settled down to wait for the door to be undone. She felt sure no girl would keep her imprisoned all night long.

Mam'zelle decided that she would now go to Miss Theobald, as she felt that no policeman would be inclined to believe a telephone call from her about three locked-up burglars. So she padded along the passage to the stairs – but just as she was about to descend them, she caught sight of yet another night-wanderer.

This time it was Anne-Marie, who was now putting on her sleep-walking act in imitation of Felicity, and was on her way to wake up Mam'zelle. Mam'zelle could not believe her eyes when she saw yet another sleep-walker. No, really she must be going mad! There could not be so many people rushing about at night in the school passages!

Anne-Marie saw Mam'zelle standing under one of the dimmed lamps, and recognized her. At first she got a shock, for she had expected Mam'zelle to be in bed and not ambling about. But as soon as she was sure it really *was* Mam'zelle, she acted exactly as if she was walking in her sleep. She glided by Mam'zelle, her eyes set and staring just as Felicity's had been, muttering a poem.

Mam'zelle hesitated to grab her, for she had heard it was bad to awaken sleep-walkers suddenly. So she did not touch Anne-Marie, but followed her, whispering under her breath.

'The poor child! Here is another who walks in her sleep! I will follow her.'

Anne-Marie led Mam'zelle a fine dance, and finally ended up outside the second-form dormitories. The girl on guard there gave the alarm when she saw the two figures coming, and there was a terrific scramble as bottles and tins and plates were pushed under beds. The candles were blown out and girls got hurriedly into bed, those who didn't belong to that dormitory squeezing into wardrobes and under beds.

Anne-Marie, still acting, wandered into the second-form dormitory, meaning to walk to the end and back – but she fell over an empty bottle, and gave an exclamation. Mam'zelle followed her into the room and switched on the light.

Anne-Marie, dazed by the sudden light, blinked in confusion, watched in amazement by girls in bed. Then, remembering her sleep-walking act, she once again became glassy-eyed and glided between the beds.

The girls sat up, giggling. 'She's pretending!' called Antoinette.

'Ah, no, she walks in her sleep, the poor, poor child,' said Mam'zelle. 'What can we do for her?'

'I will cure her, *ma tante,*' said the irrepressible Antoinette, and leapt out of bed. She took a jug of cold water and threw it all over poor Anne-Marie, who, angry and wet, turned and gave Antoinette such a ticking off that all the girls knew at once that she certainly had not been sleep-walking before, but only play-acting. Mam'zelle realized it too, and tried to haul Anne-Marie out of the room, scolding her vigorously, and telling her to go and change her wet things at once. So engrossed was she that she entirely failed to see any signs of the midnight feast, nor did she notice any of the girls squashed into the wardrobes or under the beds.

'Golly!' said Sally, as soon as Mam'zelle had gone off with Anne-Marie. 'I don't believe she even *saw* the signs of our feast, not even that bottle that rolled out from under a bed!'

'Bit of luck for us,' said Violet. 'Come on, let's finish everything up quickly, and hide the things and get to bed before Mam'zelle thinks of coming back!'

The girls giggled. Mirabel, shut in the bathroom just opposite, heard them, and knew they were still enjoying their feast. She grew very angry indeed. She felt certain one of the second formers had locked her in, and she was determined to report the whole lot of them and have them well punished.

Mam'zelle took Anne-Marie to Matron's room, and woke Matron up, explaining volubly about Anne-Marie and why she was wet. Anne-Marie, her sleep-walking act quite ruined, wept copiously, fearing that she would be the laughing stock of the school next day.

'Now stop that silly crying,' said Matron briskly, giving Anne-Marie a vigorous rub-down with a very rough towel. She had long ago sized up Anne-Marie as a silly, swollen-headed girl, just the kind to act about like this.

'I must go,' said Mam'zelle, remembering the various people she had locked up that night. 'I have burglars to see to.'

Matron stared. 'What did you say?' she inquired.

'I said, I have burglars to see to,' said Mam'zelle, with

dignity. 'I have spent the night chasing people round the corridors, and locking them up. I go to Miss Theobald now, and she will telephone to the police. Ah, the people I have chased tonight. You would not believe it, Matron!'

Matron didn't. She thought Mam'zelle must be dreaming. 'Well, you go and get Miss Theobald and the police and whatever else you like,' she said, rubbing Anne-Marie so hard that she groaned. 'But don't bring me any more wet girls to dry in the middle of the night. I don't approve of them.'

Mam'zelle went off. She came to Miss Theobald's bedroom and knocked on the door. A surprised voice came from inside.

'Yes? Who is it?'

'It is I, Mam'zelle,' said Mam'zelle, and opened the door. 'Pardon me for coming at this time of the night, Miss Theobald – but I have burglars locked up in cupboards and a sleep-walker in my bedroom.'

20
A little unlocking

Miss Theobald listened to Mam'zelle's tale in the utmost astonishment. It seemed to her as if all the corridors of St Clare's must have been peopled with burglars, robbers, thieves, and others the whole of the night – but what was even more astonishing was the thought of Mam'zelle, who was terrified even of mice and beetles, valiantly chasing the burglars and, more remarkable still, locking them up wholesale!

She could hardly believe it. She looked closely at Mam'zelle, and wondered if the French mistress could possibly have dreamt it all. She got out of bed and put on her dressing-gown.

'I think, before I telephone the police, you had better show me where you locked these men up,' she said.

Mam'zelle trotted her off to the cupboard where she had locked in little Jane Teal. There was no sound from there at all. Miss Theobald was puzzled. She rapped on the door. Still no sound. Jane had fallen into a feverish doze. Miss Theobald suddenly heard the sound of overloud breathing, quick and hoarse.

She felt sure it was no burglar there. She unlocked the door, to Mam'zelle's dismay, and switched on the light inside the big cupboard – and there, before poor Mam'zelle's startled eyes, lay little Jane Teal, obviously ill, fully-dressed, even to her hat.

'This child's ill,' said the head mistress, feeling Jane's burning hot hand. 'Flu, I should think, and a very high temperature with it. What on earth is she doing dressed up like this, with hat and coat on? Was she going out?'

Mam'zelle was dumbfounded. She could not think of a word to say. Miss Theobald gently awoke Jane, and helped her to her feet. She could hardly stand. Between them the two mistresses took her to Matron's room, who, at one glance saw that Jane was seriously ill.

'I'll carry her to the sick-bay,' she said. 'I'll sleep there with her myself tonight.'

Matron's capable, strong arms lifted the half unconscious Jane easily, and bore her away to the quiet and comfortable sick-bay where all the ill girls were nursed. There was no one there at the moment. Matron soon had Jane undressed and in bed with a hot-water bottle.

'Well,' said Miss Theobald, thankful to have found poor Jane before worse befell her, 'what about your next burglar, Mam'zelle?'

Mam'zelle fervently hoped that the next prisoner *would* prove to be a burglar, even if he leapt out at them and escaped! She led the way to the bathroom opposite the second-form dormitory.

The second formers were still awake and heard the footsteps and voices in wonder. As the footsteps passed their door, they sat up and whispered, 'Who is it? What's up?'

Antoinette leapt out of bed and padded to the door. She peeped out cautiously. To her enormous astonishment she saw the head mistress standing by the bathroom door, with Mam'zelle, her aunt! Antoinette gaped as she saw Miss Theobald rap quietly on the door and say, 'Who's in here?'

A voice answered something, an angry voice. Miss Theobald heard that it was a girl's voice and not a man's, and she unlocked the door. Out shot Mirabel, expecting to see a group of grinning second formers – and stopped short in amazement when she saw Mam'zelle and the head mistress.

Mam'zelle's eyes almost dropped out of her head. She had shut her biggest burglar – or so she thought – into the bathroom – and now it was only Mirabel, that big, detestable, loud-voiced Mirabel, whose talk was all of games, games, and yet more games. Mam'zelle snorted in disgust.

'I want to complain,' said Mirabel, in a loud voice, surprised but unabashed by the sight of the head. 'I came to see if the second formers were having a midnight feast, which I had forbidden – and one of them locked me in this beastly cold bathroom. I want to report them, Miss Theobald. I know they held a feast, and there's a most important match tomorrow. And I demand that the girl who locked me in shall be punished.'

'It was Mam'zelle who locked you in,' said Miss Theobald. 'You had no right to be wandering about at night like this. Mam'zelle thought you were a burglar and locked you in.'

Antoinette stifled a giggle and rushed back into the dormitory. She related in whispers what she had heard. The girls were half amused and half angry – amused to think that Mirabel had been locked up, and angry to think she had been sneaking round, and had reported them.

Then Mam'zelle's loud voice penetrated into the listening dormitory. 'What is this untruthful thing you say, Mirabel? The second formers had *no* feast tonight! Did not I go there to chase Anne-Marie, after I had locked you in, and the good girls were all in bed and asleep! Not a thing to be seen, not a tin, not a bottle! You are a bad untruthful girl, trying to get others into trouble to protect yourself from blame!'

Mirabel was speechless. She glared at Mam'zelle, and Miss Theobald hastened to intervene.

'Well, if Mam'zelle was in the second-form dormitory, and the girls were in bed and asleep, it seems to me that you must be mistaken, Mirabel.'

'I'm not,' said Mirabel, rudely. 'Mam'zelle isn't speaking the truth. Go into the second-form dormitory and ask the girls if I or Mam'zelle is right, Miss Theobald. Then you will see.'

'I shall do nothing of the sort,' said the head mistress, coldly. 'Be more polite, Mirabel. You forget yourself.'

Mirabel, simmering with rage, dared say no more.

'Go back to bed,' said Miss Theobald. 'I will settle this tomorrow. I do not feel very pleased with you, Mirabel.'

Mirabel went back to bed with an angry heart. She knew she was right. Those second formers *had* had a feast, and Mam'zelle must be shielding them – because of Antoinette, she supposed. Well, she would get even with the little beasts. She would cancel the match next day! No one should play. She would show those youngsters she was sports captain, and make them toe the line!

'Well,' said Miss Theobald, looking at Mam'zelle, as Mirabel retreated, 'what about your next burglar, Mam'zelle?'

Mam'zelle took the head up to the corridor that ran round the fifth-form studies. She was feeling rather nervous now that her burglars were all turning into girls. It was really most extraordinary.

Miss Theobald rapped on the cupboard in which Alma was imprisoned. Alma's voice was heard.

'Let me out! It's awful in here!'

The head unlocked the door, and Alma staggered out, stiff and cold. Miss Theobald looked at her in surprise. 'Why were you wandering about at night?' she said, sharply.

'I – er – I heard a noise,' said Alma, stammering, for she was afraid of the head. 'And someone locked me in that cupboard.'

Miss Theobald switched her torch on and lit up the inside of the cupboard. She saw at a glance that it had been used as a storing-place for food.

'You went to take food from here, I suppose, Alma?' she said. 'Was it your own food?'

'I wasn't taking any,' said Alma. 'I was – well, I was just *looking*.'

'This girl is always eating,' said Mam'zelle in disgust.

'Always she chews something, always she eats.'

'Go back to bed, Alma,' said Miss Theobald. 'I will see you in the morning.'

Alma scuttled off thankfully. Miss Theobald turned rather coldly to Mam'zelle. 'Any more burglars?' she asked.

'Oh, Miss Theobald, truly I am sorry to have made so many mistakes!' said Mam'zelle, passing her hand through her hair in bewilderment. 'I pray you to forgive me, to . . .'

'Don't worry about it,' said Miss Theobald. 'It is perhaps a good thing that all this has happened: it seems that a great deal is going on this term at St Clare's that I must inquire into. Now – who is this girl you had in your bedroom – the one you found sleep-walking?'

'Felicity,' said Mam'zelle, fervently hoping that Felicity would still be there. She hurried down the stairs to her room, and unlocked the door.

Felicity was still there, lying asleep in bed. She looked very young and thin and, even in her sleep, her face wore a harassed, worried look. Miss Theobald looked at her for some time.

'This girl is obviously over-working,' she said, and sighed. 'Her music is too much for her, but her parents insisted on her taking her exams. I think, Mam'zelle, if you don't mind, we'll leave her in your bed. You had better sleep in the bed in Miss Harry's room – she is away for a few days. I suppose you have no more locked-up girls to show me tonight?'

'No,' said Mam'zelle, looking so crestfallen that the

head smiled. She patted Mam'zelle's plump arm.

'You meant well,' she said. 'If they had all been burglars, as you thought, you would have done a good night's work. Anyway, it is a good thing that so many things have come to light. Good night.'

Miss Theobald went back to bed, worrying about little Jane Teal, Alma, Mirabel and Felicity. It looked as if Jane had been trying to run away. She must find out about that.

Mam'zelle got into a strange bed, cold and puzzled. Why had so many girls been wandering about that night? Ah, that detestable Mirabel, how dare she say that she, Mam'zelle, was telling an untruth that night? And that dreadful Alma? Did she go snooping round every night to steal food from cupboards? There was something wrong with her, that girl!

Tomorrow I will talk with Claudine and Antoinette, thought Mam'zelle, screwing up her eyes, trying to go to sleep. They have good sense, they will tell me everything. It is a pity that English girls have not the good sense of French girls. It will be a pleasure to talk to my good little Claudine and Antoinette – *they* do not wander round at night for me to lock up. Alas, to think that I made so many prisoners, and now not one remains!

21 A few upsets

The next day the whole school knew the story of the night escapades, and how Mam'zelle had locked up so many girls. There was a great deal of giggling and chattering, and Anne-Marie had her leg pulled about her sleep-walking.

'How can I help sleep-walking?' she asked, trying to assume a dignity she did not feel. 'Felicity sleep-walks too, doesn't she? And you don't laugh at *her*.'

Miss Willcox heard about Anne-Marie's sleep-walking act and laughed too. She even teased her about it in class, which hurt Anne-Marie more than anything, and made her quite determined to get even with Miss Willcox if she could.

Felicity did not appear in class that day. It was reported that she had gone to the sick-bay for a rest and would not be taking the exam, which was the next week. Jane Teal was very ill indeed. Sally had been allowed to see her and had come back rather scared.

'Matron's worried about her and so is the doctor,' said Sally. 'Her mother is there in the sick-bay, too. I'm not allowed in any more. Matron shooed me out. I heard Matron say that Jane's worried about something and she can't get out of her what it is. But *I* know! It's all this business with Mirabel and Angela, and I know Jane reads in bed late at night with a torch. She learns her English and Latin that way. She told me so.'

'Well – hadn't you better go and tell Matron what you know?' said Katie. 'She might put things right for Jane then.'

'She can't, silly,' said Sally. 'You know what worries Jane more than anything – she's upset because Mirabel believes she rang that fire-bell to stop her meeting, and that's why Mirabel is so beastly to her. If only we could find out who did ring that bell, and make them own up, it would take a great load off poor Jane's mind!'

Violet Hill was feeling uncomfortable that morning, when she heard how ill Jane was. She remembered her quarrel with Jane, and the unkind things she had said. She wished she hadn't now.

'It will be a good thing to play in the match this afternoon,' said Sally. 'Take our minds off everything! We'll feel better out on the field, playing or watching.'

But Mirabel threw a bombshell that morning. She put a notice on the board, and soon everyone was round it, astonished and angry.

'The match today is cancelled, owing to the behaviour of the team members,' said the notice, and it was signed by Mirabel.

'*Well!*' said Sally. 'Would you believe it! How has she got the nerve to stick up a notice like that? And what right has she to cancel our match?'

'She's got the right because she's sports captain,' said Violet. 'Beast! I vote we send her to Coventry and don't speak a word to her, or smile at her, or turn up at any practices at all!'

Everyone agreed. It was an unheard of thing for the lower forms to treat an upper-form girl in this way, but they felt so indignant that not one member of the first or second form backed out of the agreement. Just because they had dared to have a feast in spite of Mirabel, she was treating them abominably, and putting up a notice in public to make them look small!

Gladys saw the notice and was shocked. She went straight to Mirabel.

'Mirabel! How *could* you put up that notice? Whatever were you thinking of? You *can't* cancel the match!'

'I can and I have,' said Mirabel grimly. 'I've sent a message to the school we were playing. They won't be coming. We shall have a practice match, instead. I have just written out another notice about that – the practice is to be at three o'clock, and every girl must attend from the two lowest forms.'

'Mirabel, you must be mad,' said Gladys, quite alarmed at her friend's grim face. 'You can't put all the girls against you like this, you really can't. You'll only get the worst out of them instead of the best.'

'I've told you before that I won't have you interfering with my decisions,' said Mirabel.

'Then what is the use of my being vice-captain?' said Gladys. 'Not a bit of use! I can't help you, because you won't let me!'

'Well, you're not much use, if you really want to

know,' said Mirabel, coldly, and went out of the room to pin the lacrosse practice notice on the board.

The girls held an informal meeting about the practice, and one and all determined not to turn up. It was Saturday, and, if they wished, they could go for nature-rambles. All the first and second forms decided to do this, even Antoinette, who detested walking.

So, to the astonishment of Miss Roberts and Miss Jenks, the whole of the two lowest forms went off in the sunshine together, taking with them nature notebooks and collecting tins and jars, chattering loudly as they passed by the windows of the mistresses' common-room.

'*Well*!' said Miss Roberts, looking after the laughing girls. 'What's come over them? Why this sudden, violent and wholesale interest in nature? I thought there was to be a match or lacrosse practice or something.'

Mirabel turned up on the playing-fields at five to three, grim-faced and determined. But nobody else arrived. Mirabel waited till ten past three, and then, rather white, went back to the school. One of the third formers, hardly able to hide her smiles, told her politely that the first and second formers had all gone out for a nature-walk.

Then Mirabel knew that she had lost. It had been her will against the wills of the first and second form, and they had won. They had ignored her orders. They had shown her what they thought of her and her authority. She sat down in her study, feeling dismayed.

She saw a note on the table addressed to her and opened it. It was a formal resignation from Gladys.

I wish to resign my post as vice-captain as I feel I cannot be of any use to you.
Gladys

Mirabel threw the note on to the floor. She felt unhappy and bitter. She had been so pleased to be sports captain. She had worked so hard for that position. She had had such high hopes of putting St Clare's at the very top of the lacrosse and tennis schools. Now the girls had defied her, and even her best friend had deserted her. It was a bitter hour for Mirabel.

The girls came back from their walk, rosy-cheeked and merry. They heard from the third form how Mirabel had gone out alone to the playing field, and had waited there in vain. They also heard that Gladys had resigned as vice-captain and they were pleased.

'Good old Gladys,' they said. 'We always thought it was funny she should back Mirabel up in her unpleasant ways!'

When Mirabel appeared in public at all that weekend the girls carefully turned away from her. Almost as if I was in quarantine for something beastly! thought Mirabel, bitterly. The girl was very worried and unhappy, but far too proud to appeal even to Gladys for comfort. Gladys was miserable too, and would have made things up with Mirabel at once if her friend had turned to her, or had admitted that she had been too high-handed with the younger ones. But Mirabel was cold and stand-offish, and gave Gladys no chance to be friendly.

The exam was to be held the next week, and most of the girls were feeling the strain. Only a few, like clever Pam, or the placid Hilary, did not seem to worry. Felicity was not to take the exam.

A specialist had come from London to see her. He spoke to Miss Theobald very seriously.

'This girl is on the verge of a nervous breakdown,' he said. 'Her mind seems full of music and nothing but music. See how she plays an imaginary violin, and strains to hear the tune. She must do no more work in music for a year.'

Miss Theobald nodded. How she wished Felicity's proud parents had not insisted on their gifted girl working for that difficult music exam! How much better it would have been for her to have dropped her music for a while, and to have entered into the ordinary, normal life of the other fifth formers, instead of losing herself night and day in her beloved music. Now her music might suffer because Felicity's brain had been worked too hard.

'Parents' fault, I suppose?' said the specialist, writing a few notes in his case-book. 'Why will parents of gifted children always push them so hard?'

'Just selfishness,' said Miss Theobald. 'Well – you think we must keep Felicity in bed for a time – then let her get up and wander round a bit, without any lessons – and then gradually join in with the others, without doing any music at all?'

'She can *play* at her music, but not work at it,' said the specialist. 'Let her enjoy it without worrying about it. She will probably do that anyhow when she knows she is not to work for the music exam for at least another two years.'

Felicity's parents came to see her, worried and dismayed. They remembered how Miss Theobald had pleaded with them not to push Felicity on so quickly. They were frightened when they saw her white face and enormous, dark-rimmed eyes.

'Don't worry too much,' said Miss Theobald. 'We have stopped her in time. Her sleep-walking gave us warning. Mam'zelle discovered that, and so we have been able to deal with Felicity quickly. Soon she will be a normal, happy girl again, and when she knows she need not work night and day for her music exam, a great weight will be off her mind, and she will laugh and chatter and be as cheerful as the others.'

It was a rather subdued father and mother that went home that day. 'Miss Theobald might have said, "I told you so," to us,' said Felicity's mother. 'But she didn't. Poor Felicity – I feel we are very much to blame for all this.'

The other sleep-walker, Anne-Marie, was not having a very good time. Whenever the first or second formers saw her coming, they immediately put on glassy stares, and with out-stretched hands began to glide here and there. Anne-Marie hated this teasing, and when it spread to the fifth form too, and glassy eyes appeared there also, Anne-Marie was very near tears.

'It's beastly of you,' she said to Alison and Angela, who laughed at her. 'I know I shan't pass the exam if you all jeer at me like this. It's mean of you.'

'Well, you're pretty mean yourself,' said Alison. 'You

keep on doing beastly things to *me*, don't you? Where have you put my geometry set you hid last week?'

Anne-Marie stared in surprise. She hadn't the least idea what Alison was talking about.

'Oh, don't put on that wide-eyed innocent look,' said Alison, impatiently. 'We all know you can act, but don't try to take *us* in by it! I know jolly well you're jealous of me because Miss Willcox likes me better than she likes you, and you're trying to get back at me by hiding my things and making silly bits of trouble for me!'

'I'm not,' said Anne-Marie, her voice trembling with indignation. 'I wouldn't dream of doing such a thing. I haven't *touched* your things! And as for being jealous of you, you needn't worry! I've no time for Miss Willcox now! I'm sure she's not as clever as you think. And what's more I'll show you she isn't.'

'Don't be silly,' said Alison. 'And don't talk about Miss Willcox like that. You're just plain jealous and you're taking my things and being beastly just to get even with me.'

'I tell you I'm not playing tricks on you, and I'm not jealous,' cried Anne-Marie. 'You can keep Miss Willcox all to yourself! I don't ever want to see her again! *Deirdre* Willcox indeed! Her name is Doris, just plain Doris – I saw it written in one of her books. I bet she calls herself Deirdre just because she thinks Doris is too ordinary. She's a – a – silly pretender!'

Anne-Marie flung herself out of the room, and Alison stared after her in rage. Angela laughed.

'You two amuse me,' she said. 'I'm glad I don't go off the deep end about anyone like you do! Silly, I call it!'

'Oh, *do* you!' said Alison, in a cutting voice. 'Well, let me tell you, you're just as bad in another way – you smile sweetly at the lower-form kids and get them all round you to wait on you – then when you're tired of them, you just tick them off – and they're as miserable as can be. I bet you're partly responsible for Jane Teal trying to run away!'

Angela opened her mouth to answer heatedly, but just then the door opened and Anne-Marie popped her head in again.

'I'll show Miss Doris Willcox up tomorrow, in front of the whole class!' she said. 'You see if I don't! Then you'll have to say I'm right, and you'll be jolly sick you didn't see through her. So there!'

The door banged and Anne-Marie disappeared. 'I'm tired of Anne-Marie and her silly ways,' said Alison, who still thought that it was she who was playing tricks on her, and had no idea it had been Alma. 'Let her do what she likes. I shall always like Miss Willcox!'

Anne-Marie traps Miss Willcox

Anne-Marie had prepared her little trap for Miss Willcox, and she had prepared it very carefully. Every week Miss Willcox set the girls some kind of composition to do, and they sent in their entries, which were carefully gone through by her and marked.

This week the subject set was a poem. It had to be only eight lines long, the first and third lines had to rhyme, and the second and fourth, the fifth and seventh and the sixth and eighth. The subject was to be 'Thoughts.'

The fifth form grumbled. They didn't like writing poetry, they *couldn't* write poetry, it was a silly waste of time for them in exam week. It was just like Miss Willcox to set a poem for them to do! So they grumbled and groaned, but all the same they managed to produce something that could be called a poem.

Anne-Marie had hunted through the poets for a lesser-known poem that would suit her purpose. If only she could find one that would just do! And by great good fortune she suddenly found exactly what she wanted. It was a little eight-line poem by Matthew Arnold, called 'Despondency', which seemed to Anne-Marie to be just what she wanted.

She copied it out in her big, rather sprawly handwriting. Really it seemed as if it was her own poem, it was just as sad as the ones she liked to write!

Anne-Marie sent the poem in with those of the others of her form. She signed her name at the bottom. Now, Miss Doris Willcox, we will see if you know good poetry when you see it!

The English lesson duly arrived, and Alison glanced curiously at Anne-Marie, who seemed excited. Was she really going to carry out her silly threat and do something to Miss Willcox? Alison felt a little disturbed. Ought she to warn Deirdre?

Miss Willcox arrived, carrying the sheaf of poems in her hand. She looked as soulful as ever, and wore a trailing crimson scarf round her swan-like neck.

The first part of the lesson was given to the reading of a play. Then came the time set apart for commenting on the girls' own work. Miss Willcox pulled the sheaf of poems towards her.

'Not a very good set,' she remarked, slipping the elastic band off the papers. 'I suppose the exam has had an effect on your creative powers. Pam's is the best – quite a praiseworthy little effort, simple and honest. Claudine, I can't pass yours. You may have meant it to be funny, but it isn't.'

Claudine made a face, which fortunately for her Miss Willcox did not see. Miss Willcox dealt with everyone's poems rapidly, quoting from one or two, praising here and there, and condemning the efforts of Doris, Angela and Carlotta.

Then she came to the last one, which was Anne-Marie's. She looked round the class, a rather spiteful look in her large eyes.

'And now at last we come to the poet of the class, Anne-Marie. A sad, heart-rending poem as usual. Listen to the wailings of our poet.

'THOUGHTS

The thoughts that rain their steady glow,
Like stars on life's cold sea,
Which others know, or say they know –
They never shone for me.

Thoughts light, like gleams, my spirit's sky,
But they will not rcmain.
They light me once, they hurry by,
And never come again.'

Miss Willcox read these lines out in a mock-heroic way, exaggerating the feeling in them, making fun of the whole poem. She put down the paper.

'Anne-Marie, why must you write like this? It is all so silly and insincere and quite meaningless. What for instance can you possibly mean by "Stars on life's cold sea?" What *is* life's cold sea? Just words that came into your head and you put them down because they sounded grand. Life's cold sea! Ridiculous!'

Anne-Marie stared at Miss Willcox steadily. She felt very triumphant. That wasn't *her* poem! It was written by a great poet, not by Anne-Marie at all! That just showed that Miss Willcox didn't know a thing and wasn't any judge of good poetry!

Miss Willcox didn't like the steady, oddly triumphant look on Anne-Marie's face. She felt a wave of anger against her.

'You have the scansion and the rhyming *quite* correct,' she said scornfully to Anne-Marie, 'but all the same I consider your poem the worst of the form.'

'Miss Willcox,' said Anne-Marie, suddenly, in a high, clear voice, 'I'm so sorry – I think I must have made a mistake in sending in that poem! I don't believe it is mine after all!'

The class turned to look at Anne-Marie. She sat tensely, still with that triumphant look on her face.

'What do you mean?' said Miss Willcox, impatiently. 'Not *your* poem? Then whose is it? I must say it *sounds* exactly like yours!'

'It's – it's very kind of you to say that,' said Anne-Marie, 'because you see – that poem is by Matthew Arnold, not by me at all. I'm glad you think his poetry is like mine. I feel honoured. Though I don't suppose, if he were alive, he would be at all pleased to hear the things you have just said about his little poem – it's strange to think you consider *his* poem the worst in the form!'

There was dead silence. Alison turned scarlet, seeing the trap Anne-Marie had set for Miss Willcox, and the prompt way in which she had fallen headlong into it. Anne-Marie pulled a volume of Matthew Arnold's poems from her desk and opened it at a certain page. 'Here's the poem,' she said, getting up from her desk. 'It's called "Despondency" not "Thoughts". I'll show it to you, Miss Willcox.'

Miss Willcox had gone white. She knew it had been a trap now – Anne-Marie's revenge for the cruel words she had spoken to her some days back. She had shown her up in front of the whole class. Oh, why, why had she said that the poem was the worst in the form? Why had she said such spiteful things? Only to hurt Anne-Marie, and because she thought she wanted taking down two or three pegs.

Alison was terribly distressed. She hated to see Miss Willcox trapped like that – and she also hated to think that the teacher had allowed herself to be trapped because of her own petty spite. She looked with dislike at the triumphant Anne-Marie.

'You have cheated, Anne-Marie,' said Miss Willcox, trying to regain her dignity. 'I shall have to report you to Miss Theobald for a grave act of deceit.'

'Yes, Miss Willcox,' said Anne-Marie maliciously, and the English mistress knew that it would be no good reporting Anne-Marie – for Anne-Marie would also report her own side of the matter, and Miss Theobald would not think very much of a teacher who condemned lines by a great poet just because she thought they were written by a schoolgirl she disliked.

The bell rang, and never did Miss Willcox feel so relieved to hear it. She gathered up her books and sailed out. The girls rounded on Anne-Marie.

'That was a beastly thing to do!' said Hilary.

'I thought it was funny,' said Claudine.

'You would!' said Pat. 'It was certainly clever, but it wasn't a decent thing to do.'

'I know it wasn't,' said Anne-Marie, defiantly. 'But I wanted to get my own back. And I did.'

'Well, I hope you're happy about it,' said Alison, bitterly. 'Trying to humiliate a good teacher in front of the whole class.'

'Did she feel sorry for poor little Doris-Deirdre then?' began Anne-Marie, but Hilary was not going to allow any spite of that sort.

'Shut up, both of you,' she said. 'Maybe you won't be such an ass over Miss Willcox now, Alison – and perhaps, now you've taken your revenge, Anne-Marie, you'll cool off and try to behave decently for the rest of the term. Alison has complained to me about your behaviour to her, and it's got to stop.'

'I don't know what you mean by my "behaviour to Alison",' said Anne-Marie, puzzled. 'She complains that I take her things, and play tricks on her, but I don't. Why should I? I'm not jealous of her or anything. She can keep Miss Willcox all to herself if she wants to! *I* don't mind!'

Most of the class, although they thought it was not a nice thing to humiliate a mistress publicly, had secretly enjoyed the excitement. Alma certainly had, for she had often been held up to ridicule by Miss Willcox for her complete inability to appreciate any fine literature at all. She was glad to see her defeated by Anne-Marie – and she was glad too when she heard Alison openly accusing Anne-Marie of the tricks she, Alma, had been playing on the unsuspecting Alison!

I'll play just one more and that shall be the last, she thought. I know she had a box of sweets sent to her today. I'll slip in and take those when she isn't there, and she'll blame Anne-Marie again!

But Alma tried her tricks once too often. When she slipped into Alison's study, it was empty, and she picked up the box of sweets quickly. She hurried to her own study and ran in.

To her dismay both Alison and Angela were there, waiting to ask Pauline something! Alison immediately saw the box of sweets in Alma's hand.

'Those are my sweets!' she said. 'You beast, you took them out of my study! Alma, you're a thief! I'm sure you were a thief before too – you pilfered the cupboard outside, when the second formers hid their stuff there. Angela, isn't she absolutely awful?

Alma stood there stubbornly, trying to think of some way out. 'I wasn't going to eat them,' she said at last. 'I was only playing a trick on you because I don't like you.'

'You were stealing,' said Alison, furiously. 'You know you meant to eat them! This will have to be told to Hilary. It's simply awful for a fifth former to be caught stealing.'

Alma sat down suddenly, feeling frightened. She had had a solemn and very serious talking to by Miss Theobald about being found in the cupboard the other night, and it had been impossible to convince the head mistress that she had not been doing anything wrong. If this got to her ears, matters would be even more serious.

'I didn't steal them, Alison,' she said, desperately. 'I tell you, I was just paying you out because you stopped me going to the cupboard where the second formers put their food – though you didn't know it. I took your knitting-needles – and your geometry set – and other things. Only to spite you, though, not to steal them. They're all here, look!'

She unlocked her desk in the corner and before Alison's astonished eyes lay all the things she had missed during the last week or two!

'Bring them into my study,' said Alison, completely at a loss to know what to do or say. 'I'll have to think about this. What a beast you are, Alma – especially as you knew I was blaming Anne-Marie all the time.'

Alma took everything back, weeping. Alison took one look at the puffy, pasty face and turned away in dislike. How could a girl who had been in the top form do things like this? Perhaps that was why she had been dropped back into the fifth – maybe because of some disgrace or other!

23

A few things are cleared up

'Wait till the exams are over before you make any fuss about Alma,' said Angela to Alison. 'Oh, dear – no wonder Anne-Marie didn't know what we were talking about when we kept accusing her of taking your things!'

'I shall have to apologize to her,' said Alison, gloomily. 'Blow Alma – what a first-class idiot she is, really! Isn't she odd? I don't understand her at all. Sometimes I think she's daft.'

The exams were now pressing on the girls, and they were working feverishly. Only Pam appeared to find them easy. Hilary worked through her papers methodically, and so did Pat and Isabel, Bobby and Janet, but Carlotta, Claudine and Angela got very hot and bothered. So, oddly enough, did Mirabel, which was unusual for her, but she had given so much of her time to the organizing of the school games that she had not worked as well at her exam tasks as the others had.

'These awful questions!' she said, as she read one after another. 'I can't seem to answer any of them!'

At last the exams were over and the whole form heaved a sigh of relief. What a week it had been! The girls wanted to yell and laugh and stamp and rush about. They became very boisterous, even the quiet Pam. But the teachers turned a blind eye and a deaf ear on the yelling girls, and did not even appear to see Carlotta doing cart-wheels all round the gym.

'Thank goodness we haven't got to wait long for the results,' said Doris. 'I hate having to wait weeks. Miss Cornwallis says we shall know in a few days.'

'How's little Jane Teal?' said Pat, remembering the first former for the first time for a few days. 'Is she better?'

'She's over the flu,' said Isabel, 'but Matron says she's still worried in her mind. When she was so ill, she kept raving about the fire-bell, and Mirabel and Angela. I rather think there's going to be a few inquiries made about certain members of our form soon! Poor Jane – it's rotten to think no one ever owned up about that bell, but let Jane take the blame. It made Mirabel simply beastly to her. She is the only person who hasn't been to see Jane in the sick-bay. Did you know?'

'Just like her,' said Pat.

The exam results came out and were posted up on the board. Pam and Hilary were top with honours. The others came in turn down the list. Carlotta was glad to see she had passed. Doris just scraped through too, and so did Claudine and Alison.

Three girls failed. They were Angela, Alma – and, most surprisingly, Mirabel!

Alma had not expected to pass. Angela was amazed that *she* hadn't! As for Mirabel, she was humiliated beyond words. To think that she, sports captain of St Clare's, should have failed. She rushed off to her study, filled with shame and horror. How everyone would sneer!

Gladys, who had hardly spoken with Mirabel since she had resigned as vice-captain, stared in amazement at the exam results. Mirabel failed! She could hardly believe her eyes. With her heart full of sympathy and warmth she hurried off to find her one-time friend.

Mirabel was sitting by the window, her humiliation almost more than she could bear. Gladys went to her, and took her hand.

'Bad luck, old thing,' she said. 'I'm awfully sorry. You worked too hard at the matches and things, that's all. Don't worry too much about it. Two others have failed as well.'

Mirabel was touched by Gladys's warm sympathy. She had felt lonely and deserted. With tears in her eyes she gazed at Gladys, and tried to speak.

'I can't bear it,' she said at last. 'They'll all laugh at me. Me, the sports captain! They'll be glad to laugh too. They hate me. Everyone hates me. Where have I gone wrong? I meant to do so well.'

'Let's be friends again, Mirabel,' said Gladys. 'You need me, don't you? You wouldn't let me help you at all this term – but let me help you now. The girls don't really hate you – they admired you awfully at the beginning of the term, and there's no reason why they shouldn't again.'

Poor Mirabel – and poor Angela! Both liked to shine, and both had failed. What was the use of being sports captain, what was the use of being the most beautiful girl in the school, if your brains were so poor you couldn't even get as good marks as Doris or Alison!

Claudine had been rather quiet for a day or two. She had been to see Jane Teal and taken her a lovely little handkerchief she had embroidered for her. Then she sought out Antoinette and made a proposal to her that surprised that second former very much.

'What! Tell Miss Theobald that I rang the fire-bell!' said Antoinette, in surprise and disgust. 'Are you mad, Claudine?'

'Yes, perhaps,' said Claudine, thoughtfully. 'I am afraid I have caught a little of this English sense of honour, alas! I feel uncomfortable *here* when I think of Jane Teal worrying about the fire-bell, and of Mirabel thinking it is Jane. It is a great pity, but I fear I have caught this sense of honour, Antoinette.'

'Oh, is it catching?' said Antoinette, in alarm. 'I do not want to get it, it is an uncomfortable thing to have. See how it makes you behave, Claudine.'

'I will go to Miss Theobald and tell her it was all my fault,' said Claudine, at last. 'You do not need to come into it, Antoinette. After all, it was my idea, and you only carried it out. I will go and confess.'

She gave a huge sigh and went off. Miss Theobald was startled and amused to see Claudine arriving with a saintly and determined expression on her face.

'Miss Theobald, I have caught the sense of honour from somebody at St Clare's,' announced Claudine. 'I have come to make a confession. I told my little sister to ring the fire-bell when Mirabel was about to hold her stupid meeting. I did not mean to own up, but now I feel uncomfortable *here* about it.'

Claudine pressed her tummy, and Miss Theobald listened gravely. 'I am glad you have owned up, Claudine,' she said. 'It was a silly thing to do, but it became a serious thing when someone else was suspected of it. Please tell Hilary. I shall not punish Antoinette, but she too must own up to Jane Teal, and put her mind at rest.'

Claudine went out, knowing that her real punishment was to be owning up to the serious head girl of the form. Hilary did not favour misbehaviour of this kind now that they were top formers, and she had a way of talking that at times made Claudine feel very small. She made her feel small now.

'You don't realize that next term we shall all be in the top form,' she said to Claudine. 'From there we go out into the world. We can't behave like naughty children in the first form now. We have to set an example to the younger ones, we have to learn what responsibility means!'

'You should be a preacher, Hilary,' said Claudine, jokingly.

But Hilary was not in a mood to be joked with. She took her position as head girl very seriously, all the more so because she knew she would not be head girl of the sixth. She was only staying one term more, and the head girl must be someone staying for three terms. Everyone was wondering who would be chosen.

Claudine went off, abashed, and found Antoinette, who was highly indignant at being sent off to Jane Teal to confess. But when she saw Jane's face, she was not sorry she had gone.

'Oh,' said Jane, 'was it really you, Antoinette? Oh, I'm glad you told me. You know, I really began to feel it *might* have been me, I was so worried about it. Whatever will Mirabel say?'

Mirabel soon heard about it. Gladys told her. She flushed uncomfortably, thinking of the hard time she had given poor Jane because of her unjust suspicions. She thought for a while and then went straight off to the sick-bay, where Jane still was.

'Jane, I've heard who rang the fire-bell,' said Mirabel, hardly liking to meet Jane's eyes. 'It wasn't you, and I was sure it was. I was beastly to you – left you out of matches unfairly – and things like that. I'm – I'm sorry about it. I . . .'

'It's all right, Mirabel,' said Jane, eagerly. 'I don't mind now. Not a bit. All I want is to get up and practise hard for you again, and perhaps play in a match before the term ends.'

Jane's warm response and loyalty were very pleasant to Mirabel, who had been very miserable. She smiled at the first former, left her some barley sugar, and went back to her study, thinking how nice it was to have someone look at her with liking once again.

Mirabel's visit to Jane made a great impression on the lower forms. Jane soon spread it abroad, and spoke so glowingly of Mirabel's kind words to her, that the younger ones began to get over their dislike and defiance. They had deserted the practice field, and had shown little or no interest in games since Mirabel had cancelled their match – but now they gradually drifted back, and Mirabel found, to her delight, that they seemed as keen as ever.

Gladys took back her resignation, and Mirabel set to work humbly and happily to make out games lists again and to arrange matches – but she let Gladys do at least half of it, and was careful to listen to her and to take her advice when she gave it. The two were much happier than they had ever been before and Gladys was glad to see her friend learning from the bad mistakes she had made.

'Looks as if Mirabel will be a good captain after all,' said Bobby in surprise. 'Well, well – we're all turning over a new leaf! There's Felicity back again, not caring two hoots about her music for a bit, and being quite one of us – and there's Anne-Marie gone all friendly and jolly since Alison apologized to her for suspecting her wrongly – and there's Alison behaving sensibly too, now that she sees through dear Deirdre – and Angela isn't being such an idiot with the younger ones since she failed in her exam.'

'No – that was a shock that pulled her together a bit,' said Pat. 'She's working hard now. Did you know that Hilary gave her a most awful talking-to. She wept buckets of tears, and was furious with Hilary – but she certainly has been better since.'

'It's only Alma that's still a pain in the neck,' said Isabel. 'I hate speaking to her even. I know Hilary's gone to tell Miss Theobald about her taking those things of Alison's. I bet she'll be expelled or something if she isn't careful.'

But Alma was not expelled. Instead Hilary explained something to the girls that made them feel rather uncomfortable.

'I told Miss Theobald all about our trouble with Alma,' said Hilary, 'and she told me we must be patient with her and put up with her, because she can't help it just now. There's something wrong with her glands, that can't be put right for about six months. That's why she's so fat, and always hungry, and looks so pasty and funny. She was sent off from her last school in disgrace – but Miss Theobald wants to keep her here and help her, till she can have some sort of marvellous operation done that can put her right.'

'Poor old Pudding,' said Doris. 'She's her own enemy, I suppose – or her glands are, whatever they may be! Well – I suppose we must put up with our Alma, and grin and bear it when she chews and munches and eats.' Doris began to imitate Alma at a meal, and the girls screamed with laughter.

But there was no real unkindness in the laughter. One and all were ready to put up with Alma now and help her, even selfish little Angela, and wild Carlotta. They were growing up, they were fifth formers, they could behave decently. St Clare's put its mark on you by the time you were in the fifth form!

24

Who shall be head of the school?

After the exam the girls relaxed with pleasure and relief. The teachers gave them less prep to do, and the fifth formers spent pleasant evenings in their own studies or each other's, talking and laughing.

'Christmas will soon be upon us,' said Pat. 'The rest of this term will fly! I always like the Christmas term – it begins in summer-time, when the September sun is still hot, and it often ends in snow, with Christmas beckoning round the corner.'

'You sound quite poetic,' said Doris. 'Anne-Marie used to say things like that!'

Anne-Marie laughed. She had not written any poems for some time, for, after the success of her trick on Miss Willcox, she had felt rather ashamed of herself. After all, *she* had pretended too, just like Miss Willcox, *she* had tried to write poems that sounded very grand, but were quite worthless really. Now Anne-Marie was determined to wait till she had something to say, before she wrote poetry again.

She had had a talk with Miss Theobald, who had heard

of Anne-Marie's 'cheating' as Miss Willcox called it. The head mistress hadn't much time for the English teacher herself, sensing that she was insincere and rather conceited – but she could not allow any of the girls to flout authority, or be insolent, without reprimanding them severely.

So Anne-Marie had had a bad twenty minutes, and had come away a sadder and wiser fifth former, determined that she would write no more 'wonderful' poetry until, as Miss Theobald said, she had something real and honest and sincere in her heart to put into her writing and make it worthwhile.

Mirabel had got over the shock of failing in the exam, and was trying to make the lower forms forget her stupid arrogance and harshness. Her voice was still loud and clear, but not haughty or dictatorial, and she no longer walked as if the whole earth belonged to her. She was a wiser person altogether, and the girls respected her for being able to change herself so completely.

Jane Teal was once again working hard for Mirabel, exulting in her returned health and strength, a great weight off her mind. Angela no longer gave the younger ones so many jobs to do, and she and Alison did their mending together. Hilary had made a great impression on Angela when she had ticked her off, and had really frightened her.

'You're a poor, poor thing, Angela,' she had told her. 'You use your pretty face and smile to save yourself trouble, and you are getting a lazy mind and a lazy body, letting other people do the things *you* ought to do. No wonder you failed in the exam – and failed miserably too! If you're not careful you'll go on being a failure in all kinds of ways, and people will laugh at you instead of admiring and respecting you. What do you suppose Jane and Sally and Violet and the rest of your lower-form slaves think of their darling beautiful Angela now, when they see that she and Alma tied for bottom place in the exam? Pull yourself together a bit, for goodness' sake.'

Each term brought different things to learn, besides lessons. Those girls who faced their difficulties, saw and understood their faults, conquered their failings, and became strong characters and leaders would make the finest wives and mothers of the future. Miss Theobald watched the fifth formers carefully, and was proud of many of them.

She remembered them as silly little first formers, and a little less silly second formers. She remembered Pat and Isabel O'Sullivan, the 'stuck-up twins' as they had been called, when they first came. She remembered how Mirabel had vowed not to stay longer than half a term, and had misbehaved herself dreadfully in her first term. She remembered the wildness of Carlotta, who had come to St Clare's from circus-life, untamed and headstrong.

She remembered Bobby, whose brilliant brains were once only used in mad and clever tricks – and Claudine, untruthful, deceitful and unscrupulous, who was at last finding responsibility and a sense of honour. Here were all these girls now, dependable, honest-minded, hardworking, and responsible. Truly St Clare's was a school to be proud of.

Before the end of the term came the head mistress must choose the head girl for the whole school. All the sixth were leaving, and the fifth were to go up, with one or two new girls. Hilary was the only one of the fifth who was not staying on for one more whole year. She was only to stay one term more, and then she was to go to India to be with her parents there.

Otherwise Hilary would have been head of the sixth, and a good responsible head she would have made. But now someone else must be chosen. The girls wondered who it would be. It was a tremendous honour, for the head girl of the sixth would be the head girl of the whole school, a person of great influence.

'It won't be me, anyway,' said Doris, comfortably. 'I'm too stupid.'

'And it won't be me,' said Carlotta. 'I'm still too wild.'

'Nor me,' said Bobby, grinning. 'I'm still too much given to playing tricks. Didn't Mam'zelle jump when she drank her glass of milk this morning and found a black beetle at the bottom?'

The girls giggled. It was a silly trick, but had caused a lot of fun. Bobby had popped a little tin black beetle into Mam'zelle's glass of mid-morning milk, and her horror when she had drunk all the milk and then had suddenly seen the beetle at the bottom had been most amusing to watch.

'*Tiens*!' she had cried. 'What is this black animal I have

almost drunk? Oh là, là, that it should choose my glass and no one else's!'

The girls recalled all the tricks Bobby and Janet had played on poor Mam'zelle – the way they had made the plates dance – the dreadful stink balls – and many others. They had all been good fun, and Mam'zelle had always joined in the laughter afterwards.

'We break up in three days' time,' said Bobby. 'Then heyho for the holidays – and when we come back, we shall all be sixth formers, grave and serious and solemn! No tricks then – no giggles – no messing about!'

'Oh, rubbish!' said Carlotta. 'We shan't suddenly alter just because we're sixth formers. We shall be just the same. I do wonder who will be head girl. Perhaps one of the twins will.'

'I hope not,' said Pat, at once. 'I'd hate to be something Isabel wasn't, and she would hate it too. Otherwise we'd either of us love it. It's the thing I'd like best in the world at the moment. I love St Clare's, and I'm proud of belonging to it. If I could do something for it I would – but I don't want to do something that I can't share with Isabel.'

'I feel the same about that,' said Isabel. 'But if we *did* have the honour of being asked, either of us, to be head girl, we'd say no. Anyway, there are plenty of others who would make better head girls than we should.'

At that very moment the matter was being decided by Miss Theobald, Miss Cornwallis and Mam'zelle. They were sitting together in the head's sitting-room, discussing the very weighty and important question of who should be the next head girl. It was important because the head girl had a powerful influence on the whole school, and was, in fact, typical of the spirit of St Clare's.

They were going down the list of girls. 'Hilary can't be, of course,' said Miss Cornwallis. 'A pity, because she has had great experience of being head girl in three or four forms. Still, perhaps it is time someone else had a chance of showing leadership.'

'Janet?' said Miss Theobald.

The others shook their heads. Janet could still be hot-tempered and wilful at times. She had not yet learnt to guard her sharp tongue completely. A head girl had to have complete control of herself.

'Not Bobby, of course,' said Miss Cornwallis. 'Brilliant, trustable, but still a little unsteady. What about Gladys?'

'Too gentle – not enough of a leader,' said Miss Theobald, who knew the character of every girl in a most remarkable way. 'And Claudine I am afraid we must also cross out, Mam'zelle.'

Mam'zelle sighed. It had been a secret wish with her for two or three terms that Claudine, her little Claudine, might be head of St Clare's, the school in which Mam'zelle had taught for so many many years. But even Mam'zelle biased as she was, knew that Claudine was not fit to lead others.

'If she had been at St Clare's when she was thirteen now,' said Mam'zelle, 'ah, then my little Claudine might have had time to learn enough to become head girl!'

Both Miss Theobald and Miss Cornwallis had their

doubts about this. In fact, Miss Cornwallis thought that if Claudine had been at St Clare's ever since she was a baby, she would still not have been suitable for a head girl. But neither wanted to upset Mam'zelle, who adored her two nieces, so they said nothing.

'Alma, certainly not, poor girl,' said Miss Theobald. 'She is a most unfortunate child. Perhaps when she is in really good health, she will improve. Carlotta now – no, I think not. Still rather unaccountable and uncontrolled in her temper. I always feel she is still capable of scolding people if she doesn't approve of them.'

Mam'zelle remembered various scolding episodes in Carlotta's school-life and smiled. 'Ah, she would scold the first formers well if they did not behave!' she said. 'She would be an amusing head girl, but perhaps not a very good one.'

'Felicity, no,' said Miss Cornwallis. 'She will always be apt to forget everything when her music fills her mind. She will perhaps someday be one of the foremost musicians or composers, but only in her art will she be fit to lead others.'

'Angela and Alison – neither of them leaders in any way,' said Miss Theobald. 'How good it would be for both of them to be head girls, and feel the weight of leadership and responsibility on their shoulders – but how bad for the school! Alison is still such a feather-head, and Angela has a lot to learn yet. Three more terms to learn it in – well, maybe it will be enough.'

'Anne-Marie would be hopeless,' said Mam'zelle, 'so would Pauline.'

'That leaves Doris, Pam and the twins,' said Miss Theobald, looking at her list.

'Doris is too stupid,' said Mam'zelle. 'Still she cannot roll her Rs for me in the French way. Ah, she will be a great success on the stage, that girl, she is so clever a mimic. But she is stupid in all other ways, though a nice, nice girl.'

The others agreed. 'Pam would make an ideal head girl,' said Miss Theobald, 'but she is too young. Almost two years younger than the oldest in the fifth. She is staying on two years, so perhaps she will be head girl in the future. A nice, hard-working, quiet and dependable child.'

'That only leaves the O'Sullivan twins,' said Miss Cornwallis, 'and I am sure that we cannot choose one without the other. They are inseparable and always have been. The other twin would feel very much left out if we chose one of them.'

'Ah – I have it!' said Mam'zelle, suddenly, banging the table and making the other mistresses jump. 'I have it! Yes, we will have *two* head girls! Why not? Is not St Clare's bigger than ever it was? Has not the head girl more than enough to do? Then we will have *two* head girls, girls who will work together as one – so why not the O'Sullivan twins?'

Miss Theobald and Miss Cornwallis looked at each other. It was a good idea. Two head girls who were twins would certainly work very well together, and could share the responsibility well. Pat and Isabel had consistently done good work, and had grown into splendid, trustworthy and sensible girls.

'Yes,' said Miss Theobald, at last. 'It's a very good idea indeed. The twins will make fine head girls. It will do them a world of good, for they have never undertaken any kind of leadership here so far. They shall be joint head girls. I will make the announcement tomorrow.'

So, when the whole school was called together for the head to announce the changes in the coming term, the names of the two new head girls were given.

'We have carefully studied the question of who shall be head girl of the school for the coming year,' said Miss Theobald. 'And I think there is no doubt that our choice is wise and will be very popular. St Clare's is growing fast, and the head girl has a great deal to do; sometimes too much. So we have decided to have *two* head girls working together, and we have chosen a pair who have been with us from the first form, and have made their way up the school steadily and well, winning everyone's respect and admiration. Next term the O'Sullivan twins will be our head girls!'

There was a terrific outburst of cheering, clapping and stamping at these words. Everyone knew the like-as-pea twins, everyone liked them and trusted them. Now they were to be head girls together – splendid!

The twins were overwhelmed. They blushed scarlet, and when they heard the outburst of cheering, they felt sudden tears pricking their eyelids. It was a wonderful moment for them. To be chosen to head the school, to lead it, to hold the biggest honour St Clare's had to offer – that was something worthwhile.

'Thank you,' said Pat, standing up with Isabel, when the cheering had lessened. 'We'll – we'll do our very best!'

So they will – and their best will be very good indeed. And there we must leave them, about to have their dearest wish, head girls of St Clare's, the finest school they know.

The
SIXTH FORM
at
ST CLARE'S

Contents

Back to St Clare's

Pat and Isabel O'Sullivan walked along the station platform in a sedate manner, as befitted the head girls of St Clare's. A giggling group of second formers fell silent as they approached, looking at the twins in awe.

'They look nice,' whispered one new girl to her neighbour. 'Who are they?'

'Our head girls – the O'Sullivan twins. And they are nice – very nice.'

The twins heard and shared a secret smile, which held more than a touch of pride. 'Just think of it, Pat. You and I, head girls of St Clare's,' said Isabel. 'I still expect to wake up and find out it was all a dream.'

'More like a dream come true,' said Pat happily. 'And Mummy and Daddy were almost as pleased for us as we were for ourselves.'

'And proud,' laughed Isabel. 'I think Mummy must have rung round all our relations to tell them the news. I half expected her to put an announcement in the local paper.'

'Excuse me,' came a small, lisping voice from behind them. 'Can you help me, please?'

The twins turned and found themselves looking

down at a little girl, so tiny that she looked too young even for the first form, although she wore the school uniform. Pat and Isabel thought her rather sweet, with her halo of golden curls, rosebud mouth and wide blue eyes. They became even wider as they rested on the two identical faces.

'It's all right, kid,' said Isabel with a friendly smile. 'You're not seeing double. We're your head girls, Pat and Isabel O'Sullivan. And who are you?'

'Dora Lacey,' answered the girl. 'I seem to have lost the rest of my form.'

'Come along with us, Dora,' said Pat, putting a hand on her shoulder. 'The first form aren't usually difficult to find. Just follow the noise!'

Certainly the platform from which the St Clare's train was to leave was extremely noisy, as what seemed like hundreds of excited girls milled about, greeting one another loudly and saying goodbye to parents.

'Pat! Isabel! Over here!' The twins looked up and there, coming towards them, was their cousin Alison, along with Hilary Wentworth.

'Hi, twins! Good to see you again,' said Hilary. Then, smiling down at the first former, 'I see you've found a little stray. Miss Roberts is over there some-where, with Bobby and Janet helping her try to round up the first form and herd them on to the train, like sheepdogs.'

'Let's go and help them out,' said Alison, pulling her

heavy winter coat tightly round her. 'I'll be glad when we get on to the train ourselves. At least it should be a little warmer.'

The January day was bitterly cold and many of the girls had already boarded the waiting train rather than stand about on the cold platform.

'Dora!' said the first-form mistress, Miss Roberts, in exasperation when she saw the girl walking towards her with the sixth formers. 'I thought you were on the train already.'

'I was, but I got off again.'

'Well, get back on, and this time stay put!' said Miss Roberts firmly. Then, turning to the twins, 'It hardly seems five minutes since I had you two under my eye as unruly first formers and now here you are, head girls. Well done, both of you. I think Miss Theobald has made an excellent choice.'

'Thanks, Miss Roberts,' said Pat, flushing with pleasure. 'We'll certainly do our best.'

'I'm sure you will,' said Miss Roberts. 'Oh, Lucy, where are you going? That's the third-form carriage! Ours is here.'

'Miss Roberts is certainly going to have her hands full this term,' laughed Hilary.

'Oh, look, here come Bobby and Janet with another group.'

'Hallo all!' called out Bobby and Janet as they shepherded several small girls on to the train. 'Were we this loopy when we were first formers?'

'I suppose we must have been,' said Isabel. 'Though it seems hard to believe now. Dora! What on earth are you doing off the train again? Miss Roberts will skin you alive.'

Somehow, though none of the sixth formers had seen her get off, Dora was on the platform again.

'I thought I might buy some chocolate to eat on the train,' she said, quite unconcernedly.

'You should have done that earlier,' said Pat. 'The train's due to leave at any minute. Hey, Bobby, take this one along to her carriage, would you? And don't turn your back on her!'

'Sweet little thing,' remarked Alison as Dora boarded the train yet again. 'Rather angelic looking.'

Bobby Ellis wasn't so sure. She saw a certain mischievous twinkle in the girl's eyes, recognizing it because it was part of her own nature too. She had a distinct feeling that Dora Lacey could turn out to be more imp than angel.

At last all the first formers were settled, and the twins made their way to their own carriage, where a near-riot broke out.

'Pat! Isabel! Had a good Christmas?'

'Hi, twins! Good to see you both again!'

'Better behave ourselves now that the head girls have turned up!'

'Hallo, Doris . . . and Carlotta! And is that Gladys in the corner?'

Everyone moved along to make room for the twins

and some of the others, who had just come in, Bobby and Janet among them.

'Whew, those first formers are a handful!' said Janet, collapsing on to the seat beside Pat. 'Miss Roberts is going to have her work cut out keeping them in order.'

'Hey, who's that?' said Doris, looking out of the window. 'Must be a new arrival.'

The girls turned and saw a tall, striking-looking girl with long red curls standing on the platform, a sullen expression on her face as she spoke to the man with her.

'That must be her father,' said Gladys. 'Look how similar their colouring is.'

'Well, she's certainly in a temper about something,' said Hilary as the girl scowled fiercely at whatever her father had said. He put his hand gently on her arm and she shook it off angrily, flouncing away to board the train. Just in time, too, as the guard blew his whistle and the journey to St Clare's began.

'Wow, has she got a temper!' exclaimed Alison. 'She looks about our age, too. Let's hope she's not in the sixth.'

'Oh, I don't know. She might be rather exciting to have around,' said Bobby. 'Are we expecting any new girls in our form?'

'Miss Theobald said at the end of last term that there would be a couple,' replied Pat. 'And Priscilla Parsons of the old sixth is staying on. She's too young to leave yet.'

The listening girls groaned. 'You're kidding!' said Hilary. 'I know none of the old sixth form could stand her.'

'No wonder,' said Janet. 'Spiteful, snobbish, interfering – and those are her good points!'

The others laughed. 'Well, we'll just have to set Carlotta on to her if she tries any of her tricks on us,' said Bobby with her wicked grin. 'Remember how she dealt with old Sour Milk Prudence back in the first form?'

The girls laughed as they remembered the wild, fiery little creature Carlotta had been when she first came to St Clare's – all except Carlotta herself. In fact, Pat realized suddenly, Carlotta didn't seem her usual carefree self at all and her normally laughing brown eyes looked decidedly stormy.

'Anything up, Carlotta?' asked Pat in concern. 'Is it the thought of going back to school, or just after-Christmas blues?'

The others stopped their chatter, new girls forgotten as they, too, realized that something was wrong with their friend. Carlotta was a very popular member of the form and if she was in trouble they wanted to know about it, and help if they could.

'Neither,' said the girl, with a shadow of her wide smile, as the concern she saw on the faces around her warmed her a little. 'The fact is, I'm in a mess and I don't know if anyone can help me out of it.'

'Hey, that sounds serious!' said Doris, looking alarmed.

'It is,' said Carlotta. 'You see, my dad has got it into his head – or, to be more precise, my grandmother has *drummed* it into his head – that I need to go to some fancy finishing school once I've finished at St Clare's.'

'But you can't!' cried Bobby, horrified. 'You're coming to university with Janet, the twins and me.'

'That's what I'd *like* to do,' sighed Carlotta. 'Instead I'm supposed to learn elocution and deportment and *cordon-bleu* cookery – which, in my case, will probably be *cordon-bleurgh*!'

'You're not serious!' exclaimed Pat, quite unable to picture the spirited Carlotta fitting in at such a place. 'Finishing school! It'll probably finish you off altogether.'

Carlotta gave a bitter laugh. 'Don't I know it! But Gran's determined that I ought to learn what she calls "social graces".'

'Social graces!' snorted Doris. 'Sorry, Carlotta. No disrespect to your gran, but there are more important things in life than learning how to walk like a model and all that kind of stuff.'

'Right!' agreed Hilary warmly. Carlotta's manners had improved considerably from when she was a wild, uncontrolled first former, fresh from circus life and inclined to fly into a rage at the slightest thing. Her impulsiveness and outspokenness, however, hadn't changed a bit, part of the girl's vivacious personality. And that, thought all the sixth formers, was as it should be. It would be just awful if her individuality was crushed.

'But what's your dad thinking of to agree to such a thing?' asked Alison.

'He always thinks that Gran knows best when it comes to "feminine" matters,' said Carlotta impatiently.

'Girls, help! What am I going to do?'

The sixth formers couldn't bear to hear Carlotta sound so despairing. 'Don't you worry,' Pat reassured her. 'We'll get you out of this somehow.'

'Yes,' put in the quiet little Gladys. 'We'll get up a petition and send it to your father.'

'We'll tell him the rotten finishing school's burnt down,' added Bobby.

'If it comes to it, we'll kidnap you and smuggle you into university with us,' said Janet.

'Even better, we'll kidnap your grandmother,' said Doris quite seriously.

'Idiots!' Carlotta gave a laugh she hadn't thought she had in her. 'Do you know, you've actually cheered me up a bit.'

'Glad to hear it,' said Pat. 'Try not to get too worked up about it. After all, we've a whole year to think up a plan.'

Just then the carriage door opened and there stood little Dora Lacey. 'Oh!' she said blankly, looking surprised.

'Don't tell me,' sighed Isabel. 'You're lost again.'

Dora nodded. 'I just slipped out to the toilet, and when I came back the carriage seemed to have disappeared.' She sighed. 'I'm just not used to finding my own way around. My older sister was supposed to be starting at St Clare's this term too, but she got chickenpox and won't be back for a couple of weeks.'

'That's tough,' said Hilary sympathetically. 'All the same, you ought to be learning to stand on your own two feet a bit now, you know. Your big sister won't want to baby-sit you all the time when she does come to school. Come on.' She stood up. 'I'd better return you to Miss Roberts before she thinks you've jumped off and pulls the communication cord.'

'That bad-tempered-looking girl never joined our carriage after all,' remarked Janet as the door closed behind Hilary. 'Perhaps she's in the fifth.'

'Well, they're a good crowd this term,' said Pat. 'No doubt they'll take her in hand. Pam Boardman's staying down with them, you know. She's to be head of the form.

'I'll miss little Pam, although she was so quiet,' said Isabel.

'Me too,' said Doris in dismay. 'She was my study companion. Now what am I going to do?'

'Oh, well, I guess one of us others will have to put up with your peculiar little ways,' said Alison, earning herself a playful punch on the arm from Doris.

'Doesn't Pauline usually come by train?' asked Gladys.

'Oh, haven't you heard? She's not coming back,' said Bobby. 'Apparently she's decided to take a secretarial course, then she's going to find a job.'

'And Felicity's left too,' said Janet. 'She's to have a long rest before making any decisions about her future.'

Felicity Ray, a musical genius, had been with the girls in the fifth, but had worked so hard at her music that she had driven herself almost to a nervous breakdown.

'Poor Felicity,' said Pat. 'And poor Alma Pudden.

She's to have that operation for her glands soon, so she won't be returning either.'

The girls listened to this with mixed feelings. None of them had liked the plump, pasty Alma with her strange tempers, but once they had learnt that her problems had been due to ill health, they had all felt a little uncomfortable.

'Guess what?' said Hilary, coming back in. 'I've just seen that red-haired girl standing out in the corridor, absolutely sobbing her heart out.'

'She's a little old to be suffering from homesickness,' said Janet scornfully.

'It wasn't that kind of crying,' said Hilary thoughtfully as she took her seat. 'More sort of bitter and angry, as though she had a grudge against the whole world. I went over and asked if I could help, but she turned on me and nearly bit my head off.'

'Wonder what her problem is?' said Bobby.

No one could imagine, and Carlotta said, 'So she could be in our form after all. Who else is still to come back?'

'Claudine, Anne-Marie, Angela and Mirabel,' said Doris. 'I know that Claudine and Antoinette were due to travel back from France yesterday, and presumably the others are going by car.'

'Angela's driving herself,' put in Alison. 'Her folks bought her the neatest little sports car for Christmas. Her dad wasn't too thrilled about it, but you know what Angela and her mum are like once they've set their hearts on something.'

'I didn't know Angela and her mum possessed hearts,' said Carlotta rather maliciously. 'I'm surprised she didn't get her own chauffeur as well.'

Alison, who was Angela's friend, flushed but said nothing. No longer blind to the beautiful, but spoilt, girl's faults, she knew that Carlotta had every reason to sneer at the girl who looked down on her so terribly. The vain, feather-headed Alison had grown up a lot over the past few years, thought Pat, watching her cousin, and was now much more likeable for it.

'Will Angela and Mirabel be coming up into the sixth with us?' asked Hilary 'You know they both failed last term's exams dismally.'

'Mirabel certainly is,' said Gladys, who had spent part of the holidays with her friend. 'And she's to resit the exams. Her dad was so disappointed and gave her a dreadful lecture. The upshot was extra coaching during the holidays, and she's to have some lessons and study periods away from the rest of us so that she can concentrate on her exam work.'

'Yes, Angela's doing the same,' said Alison. 'It's tough on them, just when the rest of us are looking forward to taking things a bit easier after all our hard work last term.'

'Yes,' agreed Hilary. 'I know they brought it on themselves but, all the same, I can't help feeling sorry for them.'

2 The new girls

Claudine, the French girl, waited impatiently for the rest of her form to arrive. She and Antoinette, her third-form sister, had come back to St Clare's that morning, along with their aunt, the French teacher, Mam'zelle. Once they had reported to Matron and been to see Miss Theobald, time had hung heavy on their hands. At last some third formers had arrived and Antoinette had gone off happily with them, leaving her sister to her own devices.

Feeling a little lonely, Claudine wandered off in the direction of the sixth-form classroom, peering inside with interest. 'So,' she mused. 'This is where I shall spend my final year at this very English school. Perhaps it is where I shall, at last, catch the English sense of honour.'

'Hi, Claudine,' said a voice behind her, and the girl turned sharply.

'Anne-Marie!' she exclaimed in delight, then stepped forward and kissed the new arrival on both cheeks in true French style. Anne-Marie was as astonished as she was gratified. She had not been the most popular of girls when she had joined St Clare's last term, being rather pretentious and conceited. Then she had learnt a hard lesson and, as a result, settled down and become a much nicer, more sensible girl. Even so, she hadn't realized that Claudine thought quite so highly of her. In truth, the French girl was so heartily tired of her own company that she would even have welcomed stuck-up Angela, or the loud-voiced, domineering Mirabel.

'*Mon ami*,' she said warmly, taking Anne-Marie's arm. 'What a pleasure it is to see you again.'

'Well, it's nice to see you again, too, Claudine,' said Anne-Marie, quite overwhelmed. 'Did you have a good Christmas?'

'*Oui, très bien*,' said Claudine. 'But it is good to be back, *non*?'

'*Non*. I mean yes,' replied Anne-Marie, becoming confused. 'So this is our new classroom. Not bad, is it?'

Claudine nodded, eyes sparkling. 'Ah, what times we shall have in here, Anne-Marie. What tricks Bobby and Janet will plan. What jokes Doris will make.'

'Yes, but, Claudine, we can't mess about like that now,' objected Anne-Marie. 'We're sixth formers.'

'Oh? And can't sixth formers play tricks and jokes?' asked Claudine, crestfallen.

'Most definitely not,' answered Anne-Marie, shaking her blonde head firmly. 'It's our duty to set a good example to the younger girls.'

'*All* of the younger girls?' said Claudine, dismayed. 'Can we not set a bad example to just one or two?'

'Claudine, you're wicked!' laughed Anne-Marie. 'No, I'm afraid not. We must be well behaved and serious and – well, boring, I suppose.'

Just as Claudine was digesting this, Matron appeared in the doorway. 'Ah, sixth formers,' she said with brisk satisfaction. 'I was beginning to despair of finding any. I've new girl for you here.' She pulled forward a pretty, lively looking girl, with humorous silver-grey eyes and springy blonde curls. Claudine and Anne-Marie took to her at once and exchanged excited glances. 'I'll leave you to get acquainted,' said Matron. 'Must dash – the train girls have just arrived.'

The new girl advanced into the room, betraying not one jot of shyness. 'Hi there!' she said, grinning at the two girls. 'I'm Fizz Bentley.'

Claudine and Anne-Marie stared at her open-mouthed, surprised as much by her Cockney accent as by her unusual name.

'Fizz?' repeated Claudine. 'Surely that is not a real name?'

'No, my real name's Phyllis,' explained the girl with a grimace. 'But my little sister could never pronounce it and called me Fizz, which kind of stuck.'

'It suits you,' pronounced Anne-Marie. 'You look sort of – well – fizzy and bubbly.'

The three girls laughed together at this, which broke the ice completely.

'I've never been to boarding school before,' confided Fizz in the Cockney accent which fascinated the other two. 'But I'm looking forward to it. Do you go in for midnight feasts and that kind of stuff?'

'Alas no, not now that we are so-serious sixth

formers,' said Claudine, mindful of Anne-Marie's words. 'Always we must be so-good and set an example to the younger girls.'

Fizz looked disappointed and Anne-Marie took her arm. 'We'll still have plenty of fun, you'll see. Come on, Claudine, let's show Fizz around a bit before the bell goes for tea.'

The train girls, too, were looking forward to tea after their long journey. Pat and Isabel would have liked to take a look at their new classroom, but there was no time for that. As head girls, they had to go and see Miss Theobald before tea, so they unpacked swiftly before washing their hands and combing their hair. Both girls felt a little nervous as they made their way to Miss Theobald's room. They had had many interviews with the head over the years, but none as important as this, their first as head girls.

'Come in!' came Miss Theobald's clear, calm voice as the girls knocked at her door. She smiled as they entered.

'Twins, how nice to see you again. Refreshed after the break, I hope, and ready to help the mistresses and myself with the running of the school?'

'Yes, Miss Theobald,' chorused Pat and Isabel, liking the way the head made them feel part of her team.

'I don't intend to keep you for very long at the moment, girls,' Miss Theobald continued, 'as I will be addressing the whole of the sixth form after tea in your common-room.'

'Common-room?' repeated Pat. 'Does this mean that

we won't be having our own studies this term?'

'Oh, yes, you won't lose those.' The head smiled. 'But I've a particular reason for wanting you to have a common-room this year as well. There's a large music room along by the studies, which I've had cleared out during the holidays, and it now belongs to the sixth.'

The bell rang just then and Miss Theobald said, 'I'll explain it all to you later, along with the others. Go and have your tea now, and please see to it that everyone assembles in the common-room at six o'clock.'

'Wonder what that's all about?' said Isabel, mystified, as they made their way to the dining-room. 'It'll be a bit of gossip to pass on to the others, anyway.'

Most of the sixth form were already seated round the big dining table when the twins took their places. There was Angela, and Mirabel, both of whom had just arrived by car, and Priscilla Parsons. The sullen girl from the train was there too, so it seemed as though the sixth would have the doubtful pleasure of her company after all. And who was the vivacious-looking girl seated between Claudine and Anne-Marie? She looked like fun. It was so good to be back at school!

The sixth had their tea unsupervised, unlike the younger girls whose teachers sat at the head of each table. Pat and Isabel squeezed in between Doris and Claudine, who immediately introduced the new girl.

'Pat and Isabel, meet Fizz Bentley. Fizz, these are our so-honourable, so-dignified head girls, the O'Sullivan twins.'

The twins grinned at the new girl, at the same time shaking their heads at Claudine.

'Your pronunciation gets worse instead of better,' said Isabel. 'She can't possibly be called Fizz.'

'I am,' put in Fizz herself. 'Honest.'

The twins looked at her in amusement, then Pat stole a glance down the table at the lovely Angela, and nudged her twin. 'See Angela, looking down her nose at the new girl already?' she muttered under her breath. Priscilla looked disapproving too, but by all accounts she disapproved of most people.

'And this is another new girl, Morag Stuart,' said Hilary, who was seated beside the red-haired girl.

'Hallo, Morag,' chorused the twins. 'Welcome to St Clare's.' The girl gave a tight-lipped nod, but said nothing. She had the most stunning green eyes, noticed Isabel. What a pity they were red rimmed from her crying on the train. I bet she'd be really beautiful if only she'd smile, Isabel thought. Well, once she's got to know everyone and settled in, perhaps she'll cheer up a bit.

'*I* should be welcoming *you* to the sixth, twins,' said Priscilla Parsons, with a thin smile. 'After all, I'm the longest serving member of the form, so to speak. If you need any help or advice, don't be afraid to ask, will you?'

'Yes,' murmured Carlotta to Doris. 'If you need any advice on how to look down your nose at people, or listen outside doors, or bully the first formers, Priscilla's a walking information bureau.'

Doris gave one of her sudden, explosive snorts of laughter, which made Priscilla stare at her in astonishment, and Pat's voice trembled with suppressed amusement as she thanked the girl politely. Mirabel grinned too as she caught the twins' eyes and Isabel called out, 'Mirabel! I don't think we've had the chance to speak to you yet – or Angela. Did the two of you enjoy the holidays?'

'Apart from a terrific lecture from my father and some pretty intensive coaching, yes,' answered Mirabel with a rueful grin. 'It made me face up to myself, though, and realize what a prize dope I'd been last term. I'm going to make up for it now, though, and I aim to pass those exams if it kills me.'

The listening girls didn't doubt it. Mirabel was an extremely strong and determined character. Last term, when she had been games captain, she had been a little *too* strong and determined. Power had gone to her head, making her neglect her work and turning many of the girls against her. They were all on her side now, though, admiring her for facing up to her faults and having the courage to try to change herself.

'All wasn't exactly peace and goodwill in our household either,' put in Angela. 'My father reacted much as yours did, Mirabel, and, like you, I'm absolutely determined to pass this time as well.'

The girls were most surprised to hear this from the spoilt, lazy Angela. But there was no doubt that she meant it: she had a determined set to her pretty mouth, which gave her face unexpected character. What a turn-up it would be if Angela made an effort to change her vain, selfish ways and become one of them in her last year. Sadly, such pleasant thoughts were short lived.

'Daddy's promised that, if I pass, I can go to finishing school next year,' went on Angela with a triumphant smile. 'So you can understand that it's absolutely vital I get good results.'

'Trust you!' said Bobby in disgust. 'I would have thought that just passing the exams would have been enough, but you never do anything unless there's something in it for you.'

'Er, just where is this finishing school, Angela?' asked Carlotta in a suspiciously smooth little voice.

'Paris. It's called *St Étienne,*' said Angela, forgetting how much she despised Carlotta in her desire to boast. 'Very exclusive.'

'Of course,' said Carlotta, winking at the twins. 'As a matter of fact, I may well be going there myself next year. Isn't that nice, Angela, to think that you and I won't be going our separate ways once we're finished at St Clare's after all.'

Angela, in the act of sipping her tea, choked, so that Alison had to slap her on the back. Carlotta grinned to herself. There was a bright side to everything.

'*You*!' Angela almost spat out. 'But you can't be! It's for top-drawer people.'

'Well, what's the point of that?' exclaimed Fizz. 'I mean, top-drawer people already know all that etiquette stuff. It ought to be exclusive to bottom-drawer people – like me!'

The sixth formers fell about at this, liking Fizz all the more for making a joke at her own expense. All except Angela, who scowled angrily, and Priscilla, who didn't see anything at all amusing in this common new girl. Angela opened her mouth to make a biting retort, but Isabel saw her spiteful look and stepped in. She wasn't going to allow Angela to pick on a new girl, even though Fizz seemed quite capable of standing up for herself.

'That's enough on the subject for now,' she said firmly. 'Besides, Pat and I have a bit of news of our own.'

'Yes,' said Pat. 'Miss Theobald has turned out the music room along by the sixth-form studies and we're to have it as a common-room.'

'We're to have studies *and* a common-room?' said Anne-Marie in surprise. 'Why?'

'Your guess is as good as mine,' said Pat. 'I think the head has something up her sleeve, though I'm not sure what. Anyway, she wants to speak to us all in the common-room at six, so make sure you're there on time.'

A buzz of excitement broke out at this. Whatever did the head have to say to them? It was all very mysterious – and rather exciting!

A meeting with the head

Morag Stuart turned towards the stairs as the sixth form made their way to the new common-room, all of them talking excitedly.

'Hey, Morag!' called Pat. 'Where do you think you're going?'

'To the dormy,' replied the sulky girl in a Scottish brogue. 'I feel like some privacy.'

'At six o'clock? Don't be stupid,' said Pat shortly, sick of the girl's bad temper. 'Didn't you hear Isabel and I say that the head wanted to speak to us all?'

Morag shrugged off-handedly. 'I wasn't taking any notice.'

'Well, you won't get very far at St Clare's if you don't begin to take notice,' said Pat.

The Scottish girl glared at her. 'I don't *want* to get very far at St Clare's,' she said rudely. 'In fact, I'd like to get as far *away* from St Clare's as possible.'

The other girls, who had stopped to wait for Pat, gasped, shocked at her outburst.

'Leave her, Pat,' said Hilary, coming over to lay a hand on Pat's shoulder. 'Let her go if that's what she wants.'

But Pat had a stubborn streak and she wasn't going

to let Morag get the better of her. She had a temper of her own, too, and felt it rising. She couldn't let *that* get the better of her either, or her reign as head girl would be the shortest in St Clare's history. Isabel, who had a calmer temperament, came forward.

'Morag, Miss Theobald has instructed us all to meet in the common-room,' she said with quiet authority, looking the angry girl straight in the eye. 'As head girls, it's our duty to see that her instructions are carried out. Pat and I can't force you to come along but, if you refuse, we'll have no alternative but to report you to the head.'

Morag scowled ferociously. She had met Miss Theobald briefly on her arrival and, although she would rather die than admit it, was more than a little in awe of her. With one last scorching glare in Pat's direction, she turned away from the stairs and joined the others. Pat blew out her cheeks. Well done, Isabel!

'Thanks,' she said gratefully to her twin. 'You handled that perfectly. I was in great danger of completely losing my temper.'

'I could see that,' said Isabel with a grin. 'And that would have put you in the wrong. I know Morag's annoying, Pat, but I don't think that getting mad with her is the answer.'

Pat bit her lip and nodded, feeling a little ashamed of herself now. 'I didn't expect to lose my temper so early in the proceedings,' she said woefully.

'Don't worry about it,' said her twin, giving her a

clap on the arm. 'You got it under control again, that's what matters. And just because we're head girls doesn't mean that we're perfect and don't have faults, the same as everyone else. We just have to try to deal with them. Now, let's get a move on – I'm dying to see our common-room.'

'Very nice,' said Alison as they entered. 'Smells of new paint, though.'

It was certainly a pleasant room, newly decorated in a warm, peach shade. A large, rectangular table stood in the centre, surrounded by chairs, and more comfortable armchairs were dotted about the place.

'I must admit, I quite enjoyed having a common-room when we were lower down the school,' said Doris. 'It's great to have our studies and a little privacy, but it's nice to be able to all get together and have a good gossip too.'

'Looks as though we're going to get the best of both worlds,' said Gladys, looking round. 'Great, there's a record player and a radio!'

'I much prefer the peaceful atmosphere of the studies,' put in Priscilla heavily. 'I always feel . . .' But the girls were never to find out what Priscilla felt, because Anne-Marie, who was by the door, hissed, 'The head's coming!'

Immediately everyone lined up on one side of the big table and Miss Theobald entered.

'Good evening, girls,' she said with her pleasant smile. 'Please sit down.'

The sixth form sat, but Miss Theobald remained on her feet for a few moments, looking from one watchful face to another. 'It's nice to see you all together – those that have come up through the school from the first form, and a couple of new faces, too.' She smiled at Fizz and Morag, though the latter averted her eyes and did not smile back. The head looked at her intently for a moment, then continued, 'No doubt most of you have guessed that I've asked you here for a specific purpose and I'll come to that in due course. But first, it's my pleasant duty to announce the appointment of the new games captain.'

The girls looked at one another eagerly. Who would it be? Bobby or Janet, perhaps? Both were brilliant at sports. Probably not Hilary, as she was leaving at the end of term. Certainly not Alison or Claudine, both of whom hated games and got out of playing whenever they could. Mirabel bit her lip. It wouldn't be her, either. She'd had one stab at the job and made a complete mess of it.

'This wasn't an easy decision to make,' said Miss Theobald. 'The job requires a little more than an aptitude for sports – determination, patience, sportsmanship – and a good sense of humour! Well, many of you possess those qualities, but in the end Miss Wilton and I decided on . . . Gladys Hillman!'

Gladys turned bright red, looking round her in total disbelief while the girls congratulated her noisily, reaching across to pat her on the back. She was absolutely thrilled – but how would Mirabel feel about it? She glanced at her friend and Mirabel smiled warmly.

'Congratulations, Gladys,' she said. 'You deserve it and I know you're going to do a fantastic job.'

The head smiled at Mirabel's generous words and was pleased. The girl had much better stuff in her than she had shown last term. She held up her hand for silence and got it immediately.

'Bobby and Janet are to be joint vice-captains,' said the head. 'I'm sure that the three of you will work well together.'

Bobby and Janet exchanged delighted glances. Both took a keen interest in games and got on very well with Gladys.

'And now to the main business of the evening,' said Miss Theobald. 'As you know, St Clare's is growing all the time. This term there are more girls than ever in the two lowest forms and the mistresses find that they don't have as much time to spare for the girls' problems and worries as they would like. That's where you come in.' She paused to look round the table, and the girls stared back keenly, their curiosity thoroughly aroused. 'I want you to hold a weekly meeting in here,' she explained, 'to which any girl from the lower school can bring her worries and problems and talk them through with you. Most of you are sensible, responsible girls, and I know I can trust you to act in the best interests of the young ones.'

The girls looked at one another feeling quite

overwhelmed. What an honour, to be entrusted with a responsibility like this. And they were all determined to prove worthy of it, to do their best for the younger girls and the school.

'Of course, they must go to their form mistresses with any difficulties concerning schoolwork,' continued Miss Theobald. 'And there may be times when serious matters come to light that you feel should be reported to the mistresses or myself. But I'm sure you all know what I expect of you, without me having to draw up a list of rules. Angela and Mirabel, as you will both be working hard for your exams, neither of you will take part in the meetings for the time being.'

Angela, who had little time for anyone's problems but her own, looked unconcerned, but Mirabel was bitterly disappointed. Why had she been so stupid last term?

Miss Theobald saw her unhappy expression and said gently, 'I'm not excluding you as a punishment. But when you take time off from your studies I want you to use it to relax, not to bother over someone else's worries.' The head paused, looking directly at Mirabel, then at Angela. 'I also think it would be a good idea if the two of you shared a study until the exams are over.'

The two girls, who didn't get on at all well together, looked horrified, as did Gladys and Alison, who had been their study-mates in the fifth.

'I don't normally interfere with study allocation, but as you share a common purpose this term, it might be less distracting for you to be with one another rather than with your chosen friends.'

'Yes, Miss Theobald,' agreed both girls without enthusiasm. Angela glared at Mirabel. Loud, bossy, arrogant – she would never survive cooped up with her.

Mirabel glared right back. Of all the girls in the school, the last one she would have chosen to share with was that little madam.

'That's all I have to say,' said Miss Theobald, rising. 'I'll leave you to talk over what I've said, then if you all go along to Matron she will allocate your studies. Carlotta, I'd like a quick word with you in my room.'

'Of course,' said the girl politely, though she was a little surprised. Whatever could the head have to say to her? She followed Miss Theobald from the room, the girls beginning to chatter excitedly as soon as the door closed behind them.

'Well, I wasn't expecting this!' cried Pat.

'I'm vice-captain,' said Bobby, grinning all over her face. 'Janet, I'm vice-captain!'

'I know, dope,' laughed Janet. 'So am I, remember? This term's going to be the greatest!'

'You bet,' agreed Hilary. 'I wonder what the head wanted with Carlotta, though?'

She soon found out, for the girl returned a few minutes later.

'Come on,' Isabel said to her. 'It's time we went off to Matron to get our studies sorted out. You'll be sharing with Claudine again, I suppose?'

'I wish!' Carlotta took a quick glance round the room and lowered her voice, saying, 'The head has asked me to share with Morag.'

'*Morag*!' said Doris loudly, and Carlotta gave her a little push.

'Shh, idiot, she'll hear you.'

'But why Morag?' asked Doris more quietly. 'That's not going to be much fun, especially after sharing with someone as wacky as Claudine.'

'I can't say that I'm looking forward to it,' said Carlotta wryly. 'Miss Theobald thinks that I may be able to help Morag to settle in here. She reckons that I was very much like her when I first came to St Clare's.'

'No way!' said Hilary indignantly. 'You were *hot* tempered, Carlotta, not *bad* tempered like she is.'

'I don't think that's quite what she meant,' said Carlotta thoughtfully. 'I think she meant that we're alike in that I had trouble settling in here as well at first. Miss Theobald wouldn't tell me why Morag hates being here so much, of course. Part of the plan is that I try to encourage her to confide in me.'

'Well, I don't envy you,' said Pat, looking across at the Scottish girl who was staring broodingly out of the window.

'It'll be quite an achievement on your part if you can bring her round and turn her into one of us,' said Hilary. 'She really is hard work.'

'Well, I've given the head my word that I'll do my best,' said Carlotta. 'Oh, and she gave me a bit of good news too.'

'What?' asked the others curiously.

'Apparently Dad wrote to her, asking her to give me a reference for this finishing school,' Carlotta told them. 'And Miss Theobald doesn't think it's a good idea for me to go there at all. She's promised to speak to Dad about it on my behalf.'

'Great!' cried Doris. 'Trust Miss Theobald!'

Carlotta felt hopeful, too. Her father had the greatest respect for the wise and kindly headmistress. If anyone could change his mind, she could.

'You'd better go and break the news to Claudine that she'll have to find someone else to share with,' said Pat, nodding towards the French girl who was having an animated conversation with Fizz. 'I expect she'll be disappointed.'

Claudine was, for she had enjoyed sharing with Carlotta in the fifth form, but she accepted the news with a shrug. 'You must do what you think is right, *ma chère* Carlotta. Me, I wish you luck. That Morag, she is – how do you say – bristly.'

'Prickly,' Carlotta corrected her with a grin. 'She sure is. I'm glad you aren't offended because I'm not sharing with you, Claudine.'

Claudine seldom took offence at anything. Besides, she had taken a great liking to Fizz and decided to ask her to share. And so the sixth form paired off. Pat and Isabel shared, of course, as did Bobby and Janet. Fizz happily agreed to go in with Claudine. Alison approached Gladys, saying with her pretty smile, 'How about you and I teaming up, seeing as we've both lost our study-mates?' Gladys, who had feared that she might end up with Priscilla, said yes at once. She liked Alison, although the two of them didn't have a great deal in common. Doris and Hilary paired up too, which left Anne-Marie with Priscilla. Poor Anne-Marie wasn't at all happy, but felt a bit better when Doris whispered, 'Cheer up! Don't forget that Hilary will be leaving at the end of this term, then you can move in with me. Until then, just try to grin and bear it.'

Looking at Priscilla's tight, prim face, Anne-Marie felt that grins were going to be in short supply that term. And Carlotta hadn't fared much better, stuck with that miserable Morag. Of the two girls, Anne-Marie wasn't sure who was worse.

The girls went along eagerly to inspect their new studies. Each was furnished with a table and two armchairs, but the girls could add their own individual touches by bringing items from home. It was also a custom of the school that they could call on the first formers to do any small jobs for them. As they shut their door behind them, the twins remembered how they had felt this was beneath them when they had started at St Clare's.

'What a couple of idiots we were – the stuck-up twins!' laughed Isabel, recalling the name given to them by their class.

'Yes. Thank goodness we woke up to ourselves and realized what a great school St Clare's is,' said Pat.

'Otherwise we certainly wouldn't be head girls now.'

'It doesn't bear thinking of,' said Isabel with a shudder. 'Shall we go back to the common-room, or be by ourselves for a while?'

'Let's stay here for a bit, just the two of us,' said Pat, drawing up an armchair by the fire and snuggling down into it contentedly. 'Mm, this is nice. It'll be great having tea in here by ourselves on cold, dark evenings.'

'Lovely,' agreed Isabel, taking the chair opposite her twin and yawning. 'I'm bushed. I suppose the train journey and all today's excitement has worn me out. What time is it?'

'Only eight o'clock,' said Pat, looking at her watch. 'I don't think I'll be staying up late tonight, though.' The sixth formers were allowed to set their own bedtime, within reason.

'Me neither,' sighed Isabel. 'Much as I'd like to. There's so much to talk about. The new girls, for example. I think Priscilla and Morag are going to test our tempers this term. I like Fizz though, don't you?'

'She's great,' agreed Pat. 'Even though she's so different from the rest of us, she's good for a laugh. Generous, too.'

Fizz had produced an enormous chocolate cake at tea-time, generously sharing it with the whole table. Even Angela and Priscilla had accepted some. Only Morag had refused a slice with a curt, 'No, thank you,' but as she had eaten very little at all no one thought too much of it.

'I wonder what she's doing at St Clare's, though?' said Isabel.

'Isabel O'Sullivan!' exclaimed Pat, shocked. 'What a snobbish thing to say! I'd expect a remark like that from Angela, but not from you.'

'I didn't mean that she *shouldn't* be here,' Isabel said, ruffled. 'I thought you knew me better than that, Pat! I just wondered what made her folks suddenly decide to send her here in her final year. And did you see her clothes? Every bit as expensive as Angela's.'

'Mm, I noticed,' replied Pat. 'But I don't think there's any big mystery about Fizz. She's an open book and no doubt she'll tell us all about herself in her own good time.'

'I guess so,' Isabel said. 'Pity we can't say the same about Morag. She's all defensive and closed up somehow. I don't know about you, Pat, but I reckon that with the new girls and our weekly sessions with the kids, we're in for a pretty exciting term.'

Neither she nor Pat could begin to imagine just how exciting!

The first day

The twins slept well on their first night as head girls, waking bright and early next morning.

'Morning, Carlotta!' called out Pat, smiling at the tousle-haired girl opposite as she sat up sleepily.

'Hi, Pat.' Carlotta yawned, stretching like a cat. 'These early starts are going to take some getting used to after the long lie-ins during the holidays.'

'Mm,' agreed a sleepy voice from the next bed, as Hilary raised her head. 'And these dark mornings make it so much harder. In summer I actually *want* to get out of bed.'

'Well, there's someone who doesn't mind getting up, even on a morning like this,' joined in Isabel, nodding towards the bed nearest the door, empty and unmade.

'Morag!' exclaimed Hilary. 'Pat, you don't suppose she's done a bunk, do you?'

'Wow, I hope not!' said Pat, biting her lip. 'I wouldn't fancy having to explain to Miss Theobald that we've lost one of the new girls already.'

But as the girls began to get out of bed, the door opened and in came Morag, dressed in trousers, sweater and a warm jacket.

'Where have you been?' asked Isabel sharply.

'For a walk in the grounds.' She scowled defiantly at Isabel. 'There's no rule against that, is there?'

Pat and a few of the others glared at her. All of them felt an intense loyalty to their school and didn't like the way this newcomer seemed to mock their rules and traditions.

The girl went across to her bed and took off her jacket, before brushing out her long, red hair, which had become rather windswept. Just then a bell went, and those girls who hadn't yet risen climbed out of bed, with much groaning. Seeing that Fizz looked a little bewildered, Pat said to her kindly, 'That's the dressing-bell. In about twenty minutes it'll be breakfast time. Haven't you been to boarding school before, Fizz?'

'No, I went to the local day school,' answered the girl. 'And it was nothing like this.'

'What made your folks decide to send you to St Clare's?' asked Hilary, not feeling in the least awkward about asking such a personal question. There was something warm and open about Fizz that made you feel as if you'd known her for years. The girl glanced round and took a deep breath, before announcing, 'My dad inherited stacks of money. Millions, in fact. A relative we didn't even know about died, and Dad was the sole benefactor.'

All the girls crowded round, listening intently now, Bobby exclaiming, 'Wow, that must have been just great! But didn't you want to stay on with your friends at your old school?'

Fizz sighed. 'People started to change towards me once we moved into a big house and they heard what had happened. Suddenly I came in for a lot of spiteful remarks, even from girls I'd thought were my best friends. Everyone expected me to change and go all snobbish. Suddenly I just didn't fit in any more. I just hope that I'll fit in here.'

'You bet you will,' chorused the others, liking her open manner.

'Yes, we'll take care of you,' said Janet.

'You'll probably come up against a bit of spite from the Honourable Angela,' added Carlotta with her wicked grin. 'But don't take it personally – she looks down on all of us.'

Everyone laughed. Angela, Alison and some of the others were in the dormitory next door, and the girls couldn't wait to tell them Fizz's exciting news.

'Come on, everyone!' called Pat. 'Let's move it! We don't want to set a bad example to the young ones by being late for breakfast on the first day.' She glanced across at Morag, who had now changed into her uniform, and called out, 'Aren't you going to do your hair, Morag?'

'I've just brushed it.'

'Yes, but we're supposed to wear it tied back in class. Either that or cut short.'

Morag shrugged. 'I never wear my hair tied back.'

Pat frowned. The girl certainly had lovely hair, but Miss Harry, the sixth-form mistress, was unlikely to appreciate its beauty if Morag went into class with it tumbling about her shoulders like that. Pat was about to say so, quite bluntly, when Carlotta said softly, 'Leave her. Let her make a few mistakes. After all, we can't put her right until she does something wrong.'

'You *are* getting wise in your old age,' grinned Pat. 'All right, but I bet Miss Harry will go nuts when she claps eyes on our flame-haired beauty.'

The sixth form was filing into its new classroom when Bobby happened to spot a lone, small figure hovering in the corridor.

'Hi, Dora!' she said with a smile. 'What are you doing here? This is the sixth's classroom, you know. Don't tell me you're lost again?'

Dora Lacey nodded.

'Well, the quickest way to the first-form room is for you to go back along the corridor, out of the side door, then cut across the courtyard and in through the door by the Science Lab. Got that?'

'I think so,' lisped Dora, looking doubtful.

'Do you want me to walk you over?' offered Bobby kindly.

'No, I'll be all right. Thanks.' And with that the girl sped off, leaving Bobby grinning ruefully and shaking her head. That kid was badly in need of some geography lessons!

Going into the sixth-form room, Bobby placed her books on her desk, then glanced out of the window, what she saw making her eyes widen in amazement. 'Unbelievable!' she cried. 'I've never seen anything like it!'

'What?' asked the others in surprise.

'That first former, Dora. I left her outside that door seconds ago, and there she is now going across the courtyard. She must have run like a cheetah to have covered that distance in a few seconds.'

'She'll be one to watch at netball practice then,' said Gladys, ever the games captain. 'She's got definite possibilities if she's that fast.'

Then the girls heard the sound of brisk footsteps and became silent, those that were seated getting to their feet as their new form mistress, Miss Harry, entered.

'Morning, girls.' She smiled round the room. 'Please sit down, then we can get to know one another.'

The sixth formers liked Miss Harry, who was young and pretty with a great sense of humour. She also understood that her pupils were growing up fast and liked to be treated as young adults rather than children. But any girl who mistook Miss Harry's good nature for a lack of authority had better watch out! She soon learnt her mistake and never repeated it.

'Now, obviously I know some of you better than others,' the mistress began. 'But I'd like you all to stand up, one at a time, and introduce yourselves. That will help both me and the new girls – oh, and Priscilla, of course, to get to know you.'

Priscilla, who had chosen a desk at the front of the class, stretched her thin lips into a smile, which Miss Harry studiously ignored. Having already had the girl in her class for two terms, she knew a great deal about

Priscilla and, try as she might, could not like her.

'We'll go in alphabetical order,' said the mistress, glancing at the list in her hand. 'Starting with Phyllis Bentley.'

Fizz, quite taken aback by how young Miss Harry looked, stared with fascination at the teacher, but neither moved nor spoke.

'Fizz!' hissed Claudine, her neighbour. 'It is your turn.'

'Oh, sorry, Miss Harry,' apologized Fizz in her strong accent, blushing as she stood up. 'I'm not used to answering to Phyllis, you see. Most people call me Fizz.'

Had this been the first or second form, the girls would have burst out laughing at this. The dignified sixth stifled their amusement and merely grinned at one another. All except Priscilla, whose expression grew sour. That girl! Didn't she realize that it just wasn't done to ask a mistress to use a nickname? And such a stupid one! Priscilla sat back and waited for Miss Harry to deliver a crushing put-down. But the mistress was smiling. Something about Fizz's direct, open manner was very appealing. 'Fizz it is, then,' she said with a twinkle in her eyes.

'Carlotta Brown?'

Carlotta got up and, with a theatrical bow, introduced herself.

Priscilla's mouth became so small and mean it was in danger of disappearing altogether. What *was* St Clare's coming to, she thought disapprovingly. Carlotta didn't belong here, any more than that common Bentley girl.

Everyone knew that Carlotta had once belonged to a circus. As for Claudine – Priscilla cast a disdainful glance at Mam'zelle's daredevil niece and shuddered – if only the school was more selective about who was accepted here. Shrewd Carlotta watched her from the corner of her eye as she sat down, guessing at the girl's thoughts and despising her for them. Priscilla was the kind of person she hated most. Everything about her was thin and mean, from the shape of her face, to her long, narrow nose which, so rumour had it, she enjoyed poking into everyone's business. Even her hair was braided in a long, thin plait, more suited to a first former than one of the older girls. Yes, Carlotta was going to have her work cut out this term keeping her temper with both Prim Priscilla and Miserable Morag. Yet keep it she must. Not only was the honour of the sixth at stake, but her own future. If her father had any reports of bad behaviour, he would be more convinced than ever that she needed a course at finishing school.

Morag also watched the proceedings, but with total contempt. She didn't want to get to know these carefree, sensible girls with whom she had nothing in common, and she didn't want them prying into her business, trying to turn her into one of them. When the time came for her to stand up, she would let the class know in no uncertain terms that she wanted no part of St Clare's. Perhaps Miss Harry would report her, and no doubt that interfering Pat would tell her off, but Morag didn't care. She had been forced to come here, and certainly wouldn't abide by St Clare's rules. Arms folded, she sat back in her seat as, one by one, the girls took their turn. Then, at last, it was hers.

'Morag Stuart!' called out Miss Harry.

The girl got to her feet, the familiar scowl on her face. 'I'm Morag Stuart, and I don't want . . .'

'One moment!' interrupted Miss Harry, frowning. 'Morag, you seem to have forgotten to tie your hair back this morning.'

'I didn't forget,' replied Morag brusquely. 'At home I always wear my hair like this, and . . .'

'Well, you're not at home now,' Miss Harry said with her air of quiet authority. 'Please go up to your dormitory and do your hair properly.'

Morag narrowed her eyes. 'I don't want to tie my hair back.'

'Fine,' said the mistress unexpectedly. 'You're quite old enough to make up your own mind, and the choice is simple. There is an excellent hairdresser's in town, and if you refuse to keep your hair tied back during lessons, I suggest you pay a visit there and have it cut short.'

'Cut short?' repeated Morag, aghast.

'Yes, I think it would suit you,' said Miss Harry with a smile. 'You have a very pretty face, Morag. It would be nice to see *all* of it, rather than just catching a glimpse of it through a curtain of hair now and then.'

Morag reddened. Somehow her defiant stand had gone horribly wrong and she had merely ended up looking stupid. Far from voicing her opinion about

St Clare's, Miss Harry had barely allowed her to get a word in.

'Well, Morag?' said the mistress now. 'What's it to be?'

The sullen girl was dying to answer back, but something in Miss Harry's direct, blue-eyed stare and the firm tone of her voice stopped her. Without quite knowing how it had come about, Morag suddenly found herself outside the classroom and on her way up to the dormitory. Well done, Miss Harry, thought the class admiringly. She certainly knew how to handle the bad-tempered Scottish girl. And well done, Carlotta, thought Pat. She had foreseen what would happen and had had the good sense to stop Pat from interfering.

The sixth form had their heads bent over their work when Morag reappeared a few minutes later, a blue ribbon confining the red hair. Softly, so as not to distract the others, Miss Harry called her over to her desk and explained what the class was doing. She really *is* attractive, thought Isabel, glancing up. What I wouldn't give for those lovely, high cheekbones! Only the sulky droop of her mouth spoilt her. As though sensing eyes on her, Morag looked round sharply and Isabel gave her ready, friendly smile. Suddenly, without wanting to, Morag found herself smiling back, warmed to see a friendly face. Then she remembered the course she had set herself and switched the smile off. But Isabel was a little heartened as she turned her attention back to her work. At least the girl *could* smile. Besides, Miss

Theobald obviously thought she was worth a little trouble, otherwise she wouldn't have encouraged Carlotta to befriend her. And if the head thought so, that was good enough for Isabel.

Sixth formers and first formers

When afternoon lessons were over, Pat and Isabel, along with Hilary and Doris, went to the common-room to draft a notice concerning what had become known as their 'agony aunt' sessions. It had been decided to wait until the third week of term to hold the first meeting, giving everyone a chance to settle in properly. Then the weekly meetings would be held on Thursday evenings at seven o'clock, and a notice was to be placed in each common-room to let everyone know.

'Isn't this exciting?' said Doris. 'I can't wait for our first meeting.'

'Yes, we just *have* to make a success of this,' said Pat earnestly. 'It's quite a responsibility Miss Theobald's given us and we have to prove that we're up to it.'

'Well, we *will* prove it,' said Isabel determinedly. 'If we haven't learnt how to be responsible and make decisions after six years at St Clare's, there's not much hope for us.'

'There are some people who never learn, though,' put in Doris.

'Priscilla!' said the others at once.

'Yes, we'll have to watch her,' Hilary said. 'She's

likely to use the sessions as a chance to find out the kids' secrets and snitch on them.'

'As soon as she starts anything like that, she's out!' said Pat. 'We'll have to keep an eye on Morag, too.'

'Morag?' repeated Isabel in surprise. 'I know she's not exactly Little Miss Sunshine, but she doesn't strike me as nosey, or a sneak.'

'No, but she obviously cares nothing for St Clare's or its traditions,' Pat pointed out. 'And we don't want her passing on those ideas to the younger girls.'

'Ah, what is this?' asked Claudine, opening the door. 'Have I tripped on a secret meeting?'

'You mean stumbled on, Claudine,' laughed Doris. 'No, we were just discussing our "agony aunt" sessions. Do you mind taking onc of these notices along to Sarah in the second form? Tell her to put it up in the common-room and make sure everyone reads it.'

'*Eh bien*,' agreed Claudine, taking the sheet of paper from Doris and whisking herself from the room.

'Hilary, you and Doris go to the third's common-room,' said Pat. 'Isabel and I'll shoot along to the first form.'

'Come on, then,' said Isabel. 'I'm dying for a coffee, and the sooner we get this over with, the sooner we can get back to our study and put the kettle on.'

As they were leaving the common-room, they bumped into Dora Lacey and Pat called out, 'Dora! Be a pet – nip into our study, put the kettle on and spoon some coffee into a couple of mugs, will you? You'll find some chocolate biscuits in the cupboard as well. Help yourself to a couple. Only a couple, mind – I've counted them!'

'Will do, Pat!' The first former laughed and ran off, leaving Isabel staring doubtfully at her twin. 'I hope you know what you're doing. She's a sweet kid, but dippy. We'll probably get back to find the socket burnt out or something.'

But, by the time the twins reached the first-form common-room, Dora was there, curled up on the sofa reading a magazine.

'Dora!' exclaimed Pat in astonishment. 'Have you got motorized shoes or something? I've never known any-one move as quickly as you do.'

'Is everything OK?' asked Isabel anxiously. 'I mean, you found the kettle and everything?'

For a moment Dora looked blank, then her brow cleared and she said, 'Oh, the kettle! No problem, Isabel.'

'OK, girls, listen up!' called out Pat. 'Isabel and I have an announcement to make.'

But Isabel said nothing, staring at Dora with a puzzled frown on her face as Pat told the first form all about the weekly meetings, delighted when they were full of enthusiasm for the idea.

'Leave me to do all the talking, why don't you!' cried Pat, when they got outside. 'What's up with you?'

'Dora Lacey,' answered her twin slowly. 'Something about that kid just isn't right.'

'What do you mean?' asked Pat, surprised.

'I can't put my finger on it. But something just doesn't add up where she's concerned.'

Alison and Gladys had also sent for a first former, Joan Terry, to do their jobs. Gladys had slipped out to speak to Miss Wilton, the games mistress, when the girl arrived, and Alison greeted her with a wide smile. 'Hi, Joan! Put the kettle on and we'll have a cuppa, then you can help me find a home for this lot,' she said, busily emptying the contents of a cardboard box on to the table. 'Fudge – ugh! I used to love it when I was a kid, but I can't stand it now. Trouble is, my gran still thinks I'm a kid and sends me a box every term.'

Joan giggled. She was slightly timid and usually very much in awe of the older girls, but Alison was so friendly that she nerved herself to suggest shyly, 'Can't you tell her that you don't like it any more?'

'I couldn't,' said Alison. 'That would hurt her feelings terribly and, much as I hate fudge, I'd hate to hurt Gran's feelings even more. Do you like fudge, Joan?'

'I love it. Mum doesn't have much money to spare, so I don't often have sweets sent to me.'

Alison was touched. Joan was thin and plain, but there was something wistful and appealing about her that went straight to the girl's tender heart. 'Here, catch!' She tossed the box of sweets to Joan. 'And don't eat them all at once. I don't want Matron after me because you've been sick or come out in spots or something.'

'Thanks, Alison,' breathed the younger girl, her

grave brown eyes sparkling. 'What do you want me to do now? Shall I find a place for these books?' Alison was really nice, she thought. She had put her completely at ease. Gladys, who came in just before Joan left, was nice too. Joan had always pictured games captains as being large, domineering and loud. So it was a pleasant surprise when Gladys said in her soft voice, 'I hope we'll be seeing you at netball practice tomorrow afternoon?'

'You bet! I've never played before, though, so I hope you're not expecting too much.'

'Don't you worry about that,' said Gladys. 'If there's potential in you, we'll bring it out all right.'

Joan almost danced from the room and along the corridor, clutching the box of sweets as though it contained the crown jewels. Before she had gone more than a few steps, she ran smack into Priscilla Parsons. 'Sorry, Priscilla,' she stammered. 'I wasn't looking.'

'Evidently,' snapped Priscilla, her sharp eyes on the box Joan carried. 'Where did you get that from?'

'Alison gave it to me.'

'Are you sure?' said Priscilla, leaning forward so that her gaze bored into Joan's. 'Quite sure that you didn't . . .'

At that moment Alison put her head out of the study and said, 'Joan, would you . . . oh, Priscilla.'

'Alison.' Priscilla gave a tight smile and inclined her head. 'Joan here was just telling me that you'd given her this box of fudge.'

'That's right,' said Alison, taking in the younger girl's scared expression. Whatever could Priscilla have been saying to her? She felt a sudden wave of dislike and said, with unusual sharpness, 'Not that it's any of your business. Did you want something?'

Priscilla turned red, answering stiffly, 'No, I was just on my way to my study.'

'Well, don't let us keep you,' said Alison rudely and, after shooting her a glare, Priscilla stalked off. Joan gave a little sigh of relief and Alison frowned. She wasn't a very shrewd girl, but she was sensitive to the feelings of others and knew that something was wrong here.

'Do you know Priscilla well?' she asked gently.

'Quite well,' replied Joan. 'We live in the same village.'

'Tough luck,' Alison said with a grimace. 'It's bad enough having to put up with her during term time, never mind during the holidays as well.'

It really wasn't done for one of the top-form girls to speak against another to a member of the lower school but, thought Alison with a surge of rebellion, it was worth it to see Joan smile. She still looked a little wan, though, and Alison said kindly, 'You know, if you ever come up against any bullying, or there's anything troubling you, the sixth are here to help. Just come along to one of our Thursday sessions.' Then she remembered that Priscilla would be present at these sessions and added hastily, 'Or just come and have a word with me in private. My door's always open.'

Joan looked at Alison as though she were some

kind of goddess and said shyly, 'Thanks.'

Alison smiled. 'Now, what was I going to say before Priscilla so rudely interrupted us? Ah, yes, I was just going to ask if you'd like to come along tomorrow at the same time and give me a hand sorting out the rest of my stuff.'

'Sure,' said Joan eagerly. 'I'd love to.'

Meanwhile, Priscilla had gone to her study, pleased to find that Anne-Marie was not there. Sly and secretive by nature, Priscilla would have much preferred a study to herself. Moreover, having been in the sixth for two terms already, she thought herself superior to most of the old fifth formers, and Anne-Marie was no exception. Priscilla admired Angela because the girl was upper class and came from a wealthy family. And she would have liked to make friends with the twins, not because she liked them, but because they were head girls and it would have been pleasant to bask in their reflected glory. The twins, though, had shown clearly that they had little time for Priscilla. But the girl refused to be downhearted. There were still the Thursday night meetings to look forward to, and that appealed to her sense of self-importance enormously. Like the others, she was impatient for the first meeting. But, unlike Hilary or Bobby or Janet, Priscilla didn't think of what an honour it was to be entrusted to help the lower forms with their problems. She thought what a brilliant way it would be to find out their secrets. And if she could manage to use those secrets somehow, that would be even better. Yes, Priscilla meant to make her presence felt this term all right.

The following afternoon, Gladys, Bobby and Janet went along to watch the first formers at netball. Hilary, who took a keen interest in sports, accompanied them, and the twins, who were busy, promised to come along later.

'Susan's pretty good,' said Bobby, watching the girl move swiftly up and down the court.

'She is,' agreed Gladys. 'But then she should be, because she's been playing for a couple of years. I'm keen to see how the girls who are new to it shape up.'

Some played well, picking up the rules quickly, whilst others were slow to take to this new game. Joan Terry seemed hopeless, but when Janet suggested trying her as goalkeeper, she proved quite adept at knocking the ball away from the net.

'Good one, Joan!' called out Janet. 'Hey, Gladys, I think we've a future goalkeeper here.'

Gladys nodded, writing hurriedly in the notebook she had brought with her.

'Here's Dora,' said Bobby. 'I wonder what kind of a showing she'll make?'

The girl made a very good one, learning the rules swiftly and obviously enjoying herself as she darted all over the place, passing the ball agilely.

'Wow, she might be small, but she's good!' Gladys cried. 'And she's not afraid to tackle her opponent, even though Hilda's so much taller.'

By half-time Gladys had listed several good players who could possibly be put into a team later on. 'Brilliant!' she smiled happily at Bobby and Janet. 'I've a feeling St Clare's are going to do well at netball this term. Hey, Dora, where are you off to?'

'Stone in my shoe,' called back Dora. 'Don't worry, Gladys, I won't be long.' She was back in time for the second half, but her play had deteriorated. And she seemed to have forgotten most of the rules, too. Gladys, Bobby and Janet exchanged puzzled glances. Pat and Isabel arrived just then and, watching Dora, Pat said, 'She's fast, but that's about all you can say for her.'

'Yes, but she was playing so well in the first half,' said Gladys with a frown. 'Bobby and Janet will bear me out.'

'That's right,' Janet confirmed. 'But she seemed to go to pieces after half-time. Almost as though she'd lost her memory and forgotten everything she'd learnt.'

Miss Wilton took Dora aside and patiently explained the rules to her again, after which Dora's game improved dramatically and she even scored a goal.

'Well, Gladys, what do you think?' asked Miss Wilton, coming off the court. 'Joan Terry showed promise in goal and Dora . . . well, I don't quite know what to make of her.'

'Perhaps when she knows the game better she'll settle down,' said Gladys. 'At the moment she's a little unpredictable.'

'Yes,' agreed the games teacher thoughtfully. 'The change seemed to occur at half-time. When she came back it was as though she was a different girl!'

6
A big surprise

On Saturdays, the girls were free to do as they chose, many of them going into town to spend their allowances, or to see a film. It happened that the twins' grandmother had sent them some money, so they decided that a visit to the coffee shop was in order that afternoon. As they were getting their jackets, they bumped into Anne-Marie, looking the picture of misery.

'It's the thought of listening to Priscilla droning on and spreading poison about half the school over tea,' the girl explained when Pat asked her what was wrong. 'I'll be sorry to see the back of Hilary at the end of term, but it'll be Heaven to move in with Doris!

'Come with us,' invited Isabel, feeling sorry for Anne-Marie. 'We're going out to the coffee shop.'

'Yes, do,' said Pat. 'They do the best toasted sandwiches I've ever tasted.'

'Don't tempt me!' groaned Anne-Marie. 'It sounds great and I'm starving, but I can't. It's Mum's birthday *and* my little brother's next week, so all my allowance had to go on presents for them.'

'Our treat,' said Isabel generously. 'Pat and I are well off at the moment.'

'Thanks, girls, but I couldn't let you,' said Anne-Marie firmly.

'Sure you could,' said Pat with equal firmness, getting down the girl's jacket and handing it to her. 'Come on, I'm starving!'

So, delighted to be over-ruled, Anne-Marie slipped on her jacket, and soon the three girls were seated on high stools in the window of the coffee shop, enjoying toasted ham and cheese sandwiches washed down with large milkshakes.

'You were right, Pat – these are great!' said Anne-Marie, taking a large bite of her sandwich. 'And it's so nice to have your company after Priscilla. I'll return the favour once I get next month's allowance, that's a promise.'

It was as the twins went to the counter to pay that Anne-Marie saw something odd. Glancing out of the window, she spotted a small, familiar figure going into the bookshop opposite. That looks like little Dora, she thought, then frowned. Surely she hadn't been silly enough to come into town alone? There was a strict rule at St Clare's that the lower forms could only visit the town if they went in pairs. Only the fifth and sixth formers had the privilege of going alone if they wished. The first former would really be in trouble if the head or Miss Roberts – or even the twins – got to hear about it.

Staring out of the window, wondering whether she ought to mention the matter to Pat and Isabel, Anne-Marie's eyes widened. For there, going into the same bookshop, was Dora – *again*! The sixth former blinked and rubbed her eyes. How could that be? Anne-Marie hadn't looked away from the shop doorway for a second, and Dora certainly hadn't come out. So how could she have gone in a second time?

'Hey, Anne-Marie, you look as though you've seen a ghost!' said Pat as the twins returned to the table.

'Well, I've certainly seen something weird,' said the girl, and quickly told them her strange tale.

'Your eyes must have been playing tricks on you,' said the down-to-earth Pat. 'I expect the second girl you saw resembled Dora. After all, there are quite a few first formers with blonde hair.'

But Anne-Marie remained adamant that it was Dora she had seen and suddenly Isabel, who had been frowning thoughtfully, slapped the table. 'I've got it!' she cried. 'Pat, do you remember me saying the other day that something didn't add up about that kid? Well, I've suddenly realized what it is. She was able to tell both of us apart straight away.'

'So?' Pat said, puzzled.

'Well, you know as well as I do that most people can't. Not immediately. It usually takes them a while.'

'That's true,' put in Anne-Marie. 'I know when I first met the pair of you it took me a few weeks before I realized that your hair curls a little more than Pat's, Isabel, and that her eyebrows are just a tiny bit straighter than yours.'

'Exactly!' said Isabel triumphantly. 'But when we

spoke to Dora the other day, she called us both by our names and got them right.'

'Well, I suppose it is unusual,' Pat agreed, frowning. 'Normally the only people able to do that are other identical twins because they are so used to looking for minute differences between themselves and their own twin. Isabel! Surely you're not suggesting . . .'

'That's *exactly* what I'm suggesting!' broke in Isabel impatiently. 'I think there are *two* Doras!'

'It would certainly explain a lot,' said Anne-Marie, who had been listening open-mouthed. 'Like how she turns up unexpectedly so often, and moves from one place to another with such speed.'

'Right,' agreed Isabel. 'It would also explain her strange performance on the netball court yesterday. One twin must have played the first half, and the other the second.'

'The little monsters!' exclaimed Pat. 'No wonder Dora did our jobs so quickly the other day and managed to get back to the common-room in record time!'

'What are we going to do about it?' asked Anne-Marie, thoroughly astounded by the whole business, but relieved to know that there was nothing wrong with her eyesight.

'First we've got to get the pair of them out of that bookshop,' said Pat grimly, getting to her feet. 'Then, I'm afraid, we've no alternative but to take them to Miss Theobald.'

'Anne-Marie, you stand guard outside,' said Isabel as they crossed the road. 'Pat and I'll go in, and if either of them tries to sneak out, grab her!'

But there was no need for such measures for, as the twins were about to enter the shop, the door opened and two identical girls emerged, coming to an abrupt halt as they looked up into the stern faces of their head girls.

'Well?' demanded Pat crisply. 'What have you two got to say for yourselves?'

'It – it was just a joke, Pat,' stammered Dora – or was it her twin?

'One that may have got you into serious trouble,' said Isabel sternly. 'Which twin are you?'

'I'm Dora,' said one, hanging her head.

'And I'm Daphne,' her twin added.

The three sixth formers studied the girls closely, searching their faces for any difference, however small, that would tell them apart. The Lacey twins had tricked them once, but they were determined not to be fooled again.

'Daphne's eyes are a slightly deeper blue than Dora's,' pronounced Isabel at last. 'And she's just a fraction taller. All right, kids, now we're taking you back to St Clare's.'

'Will you have to tell the head?' asked Daphne, lip trembling as Isabel took her arm.

'I'm afraid so,' said Pat, doing likewise with Dora, as Anne-Marie brought up the rear. 'You'll get into trouble but, honestly, you really have asked for it. However have you managed to get away with it for a whole week?'

'Nothing to it, really,' said Dora, not without a touch of pride. 'I just forged a letter from Mum saying that Daphne was ill and wouldn't be able to start school for a fortnight, then sent it off to Miss Theobald.'

'Just a minute,' interrupted Isabel with a frown. 'I distinctly remember you saying that your *older* sister was coming to St Clare's.'

'Daphne *is* my older sister,' explained Dora righteously. 'She was born half an hour before me, so I wasn't lying! Only Miss Theobald and Miss Roberts knew that we were twins, though, and they didn't suspect a thing.'

The O'Sullivans and Anne-Marie exchanged glances and had to bite their lips to keep from laughing. There was something so innocent and appealing about the twins, even when they were owning up to the most outrageous behaviour.

'We've been taking turns going to lessons and having meals,' Daphne put in. 'And we've been sharing the bed in our dormitory. Dora would have it one night, while I slept on an old mattress in one of the box-rooms, then the following night we'd swap.'

'Yes, but *why*?' asked Anne-Marie, completely at a loss.

'It just seemed like a good idea,' they said in unison.

Pat and Isabel could understand this more readily than Anne-Marie. As first formers they, too, had enjoyed confusing both girls and teachers. They had never gone this far, though, and it was unlikely that the head would look upon this as a mere joke.

'Do you realize what would have happened if your folks had decided to telephone Miss Theobald to see how you were both settling in?' asked Pat sternly. 'There would have been a full-scale panic and the police would have had to have been informed that one of you was missing. Imagine how worried your mum and dad would have been.'

'We didn't think of that,' said Dora, looking ashamed.

'It seems to me that the pair of you didn't think at all,' scolded Isabel. 'Well, here we are, back at St Clare's. Take a good look at that roof, twins. Any minute now, Miss Theobald is going to go right through it!'

The younger girls' faces crumpled suddenly and they began to cry. Anne-Marie, although she thought that they had behaved irresponsibly, felt sorry for them and whispered, 'Pat, Isabel – need we report them to Miss Theobald? Couldn't we pretend that Daphne's just arrived on the train, having recovered from her illness?'

'Absolutely not!' said Pat firmly. 'Those kids deserve what's coming to them. Besides, if it did all come out later, as these things have a habit of doing, Isabel and I would probably lose our positions as head girls for not reporting it.'

'Pat's right,' Isabel agreed. 'If they get away with this, who knows *what* they might decide to do next!'

'I suppose so,' sighed Anne-Marie. 'Going into town with you two certainly isn't boring, I'll say that much!'

In the entrance hall the girls ran into Mam'zelle, who greeted them with a beaming smile. 'Ah, how good it is to see you big girls taking charge of the little ones,' she said warmly. 'The dear little Dora, is it not? And who is this behind her?' Mam'zelle's beady black eyes grew round in amazement, glasses slipping down her nose a she rubbed her eyes, much as Anne-Marie had done earlier. '*Mon dieu,* what is this?' she cried, putting a hand to her heart. 'My eyes, they are deceiving me!'

'I'm afraid it isn't your eyes that have been deceiving you, Mam'zelle,' said Isabel drily. 'But these two.'

Briefly, the girls told her the facts. The French teacher was quite horrified. Dora Lacey, although her French wasn't good, had swiftly become one of the teacher's pets, being just the kind of sweet, angelic-looking girl who appealed to her. To discover that she had been tricked by one of her favourites was too much! '*Méchantes filles*!' she cried. 'To think that you two – so young, so innocent – should be so wicked. Ah, the good Miss Theobald, she will be truly angry, and rightly so.'

The Frenchwoman suddenly seemed very frightening to the twins who, having just dried their tears, promptly began to cry again. As swiftly as it had come, Mam'zelle's anger vanished. She put a plump arm about each of the twins' heaving shoulders, saying kindly, 'Do not cry, *mes petites*. You will be punished, yes, but soon all this will be forgotten. Then you will settle down and be good, good girls, *n'est-ce pas*?'

The twins nodded, giving watery smiles, and the French mistress patted their rosy cheeks.

'We'd better take them along to the head now,

Mam'zelle,' said Isabel politely, hiding a smile at the teacher's swift change of mood.

'Of course. Miss Theobald will be just, *mes filles*, do not fear. Bear your punishment nobly.' And with these words of wisdom, she went on her way.

'Dear old Mam'zelle,' laughed Pat fondly as she watched the Frenchwoman shuffle away in her large, flat shoes. 'No matter how often she's tricked, she always forgives. Anne-Marie, are you coming to the head with us?'

'No, I'm going for a quiet sit down in the common-room,' said the girl, moving away. 'I've had quite enough excitement for one day.'

'Well, it's not over for us,' said Isabel. 'Come on, kids – time to face the music!'

7
More secrets

Miss Theobald's charming smile of welcome for Pat and Isabel turned to an expression of concern when she saw their grave faces. 'Is something wrong, twins?'

In answer they pulled forward Dora and Daphne, who had been cowering behind them, wishing that the ground would open up and swallow them.

'Daphne, I presume!' exclaimed the head in surprise. 'Your mother didn't ring to let me know that you would be back so early. I hope you're fully recovered?'

'Excuse me, Miss Theobald,' said Pat. 'But Daphne hasn't just arrived. The two of them have been here right from day one.'

Out came the full story of the Lacey twins' outrageous deception. The head's face grew more and more stern as she listened.

'Well!' she exclaimed at the end. She had been head of St Clare's for many years and had dealt with all kinds of strange situations, but never one like this before. 'Thank you, Pat and Isabel,' she said seriously. 'You can go now – and I'm grateful to you for handling this matter so responsibly and for bringing it to my attention.'

Then, as the door closed behind the head girls, she

turned her stern grey eyes on the two first formers, both of whom were shuffling uncomfortably and feeling very small. 'Never have I come across such reckless and irresponsible behaviour,' she told them coldly. 'You have deceived the teachers, the other girls and your parents. How do you suppose they would feel if they heard about your behaviour?'

'Oh, Miss Theobald, *must* you tell them?' pleaded Daphne, her mouth trembling. 'We never meant any harm, honestly. It was just a joke.'

'A joke that could have misfired badly,' said the head. 'How can the school offer you its care and protection if no one knows you are here? Imagine if a fire had broken out during the night, Daphne. Only your twin would have known that you were missing and where to find you.'

What a horrifying thought! Shivers ran down the twins' spines as they stared at one another, appalled.

'Whether or not I tell your parents depends upon the two of you and your behaviour for the rest of the term,' went on Miss Theobald. 'I believe that you meant no harm and this exploit was, in your eyes, just a bit of fun. However, you must both learn to think things through, consider the consequences of your actions and accept responsibility for them. That is one of the things your parents have sent you here to learn.' And the head intended to see that they learnt it well! 'You are both grounded for a fortnight,' she said. 'Also, as you have each only been taking half of your lessons, you will do an extra half-hour's prep every evening for a fortnight. Now, I want you both to go along to Miss Roberts and own up to her. Whether or not she chooses to impose any further punishment of her own is entirely her decision.'

'Wow!' said Dora, once they were outside the head's room. 'That was awful! My knees are still knocking.'

'Mine too,' said Daphne glumly. 'Grounded for two weeks! That's just terrible! I only hope that Miss Roberts doesn't give us a punishment too.'

Miss Roberts didn't, but she was absolutely furious and her anger was not as controlled as the head's had been. She always hated to be duped in any way, and the ears of the two first formers burnt by the time she had finished with them. Of course, the news of Dora and Daphne's escapade spread through the school like wildfire. Although Katie, the serious head of the first form, addressed a few measured words to them, most of their class were absolutely thrilled at their daring, and the twins almost became heroines to them. 'Which is only going to encourage them in further tricks,' remarked an exasperated Miss Roberts to Mam'zelle in the mistresses' common-room.

'Ah, but surely they have now learnt their lesson,' said Mam'zelle. 'They will soon settle down.'

'I wish I had your confidence, Mam'zelle,' sighed Miss Roberts. 'Well, we'll see.'

The twins, carrying out their dreaded punishment, did their best to be good, as they both hated to be confined to school. And as for an extra half-hour's prep every night . . . well, that was enough to make *anyone* think twice before stirring up trouble. Only one lapse occurred to mar their attempts at good behaviour, and that was caused by Priscilla Parsons who, spotting them in the corridor near her study one afternoon, took it upon herself to lecture them. As Dora said to Daphne later, she didn't mind being shouted at by the head girls. She didn't even resent the telling-off that Katie had given them. They were doing their duty and had the twins' welfare at heart. But Priscilla didn't. Her sole motive for scolding the girls was a love of interfering and airing her opinions. Dora and Daphne listened to her in gathering anger, feeling none of the shame or fear that had overcome them when the O'Sullivan twins had caught them out. 'I'll be keeping an eye on you both,' finished Priscilla heavily. 'And if I catch you doing anything you shouldn't be . . .'

'You'll tell on us!' said Daphne with a sneer. 'Well, you keep your eye on us, Priscilla, but you'll have nothing to report. Because Dora and I are too smart for you. Whatever we plan, you'll never find out about it until it's too late.'

'Oh!' gasped the older girl. 'How dare you?' She was furious and humiliated by their nerve, knowing that the twins wouldn't dare speak in such a way to any other sixth former, and she felt resentful of the fact that she wasn't treated with the same respect. Priscilla couldn't understand that even the youngest first former could see right through her pompous, self-righteous manner to her spiteful nature, and for this reason she would never gain the respect of the younger girls.

'What are you doing here anyway?' she asked sharply, trying to regain her dignity. 'These are the sixth form studies, you know.'

'We do,' answered Dora insolently. 'Claudine and Fizz asked us to come along and do a few jobs for them. If they ask why we're late, Priscilla, we'll explain that you kept us.'

The girl flushed angrily. Just then, Joan Terry rounded the corner and Priscilla's eyes lit up spitefully. Here was one first former she could bully easily. 'Joan!' she called out bossily. 'Come here!'

Hunching her shoulders, Joan came across and said meekly, 'Yes, Priscilla?'

'I was just telling the twins here that it's time they settled down and stopped playing stupid tricks,' said Priscilla smugly. 'Don't you agree?'

Poor Joan shifted uneasily from one foot to the other. What could she say? On the one hand she didn't want to fall out with the twins, who she sincerely liked, besides greatly admiring their audacity. On the other, she couldn't afford to offend Priscilla, who knew so much about her family. Unable to look at Dora and Daphne, the girl said tonelessly, 'Yes, Priscilla.'

The sixth former smiled triumphantly while the twins glared at Joan's bent head. 'Well, off you go then,' she ordered, and Joan scuttled thankfully away to Alison's study.

'Are you all right, Joan?' asked Alison in concern, thinking that the girl looked a little pale and worried.

'I'm OK, Alison,' said Joan, managing a little smile. 'I just bumped into Dora and Daphne, and couldn't help wishing I was more like them.'

'Well, I'm glad you're not!' said Alison with feeling. 'Pair of brats! No, Joan, I think you're just fine the way you are.'

Joan cheered up enormously, basking in these words of praise as she got happily to work. What did the twins and Priscilla matter so long as her idol, Alison, liked her as she was?

Dora and Daphne, meanwhile, were having a great time in Fizz and Claudine's study. The two older girls had been highly amused by the story of the twins' deception and were eager to hear all about it first hand.

'Ah, you bad girls!' Claudine teased them with a twinkle in her eye. 'I almost wish that I was in the first form so that I could share in your jokes and tricks.'

'I don't know how the pair of you had the nerve!' exclaimed Fizz. 'Weren't you afraid you'd be caught?'

This was music to the twins' ears, coming on top of Priscilla's hard words, but irresponsible of Fizz and Claudine. It was one thing for the sixth formers to laugh amongst themselves about the younger girls' exploit, but quite another to encourage them openly. Claudine, more versed in the ways of boarding school than Fizz, said as much when the twins had left.

'If Pat or Isabel knew how much we had laughed

with the younger girls they would think it most undignified of us,' she explained to Fizz. 'It is better that we say nothing to the others.'

Fizz looked thoughtful and, oddly for her, a little serious. 'I wonder how the sixth would like it if a member of their own form was keeping a secret from them,' she remarked at last.

'*Ma chère* Fizz, it is not to be thought of,' said the French girl, throwing up her hands in pretend horror. 'We sixth formers do not deceive or play tricks on one another. We are good, we are . . .'

'Yes, but what if someone was deceiving them for a good reason,' interrupted Fizz. 'Surely they wouldn't mind then.'

Something in the girl's tone made Claudine look at her sharply. 'Do not tell me that you, too, have a twin hiding somewhere in the school?' she said. 'It is surely not possible that I have been sharing my study with *two* Fizzes!'

Fizz laughed. 'No, there's only one of me.'

'Then why do you ask me such a question?' Claudine said suspiciously. 'You have a secret, Fizz, I know it! Come, you must serve the beans!'

'Spill the beans, dope!' laughed Fizz. 'Oh, Claudine, I don't know if I should.'

'But of course you should!' exclaimed the French girl. 'Me, I love secrets and I am so, so good at keeping them.'

Fizz studied Claudine's mischievous little face for a

moment and decided that she could trust her. The French girl had her own sense of honour, although it was a little different from the English one. Also, she had a love of the dramatic and mysterious which meant she would enjoy guarding her friend's secret.

'All right, Claudine,' said Fizz, taking a deep breath. 'I'll tell you.' So she told. And Claudine listened, silent for once, her eyes round and mouth agape.

'*C'est incredible*!' she gasped at the end, then gave a deep laugh. 'Priscilla and Angela will be so, so furious when they find out.'

'Yes, but I don't want *anyone* finding out just yet,' Fizz said firmly. 'This is between the two of us, Claudine.'

'And it shall remain so,' promised Claudine solemnly, putting a hand on her heart. 'Upon my honour.'

The first formers were laughing and chattering in their common-room, some of them dancing to music on the radio, others reading and some just enjoying sprawling around doing nothing in particular. The Lacey twins were arguing noisily over possession of a magazine when the door opened and they fell silent, drawing together as Joan Terry entered.

'Traitor!' called out Dora, giving the girl a scornful glance.

'What are you doing here, Joan?' asked Daphne. 'Tired of hanging round with the sixth form?'

'Hey, what goes on?' asked Katie, taking in the twins' contemptuous faces and Joan's pale, scared one. Some of the other girls gathered round to listen as well.

'She sided with Priscilla when she told us off earlier,' explained Daphne indignantly.

'I didn't!' protested Joan. 'But I couldn't very well argue with a sixth former, could I?'

'You could have stuck up for us a bit,' said Dora. 'But you don't seem to think much of the first form. Always hanging round that silly Alison O'Sullivan.'

'Alison isn't silly!' said Joan at once, her cheeks becoming hot.

'See! You'll defend her, but not us, your own classmates,' sneered Daphne. 'Traitor!'

'Stop it!' said Katie, looking worriedly from the twins to Joan. The first formers were, on the whole, a happy crowd and she didn't want any petty quarrels boiling up to spoil things. 'Twins, you have to learn that it isn't always easy for some of us to stand up to the likes of Priscilla,' she said with great wisdom. 'And don't forget that you always have one another for support, whereas the rest of us – like Joan – are on our own.'

Dora and Daphne listened to Katie, who they liked and respected very much, and bit their tongues.

'As for you, Joan,' she went on. 'We all know how unpleasant Priscilla can be, but she can't be allowed to get away with her sneaking and her bullying, sixth former or not. If you can just bring yourself to stand up to her a bit, we'll all back you up and be proud of you.'

Joan nodded but her thoughts were bleak. Katie's advice was sound but the girl didn't know Priscilla like she did. Nor did Katie know all about Joan, as the sixth former did.

'Something else, Joan,' said Katie, taking Joan's arm and leading her a little apart from the others. 'How about making some friends in our form? We're not a bad bunch on the whole, you know, and although Alison's really nice, you're just a kid as far as she's concerned and she can't really want you hanging round all the time.'

'OK, Katie,' said the girl listlessly. She didn't add that most of the first formers weren't interested in making friends with her because they found her quiet and boring. That was her own fault, she knew. But she hadn't always been that way. Once she had been fun-loving and happy, just like the others. Until everything had gone horribly wrong. Alison was different, though, in spite of what Katie said. She liked Joan and was kind to her. Who cared what Katie, the twins and the rest of the first form thought? Joan would stay where she was wanted – with Alison!

8 Morag in trouble

As the days went on, those members of the sixth who had come up through the school together felt as though they had never been away. Fizz, too, settled down quickly, popular with everyone but Angela and Priscilla. Whenever either of them were around, the girl took great pleasure in exaggerating her Cockney accent and talking in the strangest rhyming slang, most of which, the girls were sure, she made up as she went along. The standard of her work was high, as she had a quick intellect and only needed to look at a page to memorize it. Alison and Doris who, no matter how hard they worked, were consistently bottom of the class, envied her ability to achieve excellent results with the minimum effort. 'I can't help wondering how our Cockney sparrow will get on in French,' Pat had said with a chuckle. 'Her accent's sure to be terrible!'

But Pat had been wrong. Not only was Fizz well-grounded in the rules of French grammar, her accent was almost as perfect as Claudine's.

'At last!' Mam'zelle had cried in delight. 'Someone who speaks my language as she should be spoke. *Très bien, ma petite.*'

It was fortunate that Claudine didn't have a jealous nature, as Mam'zelle, already much taken with the girl's good looks and bubbly personality, made a great favourite of Fizz. Morag Stuart, on the other hand, was not a success. Her work was well below the standard of the sixth and she made no effort to improve. She was so rude and inattentive that Miss Harry actually threatened to send her out of the room one day, something unheard of for a sixth former. The rest of the girls had been horrified, as the disgrace would have reflected badly on the whole of the class.

'Ah, this Morag, she will turn my hair grey and white!' exclaimed Mam'zelle one day, when the girl had been particularly difficult. 'Never will you learn to roll your Rs in the French way. You are a great big stupid! Even more stupid than Doris.'

Doris, who was totally useless at French, though she could imitate Mam'zelle's accent to perfection for the amusement of the girls, grinned round the class. Morag scowled. Carlotta sighed. She was finding sharing a study with the girl very trying. Morag never initiated any conversation, responding to Carlotta's attempts with forbidding, one-word answers. Forthright Carlotta, in the habit of speaking her mind, often found it difficult to control her temper. But if she blew up and told Morag exactly what she thought of her, it would be impossible for the two of them to continue sharing, and she would feel that she had let Miss Theobald down. Morag had clashed with Pat several times too, and

Carlotta could see a terrific row boiling up there.

Things came to a head after netball one morning. Games was the one thing Morag shone at and the only lesson she appeared to enjoy. She was strong and agile, and seemed able to work off some of her aggression in the gym, or running around outside. This was the first time she had played netball, but she took to it immediately. She was a natural player, fighting fiercely for possession of the ball and sticking to Pat, the girl she was marking, like glue.

'She can certainly play,' said Bobby to Gladys. 'You'd never guess this was her first time.'

Gladys nodded. 'She needs to be more disciplined, though. Look at the way she barged into Pat just then! If this was a school match, she would have been sent off for that.'

As it was, Miss Wilton blew her whistle and took Morag aside to deliver a few measured words. Sadly for Pat, the girl ignored them! A few minutes later Hilary threw the ball and Pat, breaking away from Morag, ran to catch it. The Scottish girl wasn't far behind, though, and unfortunately she slipped on an icy patch, bringing Pat down and landing heavily on top of her. Scrambling to her feet, Morag trampled on Pat's hand and the girl yelped with pain.

Miss Wilton blew her whistle furiously, while several of the girls rushed across to Pat, who was sitting on the ground, nursing her injured hand and biting her lip in pain.

'Are you OK, Pat?' asked Isabel anxiously, before whirling round on Morag. 'You did that on purpose!'

'I didn't!' shouted the girl indignantly. 'I slipped on a patch of ice and . . .'

'Go and get changed, Morag,' ordered the games teacher sternly. 'I'll speak to you later.'

Angrily, the girl marched off the court blinking back hot tears, determined that the others wouldn't see them. It was so unfair! Games was the only thing she looked forward to, and now even that had been ruined. She really hadn't meant to hurt Pat, but it was no use telling that to the sixth form. They seemed determined to think the worst of her.

'I think you'd better take yourself off to Matron,' said Miss Wilton, looking at Pat's hand. 'Best to be on the safe side.'

So Pat went off to sickbay, knocking on the door with her uninjured hand.

'Come in!' called out Matron. 'Ah, Pat, I was just about to come looking for you. Good Heavens, whatever has happened to your hand?'

Pat told her and Matron examined the injury with gentle skill.

'No bones broken, but you'll have some beautiful bruises tomorrow,' she said briskly. 'Lucky it's your left hand. Morag's a fierce one, all right.'

Pat agreed but, now that her pain was beginning to subside and she knew that no serious damage was done, her natural sense of fair play came to the fore.

'I honestly believe it was an accident, Matron,' she said. 'The ground was pretty slippery in places because of all the frost we've had.'

'It's good of you to take it like that, but whether you'll feel so generous towards Morag after you've heard what I have to say is another matter.'

'What do you mean, Matron?' asked Pat, frowning.

'Well, if you remember, I said that I was just about to go looking for you when you came in?'

Pat nodded.

'The reason being that I had just done a spot-check on the sixth's dormitories and I'm afraid yours fell way below standard, Pat.'

'But all of the girls in my dormitory are sticklers for making their beds and keeping their things tidy,' said Pat in dismay. 'They wouldn't dare be anything else with you as Matron!'

'*Most* of them are sticklers, I agree,' said Matron meaningfully. 'But there's one girl in your form who's let the side down. Morag left her bed in a disgraceful state this morning: unmade, clothes strewn across it, and goodness knows what else. You know what that means, don't you, Pat?'

Pat's lips tightened grimly. She knew all right. An order mark! Order marks were given for misbehaviour or breaking rules and, if too many were earned, resulted in loss of privileges for the whole form. Among the lower school a few order marks weren't regarded as a very serious matter. The upper school, however, considered them a great disgrace. In fact, Pat couldn't remember any sixth form ever having an order mark against it since she had been at St Clare's. Just wait until she got hold of Morag!

'If such a thing had happened in the first or second form I would have given the girl responsible a good telling off and, perhaps, a second chance,' said Matron. 'Unfortunately I can't do that with a sixth former. At your age you're all expected to know better.'

'Yes, Matron,' agreed Pat, outwardly calm while inside she was seething. 'I'll have a word with Morag.'

'I don't doubt it, Pat,' Matron said with dry amusement at the head girl's grim expression. 'Two or three words, if I'm any judge of the matter. Don't lose your temper too badly and put yourself in the wrong, though, will you?'

'I won't,' promised Pat as she left Matron's room. Inwardly she didn't feel quite so sure.

Pat made her way down to the changing-rooms and there was the Scottish girl, sitting on a bench and changing her shoes.

'Pat,' she said, flushing as the head girl entered. 'I'm sorry about your hand. I really didn't mean . . .'

'Never mind that,' interrupted Pat, brushing the apology aside. 'Morag, why didn't you make your bed this morning?'

In a flash the girl's apologetic demeanour changed to one of stubborn anger as she snapped, 'Is that why you're here? To tell me off as though I were a first former? Well, don't waste your time, Pat, because I won't have it.' With that she got up and stalked to the door, but Pat was too quick for her. Darting in front of Morag, she slammed the door so hard that it echoed.

'Let me pass,' demanded Morag through gritted teeth as the other girl leant against the door.

'No,' said Pat, quite furious now. 'Not until you've heard me out. Thanks to you, we now have the distinction of being the only sixth form in the history of St Clare's to have an order mark against us! Can't you see that we're all sick to death of your stupid ways? It's time you grew up! You're a disgrace to the school and your parents.'

'How dare you?' gasped Morag, turning a little pale.

'I dare because I'm head girl and I care a great deal about the reputation of the sixth and the honour of St Clare's.'

Morag sneered. 'Well, I don't!'

'Tell me something I don't know!' said Pat in disgust. 'I can understand why your folks wanted to send you to boarding school, but not why Miss Theobald agreed to accept you. You've nothing to gain from your time here, because you've nothing to offer in return. Your work isn't up to first-form standard, while your behaviour belongs in the kindergarten. Well, Morag, just carry on as you are and, with a bit of luck, you'll be expelled. Your mum and dad will be upset, but I don't suppose you care for them any more than you do for anything else. One thing's for sure – the sixth won't be sorry to see the back of you.'

Morag trembled from head to foot as she listened to this scornful speech, wanting to stop the stream of angry, contemptuous words that poured from Pat's lips. But just then Pat was forced to move aside as someone pushed the door from the other side, and Carlotta entered.

'How are your fingers, Pat?' she began, then stopped, realizing that the atmosphere was tense and seeing the stormy expressions on both girls' faces. Then Morag brushed past her and walked away.

'What goes on?' asked Carlotta in astonishment. 'Have you and Morag been rowing about the way she tackled you? You look ready to explode.'

'I already have,' said Pat, and told the girl about Morag's order mark. Some of the other sixth formers came in as she was speaking, and were furious.

'What a total idiot she is!'

'It's so unfair when the rest of us take the trouble to make sure the dormitories are tidy.'

'Send her to Coventry!'

Hilary wrinkled her nose thoughtfully at this last cry. 'In Morag's case, I don't think it would make much difference,' she said. 'Because she doesn't want our company anyway.'

'Well, something's got to be done,' said Anne-Marie. 'We can't have her chalking up any more order marks for the sixth.'

The others agreed. But what?

'I feel as though I'm partly to blame,' said Carlotta

gravely. 'Miss Theobald asked me to befriend her and I've failed miserably.'

There were cries of protest at this.

'It's certainly not your fault!' said Janet. 'She's impossible, and the head will soon come to realize that, just as the other mistresses have. With a bit of luck, Morag might even be sent down into the fifth form.'

Carlotta looked sharply at Janet and said thoughtfully, 'Yes, she might. Thanks, Janet, you've just given me an idea.'

In their study that evening, Morag and Carlotta sat either side of the table, working silently at their French prep. Glancing briefly across at the other girl's book, Carlotta could see that she had covered only a few lines with her sprawling, untidy writing. And half of that had been crossed out! Looking back at her own page of neatly written work, she bit back a grin. Mam'zelle would hit the roof if Morag handed that in tomorrow. But the Scottish girl didn't seem to care, laying down her pen and pushing the book away from her with a sigh.

'Someone must have forgotten to tell Mam'zelle that we're meant to be taking it easy this term,' remarked Carlotta. 'She always gives us twice as much prep as the other mistresses. Still, you won't have to worry about it for much longer. The work's a breeze down in the fifth.'

Morag frowned. 'What do you mean?'

'Oh, only that I happened to overhear Miss Harry and the head talking together this morning, and they said . . .' Carlotta's voice trailed off and she put a hand up to her mouth. 'Oops! Maybe I shouldn't have said anything, but I assumed that Miss Harry had already spoken to you about it.'

'Spoken about what? What are you talking about?' demanded Morag impatiently.

'Well, Miss Harry told the head that your work and conduct weren't really up to the standard of the sixth,' said Carlotta innocently. 'Miss Theobald agreed that if there was no improvement over the next couple of weeks, you were to go down into the fifth.' Wicked Carlotta crossed her fingers behind her back as she said all of this, hoping that the unpredictable Morag wouldn't storm off to the head to demand the truth. She didn't, instead she looked rather pale and stricken as she said hoarsely, 'But the head can't do that!'

Carlotta raised her dark brows. 'Miss Theobald can do anything she chooses. It's quite usual, you know, for a girl to be put back a year if she can't – or won't – keep up with her class.'

Then, seeing how appalled Morag looked, she added kindly, 'You might feel more at home in the fifth. They're a good crowd and not quite so mature and responsible as our lot. Anyway, look on the bright side – you'll have a whole extra year in which to enjoy St Clare's.'

For a moment, Morag suspected Carlotta of laughing at her, but the girl had bent her head to her work again, looking the picture of innocence as she scribbled away. How she was laughing inside, though, at Morag's horror.

And, indeed, the girl *was* horrified. She had meant to be so unhappy and badly behaved that her father would take her away at half-term. Instead it seemed that she might have to endure an extra year in this rotten place! Well, she wasn't standing for that! If her only chance of getting out of it was by changing her ways and proving that she could keep up with the others, that was what she would have to do. Taking up her pen, she applied herself once more to her French book. Mam'zelle would be pleasantly surprised in tomorrow's class.

Carlotta watched her through lowered lashes, noting the changing expressions on the girl's striking face. Lying went right against her nature but, on this occasion, the girl felt that it had been justified. Certainly it seemed to have worked, Morag's pen was flying across the page. Carlotta felt encouraged. Next weekend, she decided, once the Thursday meeting was out of the way, she would make a real effort to get to know Morag better.

9
The first meeting

'I can't tell you how much I envy you,' said Mirabel to Gladys as she called into her study on Thursday evening. 'The first meeting tonight and I'll miss it! Gladys, why was I such a pig-headed idiot last term?'

'No use thinking like that,' said Gladys giving her friend a clap on the shoulder. 'You have to look forward and think what fun you'll be able to have after you've passed the exams. And you *will* pass this time, Mirabel, I know it.'

'Thanks, Gladys,' said Mirabel gruffly, flushing a little as she always did at any show of affection. 'Well, if hard work has anything to do with it, I certainly ought to pass, because I've spent every spare minute studying. So has Angela.'

'Really?' said Gladys, surprised. 'I must say, I didn't think she had it in her to work hard.'

'Oh, she can work when she wants something badly enough,' said Mirabel with a touch of scorn. 'And she's determined to get to this fancy finishing school of hers at all costs.' The girl grinned suddenly. 'Although knowing that Carlotta will be going with her has taken the edge off it a little.'

'I wouldn't be too sure about that,' said Gladys drily. 'Carlotta wants to get *out* of going every bit as badly as Angela wants to get in. And Miss Theobald has promised to have a few words with her father on the subject.'

'Great news!' cried Mirabel, pleased. 'I won't tell Angela, though. It'll do her good to think she's not going to have everything all her own way for once.'

'How are the two of you getting on?'

Mirabel wrinkled her brow. 'Well, we both spend so much time with our noses in books that there isn't much conversation. But, in a way, it's created a kind of bond between us. All the same, I'll be glad when the exams are over. How about you and Alison?'

'Oh, Alison's OK. We don't always share the same ideas, but she's kind and good natured.' She laughed. 'A little *too* good natured at times! The first former who comes to do our jobs has become very attached to her. Poor Alison's getting really bored with the way she hangs round, but can't bring herself to hurt the kid's feelings.'

Right on cue there came a soft tapping at the door, and Joan Terry put her head in. The soft brown eyes dimmed a little as she realized that Alison wasn't there. 'Hi, Gladys!' she said. 'Where's Alison?'

'Gone to see Angela,' answered Gladys. 'But what do you want her for, Joan? You came in earlier to do everything that needed doing.'

'Yes, but I was bored in our common-room,' said the girl hesitantly. 'I thought that maybe there was something else I could do for Alison.'

Gladys frowned. Although she had joked about Joan's devotion with Mirabel, something wasn't quite right here. The girl ought to be making friends in her own form and joining in the many lively activities there, instead of constantly trotting after a sixth former like a little dog. Fortunately, Alison wasn't the kind of person to take advantage of Joan's slavish loyalty, but Gladys still felt uneasy. She tried to give the girl's thoughts another direction. 'You did a great job in goal the other day, Joan. Keep up the practice, because I need all the promising players I can get.'

'You bet I will,' said Joan, flushing with pleasure. 'Will you tell Alison that I came by? And that I'll be here tomorrow at my usual time.'

'Yes, I'll tell her. Now you'd better get back to your common-room.'

Joan went and Mirabel said generously, 'You really are doing brilliantly as games captain. I haven't had much time to come and watch the young ones myself, but I'd have to be deaf not to hear the way the lower school sing your praises.'

Gladys certainly had a way with the younger girls, warmly praising those who were good and gently encouraging those who were less able. Like Mirabel, she had the gift of inspiring the girls with wanting to do their best for her. Unlike Mirabel, it hadn't gone to her head. Gladys admired her friend for being able to praise her so wholeheartedly, without a trace of bitterness, and said with her usual modesty, 'Bobby and Janet are a great help. They often spot things that I might have missed. It was Janet who thought of trying out Joan in goal. Oh, just look at the time! I'd better shoot off to the common-room or I'll be late for the first meeting. Don't feel too left out, Mirabel. I'll come and tell you all about it as soon as I have time.'

The others were already in the common-room when Gladys arrived, seated around the big table. Gladys slipped in beside Claudine and looked around. There was Priscilla, sitting up very straight and looking strangely excited for once. No doubt delighted at the prospect of sticking her nose into other people's business, thought Gladys. Beyond her sat Morag, looking rather subdued. The girls had noticed a change in the Scottish girl over the last couple of days. She actually seemed to have settled down a bit and, although she was still surly with the sixth formers, her behaviour in class had improved greatly, as had her work.

'Well, here we all are,' said Doris. 'But what do we do now?'

'Just wait until someone knocks at the door,' said Isabel. 'And hope that it won't be too long.'

'Suppose no one comes?' said Anne-Marie. 'Maybe no one has any worries or problems this week.'

'In a school of this size there's *always* someone who needs to get something off their chest,' said Hilary sagely. 'They'll come all right.'

And so they did, in a steady stream. First was a dark

girl called Hilda, who complained that her best friend was always copying her work.

'Haven't the teachers caught on?' asked Bobby. 'They must be getting suspicious if you both keep handing in identical assignments.'

'Oh, Ruth doesn't copy it word for word – just pinches my ideas! Last Saturday, for example, we were supposed to be working on a joint project. Then Ruth decided to go off roller-skating with the others and left me to do all the work. But she still took half the credit.'

'OK, Hilda,' said Pat kindly. 'You go and wait outside while we talk it through, and we'll call you back when we come up with a solution.'

This procedure had been agreed on beforehand by the girls. 'So that if we have differing ideas on how to settle a problem we can thrash it out in private,' Isabel had said. 'It's not going to look too good if we start arguing in front of the kids.'

'It's not on,' said Fizz indignantly now. 'Hilda needs to tell Ruth where to get off.'

'Yes, but not everyone's quite as blunt as you are, Fizz,' said Hilary with a smile. 'Ruth's a bit full of herself, whereas Hilda's on the shy side and not too good at sticking up for herself.'

'Ruth's cheating,' declared Priscilla pompously. 'If you ask me, she ought to be reported to Miss Roberts.'

'Trust you to come up with a solution like that!' said Bobby scornfully. The girl flushed angrily and debated whether to say something cutting in return. Then she caught the challenging look in Bobby's eye and hastily changed her mind. Anyone who engaged in a verbal battle with sharp-witted Bobby generally came second.

'I think Hilda ought to speak to her about it,' said Isabel decidedly. 'But in her own time. It won't be easy for her, but if she knows she has our support, she just might be able to work up to it. Agreed?'

There was a chorus of assent, with the exception of Priscilla, who said, 'I still think . . .'

'Well, you're out-voted, so just shut up,' said Bobby rudely. 'Great idea, Isabel. And it'll do wonders for Hilda's self-confidence if she can make a stand.'

'Shall I fetch her back?' asked Fizz. Isabel nodded and Hilda was brought back into the room. She listened intently as Isabel spoke, saying at last, 'I know you're right. I guess I've always been a bit afraid of standing up to Ruth because I don't want to lose her as a friend. She's the leader, you see, while I just sort of tag along. She's so popular while I don't find it so easy to make friends.'

'If she's any kind of a friend this shouldn't make a difference,' Fizz remarked. 'And if it does . . . well, you're better off without her.'

'Absolutely right,' agreed Pat. 'OK, Hilda, you just think about what we've said and come back in a few weeks to let us know how you're doing.'

'Well, I don't think we handled that too badly, if I do say so myself,' said Janet. 'It's great that we can reach agreement so smoothly – or at least, most of us can.' On these words she looked directly at Priscilla, who suddenly seemed to find the table fascinating, refusing to meet Janet's steady gaze. Then a timid knock sounded on the door. It opened slightly and a head appeared.

'Come in,' called Pat. 'We don't bite.'

A small figure sidled in, shaking so badly that the girls could almost hear her knees knocking.

'Lucy, isn't it?' said Pat pleasantly. 'Well, take a seat and tell us what we can do for you.'

Lucy sat, feeling very small and insignificant. Haltingly she brought out her story. 'Last week it was my friend Susan's birthday,' she began shyly. 'I'd been planning to buy her something special, because when it was my birthday she bought me a record and took me out for tea. But this month my folks were late sending me my allowance, so I was broke.'

'Don't tell me the two of you have fallen out just because you didn't get her a present?' said Gladys.

'No,' answered Lucy. 'Because as it turned out, I was able to buy her something at the last minute.'

'How come?' asked Doris. 'Did you borrow from someone?'

Lucy gulped. 'No . . . I found a ten-pound-note in the corridor and picked it up.'

'You should have handed it in to Matron immediately,' said Priscilla sharply, drawing glares from the rest of the sixth form.

'I know,' said Lucy miserably. 'And I honestly meant to. But I suddenly thought how pleased Susan would be if, for her birthday, I could buy her the bag she's had her eye on. So that's what I did. And then something awful happened!'

'What?' asked Bobby curiously.

'Well, Susan told me that she had lost the ten-pound-note her older brother had sent her as a present. Which means that *I* must have picked it up! I know that I should have told her right away but, somehow, the longer I left it, the harder it became.' Tears started in Lucy's eyes. 'I'm in such a mess, and I don't know what to do.'

Kind-hearted Alison came round the table and put her arm round the girl's heaving shoulders. 'Don't worry, Lucy,' she said, almost on the verge of tears herself. 'What you've done isn't so very bad.' She looked around the table for support and Pat said at once, 'Of course not. Just one of those spur of the moment things. Go with Alison, Lucy, while we sort it out. And don't look so upset. You haven't robbed a bank, you know.'

Lucy gave a laugh, mingled with a sob which turned into a hiccup, and allowed Alison to lead her from the room.

'Poor kid,' said Anne-Marie. 'She's obviously been worrying herself sick over this. 'Priscilla, did you have to be so sharp with her?'

'What she did was wrong,' said Priscilla piously. 'I think she should be made to tell the truth at once, otherwise it could lead to all kinds of things.'

'Don't be so stupid!' said Janet impatiently. 'It's

obvious that Lucy isn't dishonest, or she wouldn't have worked herself up into such a state.'

'Yes,' agreed Doris. 'It's the sort of thing anyone in her position might have done on the spur of the moment, and regretted later.'

Alison returned then, saying, 'She's calmed down a bit now. Any ideas, girls?'

'I think Lucy ought to tell the truth,' put in Carlotta unexpectedly. 'But not until she's saved up enough money to pay Susan back. Then she'll know Lucy's really sorry. With a bit of luck they might even be able to laugh about it.'

'Yes, and it would definitely ease Lucy's mind if she owned up,' said Pat. 'Fetch her back, would you, Alison?'

Lucy's eyes were still red when she returned, but she clearly felt a little happier for having shared her guilty secret.

'We really think that you ought to own up to Susan,' said Pat. 'But after you've saved up enough money to pay her back. If she is mad with you and the two of you fall out over it, then come back to us and we'll try to put it right for you. Personally, though, I don't think you've much to worry about.'

'Yes, I think I knew all along that owning up was the right thing to do,' Lucy said. 'I just needed someone to give me a little push. I should be able to pay her back next month – and won't it be a weight off my shoulders.'

'Phew!' said Hilary as the door closed behind the girl.

'I'm absolutely exhausted. Who would have thought that being an agony aunt could be so tiring?'

'It's not over yet,' said Isabel as someone knocked at the door. 'Next, please!'

A ride – and a revelation

Saturday morning dawned bright and clear, the sun shining although there was a chill in the air.

A perfect day for riding, thought Carlotta, who was a regular at the stables along the road, swiftly pulling on jodhpurs and a sweater before setting off. To her surprise, she found Morag there, watching as Will, the owner's son, tacked up a frisky grey mare.

'Hi, Carlotta!' he said, looking up and giving a friendly grin. 'With you in a sec.'

'No hurry, Will,' she replied with an answering smile, before turning to the Scottish girl. 'I didn't know you rode, Morag. Mind if I tag along?'

'Suit yourself,' replied the girl with a shrug. 'But I aim to go for a good, long gallop. I'm an experienced rider and if you can't keep up with me, I'll leave you behind.'

Will, who had struck up quite a friendship with Carlotta, stared narrowly at Morag and opened his mouth to say something. Then Carlotta caught his eye and winked, shaking her head. To Morag she said meekly, 'I'll try not to slow you down.'

'It's obvious your pal's never seen you in action,' murmured Will as the Scottish girl mounted her horse and he led out a handsome chestnut for Carlotta. 'I reckon you'll leave her standing.'

'She's not my pal, Will,' answered Carlotta ruefully. 'Not yet, anyhow. Don't bother with a saddle for me – mustn't keep Morag waiting.' With that she grabbed the horse's mane and, with the agility of an acrobat, vaulted lightly on to his back. 'Come on, Morag,' she called brightly. 'I'll race you to that big oak tree over there.'

Leaving Will to stare after them, the two girls trotted out of the yard, their horses picking up speed as they came into an open field, faster and faster, breaking into a canter, then a gallop. The cold air stung the girls' cheeks, bringing a rosy glow to them and an excited sparkle to their eyes. Carlotta won the race by a head and had her reward when Morag called out in admiration, 'You can certainly ride, Carlotta!'

'I was practically born on horseback,' answered the girl. 'Anyway, you weren't exactly holding back yourself.'

For the first time since she had come to St Clare's, Morag grinned and Carlotta was amazed at how different she looked, so pretty and friendly. 'Do you have a horse at home?'

'Yes, he's called Starlight,' answered Morag. 'And I miss him so much.' Then, as though afraid of revealing too much of herself, she clammed up again and trotted away.

Oh, no! thought Carlotta. Just as I was making progress. She decided to give Morag a surprise. Balancing herself very carefully, she stood on the horse's broad back. Then, with a soft chirruping noise, she coaxed him forward, catching up with Morag.

'Fancy another race?' she asked. Morag turned her head, giving a gasp of surprise as she found herself staring at Carlotta's legs where she had expected her face to be.

'Carlotta, you're mad!' she cried. 'Get down before you fall.'

'If you insist,' said Carlotta wickedly. Then, to Morag's amazement, she sprang from the horse's back, landing in side-saddle position.

'You *are* mad!' said Morag, beginning to laugh in spite of herself. 'Totally loopy, in fact!'

'I am once I get on horseback,' agreed Carlotta happily. 'There are some jumps in the paddock over there. Let's go and show one another what we can do.'

So it came about that Carlotta spent a more pleasant day than she would have believed possible with Morag, both girls showing off shamelessly and praising one another extravagantly.

'I haven't had such a good time in ages,' said Morag as the girls made their way back to school.

'It was great!' agreed Carlotta. 'We ought to make it a regular thing.'

As the day was so fine, some of the sixth formers had challenged the fifth to a friendly game of netball. They were just about to begin when Morag and Carlotta, positively glowing from their morning in the fresh air, returned to St Clare's. Pat, happening to glance round, was struck by how different Morag looked – almost happy. Perhaps now would be a good time to make amends for the harsh words she had spoken to the girl the other day. After all, Morag did seem to be making a little more effort now. Smiling, Pat walked across to the two girls and said in her friendly manner, 'Enjoyed your ride? How about joining us for netball if you're not too tired out, Carlotta? We're a player short. Morag, if you're at a loose end we could do with an umpire too.'

But, to both Pat and Carlotta's dismay, Morag's face resumed its habitual glower and she walked off without a word.

'Aargh!' cried Carlotta, clutching at her hair. 'Just as I was beginning to get through to her.'

'My fault,' said Pat ruefully. 'Evidently the only place Morag wants to bury the hatchet is in my head! She has improved in class, though – your doing?'

Carlotta grinned. 'I may have had something to do with it. I told her that the head was thinking of sending her down into the fifth and the thought of spending another year here had a strange effect on her.'

'Carlotta, you're wicked,' said Pat in mock horror. 'Still, it seems to have done the trick.'

'Hey, Pat! Carlotta!' called out Fizz. 'Come on, we're waiting to start!'

'Count me out, Pat,' said Carlotta, a sudden determined look coming over her face. 'I'm going to try and sort things out with Morag once and for all.'

'Best of luck,' said Pat, not looking very hopeful. 'All right, Fizz. Keep your hair on – I'm coming!'

Morag was cleaning her riding boots when Carlotta entered the study and said, 'You should get one of the first formers to do that.'

'I'm quite capable of doing things for myself,' replied Morag abruptly. 'I think it's a stupid, outdated custom anyway.'

Carlotta raised her eyebrows. 'It teaches the younger girls to be responsible and they get their turn at giving out orders when they reach the upper school.'

'I can do without the lecture, thanks,' retorted Morag, her green eyes icy.

'I wasn't lecturing,' said Carlotta, holding tightly on to her own temper. 'Morag, why were you so rude to Pat just then?'

'I don't like her, or they way she thinks that being head girl gives her the right to speak to me as if I was about five years old. I'm used to doing as I please.'

'Maybe, but can you imagine what St Clare's would be like if all of us went around doing and saying what we pleased?' asked Carlotta. 'And it *is* Pat's duty to see that the rules are kept.'

'I thought you weren't going to lecture me,' said Morag sullenly.

'I just wish that you'd give Pat and the rest of us a chance,' Carlotta persisted. 'If you'd just be sensible and try to join in you might . . .'

'I don't *want* to join in,' broke in Morag angrily. 'I'm not like you, or Pat, or any of the others, can't you see that? It's all right for you – you've been here for years and were brought up to this kind of life. Well, I wasn't and I hate it.' With that she slammed out of the room. Trembling with anger herself, Carlotta resisted the temptation to go after her and tell her exactly what she thought of her. Then, as suddenly as it had risen, her anger vanished and, sighing, she sank down into an armchair. She had failed! Miss Theobald had been wrong to entrust her with such a delicate task. The calm, tactful Hilary would have been a much better choice. On Monday she would go to the head and tell her so. In the meantime it was of no use to sit here brooding. She may as well join the others at netball and work off some of her temper.

Morag, meanwhile, made her way to the common-room, hoping that it would be empty. She badly needed to be alone with her thoughts. This morning she had been able to put her troubles right out of her mind in her exhilaration at being on horseback and – she had to admit – her pleasure in Carlotta's company. For a short while their mutual love of horses had created a bond between the two girls. But it had been a fragile bond, broken now. Miserably, the girl peeped round the door, pulling a face as she saw Alison and Claudine, neither of whom cared for fresh air, curled up cosily on armchairs near the fire. Morag moved away, the two girls in the room unaware of her presence as they chatted amicably. Then Claudine said something in her clear voice that made the girl pause. She knew it was wrong to eavesdrop, but Morag stood rooted to the spot, listening.

And what she heard was to help change her view of St Clare's for ever.

Carlotta felt hungry and pleasantly tired after the boisterous, good-natured netball game. Thank goodness it was Saturday and there was no prep. If it wasn't for her study-mate, she would be looking forward to tea, followed by a nice, lazy evening doing nothing. Oh, well, she supposed she could always go down to the dining-room for school tea. But when Carlotta popped into the study to change her shoes, she was happily surprised. A fresh, white cloth had been placed over the table, laid for two, and on it stood an array of sandwiches, crisps and a huge, squidgy chocolate cake.

'Oh, good, you're back.' Morag turned from the window with a hesitant smile. Gesturing towards the table she said, 'Sit down and help yourself. I thought you'd be hungry after a day spent outdoors.'

Recognising this as an olive-branch, Carlotta smiled back and said, 'I'm starving. And this looks – well, good enough to eat. It must have taken you ages to get this lot ready.'

'Oh, I got Susan from the first form to help me,' said Morag, flushing a little as she sat down. 'Tea OK? Or there's ginger beer if you'd prefer?'

'Tea's fine.' Carlotta watched Morag narrowly. Something had happened to change her mind – the question was, what?

There was silence for a few minutes as the two girls ate hungrily, then Morag cleared her throat and began,

'Look, Carlotta, I'm sorry about what I said earlier. I didn't realize that you . . .'

She broke off and Carlotta said sharply, 'Didn't realize that I what?'

Morag sighed. 'Well, the thing is, after I flounced out of here like an idiot, I went along to the common-room and heard two of the girls talking. Your name was mentioned and I listened.' She bit her lip. 'I know it was wrong of me, but I'm glad now that I did, because I learnt something. You see, I heard them saying that you had once belonged to a circus, and how you had loved the life there. Then I heard how difficult it had been for you to adapt to a completely different way of life here. But you stuck at it because you wanted to please your dad and make him proud of you.'

Carlotta nodded, her puzzled frown clearing as it dawned on her why Morag had undergone such a drastic change. The girl was so used to everyone in the school knowing about her unusual past that it simply hadn't occurred to her that to Morag it would be news. If only she had told the new girl all about herself from the start, how much easier things might have been!

'Will you tell me about your life in the circus?' asked Morag rather shyly. 'And about how you managed to settle down here?'

So Carlotta talked about her circus days, rather wistfully at times, of the people she had lived with and of how her father had come looking for her when her mother had died. Morag listened raptly. 'I should have guessed, when you performed those crazy tricks today!' she exclaimed. 'Tell me more.'

But Carlotta shook her head. 'I've talked about myself enough. I'd rather hear about Morag Stuart, and why she's so determined to be awkward and bad tempered when, deep down, she's quite nice!'

Morag blushed in earnest this time. She looked rather pensive for a moment then began, 'My mum died when I was a baby, so I was brought up by Dad. We lived in a big, rambling house in the most beautiful Scottish glen you could imagine and it was a wonderful life. I was allowed to run wild most of the time and my days were spent riding, swimming in the loch and fishing.'

'I see. But didn't you go to school?' asked Carlotta.

'I went to the village school sometimes. Dad's a writer, you see, and works from home, so we used to have what he called "bunking off" days together. Quite a lot of bunking off days! We'd just take off on horseback and go fishing, or for a picnic. Carlotta, it was the best life anyone could wish for.'

No wonder Morag couldn't settle, thought Carlotta. St Clare's must seem like a prison to her after that kind of life. But what had made her dad suddenly decide to send her away?

'Then Marian arrived,' explained the girl, as though she'd read Carlotta's mind. 'She came to our village to stay with relatives and Dad met her at a dinner party. Suddenly our bunking off days were over, and he was spending every spare minute with her. And before I knew what had happened, they were married.'

And Morag, having had her father to herself all her life, had resented it bitterly, Carlotta guessed. So it seemed, as Morag poured out the rest of her tale.

'She disapproved terribly of me, and the way Dad had brought me up. And she thought I spent too much time with Starlight and not enough on my school work.' Morag paused, turning a little red. 'It wasn't all her fault, though. I went out of my way to be rude and make life difficult for her. In the end, the house just wasn't big enough for the two of us, so here I am.'

Carlotta eyed her thoughtfully for while, then said, 'No wonder you're so fed up here. But I reckon your dad's to blame as well. If he'd included you in his plans and let you get to know Marian before they married, instead of pushing you out, perhaps you wouldn't have felt so hostile towards her. But I think that you ought to be pleased for your dad. I know I'd be delighted if mine found someone who could make him happy.'

'I never thought of it that way,' said Morag slowly. 'Too wrapped up in myself, I suppose.'

'Yes, you have been,' said Carlotta in her forthright way. 'But I think your stepmother might have done you a favour by insisting you come here.'

'Oh?' Morag looked extremely doubtful.

'Well, how can you know what you really want from life if you don't experience different things?' said Carlotta, sounding very mature and wise to the confused girl at that moment. 'When you leave St

Clare's you may decide to return to your beautiful Scottish glen. Or you may choose to do something quite different, like train for a career or go to college. The point is, if you hadn't left home then your view of the world and your choices would have been far narrower.'

'You're right,' said Morag, things seeming to fall into place. 'I've been a bit of an idiot, haven't I? But I won't be again, believe me.'

Carlotta did.

'Will you promise me something, Carlotta?' asked the Scottish girl, looking solemn.

'Anything,' agreed Carlotta, already liking this new Morag.

'If you see me slipping back into my old, stupid, sullen ways, kick me – good and hard.'

'I will,' Carlotta laughed. 'Although somehow I don't think I'll need to. Now, did you say something about ginger beer? All this straight talking has given me a thirst!'

Priscilla stirs things up

Mischief was brewing in the first-form common-room. The Lacey twins, their long punishment now behind them, were finding the strain of trying to be good too much and were in the mood for excitement.

'I feel a trick coming on,' announced Dora. 'Possibly in maths tomorrow.'

Katie turned down the corners of her mouth and shook her head.

'Oh, Katie! Don't say you're going to be a wet blanket about playing tricks just because you're head of the form?' Dora pleaded.

'Not at all,' answered Katie. 'But everyone knows Mam'zelle is the best person to play tricks on. You'll never manage to put one over on Miss Roberts – she's too sharp.'

'*You* might not,' said Dora haughtily. 'But *I* would. I just love a challenge, isn't that right, Daphne?'

Her twin nodded absent-mindedly. 'Mm. But if you ask me, a midnight party's a better way to relieve boredom.'

This suggestion found instant favour, a dozen or more voices chorusing, 'Brilliant! Let's do it!'

'Well, it is a kind of tradition, I suppose,' said Katie.

'Anyone got a birthday coming up?'

'Mine's in a fortnight,' said a girl called Rita. 'My folks usually send me money, and I don't mind putting some of it towards a party.'

'Great!' cried Daphne. 'So, if the rest of us buy some food as well, we can celebrate Rita's birthday in style.'

Joan Terry was not present at this meeting, being busy in Alison's study. Her jobs finished, she made her way back to the common-room and had just turned a corner when she gave a sudden gasp. There outside the door, nose practically in the keyhole, stood Priscilla. She tried to draw back, but her gasp had given her away and Priscilla turned sharply, her mean eyes narrowing. Joan was shocked, for although she knew that the sixth former had a reputation for snooping, to catch her in the act like this was just awful. Worse still, the girl could do nothing about it. If she told the first formers, or put them on their guard in any way, Priscilla would pay her back in the cruellest way possible.

Silently Priscilla beckoned Joan forward and, as she reached Priscilla's side, she heard Katie's voice saying quite clearly, 'A midnight party it is, then. We've two weeks to organize everything, so that should give us plenty of time.'

Joan's hand flew to her mouth in horror as she saw Priscilla's thin lips stretch into a queerly triumphant smile and, bravely, she stepped forward, placing her hand on the doorknob. She had to stop the first form giving anything else away. But her action came too late, for at that moment the door swung away from her, opened from the inside, and Rita stood there, the colour leaving her face as she saw who Joan was with. Poor Joan was very flustered and showed it, but Priscilla carried off the situation in her usual arrogant manner, walking calmly into the common-room and turning off the radio. The first formers felt uncomfortable, yet angry as well. Not one of the other sixth formers would have dreamt of invading the younger girls' privacy in such a way.

'Girls,' began Priscilla in a silky tone that they mistrusted at once. 'I'm looking for a volunteer to do a little work for me.' She looked round the room, but none of the girls would meet her gaze. Her eyes snapped coldly and she said angrily, 'Well, I don't think I've ever met such a set of rude, unhelpful kids! When I was your age, if a senior girl snapped her fingers we jumped, and . . .'

'Pity you didn't jump in the river,' muttered Daphne under her breath.

Priscilla's sharp ears caught the remark and she rounded on the girl, demanding, 'What did you say?'

Daphne, unabashed, stared at Priscilla, obviously quite ready to repeat her remark. But as she opened her mouth, Joan, shaking in her shoes and unable to bear the tension a moment longer, said nervously, 'I'll do your jobs for you, Priscilla.'

Every head turned in her direction and the girl wished that the ground would open up as she read the others' scornful thoughts. Coward! Traitor! Much to her surprise, Priscilla declined her offer, patting her shoulder and saying in a smooth voice, 'Thank you, Joan. It's nice to know that *one* member of the first form is willing to help. But you've already been working hard for Alison and I couldn't possibly expect you to do my jobs as well. Susan!' She picked on the girl whose ten-pound-note Lucy had mistakenly picked up. 'And you, Ruth.' This was the first former Hilda had complained of. 'You two will do. Come on.'

Reluctantly, pulling faces at Priscilla behind her back that made the others want to giggle, the two first formers followed her from the room. Once the door was closed behind them, the twins rounded on Joan.

'I'll do your jobs for you, Priscilla,' mimicked Dora cruelly. 'And can I lick your boots clean for you?'

'Yes, and what were you doing listening outside the door with her?' demanded Rita, pushing Joan roughly in the shoulder. 'Just what did you hear, you little snitch?'

'Nothing!' said Joan, almost in tears. 'I wasn't listening. Honestly I wasn't.'

'I'll bet that sneak Priscilla was, though,' said Daphne. 'And it wouldn't surprise me if you were covering up for her. Well, she'd better not get to know any first-form secrets, that's all. Because if she does, we'll know who told her.'

But, of course, Priscilla already knew some of the first form's secrets. Things that she hadn't learnt from Joan or from listening outside doors, but that she had discovered from the Thursday meeting. And the girl meant to use them to stir up trouble for the two first formers who were helping tidy her study – although this was so neat that there was hardly anything for them to do and they began to wonder why Priscilla wanted them there. They soon found out.

'I hear you lost ten pounds last week, Susan,' she said. 'Rather careless of you.'

Susan flushed. 'I didn't realize there was a hole in my pocket,' she said shortly. 'But how did you get to hear about it?'

'Oh, Lucy told me about it, after she found it,' said Priscilla innocently.

'But Lucy didn't find it!' said Susan, her eyes sparkling angrily. 'She's my friend and she'd have handed it back to me straight away.'

'If you're so sure why don't you ask her?' suggested Priscilla, with a smug smile.

'I will,' retorted Susan. 'And you'll be proved wrong, you'll see.' But inwardly the girl felt uneasy. It seemed impossible that her friend could have done something so low, yet Priscilla sounded sure.

'You'd be surprised how much I know about the goings-on in your form,' said Priscilla slyly. 'For example, I know all about your nasty little ways, Ruth.'

'Me?' said Ruth, startled. 'What have *I* done?'

'You cheat,' said Priscilla. 'And you make use of a girl who's supposed to be your friend.'

'I don't know what you're talking about!' cried Ruth, completely bewildered.

'No? The only reason you're friends with Hilda is because she gets good marks and you can copy her work, isn't it? And I happen to know that Hilda feels pretty sore about it, because she told me so herself.'

'That's not why I'm her friend at all!' gasped Ruth, turning pale. 'And if Hilda was mad at me, she'd say so to my face, not go behind my back – and to you, of all people!'

Priscilla flushed angrily. 'Just remember to show a little respect when you're speaking to your elders,' she snapped.

Respect, however, was the last thing either girl felt for Priscilla at that moment. Hurt and angry, they hurried over their tidying, anxious to get away from her spiteful accusations and get to the bottom of things.

'Hi, you two,' said Katie with a sympathetic grin when they got back to the common-room. 'Had a nice time with dear Priscilla?'

'We've had a most informative time,' replied Susan coldly as she spotted Lucy sitting in the corner. 'Hey, Lucy! I want a word with you.'

'Well, whatever's got into *her*?' asked Katie, astonished.

'A little bit of poison – courtesy of Priscilla,' answered Ruth grimly. 'Hilda, come here! You've got some explaining to do!'

After that, recriminations and accusations flew in all directions.

'I can't believe you would do something so low, Lucy,' burst out Susan. 'You *knew* I was upset about losing that money, and all the time *you* had it!'

'Hilda, I thought we were friends!' cried Ruth. 'Couldn't you have come and told me what was bothering you, instead of running to Priscilla? How you turn to *her*, of all people, beats me!'

'What's going on?' demanded Katie, pushing her way through the group that had gathered around the four girls – who looked as though they were about to have a free fight – and taking charge. Four angry voices spoke at once and Katie winced, holding up her hand for silence. 'One at a time! Lucy, you first.'

Stammering, her face red, Lucy told her story. A couple of the girls looked at her with contempt, but she was a well-liked girl and most of them felt for her, understanding that she had been sorely tempted. Even Susan calmed down and gave her friend a hug, saying warmly, 'I understand why you did it. Maybe I'd have done the same in your place. But next time you can't afford to buy me a present, just say so!'

Hilda spoke next and Ruth bit her lip. It was true, she realized in shame. She had used Hilda, never thinking how the girl felt about it. And poor Hilda had been afraid to confront her about it in case she lost her friendship. Suddenly Ruth felt about two feet tall. 'I'm sorry, Hilda,' she said humbly. 'I honestly thought you didn't mind me cribbing from you. You should have said. And it's not true that I'm friends with you just so that I can copy your work. We can *still* be friends, can't we?'

'You bet,' replied Hilda, her voice a little shaky.

'Thanks,' said Ruth. 'And if I ever ask to crib from you again, just tell me where to get off.'

'Well, I'm glad that's all been sorted out!' exclaimed Katie, wondering if there was a jinx on the first form today.

'There's one more thing to get sorted out,' put in Daphne. 'And that's the sixth form and their meetings. What's the point of us going to them with our personal problems if they're going to blab about them?'

'That's a bit unfair, Daphne,' protested Katie. 'It was only Priscilla who blabbed, with the intention of causing trouble. I'm sure that none of the other sixth formers would dream of breaking a confidence.'

'I agree,' said Rita. 'They're all really nice, apart from Priscilla. So what are we going to do about her?'

'Well, it's not really our place to do anything,' said Susan. 'It's up to the rest of the sixth to deal with her.'

'I don't like snitching – even on someone who deserves it – and Priscilla certainly deserves it!' said Hilda. 'But she'll make our lives a misery if we don't.'

'Mm,' said Katie thoughtfully. Then her brow cleared. 'I know what! We'll boycott the next meeting. Then, next day, when the sixth have been left high and dry, wondering why no one's turned up, we'll go along to the head girls and tell them all about Priscilla.'

'Good idea,' said Dora. 'Daphne and I'll shoot off to the second and third forms and put them in the picture as well. Oh, and someone had better keep an eye on *her*.' She nodded scornfully in Joan's direction and the girl cowered miserably in her chair.

'Yes,' agreed Daphne. 'Otherwise we'll have her running off to Priscilla as soon as our backs are turned to warn her of what we're planning.'

Poor Joan made no attempt to defend herself. What was the point? Seeing how unhappy the girl looked, Katie said sharply, 'Now that's enough. Go on then, twins, and remember, everyone – no matter how serious your problems are, the sixth's meeting is strictly out of bounds on Thursday.'

A week of shocks and surprises

The following day, Pat had a surprise when Morag approached her in the dormitory before breakfast and said in a low voice, 'Can you spare me a moment, Pat?'

'I suppose so,' she answered, not very graciously, for she was thoroughly fed up with the girl's sullen manner.

'I just wanted to apologize,' said Morag quietly. 'I was really rude to you yesterday. In fact, I've been rude and aggressive to everyone, behaving like a spoilt, stupid kid.' She gave a sad smile and went on, 'I just hope you haven't given up on me altogether, because things are going to be different from now on.'

'Well, you don't know how pleased I am to hear that!' said Pat, amazed and unable to stop herself from responding to the girl's infectious smile. She admired Morag for having the courage to own up to her faults and apologize so unreservedly. 'What's brought this on?'

'Oh, Carlotta gave me a good talking to, and suddenly I seemed to see things in a different light,' answered Morag.

And, certainly, she seemed like a different person this morning, thought Pat. Good one, Carlotta!

The rest of the sixth were astonished to see Pat and

Morag come into breakfast together, chattering away like old friends and Doris, as she said later, almost fainted into her cereal when the Scottish girl beamed round the table and greeted everyone with a cheerful 'Good morning'. Isabel blinked and, as her twin sat down beside her, said, 'She *looks* like Morag and she *sounds* like Morag, but I think she's been taken over by an alien being!'

'Idiot,' laughed Pat, helping herself to toast. 'Hey, where's Alison? Don't tell me she's still in bed.'

'Either that or she's curling her hair, or painting her toe-nails,' said Isabel.

'Oh, well, I'm not going to look for her. Alison's old enough now to be responsible for herself, and if she misses breakfast, it's her own fault.'

Alison was neither asleep nor gazing into her mirror. She had been waylaid by Joan Terry, who she had found waiting for her outside the dormitory.

'Joan!' she exclaimed, surprised and none too pleased. 'What are you doing here? You really aren't supposed to be in this area, you know.'

'Oh, Alison, don't be mad with me,' said Joan, her brown eyes pleading. 'I came to see if there was anything you might need doing in your dormitory. Perhaps I could make your bed, or tidy your locker or . . .'

'My bed is made and I'll tidy my locker at break-time,' said Alison with unusual firmness. 'You know it's the rule that we do those things ourselves. Matron would be absolutely furious if she thought I was getting you to do them for me.'

'But you're not – I offered,' persisted Joan. 'I like doing things for you, Alison.'

'Yes, and I appreciate it,' said Alison, feeling a bit hounded. 'But enough's enough, Joan. Now hurry, or we'll both be late for breakfast.' With that she walked briskly away before the younger girl could wear her down. Alison was well aware that hers was a weak character, and the first former had an unexpectedly determined side to her when she badly wanted to do something. And it seemed that what she most wanted to do was make a willing slave of herself to Alison. Alison liked the girl and, at first, had enjoyed the novelty of being looked up to. Now, however, it had worn thin and Joan was definitely becoming a nuisance. Fortunately, Alison managed to slip into the dining-room unnoticed by any mistress and Pat hissed, 'Where have you been?'

'I really don't want to talk about it,' snapped Alison, still feeling ruffled. 'Pass the marmalade, please.'

Pat did so, looking at her cousin in surprise. Normally Alison chattered non-stop about every trivial detail of her life to anyone who would listen. Nor was it like her to snap. She was certainly preoccupied about something, though – and why did she keep looking over at the first-form table like that?

Of course, Alison was looking out for Joan, half afraid that the girl might try to join her at the sixth's table. But the meal went on and still she didn't appear. Wherever could she have got to?

Alison found out at break-time when she slipped to the dormitory to tidy her locker.

'I'll come with you,' said Doris. 'Mine's an absolute tip and we don't want Matron dishing out another order mark.'

Both girls were in for a shock when they entered the dormitory. For on the floor lay a framed photograph of Alison's parents, which she kept on her locker, the glass smashed to pieces.

'Oh, no!' cried Doris, taking a look at Alison's white face. 'However could that have happened?'

Poor Alison was too upset to reply, though she knew who was responsible. But had Joan deliberately smashed the photograph in anger at Alison's coolness? Or had it been an accident? Stepping carefully over the broken glass, Alison pulled open the door of her locker. Not a thing out of place! So Joan had ignored her and tidied her locker after all, which meant that the photograph must have been broken by accident. That was some comfort, for Alison would have hated to think that Joan could have done it deliberately. All the same, she wished she had the girl in front of her now, because she'd like to shake her! Probably the silly kid had panicked and run off as soon as the accident happened. Doris, who had popped out to fetch a dustpan and brush, came back and exclaimed, 'Why, your locker was an absolute shambles before breakfast and now it's tidy! What *is* going on?'

As they swept up the glass Alison told her, and Doris

exclaimed, 'The nerve of her! Sneaking in here after you'd told her not to! I hope you're going to give her a rocket, Alison.'

'You can count on it!'

That afternoon Joan sought her out and owned up in a trembling voice. 'I'm so sorry, Alison. It was an accident, but I'll save all my money to buy you a new frame, honestly.'

Remembering that Joan had once said that she didn't get very much money from home, Alison's tender heart melted and she found herself patting the girl on her shoulder. 'Accidents will happen,' she said. 'Just be more careful next time.'

'I will, Alison,' said Joan, happy again now that she had been forgiven.

Only after the girl had gone did it occur to Alison that she hadn't told Joan off for disobeying her orders. What was worse, she might just take that 'next time' Alison had warned her about as an open invitation to go into her dormitory and tidy up whenever she felt like it. With a groan Alison sank down on to a chair and buried her face in her hands. Whatever had she done to deserve this?

If Alison was down in the dumps, Morag's new happiness showed no signs of abating, to the delight of the sixth form who had feared it might be a flash in the pan. The mistresses were pleased with her too, Miss Harry confiding to Mam'zelle that she had hardly believed her eyes when the girl had not only held open the door for her that morning, but had actually *smiled* at her.

'Ah, yes, even in her French she is trying hard,' said Mam'zelle beaming. 'She made so brave an effort to roll her Rs correctly yesterday.' Her smile became a little less warm. 'Sadly, she did not succeed, but no matter. At least she tries.'

Morag had indeed tried, much to the amusement of the class. Her Scottish brogue did not make for a smooth French accent and, in the common-room later, Doris had imitated her efforts, to the hilarity of the others. And Morag had laughed louder than anyone, tears pouring down her cheeks.

Doris is a real comedienne, she thought in surprise. And I've only just discovered it. She looked around at the others, all of them holding their sides helplessly. It makes me realize how little I know about *any* of the sixth really, apart from Carlotta. Well, it's time I started taking an interest in others, including the little ones. Tomorrow's meeting will be an excellent place to start.

Alas for such good intentions! At seven precisely, the sixth form gathered round the big table and waited . . . and waited. At seven-thirty Fizz looked at her watch and said with a sigh, 'Looks as though no one's coming, girls.'

'I can't understand it,' said Isabel with a frown. 'Surely the advice we dished out last week wasn't so bad that no one wants to give us another chance?'

'I think we did very well,' said Anne-Marie stoutly. 'If you ask me, something's up.'

'What?' asked Pat.

'Well, I don't know. But it's very strange that not one person has come.'

Morag cleared her throat. 'As we're at a loose end, would you mind if *I* say something? You've all been patient with me and I think I owe you an explanation as to why I behaved so badly.'

'Go ahead,' said Pat curiously.

So Morag told the rest of the sixth form what she had already confided in Carlotta, and they listened intently.

'Wow, your dad really messed things up!' said Janet in her direct way. 'I often think that someone ought to start a school for parents.'

'Yes, but maybe your stepmum won't be so bad once you really get to know her,' said Gladys thoughtfully. 'You said yourself that you'd set out to make life hard for her.'

'Well, I mean to try to get to know her better now,' said Morag, looking a little shamefaced. 'She and Dad are coming to take me out at half-term, so it'll be a chance to show her that I can act like a normal human being!'

'It's really good that you felt you could tell us all this,' said Bobby. 'It makes you belong more, somehow, knowing that you trust us enough to share your secret with us.'

'Of course!' said Doris suddenly. 'That's what these meetings are all about, aren't they? Alison, come on, share *your* problem and see what words of wisdom the sixth have to offer.'

Alison turned pink. 'I couldn't possibly! We're supposed to help the younger girls.'

'Well, it's a bad job if we can't help one of our own,' insisted Doris.

'What are you two talking about?' asked Hilary impatiently. 'Alison, is there something you're worried about?'

'Well, yes, actually,' said Alison hesitantly, and began to tell the girls about 'the Joan affair' as she had come to think of it. 'It's as though I can't turn round without finding her there,' she finished plaintively. 'If I wake up in the middle of the night I expect to find her standing by my bedside.'

'I see,' said Janet, her lips quivering as she looked at Alison rather oddly. 'Well, if you ask me . . .'

But Janet couldn't go on, overcome by a spasm of coughing so violent that Bobby had to slap her on the back.

'Er . . . I think that what Janet is trying to say,' began Hilary, in a strange, quavery voice, 'is . . . oh dear, oh I can't!' Then she burst out laughing and clutched at Doris, who promptly did the same. Alison looked offended. 'Well,' she said stiffly. 'I'm glad you think it's funny.'

'Of course we don't, Alison,' said Pat soothingly. 'It's just that . . . oh, tell her, Isabel. I can't speak!' And before her cousin's astonished gaze, Pat too creased up laughing.

The normally good-natured Alison looked fit to explode and, seeing it, Isabel patted her on the arm. 'The thing is, Alison, it's normally *you* who goes around worshipping people and now . . .' Isabel's voice cracked and Bobby went on, 'Now you're getting a taste of your own medicine. Alison, you of all people should know how to handle this situation – after all, you've been in Joan's position often enough.'

Dumbfounded, Alison thought back over her years at St Clare's. There had been Sadie, the glamorous American girl in the first form. Then Miss Quentin, the drama teacher in the second. And how badly both of them had let her down! In the fourth she had attached herself to Angela, then last year it had been Miss Willcox, the English teacher. Sadly, both Alison and Anne-Marie, who had also adored the teacher, had discovered that Miss Willcox wasn't all that she seemed. Yes, Alison had worshipped all of these people and now here was Joan doing the same to her – and she didn't like it one little bit! Crossly she glared round the table at the laughing girls. It wasn't funny at all! Well . . . maybe just a little. Slowly one corner of Alison's mouth lifted, then the other. Soon she was laughing with the others, and how they liked her for it. She might be vain and empty headed in some ways, but Alison could take a joke against herself.

'Oh,' gasped Doris, wiping her eyes. 'I don't remember when I last laughed so much. You're a good sort not to take offence, Alison.'

So the meeting broke up on a happy note but later, back in their studies, the girls began to wonder again why none of the younger girls had attended.

The head girls discovered why the following afternoon, when Katie and Hilda knocked at their study door.

'Hi, kids!' said Pat in surprise as the two entered. 'Isabel and I didn't send for you.'

'Hilda and I'd like a word with you both, please,' said Katie, and the twins frowned at her unusually grave expression. 'It's about a certain member of the sixth.'

'Go on,' said Isabel, catching Pat's eye. The same thought was in both their minds. Only one member of the sixth could have brought such a sober expression to the girls' faces – Priscilla!

So indeed it proved. As Katie and Hilda poured out their story, the twins' faces became more and more grim. 'Our class is planning a midnight party,' Hilda finished indignantly. 'And Priscilla is always hanging round outside our common-room, trying to find out the details. We're pretty sure she means to spoil it in some way.'

'Dummy!' hissed Katie, elbowing the unfortunate Hilda.

'Don't worry, Katie,' said Pat, an amused gleam in her eye. 'If Isabel and I knew when and where you were holding the party then, naturally, it would be our duty to stop it. But as we don't know anything about it, there's nothing we can do.'

Hilda and Katie exchanged delighted glances. The O'Sullivan twins were just the greatest!

'Mm,' said Isabel thoughtfully. 'I think the best thing to do is tell Priscilla exactly when and where it's to be held, then she can try to stop it.'

'Isabel!' exclaimed Pat in amazement. 'Have you gone completely mad?'

'Far from it,' said Isabel calmly. 'I was just thinking of Elsie Fanshawe. Remember her from our days in the second form, Pat?'

'Elsie Fanshawe,' repeated Pat, light dawning. 'What a great idea, Isabel.'

The first formers listened to this exchange in bewilderment. Who was Elsie Fanshawe and what did she have to do with their present predicament? They were soon to find out.

'Elsie Fanshawe was with us back in the second form – and she was every bit as spiteful and sneaky as Priscilla! She discovered that we'd planned a midnight party and decided to ruin it,' explained Pat.

'What did you do?' asked Hilda curiously.

'Spiked her guns,' said Isabel with a laugh. 'We led Elsie to believe that our party was going to be on a certain night – then secretly held it the night before. And did we have some fun the following night, slipping out of our dormitory and hiding until she had gone off to sneak to Miss Jenks. Of course, by the time Elsie and Miss Jenks came back, we were all tucked up in bed and pretending to be fast asleep.'

'Wow!' gasped Hilda. 'What a great idea!'

'Are you saying that we ought to try the same trick on Priscilla?' asked Katie, staring hard at the twins.

'It would be most improper for us to suggest anything of the kind,' replied Isabel, a twinkle in her eye. 'Isn't that right, Pat?'

'Extremely improper,' agreed Pat, with an answering twinkle. 'Of course, if Priscilla *were* to be caught out by the "Elsie" method, I'm quite sure that Miss Theobald would bar her from any of our future Thursday meetings.'

'I see,' said Katie grinning. 'Come on, Hilda. Time to call a form meeting, I think. Thanks for your help, twins.'

'Aren't they just great?' said Hilda in delight, once they were outside. 'More or less giving us permission to trick Priscilla, *and* telling us how to go about it.'

'I'll say,' agreed Katie, adding gravely, 'There are bad head girls and there are good head girls. And then there are the O'Sullivan twins. They're in a league of their own!'

A shock for Priscilla

Half-term came and went, the girls thrilled to see their parents again. Carlotta, whose own father was away, went out with Morag, her father and stepmother. Fizz's parents couldn't come either, but her older brother Harry arrived and got permission from Miss Theobald to take out both his sister and Claudine. The three of them had a great time, Harry's sense of humour being every bit as wicked as his sister's, and the two girls returned to school in high spirits.

Joan Terry earned herself another black mark with the first form when Priscilla, knowing that the younger girl's mother and father wouldn't be there, invited Joan to spend the day with her and her own parents. There was nothing Joan would rather do less, but she didn't know how to refuse. The scornful stares of her form as they watched her drive off with Priscilla seemed to burn into her skin. 'Going off to spill our secrets,' said Rita scornfully. 'Little traitor!'

'Never mind, Rita,' said Dora, with an angelic smile. 'Joan might turn out to be very useful to us – very useful indeed!'

Priscilla also intended to make use of Joan. As soon

as they returned to school and said goodby to Mr and Mrs Parsons, Priscilla took the girl aside and said smoothly, 'Now, Joan, there's a little favour you can do for me in return for your day out.'

Joan said nothing, but waited with a sinking heart for what was to come next. 'I want you to find out when and where the first form are holding their party and tell me,' said Priscilla.

'I can't!' refused Joan, horrified. 'The others would never speak to me again!'

'Well, it's up to you, of course,' Priscilla said with a shrug. 'But if I were to let slip – purely by accident, naturally – what I know about you, no one in the whole *school* would want to speak to you.'

Joan was trapped and she knew it. Priscilla had the upper hand.

'OK, Priscilla,' said Joan woodenly. 'Whatever you want.'

'Now you're being sensible.' Priscilla smiled her thin smile. 'As soon as you find anything out, let me know.'

Spying for Priscilla proved to be an unexpectedly easy task. Joan had fully expected to be left out of the party, well aware that she wasn't exactly popular with her class. But, to her surprise, the others discussed their plans quite openly in front of her.

'So, Wednesday night is party night,' said Susan one afternoon in the common-room. 'Where's it to be?'

'In here,' said Katie. 'At midnight precisely.'

Joan sat gazing unseeingly at the book open on

her lap for a few moments, then got up and quietly slipped out.

'Straight off to Priscilla, I'll bet,' said Katie. 'Follow her, Dora. We want to make sure that she delivers the message.'

Dora did so, silently, keeping her distance and darting into doorways when Joan glanced over her shoulder. Sure enough, the girl went straight to Priscilla's study. 'Mission accomplished,' said Dora, when she reported back. 'I can't get over the way Joan's acting. We ought to get our own back on *her*, as well as Priscilla.'

'We will,' promised Katie. 'After we've had our party – on *Tuesday* night – and dealt with Priscilla!'

The party was a great success, the first formers having sneaked out of their dormitory without waking Joan. As Daphne said later, they had the most fantastic time, wolfing down crisps, sausage rolls, cakes and biscuits, all washed down with gallons of lemonade. A few of them regretted it next morning, though, finding it impossible to get out of bed.

'I don't feel well,' complained Rita as they trooped down to breakfast.

'I'm not surprised, you pig,' said Katie. 'What do you expect after eating nearly a whole tin of biscuits?'

'Ugh, don't!' groaned Rita, screwing up her face. 'I'll be sick!'

'You will not!' said Katie firmly. 'We don't want anyone getting suspicious.' She nodded towards Joan, walking a little way in front. 'Just have a cup of tea for breakfast and don't eat anything. If Miss Roberts asks why, tell her you're trying to get rid of some of that fat!' And with a wicked grin, Katie ran off towards the dining-room, Rita, forgetting her sickness for a moment, in hot pursuit. 'I'll get you for that! Oof, sorry, Mam'zelle!'

The first formers weren't the only ones waiting in anticipation for Priscilla's downfall. Pat and Isabel had told the sixth about her behaviour towards the younger girls and they had been furious.

'She's unbelievable! We'll have to bar her from our meetings, that's for sure.'

'I just hope the first form manage to set her up and she falls for it!'

'She will,' said Isabel confidently. 'Priscilla might be sly and cunning, but she's got the brains of a flea!'

Priscilla found it easy to keep awake that night, her spiteful nature rejoicing in what was to come. At a quarter to midnight she slipped silently out of bed, put on her slippers and dressing-gown, and made her way stealthily to the first-form dormitories. Hiding in a bathroom opposite, she opened the door a crack and peeped out. The first form, who had been waiting quietly and patiently, heard the soft clicking of the door.

'OK,' whispered Katie. 'You know what to do, everyone – let's go!'

The girls put into action their carefully thought out plan. Daphne and Lucy went first, leaving the dormitory with much giggling and whispering. Winking, Daphne stopped directly outside the bathroom where Priscilla was hidden and, not troubling to lower her voice, said, 'Let's go and fetch the food! This is going to be just great!'

Priscilla waited until the girls had moved away and rounded the corner before tiptoeing after them. Sadly for her, the girl didn't realize that she, too, was being shadowed – by Dora! The strange little crocodile made its way to a cupboard near the first-form common-room, from which, with a lot of unnecessary noise, Lucy and Daphne produced a large cardboard box. It was empty, of course, but Priscilla assumed that it contained food for the party. Just then the school cat, who had been peacefully sleeping in a corner, stretched and came to life, deciding that he rather liked the look of Priscilla. Silently he padded forward, tripping her up. The girl gave a gasp and stumbled, managing to regain her balance, but losing a slipper. There was no time to retrieve it, as the first formers were coming back and she had to dart behind a long curtain.

'Time to wake the others,' said Lucy, in a carrying voice. 'Not long now to party-time!'

They walked on, voices fading and, with a sigh of relief, Priscilla left her hiding place. Now to go back for her slipper. But, to the girl's annoyance, it seemed to have vanished off the face of the earth. Well, no time to worry about that now. By the time she reached the mistresses' sleeping quarters, the girls should be in their common-room and the party well under way. But not for long, thought Priscilla, grinning to herself. She had carefully planned which mistress she would go to. Miss

Roberts! She was in charge of the first form and would, no doubt, be grateful to Priscilla for the information. Miss Roberts had a sarcastic streak, too, and would soon reduce the first formers to the status of four year olds, thought Priscilla gleefully.

Stepping out of the dark shadows, Dora smiled to herself as she tapped Priscilla's slipper against the palm of her hand. She had a fair idea of the girl's plans which, unfortunately for Priscilla, didn't coincide with her own at all.

Ah, there was Miss Roberts' room, next door to Mam'zelle's. Priscilla moved towards it and raised her hand to knock. But, before it descended, something flew past her shoulder and hit Mam'zelle's door with a resounding thud. Everything seemed to happen at once after that. She heard the sound of running footsteps along the corridor, Mam'zelle's sharp '*Tiens*!' from behind her door and another voice crying, 'What on earth was that?'

Stooping to pick up the missile that had caused all the commotion, Priscilla was amazed to discover that it was her lost slipper. Suddenly Mam'zelle's door opened and, at the sight of Priscilla standing there with the incriminating slipper in her hand, the French teacher cried, '*Mon dieu*, what is the meaning of this? How dare you come here at night to throw footwear at my door? Miss Harry, come! See who is responsible for this outrage!'

The girl's jaw dropped in dismay as her own form

mistress appeared behind Mam'zelle. She hadn't known that Miss Harry was using the spare bed in Mam'zelle's room while her own room was being redecorated. Wicked little Dora had known it, though, and planned accordingly. The hot-tempered Mam'zelle and Miss Harry, who knew Priscilla's underhand ways only too well, would see to it that she got what she deserved.

'I trust you have some explanation for this extraordinary behaviour?' Miss Harry demanded, so coldly that Priscilla shook. There was nothing for it but to explain about the party, though she would far rather have told Miss Roberts. As she told her tale, the expressions on the faces of the two mistresses grew more contemptuous.

'Ha! You come to sneak!' said Mam'zelle scornfully. 'You have no honour, no decency.'

'None at all,' agreed Miss Harry, looking at the red-faced girl with dislike. 'Well, I suppose we'd better investigate, Mam'zelle. And for your sake, Priscilla, I just hope you've got your facts right.'

It was a very deflated Priscilla who followed the two mistresses to the first-form common-room, cowering back in the shadows as Miss Harry threw open the door and snapped on the light.

'I – I don't understand,' spluttered the girl, staring in horror at the empty room. 'They must have decided to hold it in the dormitory instead.'

But when they reached the dormitory it was in darkness, with only the sounds of deep breathing and an occasional gentle snore to be heard.

'Who's there?' asked Katie sleepily. 'Miss Roberts, is it you?'

'No, *ma petite,* it is I, Mam'zelle,' said the French mistress. 'And the good Miss Harry.'

'Is something wrong?' asked Katie.

'Very wrong,' said Miss Harry, with an angry look at Priscilla. 'But it's nothing for you to worry about, Katie. Go back to sleep now, dear.'

In fact, very few of the first formers had been asleep, all of them eager to learn the outcome of their trick. They were rewarded as they heard Miss Harry say to the crestfallen Priscilla, 'Thanks to your spite, Mam'zelle and I have had a disturbed night for nothing. Now, as you've done a little sneaking tonight – quite wrongly as it turns out – I'll be doing some of my own tomorrow. On you! Report to the head after breakfast!'

A bad time for the sixth

Priscilla was in trouble – big trouble! The whisper flew round the school the next morning and no one felt the slightest bit sorry for her. The girl herself was furious, guessing that she had been tricked – and that stupid little Joan had been in on it, feeding her false information. Well, she'd be sorry.

Joan was already sorry. She knew what Priscilla must be thinking and she had been taunted by the first formers that morning.

'Thanks for helping us set Priscilla up, Joan,' Susan had said cheerfully.

'Yes, we'll know who to turn to next time we're looking for a mug,' sneered Daphne.

'Dummy!' laughed Dora scornfully. 'Did you really think we'd let you in on our secret? You're not one of us!'

'Go somewhere else if you want to cry!' said Katie impatiently, as Joan began to sniff. 'Maybe your good friend Priscilla will comfort you.'

Priscilla was feeling sorely in need of comfort herself, after a long and painful interview with Miss Theobald. Every defect in the girl's character – and the head had found many – was discussed at length.

'You learnt that the first form were to hold a party and decided to spoil it,' said the head icily. 'But instead of going to the girls yourself and nipping it in the bud, you wanted to wait until the party had started, then inform on them. I'm glad that they outsmarted you! You're a troublemaker, Priscilla, and this time you've made trouble for yourself. I only hope that this will make you look at yourself long and hard, and that you'll make some attempt to change your ways. I've no choice but to recommend to the head girls that you be banned from their weekly meetings, since you're clearly not fit to deal with anyone's problems until you've sorted your own out. Go now, Priscilla, and if you're brought before me again this term, the consequences will be severe!'

Another girl might have taken Miss Theobald's words to heart, taken the opportunity to try to overcome the flaws in her character. Priscilla was too weak to do this, instead feeling bitter and resentful. And her bitterness was directed towards those who were the cause of her disgrace, as she saw it. Her first act, on leaving the head's office, was to find Joan.

The girl was standing alone in the courtyard, a forlorn figure as she watched the other first formers laughing together. If only there was someone she could confide in. Someone kind and understanding – like Alison. But the thought of her idol turning from her in disgust when she heard Joan's awful secret was worse than anything, so the girl kept it to herself, growing more withdrawn and unhappy.

'Joan, there you are! Come here!'

She turned to see Priscilla standing at the corner and went over.

'Well, you and your classmates made a complete fool of me, didn't you?' said Priscilla angrily. 'You'll pay for it, though! I warned you what would happen if you crossed me.'

'But I wasn't in on it!' protested Joan, scared. 'The others guessed that you'd try and find out about the party from me and used me.'

Looking down into the first former's scared face, Priscilla believed her. 'All right then, tell me whose idea it was,' demanded the older girl, taking Joan by the shoulders. 'Those cheeky Lacey twins, I suppose – or Katie, maybe?'

'Ow, you're hurting me,' squealed Joan, struggling to escape from Priscilla's long, bony fingers. 'All right, I'll tell! I overheard Katie saying this morning that it was the sixth's idea. They put Katie up to it.'

'The sixth!' Priscilla's hands fell from Joan's shoulders, her face darkening with fury. She was so angry that she shook. How could they! To side with the first form against her and plan her downfall! Well, if they thought they were going to get away with it, they could think again. She'd get her own back on the lot of them!

Shortly afterwards, strange things began to happen in the sixth form. It started with Pat and Isabel, who had just bought their mother a bottle of her favourite perfume for her birthday. But when the time came for them to wrap it up and post it, it had completely vanished.

'I'm sure I put it in this cupboard,' said Isabel, scratching her head.

'You did,' Pat said. 'I saw you. But it's certainly not there now.'

The perfume didn't turn up, and the twins had to spend what money they had left on a box of chocolates for their mother instead, which didn't please them at all.

The following day, Hilary's watch disappeared, along with Janet's fountain pen. Within a few days nearly all of the sixth had lost something.

'Lost!' snorted Bobby as she discussed the matter with the twins, Janet and Hilary in the common-room one afternoon. 'We all know that our things haven't just been mislaid. Let's face it, girls, they've been stolen!'

'I think you're right,' admitted Pat reluctantly. Try as they might, she and Isabel had been unable to come up with another explanation. 'But who could it be?'

'There is one rather obvious suspect,' said Janet drily.

'Priscilla!' chorused the others.

'She's got the motive,' said Isabel. 'She was absolutely furious about being barred from our meetings.'

'And she'll be out to get her own back, if I know anything about her,' said Hilary.

'Hold on a minute!' put in Bobby, who had been looking thoughtful. 'It can't be Priscilla. Anne-Marie had a fiver taken from her study last night, while she was at that debate with the fifth, and Priscilla was there too.'

'Are you sure?' asked Pat.

'Absolutely. I was there myself, and Priscilla was sitting right in front of Anne-Marie and me. I remember particularly, because I had to tell her to move her big head,' Bobby said.

'Couldn't she have slipped out early or something?' asked Janet.

Bobby shook her head. 'She was already in her seat when Anne-Marie arrived, and didn't move until we'd left. Sorry, folks, but it looks as though that rules Priscilla out.'

'Then who?' asked Janet uncomfortably. 'I'd hate to think it could be one of the others who've come up through the school with us.'

'Of course it isn't,' Hilary said firmly.

'Well, that only leaves Morag and Fizz,' said Isabel. 'And I can't believe either of them would do such a thing.'

'Just a second!' Bobby snapped her fingers suddenly, looking excited. 'There is one member of our class who hasn't had anything taken yet – Alison!'

'Hang on, Bobby!' said Pat, firing up. 'I know Alison's got her faults, but she doesn't have a dishonest bone in her body. She'd never . . .'

'I'm not accusing Alison, you feather-brain!' interrupted Bobby, thumping Pat on the arm. 'I know she's straight.'

'Oh. Sorry, Bobby,' said Pat, looking a little sheepish. 'What *are* you suggesting, then?'

'That the thief is someone who has a soft spot for Alison and wants to leave her out of this campaign that she's waging against the rest of us.'

'Joan!' cried Isabel, adding, as the others stared at her, 'Well, she's always in and out of Alison's study, so it would be easy for her to nip into ours when they're empty, and take something.'

'That's true,' Pat said. 'But what on earth could that little shrimp have against us?'

'Search me,' sighed Hilary. 'I've a feeling we're on the right track, though. Look, let's get Alison in and see what she thinks. She knows Joan better than any of us.'

Janet sped off to fetch Alison from her study, and within moments the two girls were back. Swiftly Pat told her cousin what they had been discussing, and the girl's blue eyes widened.

'No!' she protested, shocked. 'She's a strange girl in some ways, but I'd never have thought her a thief.'

'Well, she's the only person we can think of,' said Janet. 'So one of us ought to tackle her about it.'

'I think it ought to be you, Alison,' said Isabel at once.

'Oh, no!' Alison shook her head firmly. 'You, or Pat, or Hilary are much better at that kind of thing than I am.'

'But Joan doesn't look up to us in the way she looks up to you,' Pat pointed out. 'Come on, Alison! Do it for the sixth.'

'Oh, all right. But there's something I need to do first. Miss Roberts has taken the first form on a nature-walk this afternoon, hasn't she?'

'That's right,' said Pat. 'You'll have to wait until after tea to see Joan.'

'Good,' Alison said. 'Because first I intend to search her locker.'

'Alison!' cried Hilary. 'You can't go snooping around in the first-form dormitories.'

'Oh, yes I can! If I'm to accuse her of stealing – which, by the way, I am still not convinced of – then I'd feel far happier if I had some proof.'

'Well, if you put it like that, I suppose it might not be such a bad idea,' agreed Bobby. 'I'll come with you, Alison, and keep look-out.'

'Now, which do you suppose is Joan's bed?' mused Alison, once she and Bobby were in the dormitory. Then she spotted a pair of shoes beside one of the beds. 'Those are hers, I'm sure of it!'

'Well, get on with it!' said Bobby impatiently from the doorway. 'If Matron catches us poking around in here, we're in deep trouble.'

So Alison opened the locker beside the bed and removed a wash-bag, two books – aha, what was that, right at the back? Her fingers touched a box and she pulled it forward, removing the lid. 'Bobby!' she gasped. 'Take a look at this!'

With a swift glance up and down the corridor, Bobby left her post, giving a low whistle as she saw the contents of the box. 'The twins' perfume,' she said. 'Hilary's watch – and the record I bought last week! The little thief!'

'I can't believe it,' said Alison sadly.

'Never mind,' said Bobby kindly, resting a hand on her shoulder. 'At least you won't have to tackle her about it now. With this lot as proof, we can go straight to the head.'

'If you don't mind, Bobby, I'd rather talk to her first,' said Alison soberly. 'I just want to know *why*!'

Bobby shrugged. 'Fair enough. Now we'd better put everything back just as we found it. We don't want Joan to guess we're on to her until we're good and ready.'

Alison was on tenterhooks until after tea, very little of which she managed to eat. Then she sent someone to find Joan. Alison studied the girl closely when she arrived, noticing that, despite an afternoon in the fresh air, her cheeks were pale and there were dark circles beneath her eyes. She managed to smile, though, and said brightly, 'Hi, Alison! Did you want me?'

'Sit down, Joan,' said Alison seriously. 'I want to talk to you.' Then, in her mind, she ran over the little speech she had rehearsed. It was no use beating about the bush, she had decided. She must come straight to the point. 'Joan, we know that you've been stealing things from the sixth formers,' she said directly. 'I want to know why.'

If Joan had looked pale before, she was positively white now. For a moment she was tempted to deny the accusation, then she saw the grave look in Alison's eyes and knew that it was no use. 'How did you find out?' she asked bleakly.

'We suspected you because nothing was taken from me,' answered Alison. 'Then I searched your locker this afternoon and found the things that the others had missed. Oh, Joan, why did you do it?'

The first former buried her face in her hands. 'I'm sorry, Alison!' she cried. 'So sorry. I've never done anything like it before.'

'Then why now? Come on, Joan, you must tell me everything if I'm to help you.' Alison's tone was kind and Joan looked up.

'Oh, if only you could. But I'm in such a mess and I just can't see a way out.'

Alison said nothing, but took the girl's hand and squeezed it gently.

'Someone else made me take those things,' said Joan at last. 'Someone who's got it in for the sixth. I can't tell you who.'

'You don't need to,' Alison said grimly. 'There's only one person I can think of who's got something against us – Priscilla Parsons!'

'Oh!' Joan became very agitated and began to cry. 'Now I've made things worse!'

'Well, I don't see how things *can* get worse,' said Alison frankly. 'Joan, what made you agree to do such a thing? You must have known it was wrong. Why didn't you tell someone what was happening?'

'I couldn't,' sobbed the first former. 'I have to do

what Priscilla wants. You see, she knows something about me – something bad – and threatened to tell the whole school.'

Alison's gentle blue eyes grew hard and angry. Just wait until the others heard this. Then Priscilla would be sorry.

'Joan, whatever Priscilla knows, you *must* tell me,' she said urgently. 'Once your secret's out, her hold over you will be broken.'

'I know, but you'll hate me, and I couldn't stand that,' hiccuped Joan, dabbing at her eyes.

'Of course I won't hate you!' cried Alison. 'Please, Joan! This is the only way we can stop Priscilla.'

Joan took a deep breath and said bravely, 'It's my dad. He's been accused of embezzling money from the firm he worked for, and now he's in prison awaiting trial. Alison, he didn't do it, I know he didn't! But everyone at home knows all about it, including Priscilla. Some people have been kind and stood by us, but others haven't and it's all been so horrid for Mum and me.'

'Oh, Joan,' whispered Alison, absolutely horrified. 'What a burden to carry all by yourself. And on top of that, to have Priscilla taking advantage of your misery. Well, that's one thing I *can* put a stop to!'

Alison got purposefully to her feet and Joan said, in alarm, 'Where are you going? What's going to happen?'

The older girl patted Joan's arm reassuringly. 'I need to discuss this with the others,' she said. 'But you can trust them not to spread it around. And nothing terrible is going to happen to you, I promise. Now, Joan, I want you to go back to the first form and, if you should bump into Priscilla, say nothing about all this. That girl isn't going to know what hit her!'

15
Things are sorted out

Alison shot off to the studies and rounded up the sixth formers – all except Priscilla, of course. In the common-room she told them Joan's story and, as she had expected, they were outraged.

'I'd like to get my hands on her!' cried Doris, shaking with anger. 'I hate bullying more than anything!'

'She's evil!' shuddered Anne-Marie. 'To use one of the kids like that.'

'Where is she?' demanded Bobby. 'Fetch her, some-one, and we'll show her what happens to people who pick on little kids!'

'OK, calm down, everyone!' Pat raised her voice. 'I understand how you're all feeling, because I feel just the same. But we have to do this by the book. I think Isabel and I ought to see Miss Theobald first. Alison, you'd better come with us. Well done for getting to the bottom of this.'

'Yes, nice work!' called out some of the others, and Alison flushed. Used to being the class feather-head for years, it was rather nice to be praised for once. Fortunately the head was in and she listened gravely as the three girls explained the extraordinary happenings in the sixth form and the parts Priscilla and Joan had played.

'What will happen to Joan?' asked Alison anxiously, once they had finished.

'Nothing very terrible, though I'll have a serious talk with her, of course. I think she's been punished quite enough already, poor child,' said Miss Theobald heavily. 'There's only one person to blame in all this, and I intend to deal with her severely. Thank you, twins – and Alison. I'm very pleased with the way you've all handled this matter. Now, send Priscilla to see me, please.'

Priscilla was puzzled when told that the head wanted to see her, but not concerned. What was there to worry about, after all? She had got her own back on the sixth, and no one was any the wiser. Perhaps Miss Theobald had changed her mind and was going to allow her to attend the meetings again. But one look at the head's stern face was enough to tell the girl that she was in very serious trouble. Miss Theobald wasted no time in telling her why she had been sent for, watching without pity as the girl turned white and she began to shake.

'You're a disgrace to St Clare's, Priscilla. What upsets me most about the whole affair is that you used blackmail on a younger girl to carry out your nasty little schemes.'

Priscilla flinched and the head went on ominously, 'Yes, blackmail is an ugly word, isn't it? And an ugly act – a criminal act!'

The girl was terrified now, and asked in a shaky voice, 'What will happen to me?'

'Hopefully you'll learn from this experience and use that knowledge to become a better person in the future,' said Miss Theobald. 'But I cannot keep you at St Clare's, Priscilla. I've already called your parents and they are on their way.'

Priscilla stared at the head, too shocked to speak. Expelled! The disgrace of it! What would her mum and dad say? Then she began to cry, pleading, 'Miss Theobald, give me another chance, please. I'll make it up to the sixth form, and to Joan.'

But Miss Theobald shook her head. 'It's too late, Priscilla. I have the welfare of the younger girls to consider. This is for your sake, too, because I'm afraid that what you've done is something the others will never be able to forgive or forget. Now go and pack, and try to accept your punishment bravely. It could be the making of you.'

At last the door closed behind the girl and Miss Theobald heaved a sigh. Thank goodness that, for every girl like Priscilla, there were dozens like the O'Sullivan twins.

Joan was sent for too, but the head spoke to her gently and reassuringly. 'It's never any good bottling things up, Joan – as I think you've learnt to your cost. In future, if something is troubling you, do talk to someone about it.'

'I will, Miss Theobald,' promised the girl earnestly, and left the head's room feeling as though a huge weight had been lifted from her shoulders. If only she could put things right for her father. And if only she could settle things with the rest of her form. Well, there was nothing she could do for her father, sadly, but maybe there was a solution to the second of her problems. Miss Theobald was right – she would go to the sixth's next meeting and see what they could do for her.

The sixth form was a much happier place without Priscilla in it. Only Angela and Mirabel, who were taking their exams that week, were down in the dumps. They grew very short tempered with the strain of it, but the others understood how they were feeling and made allowances for them.

'All the same, I'll be glad when it's over,' said Hilary, who had broken in on Mirabel's studies to ask if she felt like a walk into town and got her head bitten off for her trouble. 'Let's just hope they pass after all this.'

Miss Harry gave out the results in class the following week, a solemn look on her face that made both girls' hearts sink as she handed them identical brown envelopes. Silently, the two girls opened them. Then Mirabel gave a yell. 'I've passed! And I've got the grades I wanted. I've passed! How about you, Angela?'

'Yes!' A wide grin spread over Angela's lovely face. 'Yes! I can't believe it! And you too! Well done, Mirabel!'

'Well done yourself!' returned Mirabel gruffly, turning pink. Then Angela surprised the class, and herself, by giving Mirabel a sudden hug, and the whole form erupted, gathering round to congratulate the girls and thumping them on the back, while Miss Harry watched, smiling.

'I'd just like to apologize to everyone for being a bit short this last week,' said Mirabel frankly. 'Exam nerves. I'll make it up to all of you.'

'The same goes for me, too,' agreed Angela, behaving pleasantly for once. She was thrilled that she could go to finishing school, of course, but she also felt an unexpected sense of achievement at having worked so hard and succeeded at something. Even spoilt Angela was feeling the effects of St Clare's.

There was good news for Carlotta that day, too. True to her word, Miss Theobald had written to the girl's father, urging him most strongly to reconsider his decision about sending Carlotta to finishing school. Mr Brown had been impressed by both her words, and her high regard for his daughter, and decided that if Miss Theobald thought Carlotta was fine as she was, that was good enough for him. Both the head and Carlotta were delighted to receive letters from him informing them of his change of heart, and the sixth form were almost as thrilled by Carlotta's news as they were over Angela and Mirabel's success.

'Things are really going our way,' commented Pat happily at the beginning of their next Thursday meeting. 'Priscilla's gone, and as for Morag – well, she's like a different person.'

'Yes, we've solved our own problems,' said Hilary. 'Now let's see what we can do for the kids. Wonder who'll be first tonight?'

It was Joan, looking a little apprehensive. The sixth

formers had all felt extremely sorry for her when Alison told them about her father, and none of them blamed her in the least for her part in the thefts. Isabel smiled and said pleasantly, 'What can we do for you, Joan?'

'I'm not very popular with the girls in my form,' said Joan, getting straight to the point. 'None of them likes me because I always seemed to side with Priscilla, and she made me tell her about the midnight party. Daphne and Dora have really got it in for me, and I just can't seem to change their opinion.'

'Well, I reckon if anyone deserves a chance, it's you, Joan,' said Carlotta. 'The first form aren't a bad lot, and I'm sure if you explained about your dad they'd understand.'

'I couldn't,' said Joan, with a firm shake of the head. 'I don't mind you knowing, because I know you'll keep it to yourselves, but I couldn't stand it if the whole school knew. It's bad enough at home, with all the stares and whispers, but I thought that here I'd be able to get away from it.'

'Hmm, we need to talk this through, I think,' said Pat. 'Joan, go back to the common-room and we'll send for you soon. In the meantime, try not to worry.'

'Wow, this is a tricky one,' said Janet. 'You can't really blame the first form for thinking the worst of Joan.'

'Actually, I've an idea,' said Isabel, going to the door. Putting her head out, she called to a passing second former. 'Sheila! Fetch Daphne and Dora Lacey for me, would you?'

'Will do, Isabel,' answered the girl, and sped off.

'What are you up to?' asked Pat suspiciously, but Isabel shook her head. 'Just wait and see, Pat,' she said.

'Well, if it isn't the Heavenly Twins,' said Bobby, grinning at the identical, innocent faces when Daphne and Dora appeared.

'Are we in trouble?' they asked in unison.

'Not so far as we know,' answered Isabel drily. 'But we need you to do us a favour. You see, girls, there's a girl in your class who's not very happy, and we want you to look after her, try to cheer her up a bit.'

The twins glanced at one another in surprise. They hadn't had the slightest inkling as to why the sixth had sent for them, but they certainly hadn't expected this! It was quite an honour really, being singled out and entrusted with such an important task, thought Dora. Evidently Daphne thought so too. Her head high and a note of pride in her voice she answered, 'Leave it to us, Isabel. Who is it?'

'Joan Terry,' answered Isabel, watching the two girls' expressions carefully.

'Oh, no!' wailed Dora. 'Anyone but her. She's so wet, and the most awful snitch besides. Honestly, Isabel, you don't know the half of it.'

'I'm afraid it's you two who don't know the half of it,' put in Pat. 'Now listen! Joan has serious problems at home. I can't tell you what, exactly, because that would be breaking a confidence. Just take my word for it that she's going through a very bad time at the moment. To make things worse, Priscilla knew all about Joan's troubles and threatened to spread gossip about her round the school if she didn't do everything Priscilla said.'

The two pairs of round blue eyes grew rounder still. 'We had no idea,' said Daphne in dismay.

'If only we'd known, we wouldn't have been quite so hard on her,' added Dora, looking a little ashamed of herself.

'Well, now's your chance to make up for it,' said Pat.

'We will,' said Dora fervently.

'Yes, you can count on us. We'll cheer her up, all right,' Daphne promised.

'I'll just bet you will,' said Bobby with a grin. 'Now shove off – and behave yourselves!'

16

A lovely end to the term

The Lacey twins were as good as their word, changing completely towards Joan and including her in everything. She was a little wary of their friendship at first, suspecting them of some trick, but once she realized they were in earnest, she opened up a little. They, in turn, were happily surprised to discover that Joan had a wicked sense of humour. And if she was a little quiet and withdrawn at times, the twins remembered the problems Isabel had spoken of and did their best to take her out of herself. The rest of the first form followed the twins' lead and Joan's popularity increased by the day as the business with Priscilla was forgotten. Alison, too, was pleased, for although Joan still came faithfully to do her jobs, the girl no longer hung round her so much.

One day towards the end of term, Joan was summoned to Miss Theobald's room. Rather fearfully she went in, hoping that the head hadn't got to hear about the trick she and the twins were planning for Mam'zelle's next French lesson. It seemed not, for Miss Theobald was wearing her most charming smile. 'Sit down, dear,' she said warmly. 'I have wonderful news. Your mother has called me to say that your father's name has been cleared. Evidently another man has confessed to taking the money he was accused of stealing.'

'Oh, Miss Theobald, is this really true?' breathed Joan, hardly daring to believe it.

'Indeed it is,' laughed the head. 'So you can look forward to the holidays, knowing that your family will be complete again. Now, your mother wants you to ring her, and she'll give you all the details. I'll go outside and give you some privacy.'

After a laughter-and-tear-filled conversation with her mother, Joan practically sprinted back to class, bumping into a group of sixth formers on the way.

'Hey, slow down, Joan!' called out Janet. 'Are you training for the Olympics, or something?'

'Sorry! Oh, Janet, Bobby, twins – I've just had the most incredible news!' said the happy first former, her face glowing. 'My dad's name has been cleared. Another man's confessed to taking the money. I *knew* he was innocent!'

'That's just wonderful!' exclaimed Isabel. 'I'm really pleased for you, Joan.'

'That goes for all of us,' agreed Bobby, with her ready smile. 'Good for you!' Joan went happily on her way and Pat said, 'Suddenly there seems an awful lot to celebrate, what with Angela and Mirabel's exams and Carlotta not having to go to that awful finishing school.'

'I was thinking that we ought to do something to mark Hilary's leaving, too,' said Bobby. 'You know she won't be coming back next term.'

There was a subdued silence as everyone digested

this. Hilary was a very popular girl, and St Clare's just wouldn't be the same without her.

'Let's have a party!' cried Pat. 'A celebration and a leaving party for Hilary all in one.'

'Great idea!' said Isabel at once. 'What a shame we're too old and responsible to have a midnight party. That really would finish the term off with a bang.'

'Wouldn't it just,' sighed Janet. Then she brightened. 'I bet if we asked Miss Theobald, she'd let us hold a party in the common-room one evening. We could get in some food and it would be just like a midnight-do, but earlier.'

'Yes!' chorused the others. 'That would be fantastic!'

'Let's not say anything to Hilary,' suggested Bobby. 'We'll make it a surprise party.'

'Better and better,' said Isabel happily. 'Come on, let's find the others – all except Hilary, of course – and make plans. We haven't got long.'

Miss Theobald was delighted to give permission for the party, and the evening before the end of term saw the sixth busily setting out plates of food in the common-room. What a surprise Hilary would have had if she had been able to see what was going on in there! Claudine and Fizz had decorated the room with colourful paper streamers, and a checked cloth covered the big table on which stood plates loaded with sandwiches, sausage rolls, crisps – and everything the girls liked best!

'I'm starving,' said Doris, looking longingly at the

food. 'Do you think I could have just *one* sandwich?'

'Certainly not,' said Pat sternly, slapping her hand away. 'We've all missed out on tea today.'

The girls had all voted not to eat at tea-time, in anticipation of the evening's party. Only Hilary was in the dark – which was where Carlotta and Morag had come in. The two of them had taken Hilary out riding late that afternoon, pretending to get hopelessly lost on the way back to the stables and arriving back at school far too late for tea.

Just my luck! Hilary had thought crossly. I'm starving, too, after that ride. I wonder if Doris has any of those biscuits left?

But Doris was nowhere to be found – and nor were any of the other sixth formers. What was more, when Hilary tried the door to the common-room, it was locked. It really was very strange! By eight o'clock, Hilary was feeling lonely and fed-up – not to mention hungry – when Claudine suddenly burst into her study.

'Ah, Hilary, you must come to the common-room at once!' she demanded.

'The common-room's locked,' said Hilary, puzzled. 'I tried the door earlier.'

'Now it is open. Please, Hilary,' Claudine pulled the girl to her feet. 'Something most strange is happening in there.'

'Heavens, what?' asked Hilary, following the girl.

But Claudine took refuge in a torrent of rapid, excited French, which she kept up until they reached the common-room. Then she threw open the door. All was dark and silent as Hilary stepped inside, then Claudine switched on the light.

'Surprise!'

Hilary gasped, hardly able to believe her eyes. 'How fantastic! Oh, what angels you all are!' she cried. 'You must have worked like slaves! It looks gorgeous!'

'Well, we couldn't let you go without a proper send-off,' said Bobby. 'Pat, Isabel – I think you have something for Hilary before we eat.'

The head girls came forward, carrying between them a large, flat parcel, which they handed to the surprised girl.

'A little memento of the happy times we've all shared,' said Pat, smiling.

'Yes, we can't have you forgetting all about us,' added Isabel.

'As if!' Hilary exclaimed, tearing open the parcel. 'Oh, this is just lovely!'

Miss Theobald had arranged for the sixth formers and the teachers to have a group photograph taken, then everyone had clubbed together to buy a silver frame for it. The mistresses had even contributed towards the food, and many of them had promised to look in during the evening. Hilary was a very popular girl. Tears misted her eyes now as she looked at the photograph and said in a choked voice, 'I'm going to miss you all so much.'

Alison, always easily moved, gave a loud sniff and

Doris called out, 'Don't start blubbing, Hilary! You'll set us all off!'

'Yes, this is supposed to be a happy occasion,' Anne-Marie put in. 'Come on, everyone – let's party!'

And party they did! The piles of food disappeared rapidly as the hungry girls attacked it. Then the table was pushed back against the wall, a record player was produced and the girls held an impromptu dance. Mam'zelle arrived just as the dancing began and joined in enthusiastically, keeping the girls in stitches.

'Go, Mam'zelle!' yelled Bobby. 'Isn't she just great?'

'I'll say,' agreed Carlotta. 'What a brilliant end to the term this is, Bobby!'

There was one more surprise to come before the evening was over. Worn out with dancing, the girls had turned the music down low and were sitting about chatting as they sipped ginger beer and lemonade from paper cups.

'This certainly beats day school,' declared Fizz. 'Nothing like this ever happened there.'

A sudden silence descended and all the girls stared at her. The voice in which she had spoken was quite different from the Cockney accent they had become used to.

'Heavens, Fizz, have you been taking elocution lessons or something?' asked Mirabel.

Fizz laughed, turning slightly red, and shook her head. 'No. I'm afraid I haven't been quite honest with you. I hope you won't be mad with me, but it was all in a good cause.'

'Whatever do you mean?' asked Pat, quite unable to get used to the girl's new, refined tone.

'What I told you about not fitting in at my day school was quite true. But it wasn't because my family had suddenly become wealthy,' Fizz explained. 'You see, we've *always* been wealthy. My parents are the Duke and Duchess of Delchester and I'm *Lady* Phyllis Bentley.'

The girls listened with their mouths agape. Many of them felt rather disappointed in Fizz for having lied to them, and the girl saw it in their faces.

'Please don't judge me too harshly!' she pleaded. 'Not until you've heard me out.'

'Go on,' said Janet coolly.

'Well, until last year, I was educated at home by a tutor. Then my parents decided I ought to mix with people my age more, and sent me to our local school.'

She grimaced and Alison asked, 'Weren't you popular there?'

'Oh, I was popular, all right,' said Fizz drily. 'But for all the wrong reasons. Everyone wanted to be friends with Lady Phyllis, to be invited to her big house, and meet the Duke and Duchess! But no one really wanted to take the trouble to get to know *me*, Fizz, as a person.'

'Wow!' exclaimed Bobby. 'Well, it just goes to show that the upper classes have their problems too.'

'Yes, having everyone want to know you because of *what* you are rather than *who* you are isn't much fun,' said Fizz with a sigh. 'So I decided I wanted to start afresh, somewhere no one knew about my parents or my title, to see if anyone really did like me for myself.'

'And we do, Lady Fizz,' Claudine spoke up. 'Very much.'

'Does Miss Theobald know about this?' asked Isabel.

'Yes, and she agreed to it.' Fizz grinned. 'You've all been so sweet to me that now I can come clean – and I'm glad of it, too, because I haven't felt good about not being straight with you. Well, what's the verdict? Am I forgiven?'

There was a moment's silence – then a roar of agreement, all of the girls seeing Fizz's point; they were delighted that she wanted to be accepted as one of them. All but one girl, and that was Angela. She turned crimson with mortification when she remembered how she had snubbed Fizz and looked down on her. And all the time her family were aristocrats! How impressed her mother would have been if she could have gone home tomorrow and boasted that Lady Phyllis Bentley was her friend. Instead, she was probably the most unpopular girl in the class, as far as Fizz was concerned. She watched the girl now, joking with Claudine and laughing as Janet teased, 'Come on, Lady Fizz, we have to clear up before bed-time – we've given the help the night off!'

Despite their late night, the girls were up bright and early the next morning, looking forward to the holidays.

'Our first term as head girls over already,' said Pat rather sadly, as she and Isabel packed. 'Hasn't it just flown?'

'Yes, but the holidays will go even faster,' replied

Isabel. 'And then we'll be back. Hey, Claudine, those are *my* slippers you're packing! Were you thinking of taking them on holiday to France?'

'*Pardon,* Isabel,' apologized the French girl, handing them back. 'My head is in the sky today.'

'The clouds, dope, not the sky!' laughed Pat. 'Why's that, Claudine?'

'Because I do not go to France this holiday,' said Claudine. 'I have been invited to stay with Fizz and her so-wonderful parents. And I am to go to the ball they are holding. Ah, I shall probably be engaged to a lord, at the very least, when I return next term.'

The others laughed loudly – apart from Angela, who could hardly contain herself as she heard this. If only she hadn't been such a snob, she might be going home with Fizz for the holidays, a guest at the Duke and Duchess's ball, instead of that awful Claudine.

Hilary, meanwhile, who had finished her packing earlier, was looking out of the window with rather a wistful expression.

'Everything all right?' asked Pat gently, going across to her.

'Yes, I was just thinking back over the last six years,' said the girl. 'In some ways I wish I was a first former again, with it all to look forward to.'

'Yes, but you've a whole new life ahead of you now,' said Isabel, joining them. 'It'll be great for you to live with your folks again. Here, write down your address for us, and make sure you keep in touch.'

Soon everyone was crowding round, asking for Hilary's address and Janet joked, 'You're going to have writer's cramp, with all the people you've promised to keep in touch with, Hilary. Oh, here are the coaches! Come on, girls! Time we made a move.'

Picking up their hand luggage, the girls made their way down to the big hall, where many of the younger girls and some of the mistresses were already gathered.

'Hilary!' called out Miss Harry. 'I'm glad to have this chance to say goodbye. It was nice to have you in my class, if only for one term.'

'And it was nice to be there, Miss Harry,' Hilary said.

'*Ma chère* Hilary!' cried Mam'zelle, tears gathering in her eyes as she enveloped the girl in a great hug. 'Be happy. We shall miss you.'

'And I'll miss you, Mam'zelle,' Hilary gulped, hoping that she wasn't going to cry.

Miss Theobald, coming out of her study at that moment, saw the girl's lips begin to tremble and went across. 'My dear,' she said warmly, taking her hand. 'Go forward into your new life with many happy memories of us . . . as we have of you. And remember, a little part of you will always remain here, in the spirit of St Clare's.'

'Thank you, Miss Theobald. I'm so proud to have been here, to have known you – Mam'zelle – everyone . . .' Suddenly Hilary couldn't speak any more for the lump in her throat.

'Hilary, come on! We'll miss the coach.' Pat came up then and took her arm. 'Oh, excuse me, Miss Theobald.'

'It's all right, Pat,' said the head. 'Goodbye, Hilary.'

'Goodbye, Miss Theobald.'

And goodbye, St Clare's, thought Hilary, as she walked outside – away from the school she loved so much – and into a new life.

Enid Blyton®

Enid Blyton was born in London in 1897. After school, she trained as a kindergarten teacher, and married Hugh Pollock when she was 27. They had two children, and soon afterwards Enid wrote her first novel, The Adventures of the Wishing-Chair.

Enid divorced Hugh after almost 20 years of marriage, and married Kenneth Waters in 1943. Throughout the 40s and 50s, Enid wrote books at a colossal pace: adventure stories, mysteries, magical stories, farming stories, stories for younger children, and best-selling series like Malory Towers and Amelia Jane. Blyton died in 1968, but her stories remain timeless classics, adored throughout the world.

Join the twins in their first exciting year at the best school ever – ST CLARE'S!

Pat and Isabel are going to a new school, but will they like it? And will the others like them? They needn't have worried. There are teachers to play tricks on, sports matches to win, friends to be made and midnight feasts to scoff. Pat and Isabel are going to have so much fun . . .

This bumper volume includes:

The Twins at St Clare's

The O'Sullivan Twins

Summer Term at St Clare's

The *O'Sullivan twins* are back in this bumper collection!

Isabel and Pat are now in their second year at St Clare's, and they're determined to enjoy themselves! There are new girls to play tricks on, midnight feasts to organise – and plenty of drama, too!

This bumper volume includes:

Second Form at St Clare's

The Third Form at St Clare's

Kitty at St Clare's

Darrell Rivers is off to a new school, the famous Malory Towers. How is she going to fit in, let alone find her way around? And what adventures will she have?

Join Darrell and her new friends as they learn about boarding school life. Along the way there will be lessons, quarrels and sporting contests, teachers to play tricks on – and plenty of mischief, mayhem and midnight feasts!

This bumper volume includes the first three Malory Towers stories:

First Term at Malory Towers
Second Form at Malory Towers
Third Year at Malory Towers

'Off to Malory Towers again!' she said, joyfully.
'Good old Malory Towers!'

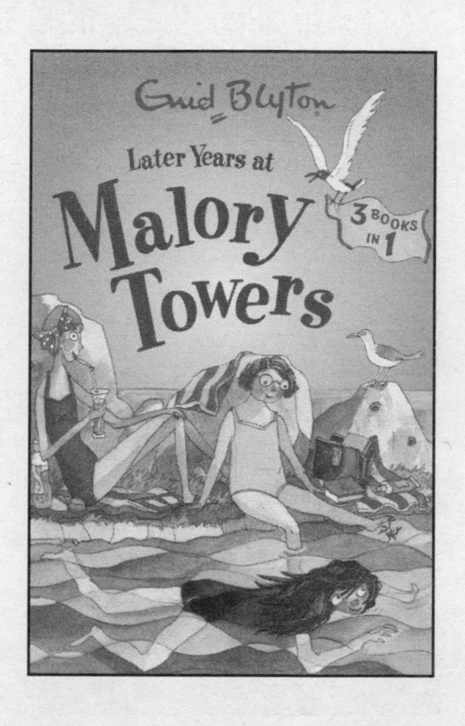

Darrell and her friends are back at boarding school again for more drama, fun and excitement! There are new girls to get to know, plays to produce and matches to win on the sports fields – and the girls of Malory Towers are just guaranteed to get into mischief!

This bumper volume includes another three Malory Towers stories:

Upper Fourth at Malory Towers
In the Fifth at Malory Towers
Last Term at Malory Towers

Felicity is the new head of the third form at Malory Towers, and what a lot she has to deal with!

There are new girls to get to know, mysteries to uncover, and even a concert to put on – not to mention plenty of midnight feasts. Whatever each new term brings, Felicity and her friends know one thing is for sure. There will always be mischief and adventure!

This bumper volume includes the next three Malory Towers stories:

New Term at Malory Towers
Summer Term at Malory Towers
Winter Term at Malory Towers

COMING SOON . . .

Final Years at Malory Towers

It's nearly the end of her time at Malory Towers, and Felicity is determined to have lots of fun and games with her school friends. But they weren't expecting to find a thief in their midst, or be put in charge of naughty first-formers . . . or to see the return of a very old friend.

This bumper volume includes the final three Malory Towers stories:

Fun and Games at Malory Towers
Secrets at Malory Towers
Goodbye Malory Towers

EGMONT PRESS: ETHICAL PUBLISHING

Egmont Press is about turning writers into successful authors and children into passionate readers – producing books that enrich and entertain. As a responsible children's publisher, we go even further, considering the world in which our consumers are growing up.

Safety First
Naturally, all of our books meet legal safety requirements. But we go further than this; every book with play value is tested to the highest standards – if it fails, it's back to the drawing-board.

Made Fairly
We are working to ensure that the workers involved in our supply chain – the people that make our books – are treated with fairness and respect.

Responsible Forestry
We are committed to ensuring all our papers come from environmentally and socially responsible forest sources.

For more information, please visit our website at www.egmont.co.uk/ethical

Egmont is passionate about helping to preserve the world's remaining ancient forests. We only use paper from legal and sustainable forest sources, so we know where every single tree comes from that goes into every paper that makes up every book.

This book is made from paper certified by the Forestry Stewardship Council (FSC®), an organisation dedicated to promoting responsible management of forest resources. For more information on the FSC, please visit **www.fsc.org**. To learn more about Egmont's sustainable paper policy, please visit **www.egmont.co.uk/ethical**.